Lady Mary Wortley Montagu, Sarah J. B. Hale

The Letters of Lady Mary Wortley Montagu

Lady Mary Wortley Montagu, Sarah J. B. Hale

The Letters of Lady Mary Wortley Montagu

ISBN/EAN: 9783337121204

Printed in Europe, USA, Canada, Australia, Japan

Cover: Foto ©Andreas Hilbeck / pixelio.de

More available books at **www.hansebooks.com**

THE LETTERS

OF

LADY MARY WORTLEY MONTAGU.

EDITED BY

MRS. HALE,

AUTHORESS OF "WOMAN'S RECORD," "NORTHWOOD," "MANNERS," ETC.

"The equal lustre of the heavenly mind,
Where every grace with every virtue joined,
Learning not vain, and wisdom not severe,
With greatness easy, and with wit sincere." — POPE.

REVISED EDITION.

BOSTON:
ROBERTS BROTHERS.
1884

PREFACE TO THE REVISED EDITION.

THERE are many by-paths to the knowledge of mankind in general, and of illustrious individuals in particular, where the dignified Muse of History never deigns to lead us. She shows us kings and heroes, describes wonderful spectacles and great battles, embodies religious movements and mighty revolutions, — subjects that we ought to know and that we like to know; but there are many subordinate personages, incidents, circumstances, perhaps more interesting because nearer to us in feeling, that we can only learn through the aid of familiar memoirs, autobiographies, and especially private and contemporaneous letters. These last give us the surest information about the ways and means of actual life, the most minute details and various images of the real thoughts, feelings, passions, and pursuits of people and of periods.

Every age (and every society) has its peculiar tone, acting, for the time, as a sort of atmosphere, which, in spite of any isolation or eccentricity of character, will influence every person it surrounds. This tone is nowhere to be seized so easily, and understood so well, as in the familiar letters of each epoch. How stiff, stupid, and dead is the most elaborate description of dress, manners, and etiquette, presented in the pictures drawn by general authors and astute diplomatists, compared with the real talk, the frank opinions, the ill-natured gossip, the spontaneous admiration, that enlighten as well as amuse us in contemporary correspondence.

The name of Lady Mary Wortley Montagu is familiar to our people, yet her celebrated "Letters" have never been made easily accessible, and therefore are little known. In preparing this volume for popular use, great care has been taken to preserve the unity of each division of the "Letters," so that the history of the writer might be elucidated, as well as the sketches of events she records be understood in their true connection. The complete edition of her works, edited by her great-grandson, Lord Wharncliffe, has been followed as the best authority. The work can scarcely fail of interesting deeply the American reader. Lady Mary lived and wrote in the first half of the eighteenth century, when our land was a component portion of the British Empire, consequently her genius and her fame are ours by inheritance. Her letters will be found valuable as well as amusing, aiding the students of history to catch the manners and opinions of English society in high life — then the dominant power of the realm — at the time Benjamin Franklin and his co-patriots in this Western World were working out the problem of American independence and popular sovereignty.

The contrast in the condition of the two countries then and now is curious and instructive; so, also, is the contrast between the description of Constantinople, as it then appeared to Lady Mary, and its present state.

An article in a late number of "Blackwood's Magazine" thus describes her visit: —

"Change, adventure, movement, new things to see and hear and find out — every thing her brilliant and curious intelligence required — were thus supplied to her; and there never had been so clear a picture of the mysterious East as that which the gay young English Ambassadress sent thereafter in long letters, sparkling with wit and observation and real insight, to all her English friends. . . . She is even so good-natured as to describe a camel for some good rural gentlewoman. Altogether, there never was a more spontaneous, sprightly, and picturesque narrative of travel than this which the light-hearted young woman with bright English eyes, which noted every thing under her flowing Eastern veil, despatched to the little knot of men and women at home."

But Lady Mary showed even higher qualities than wit and observation. The practice of inoculation for small-pox was universal in Turkey. She examined it, perceived its utility, tested it upon her little son, and came back to England resolved to introduce it. For five years she struggled against the doctors and the conservatives, and at length forced its beneficent character upon the unwilling Faculty.

Near the close of her life we find her quiet heroism especially admirable. "She sets forth in her letters all her surroundings, all her occupations, not by way of amusing her correspondent alone, but by way of showing that her own life is yet worth living, and her individuality unimpaired. In her Italian villa, queen of the alien hamlet, legislator for her neighbor cottages, the English lady took her forlorn yet individual place; filling her days with a thousand occupations ; dazzling the strange little world about her with brilliant talk ; seeking forgetfulness in books ; living and growing old in her own way with a certain proud reasonableness and philosophy ; deluding herself with no dreams, forbidding her heart to brood over the past, and making a heroic and partially successful attempt to be sufficient to herself. We follow her brave spirit through the haze of years with a certain wondering sympathy, a surprised respect. 'Keep my letters,' said Lady Mary, in the heyday of her life; 'they will be as good as Madame de Sévigné's forty years hence.' "

All this long and eventful life is mirrored in her letters. They are vivid, animated, sparkling with caustic and kindly observations. Like Madame de Sévigné's, they are eminently fit to form the style of youth; and no better adjuncts to the school composition could be had than the careful reading of these interesting volumes.

In the original Preface, written by "Mistress Mary Astell, of learned memory, the Madonilla of the 'Tatler,'" are these sentiments, which American ladies may well approve and adopt: "Let her own sex do justice to Lady Mary Wortley Montagu. Let us freely own the superiority of her genius, pleased that a *Woman* triumphs; that the Giver of all good gifts intrusted and adorned her with most excellent talents."

SARAH JOSEPHA HALE.

PHILADELPHIA, Nov. 26, 1868.

MEMOIR

OF

LADY MARY WORTLEY MONTAGU.

LADY MARY PIERREPONT was the eldest daughter of Evelyn Duke of Kingston and the Lady Mary Fielding, daughter of William Earl of Denbigh. We shall say no more upon her pedigree, except to note that she was, by the mother's side, cousin of Henry Fielding, the novelist. The kindred of genius is an interesting point of genealogy to all who study human nature instead of the peerage. The novelist is now the most celebrated of her kindred. She was born at Thoresby, about the year 1690, and lost her mother in 1694, when Lady Mary and her two sisters had scarcely passed the years of infancy. Their father, a dissipated, selfish, worldly man, appears to have concerned himself very little with their training, though one of her biographers* asserts that Lady Mary displayed in her childhood such tokens of genius that she was placed under the same preceptors as her only brother, the Viscount Newark, and that "she acquired the elements of the Greek, Latin, and French Languages with the greatest success." He goes on to say that "when she had made a singular proficiency, her studies were superintended by Bishop Burnet, who fostered her superior talents with every expression of dignified praise."

Lord Wharncliffe seems to doubt this statement; he thinks her improvement was mainly owing to her own indomitable eagerness for knowledge. However this may be, the following anecdote† shows that the beauty and precocity of his celebrated daughter had made her in her childhood a pet with the duke,

---

* Mr. Dillaway.

† From Biographical Anecdotes collected by Lord Wharncliffe.

her father; but his neglect in her after years, and the unkindness and mercenary tyranny he exercised toward her at the time of her marriage, speak plainly of the want of all real fatherly interest and affection. "A sprightly, beautiful child, while it *is* a child, reflects luster upon a young father, from whom it may be presumed to have partly inherited its charms. Accordingly, a trifling incident, which Lady Mary loved to recall, will prove how much she was the object of Lord Kingston's pride and fondness in her childhood. As a leader of the fashionable world, and a strenuous Whig in party, he of course belonged to the Kit-cat Club. One day, at a meeting to choose toasts for the year, a whim seized him to nominate her, then not eight years old, as a candidate, alleging that she was far prettier than any lady on their list. The other members demurred, because the rules of the club forbade them to elect a beauty whom they had never seen. 'Then you shall see her,' cried he; and in the gayety of the moment sent orders to have her finely dressed, and brought to him at the tavern; where she was received with acclamations, her claim unanimously allowed, her health drunk by every one present, and her name engraved in due form upon a drinking-glass. The company consisting of some of the most eminent men in England, she went from the lap of one poet, or patriot, or statesman, to the arms of another, was feasted with sweetmeats, overwhelmed with caresses, and, what perhaps already pleased her better than either, heard her wit loudly extolled on every side. Pleasure, she said, was too poor a word to express her sensations; they amounted to ecstasy: never again, throughout her whole future life, did she pass so happy a day. Nor indeed could she; for the love of admiration, which this scene was calculated to excite or increase, could never again be so fully gratified: there is always some alloying ingredient in the cup, some drawback upon the triumphs of grown people. Her father carried on the frolic, and, we may conclude, confirmed the taste, by having her picture painted for the club-room, that she might be enrolled a regular toast."

Like all persons of genius whose writings are worth any thing, Lady Mary was a great reader, and had a wonderfully retentive memory. She complains that her education was "one of the worst in the world;" but we find that her own efforts and zeal for improvement made up for deficiencies in instruction. Her letter to Bishop Burnet (see page 402) shows what obstacles she had to encounter in that age, when learning was considered almost as disgraceful for an English lady as the use of full-grown feet would now be to a Chinese beauty.

In one kind of lady-like accomplishment, that of presiding at the dinner-table, she was early and thoroughly instructed. As her mother died when she was only four years old, and her father continued a widower till all his children were grown up and married, Lady Mary, as eldest daughter, was placed at the head of the great household-establishment, when she was a mere child—as soon as she had bodily strength for the office, which, in those days, required no small share.*

Thus passed the early youth of Lady Mary, her time being principally spent at Thoresby and at Acton near London; and her society confined to a few friends, among whom the most confidential was Mrs. (or Miss) Anne Wortley, the favorite sister of the Honorable Edward Wortley Montagu.† He was a scholar, and had traveled; his companions were Steele, Garth, Congreve, Mainwaring, etc.; and Addison was his bosom friend. Such a man, if not possessed of brilliant genius, must have admired it; and that he had a clear understanding and great integrity of character, his own letters and the respect Lady Mary always testifies for his abilities, clearly show.

Her intimacy with his sister was the means of first bringing them together. We give the scene as described by Lord Wharncliffe:

" Mr. Wortley's chief intimates have been already named. His

---

* At the table each joint was carried up in its turn, to be operated upon by her, and her alone—since the peers and knights on either hand were so far from being bound to offer their assistance, that the very master of the house, posted opposite to her, might not act as her croupier; his department was to push the bottle after dinner. As for the crowd of guests, the most inconsiderable among them—the curate, or subaltern, or squire's younger brother—if suffered through her neglect to help himself to a slice of the mutton placed before him, would have chewed it in bitterness, and gone home an affronted man, half inclined to give a wrong vote at the next election. There were then professed carving-masters, who taught young ladies the art scientifically; from one of whom Lady Mary said she took lessons three times a week, that she might be perfect on her father's public days; when, in order to perform her functions without interruption, she was forced to eat her own dinner alone an hour or two beforehand.—WHARNCLIFFE.

† His father was second son of Admiral Montagu, first Earl of Sandwich. Upon marrying the daughter and heiress of Sir Francis Wortley, he was obliged by the tenor of Sir Francis's will to assume his name.

society was principally male; the wits and politicians of that
day forming a class quite distinct from the " white-gloved beau"
attendant upon ladies.   Indeed, as the education of women had
then reached its very lowest ebb, and if not coquettes, or gossips,
or diligent card-players, their best praise was to be notable
housewives, Mr. Wortley, however fond of his sister, could have
no particular motive to seek the acquaintance of her companions.
His surprise and delight were the greater, when one afternoon,
having by chance loitered in her apartment till visitors arrived,
he saw Lady Mary Pierrepont for the first time, and, on entering
into conversation with her, found, in addition to beauty that
charmed him, not only brilliant wit, but a thinking and cultivated mind. He was especially struck with the discovery that she
understood Latin, and could relish his beloved classics.   Something that passed led to the mention of Quintus Curtius, which
she said she had never read.   This was a fair handle for a piece
of gallantry; in a few days she received a superb edition of the
author, with these lines facing the title-page :

> Beauty like this had vanquished Persia shown,
> The Macedon had laid his empire down,
> And polished Greece obeyed a barbarous throne.
> Had wit so bright adorned a Grecian dame,
> The amorous youth had lost his thirst for fame,
> Nor distant India sought through Syria's plain ;
> But to the Muses' stream with her had run,
> And thought her lover more than Ammon's son."

Lady Mary and Anne Wortley were then writing to each other
in young lady fashion, though both writers evinced talents of no
common order.   Edward Wortley seems to have found a chan-
nel for his admiration of his sister's friend through the letters to
Lady Mary, till the death of Anne Wortley, which occurred soon
after, left the correspondence to be continued by the lovers—as
they then were.   Mr. Wortley, after his acceptance by Lady
Mary, made his proposals to the Duke of Kingston in form, and
was cordially approved till the marriage settlements came under
consideration.   Mr. Wortley had a large landed estate, but he
was, on principle, opposed to the practice of entail.   He offered
to make the best provision in his power for Lady Mary, but
positively refused to settle his landed property upon his first-born

son, who, for aught he knew, might prove unworthy to possess it—might be a spendthrift (as his son afterward proved), an idiot, or a villain.

The Duke of Kingston allowed that these theories might be fine, but declared that *his* grandchildren should never be left beggars; and so the treaty of marriage was broken off.

The secret correspondence and meetings between the lovers went on, however; but shortly afterward Lady Mary received offers from another suitor, whom her father commanded her peremptorily to accept; if she did not comply, she was to be immediately sent to a remote place in the country, there to reside during his life, and at his death have no portion save a small annuity. Then it was that she consented to a clandestine marriage with the man she truly loved. Her letters written during their courtship are given in this volume, but one of Lady Mary's, the last she wrote before her marriage, is so fraught with interest in its display of the writer's character and feelings in the most important action of her life, that we reserved it to elucidate more clearly her nobleness of mind, as shown in her sincerity and her devoted, yet self-denying love.

"TO E. W. MONTAGU, ESQ.
"Sunday Morning.

" I wrote you a letter last night in some passion. I begin to fear again; I own myself a coward. You made no reply to one part of my letter concerning my fortune. I am afraid you flatter yourself that my father may be at length reconciled and brought to reasonable terms. I am convinced, by what I have often heard him say, speaking of other cases like this, that he never will. Reflect now for the last time in what manner you must take me. I shall come to you with only a nightgown and petticoat, and that is all you will ever get by me. I told a lady of my friends what I intended to do. You will think her a very good friend when I tell you, she proffered to lend us her house. I did not accept of this till I had let you know it. If you think it more convenient to carry me to your lodgings, make no scruple of it. Let it be where it will: if I am your wife, I shall think no place unfit for me where you are. I beg we may leave London next morning, wherever you intend to go. I should wish to go out of England if it suits your affairs. You are the best judge of your father's temper. If you think it would be obliging to him, or necessary for you, I will go with you immediately to ask his pardon and his blessing. If that is not proper at first, I think the best scheme is going to the Spa. When you come back, you may endeavor to make your father admit of seeing me, and treat with mine (though I persist in believing it will be to no purpose). But I can not think of living in the midst of my relations and acquaintances after so unjustifiable a step:—so unjustifiable to the world—but I think I can justify myself to myself. I again beg you to have a coach to be at the door early Monday morning, to carry us some part of our way, wherever you resolve our journey shall be. If you determine to go to the lady's house, you had best come with a coach and six at seven o'clock to-morrow. She and I will be in the balcony which looks on the road ; you have nothing to do but stop under it, and we will come down to you. Do in this what you like; but after all think very seriously. Your letter, which will be waited for, is to determine every thing.

"You can show me no goodness I shall not be sensible of. However, think again, and resolve never to think of me if you have the least doubt, or that it is likely to make you uneasy in your fortune. I believe, to travel is the most likely way to make a solitude agreeable, and not tiresome : remember you have promised it.

" 'Tis something odd for a woman that brings nothing to expect any thing; but after the way of my education, I dare not pretend to live but in some degree suitable to it. I had rather die than return to a dependency upon relations I have disobliged. Save me from that fear if you love me. If you can not, or think I ought not to expect it, be sincere and tell me so. 'Tis better I should not be yours at all than, for a short happiness, involve myself in ages of misery. I hope there will never be occasion for this precaution; but, however, 'tis necessary to make it. I depend entirely upon your honor, and I can not suspect you of any way doing wrong. Do not imagine I shall be angry at any thing you can tell me. Let it be sincere; do not impose on a woman that leaves all things for you."

The result is well known. The lovers were privately married, by special license, which bears date, August 12th, 1712. Their residence was in the country for about two years, till the death of Queen Anne, in 1714, and the accession of George I., brought a change in the administration, and gave Mr. Montagu a place at court. Lady Mary's first appearance at St. James's was a triumph for her; her beauty and wit, the elegance of her form and the charms of her conversation were unrivaled in the first private circles of the nobility. She had a familiar acquaintance both with Addison and with his rival, Pope, who then contemplated her uncommon genius without envy. His enthusiastic admiration of her is sufficiently apparent in his letters which will be found in this volume. That he became her vindictive enemy in after years was his fault, not hers.

In 1716, the Honorable Edward Wortley Montagu was appointed embassador to the Porte, and, with his accomplished wife and infant son, prepared for his journey to the East. This was, for Lady Mary, a perilous task, as traveling in those days was dangerous as well as most fatiguing, and seldom attempted by women; but she would not be separated from her husband. "When she arrived at Constantinople her active mind was readily engaged in the pursuit of objects so novel as those which the Turkish capital presented. While they excited her imagination, she could satisfy her curiosity, in her ideas of its former splendor as the metropolis of the Roman empire. Her classical acquirements rendered such investigations interesting and successful. Among her other talents was an extraordinary facility in learning languages; and in the assemblage of ten embassies from different countries, of which the society at Pera and Belgrade was composed, she had daily opportunities of extending her knowledge and practice of them. The French and Italian were familiar to her before she left England; and we find in her letters that she had a sufficient acquaintance with the German to understand a comedy, as it was represented at Vienna. She even attempted the Turkish language, under the tuition of one of Mr. Wortley's dragomans, or interpreters, who compiled for her use a grammar and vocabulary in Turkish and Italian. Of her proficiency in that very difficult dialect of the Oriental tongues, specimens are seen in her letters, in which a translation of some popular poetry appears." Thus testifies her English biographer; but more important to the world are the results of her foreign residence, as it developed her genius and widened the sphere of her observance. Her correspondence, while abroad, has gained her such wide-spread celebrity as places her among the first of female writers in the English language. But a still higher praise is hers—that of benefactor to humanity, for to her brave, unprejudiced mind, the Christian world owes the introduction of inoculation for the small-pox. While residing at Belgrade, during the summer months, Lady Mary observed a singular custom prevalent among the Turks—that of *engrafting*, as they styled it, to produce a mild form of small-pox and stay the ravages of that loathsome disease. She examined the process with more than philosophical curiosity—with deep earnestness to learn if it was good; she had lost her only brother by the small-pox, and her own life had been scarcely saved; she knew how terrible was the disease, and sought to save her country from the scourge. Becoming convinced of its efficacy, she did not hesitate to apply it to her own son, a child of three years old. On her return home, she introduced the art into England, by means of the medical attendant of the embassy. Its expediency was questioned by scientific men, and an experiment, by order of government, was made upon five persons under sentence of death, which was perfectly successful.

At that time it was computed that one person in every seven died of the small-pox taken in the natural way, and many who lived were terribly disfigured. It might have been supposed that such an amelioration as this way of *engrafting* offered would have been received with joy, and that Lady Mary would have been acknowledged as a public benefactor. So far from this was the result, that she was persecuted with the most relentless hostility. The clamors raised about her were beyond belief at this day. The faculty rose to a man against her; the clergy descanted from their pulpits on the awful impiety of seeking to take events out of the hands of Providence. The common people were taught to hoot at her as an unnatural mother who had risked the lives of her own children. So fierce was the clamor that, with all her bravery in the cause of truth and humanity, she admitted "that if she had foreseen the persecution and obloquy she was to endure, she would not have attempted to introduce inoculation."

However, she soon gained supporters. The Princess of Wales, afterward Queen Caroline, stood her friend, and truth and reason finally prevailed.* She gave much of her time to advice and superintendence in the families where inoculation was adopted, constantly carrying her little daughter with her into the sick room, to prove her security from infection.

On her return to England, Lady Mary Wortley, at the solicitation of Mr. Pope, took up her residence at Twickenham. Pope had been her most intimate friend and admirer, as his letters to her in this volume will show. Both of them witty, sarcastic, fond of elegant literature, there were many points of similarity of taste and character which must have cemented an intimacy that Lady Mary permitted, if she did not encourage. On this intimacy he presumed to make love to her, as she said—such passionate love that in spite of her utmost endeavors to be angry, and look grave, she was provoked to an immoderate fit of laughter; from which moment he became her implacable enemy. His conduct toward her was as mean as his hatred was malicious. He libeled her almost by name in his poems, and then denied in his letters that his satire was intended for her. The affair has injured both, and must be reckoned among the most unhappy "quarrels and calamities of authors."

While residing in England, Lady Mary carried on her corres-

* In the "Plain-Dealer," then edited by Steele, appeared, in 1724, the following paper:

"It is an observation of some historian that England has owed to women the greatest blessings she has been distinguished by. In the case we are now upon, this reflection will stand justified. We are indebted to the reason and the courage of a lady for the introduction of *this art*, which gains such strength in its progress that the memory of its illustrious foundress will be rendered sacred to it to future ages. This ornament to her sex and country, who ennobles her own nobility by her learning, wit, and virtues, accompanying her consort into Turkey, observed the benefit of this practice, with its frequency even among those obstinate predestinarians, and brought it over for the service and the safety of her native England, where she consecrated its first effects on the persons of her own fine children; and has already received this glory from it, that the influence of her example has reached as high as the blood royal, and our noblest and most ancient families, in confirmation of her happy judgment, add the daily experience of those who are most dear to them. It is a godlike delight that her reflection must be conscious of, when she considers to whom we owe, that many thousand British lives will be saved every year to the use and comfort of their country, after a general establishment of this practice. A good, so lasting and so vast, that none of those wide endowments and deep foundations of public charity which have made most noise in the world deserve at all to be compared with it.

"High o'er each sex in double empire sit
Protecting beauty and inspiring wit."

pondence with her sister Lady Mar, and superintended the education of her only daughter, who married the Marquis of Bute.
Soon after this event Lady Mary, whose health was suffering
from the incipient but fatal disease (cancer), which terminated
her life, went to Italy.   Her husband approved of her plan, and,
it seems from her letters, engaged to join her; but parliamentary
business and other duties detained him in England; they corresponded constantly and kindly; but they never met again.

The letters of Lady Mary to her beloved daughter, Lady Bute,
(in this volume) give a graphic description of her travels, and
living pictures, as it were, of the scenes and persons she met
and observed.   They show also her tender care for her daughter, and that the ties of domestic life were the sweetest to her
heart.   And she sincerely enjoyed her repose from the entangle-
ments of the gay world of fashionable life.   She was residing
in Venice when intelligence of the death of Mr. Wortley, her
husband, reached her in 1761.   Her daughter urged her return
home so earnestly that Lady Mary yielded; and after an absence
of twenty-two years, she began her journey to England, where
she arrived in October.   But her health had suffered much, and
a gradual decline terminated in death, on the 21st of August,
1762, and in the seventy-third year of her age.

Lady Mary Wortley Montagu ranks in the first class of learned
women.   Of this learning, with the true simplicity character-
istic of sensible people, she herself makes small account; but
her familiarity with classic authors is evident in her letters to
Pope and other learned men.   Her acquaintance with general
literature was extensive.   These acquirements, however, may
now be often met with among her sex; but the fertility of her
genius, the flashing of her wit, and her solid good sense, seldom
found united in the same mind, place her among the greatest writers of her day.   Her style and her thoughts are alike free from affection or pretension.   She loved truth and hated shams; this
sincerity of character and her brilliant talents made her many
envious and bitter enemies.   Her English biographer says:

"During her long life, her literary pretensions were suppressed
by the jealousy of her cotemporaries, and her indignant sense of
the mean conduct of Pope and his phalanx, the self-constituted
distributers of the fame and obloquy of that day, urged her to
confine to her cabinet, and a small circle of friends, effusions of

wisdom and fancy, which otherwise had been received by society at large with equal instruction and delight."

But the acknowledgment of her merits, if long delayed, has been fully made. (Her Letters, published in many editions, have been conceded to be the most perfect productions of their kind to be found in our tongue.) An eminent British critic says: "They are truly *letters*, not critical or didactic essays, enlivened by formal compliment and elaborate wit, like the correspondence of Pope."

Still there was one sad defect in the writings of this celebrated lady, which is now far more apparent than when she lived, namely, her lack of religious feeling. True, her lot was cast in an age of practical unbelief, when the English Church was like that of Sardis of old, and rank had the privilege of low sensuality and sin, and public morality was derided as foolishness. Gross darkness was around her path. It is not much to be wondered at that she did not seek the true light, but it is to be deeply regretted that a mind like hers should have been bound to earth, when it had such clear conceptions of the emptiness of worldly pleasures. Piety of heart would have imparted tenderness to her character, and that sweet pity for the faults of others which would have polished her style and given a lovelier light to the diamond sparkle of her wit.

The poems of Lady Mary were written as suggested by particular occasions, and she never took any pains to correct or polish her verses. But she had true poetic talent, and if the same incitements could have been brought to bear on her mind as those that influenced Pope in his pursuit of excellence in versification, she would probably have borne away the palm of genius. However, she won a higher palm than that of a poet—she was the benefactor of her nation. Had Lady Mary Wortley lived in the days of heathen Greece or Rome, such service as she performed in the introduction of inoculation, would have enrolled her name among the deities who have benefited mankind. But in Christian England, her native land, on which she bestowed such a vital blessing, and through it, to all the people of the West, what has been her recompense? We read of princely endowments bestowed by the British government upon great generals; of titles conferred and pensions granted, through several generations, to those who have served their country; of monuments erected by the British

people to statesmen and warriors, and even to weak and worthless princes; but where is the national monument to Lady Mary
Wortley Montagu? Is it in Westminster Abbey? Or has it
been only by the private bounty of a woman that her good
deed has a record?*   On the pages of history, and in the an-
nals of medicine, the name of Lady Montagu must find its place;
but should not England be proud to honor her noble daughter,
whose memory, from royal palace to pauper's hut, ought to be
held in grateful affection?

S. J. H.

* In the cathedral at Litchfield, a cenotaph is erected to her memory, with the
following inscription:

Sacred to the memory of
The Right Honorable
LADY MARY WORTLEY MONTAGU,
who happily introduced from Turkey,
into this country,
the salutary art
of inoculating the small-pox.
Convinced of its efficacy,
she first tried it with success
on her own children,
and then recommended the practice of it
to her fellow-citizens.
Thus by her example and advice
we have softened the virulence,
and escaped the danger of this malignant disease.
To perpetuate the memory of such benevolence,
and express her gratitude
for the benefit she herself received
from this alleviating art;
this monument is erected by
HENRIETTA INGE,
relict of THEODORE WILLIAM INGE, Esq.,
and daughter of SIR JOHN WROTTESLEY, Bart.,
in the year of our Lord M,DCC,LXXXIX.

The monument consists of a mural marble, representing a female figure of
beauty, weeping over the ashes of her preserver, supposed to be inclosed in the
urn, inscribed with her cypher, M. W. M.

LETTERS OF

LADY MARY WORTLEY MONTAGU,

FROM 1710 TO 1716.

ADDRESSED TO EDWARD WORTLEY MONTAGU, ESQ.

(WRITTEN DURING THEIR COURTSHIP AND THE FIRST FIVE YEARS OF MARRIED LIFE.)

LETTER I.*

No date.

PERHAPS you 'll be surprised at this letter; I have had many debates with myself before I could resolve upon it. I know it is not _acting in form_, but I do not look upon you as I do upon the rest of the world; and by what I do for *you*, you are not to judge of my manner of acting with others. You are brother to a woman I tenderly loved; my protestations of friendship are not like other people's—I never speak but what I mean, and when I say I love, 'tis forever. I had that real concern for* Mrs. Wortley, I look with some regard on every one that is related to her. This and my long acquaintance with you may in some measure excuse what I am doing. I am surprised at one of the Tatlers you sent me; is it possible

* A remarkable letter, the first she ever wrote to him. There is a copy of it in his handwriting: it appears by it that his sister was then dead.

† Miss or Mrs. Anne Wortley was the favorite sister of Edward Wortley Montagu. She had been the friend and confidante of Lady Mary Pierrepont, and their correspondence was the medium through which the lovers had communicated till the death of the sister.-*Am. Ed.*

to have any sort of esteem for a person one believes capable of having such trifling inclinations ? Mr. Bickerstaff has very wrong notions of our sex. I can say there are some of us that despise charms of show, and all the pageantry of greatness, perhaps with more ease than any of the philosophers. In contemning the world, they seem to take pains to contemn it ; we despise it without taking the pains to read lessons of morality to make us do it. At least, I know I have always looked upon it with contempt, without being at the expense of one serious reflection to oblige me to it. I carry the matter yet further : was I to choose £2,000 a year, or £20,000, the first would be my choice. There is something of an unavoidable *embarras* in making what is called a great figure in the world ; (*it*) takes off from the happiness of life ; I hate the noise and hurry inseparable from great estates and titles, and look upon both as blessings which ought only to be given to fools, for 'tis only to them that they are blessings. The pretty fellows you speak of, I own entertain me sometimes ; but is it impossible to be diverted with what one despises ? I can laugh at a puppet-show, and at the same time know there is nothing in it worth my attention or regard. General notions are generally wrong. Ignorance and folly are thought the best foundations for virtue, as if not knowing what a good wife is was necessary to make one so. I confess that can never be my way of reasoning ; as I always forgive an *injury* when I think it not done out of malice, I can never think myself *obliged* by what is done without design. Give me leave to say it (I know it sounds vain), I know how to make a man of sense happy ; but then that man must resolve to contribute something toward it himself. I have so much esteem for you, I should be very sorry to hear you were unhappy ; but, for the world, I would not be the instrument of making you so ; which (of the humors you are) is hardly to be avoided if I am your wife. You distrust me—I can neither be easy, nor loved, where I am distrusted. Nor do I believe your passion for me is what you pretend it ; at least, I am sure was I in love, I

could not talk as you do. Few women would have wrote so
plain as I have done; but to dissemble is among the things I
never do. I take more pains to approve my conduct to myself than to the world; and would not have to accuse myself
of a minute's deceit. I wish I loved you enough to devote
myself to be forever miserable, for the pleasure of a day or
two's happiness. I can not resolve upon it. You must think
otherwise of me, or not at all.

I don't enjoin you to burn this letter—I know you will.
'Tis the first I ever wrote to one of your sex, and shall be the
last. You may never expect another. I resolve against all
correspondence of the kind; my resolutions are seldom made,
and never broken.

LETTER II.

Reading over your letter as fast as ever I could, and answering it with the same ridiculous precipitation, I find one
part of it escaped my sight, and the other I mistook in several
places. Yours was dated the 10th of August; it came not
hither till the 20th: you say something of a packet-boat, etc.,
which makes me uncertain whether you 'll receive my letter,
and frets me heartily. Kindness, you say, would be your destruction. In my opinion, this is something contradictory to
some other expressions. People talk of being in love just as
widows do of affliction. Mr. Steele has observed, in one of his
plays, " that the most passionate among them have always
calmness enough to drive a hard bargain with the upholders."
I never knew a lover that would not willingly secure his interest as well as his mistress; or, if one must be abandoned,
had not the prudence, among all his distractions, to consider,
that a woman was but a woman, and money was a thing of
more real merit than the whole sex put together. Your letter
is to tell me, you should think yourself undone, if you married

me ; but if I would be so tender as to confess I should break
my heart if you did not, then you 'd consider whether you
would or no ; but yet you hoped you should not. I take this
to be the right interpretation of—" even your kindness can't
destroy me of a sudden"—" I hope I am not in your power"—
" I would give a good deal to be satisfied," etc.

" As to writing—that any woman would do who thought
she writ well." Now I say, no woman of common good sense
would. At best, 'tis but doing a silly thing well, and I think
it is much better not to do a silly thing at all. You compare
it to dressing. Suppose the comparison just :—perhaps the
Spanish dress would become my face very well ; yet the whole
town would condemn me for the highest extravagance if I
went to court in it, though it improved me to a miracle. There
are a thousand things, not ill in themselves, which custom
makes unfit to be done. This is to convince you I am so far
from applauding my own conduct, my conscience flies in my
face every time I think on 't. The generality of the world
have a great indulgence to their own follies : without being a
jot wiser than my neighbors, I have the peculiar misfortune to
know and condemn all the wrong things I do.

You beg to know whether I would not be out of humor.
The expression is modest enough ; but that is not what you
mean. In saying I could be easy, I have already said I should
not be out of humor : but you would have me say I am violently in love ; that is, finding you think better of me than
you desire, you would have me give you a just cause to contemn me. I doubt much whether there is a creature in the
world humble enough to do that. I should not think you more
unreasonable if you were in love with my face, and asked me
to disfigure it to make you easy. I have heard of some nuns
that made use of that expedient to secure their own happiness ; but, among all the popish saints and martyrs, I never
read of one whose charity was sublime enough to make themselves deformed, or ridiculous, to restore their lovers to peace
and quietness. In short, if nothing can content you but de-

told I am in the wrong, but tell it me gently. Perhaps I have been indiscreet; I came young into the hurry of the world; a great innocence and an undesigning gayety may possibly have been construed coquetry and a desire of being followed, though never meant by me. I can not answer for the observations that may be made on me: all who are malicious attack the careless and defenseless: I own myself to be both. I know not any thing I can say more to show my perfect desire of pleasing you and making you easy, than to proffer to be confined with you in what manner you please. Would any woman but me renounce all the world for one? Or would any man but you be insensible of such a proof of sincerity?

LETTER V.

I have this minute received your two letters. I know not how to direct to you—whether to London, or the country; or if in the country, to Durham, or Wortley. 'Tis very likely you 'll never receive this. I hazard a great deal if it falls into other hands, and I wrote for all that. I wish with all my soul I thought as you do; I endeavor to convince myself by your arguments, and am sorry my reason is so obstinate, not to be deluded into an opinion that 'tis impossible a man can esteem a woman. I suppose I should then be very easy at your thoughts of me; I should thank you for the wit and beauty you give me, and not be angry at the folly and weaknesses; but, to my infinite affliction, I can believe neither one nor t'other. One part of my character is not so good, nor t'other so bad, as you fancy it. Should we ever live together, you would be disappointed both ways: you would find an easy equality of temper you do not expect, and a thousand faults you do not imagine. You think, if you married me, I should be passionately fond of you one month, and of somebody else the next: neither would happen. I can esteem, I can be a friend, but I don't know whether I can love. Expect all that is complaisant and easy, but never what is fond, in me. You judge very wrong of my heart when you suppose me capable of views of interest, and that any thing could oblige me to flatter any body. Was I the most indigent creature in the world, I should answer you as I do now, without adding or diminishing. I am incapable of art, and 'tis because I will not be capable of it. Could I deceive one minute, I should never regain my own good opinion; and who could bear to live with one they despised?

If you can resolve to live with a companion that will have all the deference due to your superiority of good sense, and that your proposals can be agreeable to those on whom I depend, I have nothing to say against them.

As to traveling, 'tis what I should do with great pleasure, and could easily quit London upon your account; but a retirement in the country is not so disagreeable to me, as I know a few months would make it tiresome to you. Where people are tied for life, 'tis their mutual interest not to grow weary of one another. If I had all the personal charms that I want, a face is too slight a foundation for happiness. You would be soon tired with seeing every day the same thing Where you saw nothing else, you would have leisure to remark all the defects; which would increase in proportion as the novelty lessened, which is always a great charm. I should have the displeasure of seeing a coldness, which, though I could not reasonably blame you for, being involuntary, yet it would render me uneasy; and the more, because I know a love may be revived, which absence, inconstancy, or even infidelity, has extinguished; but there is no returning from a *dégoût* given by satiety.

I should not choose to live in a crowd: I could be very well pleased to be in London, without making a great figure, or seeing above eight or nine agreeable people. Apartments, table etc., are things that never come into my head.

But I will never think of any thing without the consent of my family, and advise you not to fancy a happiness in entire solitude, which you would find only fancy.

Make no answer to this, if you can like me on my own terms. 'Tis not to me you must make the proposals : if not, to what purpose is our correspondence ?

However, preserve me your friendship, which I think of with a great deal of pleasure, and some vanity. If ever you see me married, I flatter myself you 'll see a conduct you would not be sorry your wife should imitate.

LETTER VI.

I am going to comply with your request, and write with all the plainness I am capable of. I know what may be said upon such a proceeding, but am sure you will not say it. Why should you always put the worst construction upon my words? Believe me what you will, but do not believe I can be ungenerous or ungrateful. I wish I could tell you what answer you will receive from some people, or upon what terms. If my opinion could sway, nothing should displease you. Nobody ever was so disinterested as I am. I would not have to reproach myself (I don't suppose you would) that I had any ways made you uneasy in your circumstances. Let me beg you (which I do with the utmost sincerity) only to consider yourself in this affair ; and since I am so unfortunate to have nothing in my own disposal, do not think I have any hand in making settlements. People in my way are sold like slaves ; and I can not tell what price my master will put on me. If you do agree, I shall endeavor to contribute, as much as lies in my power, to your happiness. I so heartily despise a great figure, I have no notion of spending money so foolishly, though one had a great deal to throw away. If this breaks off, I shall not complain of you : and as, whatever happens, I shall

still preserve the opinion that you have behaved yourself well,
let me entreat you, if I have committed any follies, to forget them ; and be so just as to think I would not do an ill thing.

I say nothing of my letters : I think them entirely safe in your hands.

I shall be uneasy till I know this is come to you. I have tried to write plainly : I know not what one can say more upon paper.

LETTER VII.

Indeed, I do not at all wonder that absence, and variety of new faces, should make you forget me ; but I am a little surprised at your curiosity to know what passes in my heart (a thing wholly insignificant to you), except you propose to yourself a piece of ill-natured satisfaction, in finding me very much disquieted. Pray, which way would you see into my heart ? You can frame no guesses about it from either my speaking or writing ; and supposing I should attempt to show it you, I know no other way.

I begin to be tired of my humility : I have carried my complaisances to you farther than I ought. You make new scruples : you have a great deal of fancy ; and your distrusts being all of your own making, are more immovable than if there were some real ground for them. Our aunts and grandmothers always tell us that men are a sort of animals ; that if ever they are constant, 'tis only where they are ill used. 'T was a kind of paradox I could never believe : experience has taught me the truth of it. You are the first I ever had a correspondence with, and I thank God I have done with it, for all my life. You needed not to have told me you are not what you have been : one must be stupid not to find a difference in your letters. You seem, in one part of your last, to excuse yourself from having done me any injury in point of fortune.   Do I accuse you of any?

I have not spirits to dispute any longer with you. You say you are not yet determined: let me determine for you, and save you the trouble of writing again. Adieu forever: make no answer. I wish, among the variety of acquaintance, you may find some one to please you; and can't help the vanitv of thinking, should you try them all, you won't find one that will be so sincere in their treatment, though a thousand more deserving, and every one happier. 'Tis a piece of vanity and injustice I never forgive in a woman, to delight to give pain; what must I think of a man that takes pleasure in making me uneasy? After the folly of letting you know it is in your power, I ought in prudence to let this go no further, except I thought you had good-nature enough never to make use of that power. I have no reason to think so: however, I am willing, you see, to do you the highest obligation 'tis possible for me to do:—that is, to give you a fair occasion of being rid of me.

LETTER VIII.

29 March.

Though your letter is far from what I expected, having once promised to answer it, with the sincere account of my inmost thoughts, I am resolved you shall not find me worse than my word, which is, whatever you may think, inviolable.

'Tis not affectation to say that I despise the pleasure of pleasing people whom I despise; all the fine equipages that shine in the ring never gave me another thought than either pity or contempt for the owners that could place happiness in attracting the eyes of strangers. Nothing touches me with satisfaction but what touches my heart; and I should find more pleasure in the secret joy I should feel at a kind expression from a friend I esteemed, than at the admiration of a whole play-house, or the envy of those of my own sex, who could not attain to the same number of jewels, fine clothes, etc., supposing I was at the very summit of this sort of happiness.

You may be this friend if you please : did you really esteem me, had you any tender regard for me, I could, I think, pass my life in any station, happier with you, than in all the grandeur of the world with any other. You have some humors, that would be disagreeable to any woman that married with an intention of finding her happiness abroad. That is not my resolution. If I marry, I propose to myself a retirement ; there is few of my acquaintance I should ever wish to see again ; and the pleasing one, and only one, is the way in which I design to please myself. Happiness is the natural design of all the world ; and every thing we see done, is meant in order to attain it. My imagination places it in friendship. By friendship, I mean an entire communication of thoughts, wishes, interests, and pleasures, being undivided ; a mutual esteem, which naturally carries with it a pleasing sweetness of conversation, and terminates in the desire of making one or another happy, without being forced to run into visits, noise, and hurry, which serve rather to trouble, than compose the thoughts of any reasonable creature. There are few capable of a friendship such as I have described, and 'tis necessary for the generality of the world to be taken up with trifles. Carry a fine lady or a fine gentleman out of town, and they know no more what to say. To take from them plays, operas, and fashions, is taking away all their topics of discourse ; and they know not how to form their thoughts on any other subjects. They know very well what it is to be admired, but are perfectly ignorant of what it is to be loved. I take you to have sense enough not to think this science romantic ; I rather choose to use the word friendship, than love ; because, in the general sense that word is spoke, it signifies a passion rather founded on fancy than reason : and when I say friendship, I mean a mixture of friendship and esteem, and which a long acquaintance increases, not decays. How far I deserve such a friendship, I can be no judge of myself: I may want the good sense that is necessary to be agreeable to a man of merit, but I know I want the vanity to believe I have; and can promise you shall never like me less, upon knowing me better; and that I shall never forget that you have a better understanding than myself.

And now let me entreat you to think, if possible, tolerably of my modesty, after so bold a declaration: I am resolved to throw off reserve, and use me ill if you please. I am sensible, to own my inclination for a man, is putting one's self wholly in his power: but sure you have generosity enough not to abuse it. After all I have said, I pretend no tie but on your heart: if you do not love me, I shall not be happy with you; if you do, I need add no further. I am not mercenary, and would not receive an obligation that comes not from one who loves me.

I do not desire my letter back again: you have honor, and I dare trust you.

I am going to the same place I went last spring. I shall think of you there: it depends upon you in what manner.

LETTER IX.

I am going to write you a plain long letter. What I have already told you is nothing but the truth. I have no reason to believe that I am going to be otherwise confined than by my duty; but I, that know my own mind, know that is enough to make me miserable. I see all the misfortune of marrying where it is impossible to love; I am going to confess a weakness may perhaps add to your contempt of me. I wanted courage to resist at first the will of my relations; but, as every day added to my fears, those, at last, grew strong

enough to make me venture the disobliging them. A harsh
word always damps my spirits to a degree of silencing all I
have to say. I knew the folly of my own temper, and took
the method of writing to the disposer of me. I said every
thing in this letter I thought proper to move him, and proffered, in atonement for not marrying whom he would, never
to marry at all. He did not think fit to answer this letter,
but sent for me to him. He told me he was very much surprised that I did not depend on his judgment for my future
happiness; that he knew nothing I had to complain of, etc.;
that he did not doubt I had some other fancy in my head,
which encouraged me to this disobedience; but he assured
me, if I refused a settlement he had provided for me, he gave
me his word, whatever proposals were made him, he would
never so much as enter into a treaty with any other; that, if
I founded any hopes upon his death, I should find myself mistaken—he never intended to leave me any thing but an annuity of £400 per annum; that, though another would proceed in this manner after I had given so just a pretense for it,
yet he had the goodness to leave my destiny yet in my own
choice, and at the same time commanded me to communicate
my design to my relations, and ask their advice. As hard as
this may sound, it did not shock my resolution: I was
pleased to think, at any price, I had it in my power to be
free from a man I hated. I told my intention to all my
nearest relations. I was surprised at their blaming it, to the
greatest degree. I was told they were sorry I would ruin myself; but, if I was so unreasonable, they could not blame my
father, whatever he inflicted on me. I objected, I did not
love him. They made answer, they found no necessity for
loving: if I lived well with him, that was all was required
of me; and that if I considered this town, I should find very
few women in love with their husbands, and yet a many
happy. It was in vain to dispute with such prudent people;
they looked upon me as a little romantic, and I found it impossible to persuade them that living in London at liberty

was not the height of happiness. However, they could not change my thoughts, though I found I was to expect no protection from them. . When I was to give my final answer to ——, I told him that I preferred a single life to any other; and, if he pleased to permit me, I would take that resolution. He replied, that he could not hinder my resolutions, but I should not pretend after that to please him; since pleasing him was only to be done by obedience; that if I would disobey, I knew the consequences; he would not fail to confine me, where I might repent at leisure; that he had also consulted my relations, and found them all agreeing in his sentiments. He spoke this in a manner hindered my answering. I retired to my chamber, where I writ a letter to let him know my aversion to the man proposed was too great to be overcome, that I should be miserable beyond all things could be imagined, but I was in his hands, and he might dispose of me as he thought fit. He was perfectly satisfied with this answer, and proceeded as if I had given a willing consent.—I forgot to tell you, he named you, and said, if I thought that way, I was very much mistaken; that if he had no other engagements, yet he would never have agreed to your proposals, having no inclination to see his grandchildren beggars.

I do not speak this to alter your opinion, but to show the improbability of his agreeing to it. I confess I am entirely of your mind. I reckon it among the absurdities of custom, that a man must be obliged to settle his estate on an eldest son, beyond his power to recall, whatever he proves to be, and make himself unable to make happy a younger child that may deserve to be so. If I had an estate myself, I should not make such ridiculous settlements, and I can not blame you for being in the right.

I have told you all my affairs with a plain sincerity. I have avoided to move your compassion, and I have said nothing of what I suffer; and I have not persuaded you to a *treaty*, which I am sure my family will never agree to. I can have no fortune without an entire obedience.

Whatever your business is, may it end to your satisfaction. I think of the public as you do. As little as *that* is a woman's care, it may be permitted into the number of a woman's fears. But, wretched as I am, I have no more to fear for myself. I have still a concern for my friends—I am in pain for your danger. I am far from taking ill what you say—I never valued myself as the daughter of ——; and ever despised those that esteemed me on that account. With pleasure I could barter all that, and change to be any country gentleman's daughter that would have reason enough to make happiness in privacy. I beg your pardon. You may see by the situation of my affairs 'tis without design.

LETTER X.

Thursday night.

If I am always to be as well pleased as I am with this letter, I enter upon a state of perfect happiness in complying with you. I am sorry I can not do it entirely as to Friday or Saturday. I will tell you the true reason of it. I have a relation that has ever showed an uncommon partiality for me. I have generally trusted him with all my thoughts, and I have always found him sincerely my friend. On the occasion of this marriage, he received my complaints with the greatest degree of tenderness. He proffered me to disoblige my father (by representing to him the hardship he was doing) if I thought it would be of any service to me ; and, when he heard me in some passion of grief assure him it could do me no good, he went yet further, and tenderly asked me if there was any other man, though of a smaller fortune, I could be happy with ; and, how much soever it should be against the will of my other relations, assured me he would assist me in making me happy after my own way. This is an obligation I can never forget, and I think I should have cause to reproach myself if I did this without letting him know it, and I believe he will approve of it. You guess whom I mean.—The generosity and the goodness of this letter wholly determines my softest inclinations on your side. You are in the wrong to suspect me of artifice; plainly showing me the kindness of your heart (if you have any there for me) is the surest way to touch mine. I am at this minute more inclined to speak tenderly to you than ever I was in my life—so much inclined, I will say nothing. I could wish you would leave England, but I know not how to object to any thing that pleases you. In this minute I have no will that does not agree with yours. Sunday I shall see you, if you do not hear from me Saturday.

LETTER XI.

Friday night.

I tremble for what we are doing.—Are you sure you shall love me forever? Shall we never repent? I fear and I hope. I foresee all that will happen on this occasion. I shall incense my family in the highest degree. The generality of the world will blame my conduct, and the relations and friends of —— will invent a thousand stories of me; yet, 'tis possible you may recompense every thing to me. In this letter, which I am fond of, you promise me all that I wish. Since I writ so far, I received your Friday letter. I will be only yours, and I will do what you please.

LETTER XII.*

Walling Wells, Oct. 22, 1712.

I don't know very well how to begin; I am perfectly un acquainted with a proper matrimonial style. After all, I

* The following letters, written during the first four years of Lady Mary's married life, are deeply interesting from the insight they give ns of her character as a wife and mother. Her warm, unselfish feel-

think 'tis best to write as if we were not married at all.   I
lament your absence as if you were still my lover, and I am
impatient to hear you have got safe to Durham, and that you
have fixed a time for your return.

I have not been very long in this family; and I fancy myself in that described in the Spectator.   The good people here
look upon their children with a fondness that more than rec-
ompenses their care of them.   I don't perceive much distinction in regard to their merits ; and when they speak sense or
nonsense, it affects the parents with almost the same pleasure.
My friendship for the mother, and kindness for Miss Biddy,
make me endure the squalling of Miss Nanny and Miss Mary
with abundance of patience ; and my foretelling the future
conquests of the eldest daughter, makes me very well with the
family.   I don't know whether you will presently find out,
that this seeming impertinent account is the tenderest expressions of my love to you : but it furnishes my imagination
with agreeable pictures of our future life ; and I flatter myself with the hopes of one day enjoying with you the same
satisfactions ; and that, after as many years together, I may
see you retain the same fondness for me as I shall certainly do
for you, when the noise of a nursery may have more charms
for us than the music of an opera.

Amusements such as these are the sure effect of my sincere love, since 'tis the nature of the passion to entertain the
mind with pleasures in prospect, and I check myself when I
grieve for your absence, by remembering how much reason I
have to rejoice in the hope of passing my whole life with you.
A good fortune not to be valued !   I am afraid of telling you
that I return thanks for it to Heaven, because you will charge
me with hypocrisy ; but you are mistaken ; I assist every day
at public prayers in this family, and never forget in my private
ejaculations how much I owe to Heaven for making me yours.

ings contrast most strikingly with her husband's cold manners and
neglectful habits toward her.   The revealings are painful, but justice
to her memory forbids them to be suppressed.

'Tis candle-light, or I should not conclude so soon. Pray, my love, begin at the top, and read till you come to the bottom.

LETTER XIII.

Your short letter came to me this morning; but I won't quarrel with it, since it brought me good news of your health. I wait with impatience for that of your return. The Bishop of Salisbury writes me word that my Lord Pierrepont* declares very much for us. As the bishop is no infallible prelate, I should not depend much on that intelligence; but my sister Frances tells me the same thing. Since it is so, I believe you 'll think it very proper to pay him a visit, if he is in town, and give him thanks for the good offices you hear he has endeavored to do me, unasked. If his kindness is sincere, 'tis too valuable to be neglected. However, the very appearance of it must be of use to us. I think I ought to write him a letter of acknowledgment for what I hear he has already done. The bishop tells me he has seen Lord Halifax, who says, besides his great esteem for you, he has particular respect for me, and will take pains to reconcile my father, etc. I think this is nearly the words of my letter, which contains all the news I know, except that of your place; which is, that an unfortunate burgess of the town of Huntingdon was justly disgraced yesterday in the face of the congregation, for being false to his first lover, who, with an audible voice, forbid the banns published between him and a greater fortune. This accident causes as many disputes here as the duel could do where you are. Public actions, you know, always make two parties. The great prudes say the young woman should have suffered in silence; and the pretenders to spirit and fire would have all false men so served, and hope it will be an ex-

* Gervase Pierrepont, created Baron Pierrepont of Hanslope, 1714, great-uncle of Lady Mary Wortly Montague, being, at that time, an Irish baron.

ample for the terror of infidelity throughout the whole country.   For my part, I never rejoiced at any thing more in my
life.   You 'll wonder what private interest I could have in this
affair.   You must know it furnished discourse all the afternoon, which was no little service, when I was visited by the
young ladies of Huntingdon.   This long letter, I know, must
be particularly impertinent to a man of business ; but idleness
is the root of all evil ; I write and read till I can't see, and
then I walk ; sleep succeeds ; and thus my whole time is
divided.   If I were as well qualified all other ways as I am by
idleness, I would publish a daily paper called the *Meditator.*
The terrace is my place consecrated to meditation, which I
observe to be gay or grave as the sun shows or hides his face.
Till to-day I have had no occasion of opening my mouth to
speak, since I wished you a good journey.   I see nothing, but
I think of every thing, and indulge my imagination, which is
chiefly employed on you.

LETTER XIV.

December 3, 1712.

I am not at all surprised at my Aunt Cheyne's conduct :
people are seldom very much grieved (and never ought to be)
at misfortunes they expect.   When I gave myself to you, I
gave up the very desire of pleasing the rest of the world, and
am pretty indifferent about it.   I think you are very much in
the right for designing to visit Lord Pierrepont.   As much as
you say I love the town, if you think it necessary for your
interest to stay some time here, I would not advise you to
neglect a certainty for an uncertainty ; but I believe, if you
pass the Christmas here, great matters will be expected from
your hospitality : however, you are a better judge of that
than I am.   I continue indifferently well, and endeavor as
much as I can to preserve myself from spleen and melancholy ;
not for my own sake ; I think that of little importance · but

in the condition I am, I believe it may be of very ill consequence; yet, passing whole days alone as I do, I do not always find it possible : and my constitution will sometimes get
the better of my reason. Human nature itself, without any
additional misfortunes, furnishes disagreeable meditations
enough. Life itself, to make it supportable, should not be
considered too nearly: my reason represents to me in vain
the inutility of serious reflections. The idle mind will sometimes fall into contemplations that serve for nothing but to
ruin the health, destroy good-humor, hasten old age and
wrinkles, and bring on an habitual melancholy. 'Tis a maxim
with me to be young as long as one can : there is nothing
can pay one for that invaluable ignorance which is the companion of youth : those sanguine groundless hopes, and that
lively vanity, which make all the happiness of life. To my
extreme mortification, I grow wiser every day.—I don't believe Solomon was more convinced of the vanity of temporal
affairs than I am : I lose all taste of this world, and I suffer
myself to be bewitched by the charms of the spleen, though I
know and foresee all the irremediable mischiefs arising from
it. I am insensibly fallen into the writing you a melancholy
letter, after all my resolutions to the contrary; but I do not
enjoin you to read it: make no scruple of flinging it into the
fire, at the first dull line. Forgive the ill effects of my solitude, and think me, as I am, ever yours.

LETTER XV.

No date.

I don't believe you expect to hear from me so soon ; I remember you did not so much as desire it, but I will not be so
nice to quarrel with you on that point; perhaps you would
laugh at that delicacy, which is, however, an attendant upon
tender friendship.

I opened a closet where I expected to find so many books :

to my great disappointment, there were only some few pieces of the law, and folios of mathematics; my Lord Hinching-brook and Mr. Twinam having disposed of the rest. But as there is no affliction, no more than no happiness, without alloy, I discovered an old trunk of papers, which, to my great diversion, I found to be the letters of the first Earl of Sandwich; and am in hopes that those from his lady will tend much to my edification, being the most extraordinary lessons of economy that ever I read in my life. To the glory of your father, I find that *his* looked upon him as destined to be the honor of the family.

I walked yesterday two hours on the terrace. These are the most considerable events that have happened in your absence; excepting, that a good-natured robin red-breast kept me company almost the whole afternoon, with so much good-humor and humanity, as gives me faith for the piece of charity ascribed to these little creatures in the " Children in the Wood," which I have hitherto thought only a poetical ornament of history.

I expect a letter next post to tell me you are well in London, and that your business will not detain you long from her who can not be happy without you.

LETTER XVI.

No date.

I am alone, without any amusement to take up my thoughts I am in circumstances in which melancholy is apt to prevai even over all amusements, dispirited and alone, and you write me quarreling letters.

I hate complaining: 'tis no sign I am easy that I do not trouble you with my headaches and my spleen; to be reasonable, one should never complain but when one hopes redress. A physician should be the only confidant of bodily pains; and for pains of the mind, they should never be spoke of but to them that can and will relieve them. Should I tell you that I am uneasy, that I am out of humor, and out of patience, should I see you half an hour the sooner? I believe you have kindness enough for me to be very sorry, and so you would tell me; and things remain in their primitive state; I choose to spare you that pain; I would always give you pleasure. I know you are ready to tell me that I do not ever keep to these good maxims. I confess I often speak impertinently, but I always repent of it. My last stupid letter was not come to you before I would have had it back again, had it been in my power: such as it was, I beg your pardon for it. I did not expect that my Lord Pierrepont would speak at all in our favor, much less show zeal upon that occasion, that never showed any in his life. I have writ every post, and you accuse me without reason. I can't imagine how they should miscarry; perhaps you have by this time received two together. Adieu! je suis à vous de tout mon cœur.

LETTER XVII.

No date.

I was not well when I wrote to you last. Possibly the disorder in my health might increase the uneasiness of my mind. I am sure the uneasiness of my mind increases the disorder of my health; for I passed the night without sleeping, and found myself the next morning in a fever. I have not since left my chamber. I have been very ill, and kept my bed four days, which was the reason of my silence, but I am afraid you have attributed it to being out of humor; but was so far from being in a condition of writing, I could hardly speak; my face being prodigiously swelled, that I was forced to have it lanced, to prevent its breaking, which they said would have been of worse consequence. I would not order Grace to write to you, for fear you should think me worse than I was;

though I don't believe the fright would have been considerable enough to have done you much harm. I am now much —better, and intend to take the air in the coach to-day ; for keeping to my chair so much as I do, will hardly recover my strength.

I wish you would write again to Mr. Phipps, for I don't hear of any money, and am in the utmost necessity for it.

LETTER XVIII.

No date.

I am at present in so much uneasiness my letter is not likely to be intelligible, if it at all resembles the confusion of my head. I sometimes imagine you not well, and sometimes that you think it of small importance to write, or that greater matters have taken up your thoughts. This last imagination is too cruel for me. I will rather fancy your letter has miscarried, though I find little probability to think so. I know not what to think, and am near being distracted, among my variety of dismal apprehensions. I am very ill company to the good people of the house, who all bid me make you their compliments. Mr. White begins your health twice every day. You don't deserve all this, if you can be so entirely forgetful of all this part of the world. I am peevish with you by fits, and divide my time between anger and sorrow, which are equally troublesome to me. 'Tis the most cruel thing in the world to think one has reason to complain of what one loves. How can you be so careless ?—is it because you don't love writing ? You should remember I want to know you are safe at Durham. I shall imagine you have had some fall from your horse, or ill accident by the way, without regard to probability ; there is nothing too extravagant for a woman's and a lover's fear. Did you receive my last letter ? If you did not, the direction is wrong, you won't receive this, and my question is in vain. I find I begin to talk nonsense ; and 'tis time to leave off. Pray, my dear, write to me, or I shall be very mad.

LETTER XIX.

No date.

I am at this minute told I have an opportunity of writing a short letter to you, which will be all reproaches. You know where I am, and I have not once heard from you. I am tired of this place because I do not; and if you persist in your silence, I will return to Wharncliffe. I had rather be quite alone and hear sometimes from you, than in any company and not have that satisfaction. Your silence makes me more melancholy than any solitude, and I can think on nothing so dismal as that you forget me. I heard from your little boy yesterday, who is in good health. I will return and keep him company.

The good people of this family present you their services and good wishes, never failing to drink your health twice a day. I am importuned to make haste; but I have much more to say, which may, however, be comprehended in these words—I am yours.

LETTER XX.

No date.

I should have writ to you last post, but I slept till it was too late to send my letter. I found our poor boy not so well as I expected. He is very lively, but so weak that my heart aches about him very often. I hope you are well : I should be glad to hear so, and what success you have in your business. I suppose my sister is married by this time. I hope you intend to stay some days at Lord Pierrepont's ; I am sure he 'll be very much pleased with it. The house is in great disorder, and I want maids so much that I know not what to do till I have some. I have not one bit of paper in the house, but this little sheet, or you would have been troubled with a longer scribble. I have not yet had any visitors. . Mrs. Elcock has writ me word that she has not found any cook. My first inquiries shall be after a country-house, never forgetting any of my promises to you. I am concerned I have not heard from you; you might have writ while I was on the road, and your letter would have met me here. I am in abundance of pain about our dear child: though I am convinced, in my reason, 'tis both silly and wicked to set my heart too fondly on any thing in this world, yet I can not overcome myself so far as to think of parting with him, with the resignation that I ought to do. I hope and I beg of God he may live to be a comfort to us both. They tell me there is nothing extraordinary in want of teeth at his age, but his weakness makes me very apprehensive; he is almost never out of my sight. Mrs. Bêhn says that the cold bath is the best medicine for weak children, but I am very fearful, and unwilling to try any hazardous remedies. He is very cheerful, and full of play. Adieu, my love; my paper is out.

LETTER XXI.

[Dated, by Mr. Wortley, 24th November.]

I have taken up and laid down my pen several times, very much unresolved in what style I ought to write to you: for once I suffer my inclination to get the better of my reason. I have not often opportunities of indulging myself, and I will do it in this one letter. I know very well that nobody was ever teased into a liking; and 'tis perhaps harder to revive a past one, than to overcome an aversion, but I can not forbear any longer telling you I think you use me very unkindly. I don't say so much of your absence, as I should do, if you were in the country and I in London; because I would not have you believe that I am impatient to be in town, when I say I am impatient to be with you; but I am very sensible I parted with you in July, and 'tis now the middle of November. As if this was not hardship enough, you do not tell me you are sorry for it. You write seldom, and with so much indifference as shows you hardly think of me at all. I complain of ill health, and you only say you hope 'tis not so bad as I make it. You never inquire after your child. I would fain flatter myself you have more kindness for me and him than you express; but I reflect with grief that a man that is ashamed of passions that are natural and reasonable, is generally proud of those that are shameful and silly.

You should consider solitude, and spleen, the consequence of solitude, is apt to give the most melancholy ideas, and there needs at least tender letters and kind expressions to hinder uneasinesses almost inseparable from absence. I am very sensible how far I ought to be contented when your affairs oblige you to be without me. I would not have you do yourself any prejudice; but a little kindness will cost you nothing. I do not bid you lose any thing by hasting to see me, but I would have you think it a misfortune when we are asunder. Instead of that, you seem perfectly pleased with our separation, and indifferent how long it continues. When I reflect on your behavior, I am ashamed of my own, and think I am playing the part of my Lady Winchester. At least be as generous as my lord; and as he made her an early confession of his aversion, own to me your inconstancy, and upon my word I will give you no more trouble about it. I have concealed as long as I can the uneasiness the nothingness of your letters have given me, under an affected indifference; but dissimulation always sits awkwardly upon me; I am weary of it; and must beg you to write to me no more, if you can not bring yourself to write otherwise. Multiplicity of business or diversions may have engaged you, but all people find time to do what they have a mind to. If your inclination is gone, I had rather never receive a letter from you, than one which, in lieu of comfort for your absence, gives me a pain even beyond it. For my part, as 'tis my first, this is my last complaint, and your next of the kind shall go back inclosed to you in blank paper.

LETTER XXII.

No date.

* * * * I thank God this cold well agrees very much with the child; and he seems stronger and better every day. But I should be very glad, if you saw Dr. Garth, if you would ask his opinion concerning the use of cold baths for young children. I hope you love the child as well as I do; but if you love me at all, you 'll desire the preservation of his health, for I should certainly break my heart for him.

I writ in my last all I thought necessary about my Lord Pierrepont.

LETTER XXIII.

1714.

I can not forbear taking it something unkindly that you do not write to me, when you may be assured I am in a great fright, and know not certainly what to expect upon this sudden change. The Archbishop of York has been come to Bishopthorp but three days. I went with my cousin to-day to see the king proclaimed, which was done; the archbishop walking next the lord-mayor, and all the country gentry following, with greater crowds of people than I believed to be in York, vast acclamations, and the appearance of general satisfaction. The Pretender afterward dragged about the streets and burned. Ringing of bells, bonfires, and illuminations; the mob crying "Liberty and property!" and "Long live King George!" This morning all the principal men of any figure took post for London, and we are alarmed with the fear of at tempts from Scotland, though all the Protestants here seem unanimous for the Hanover succession. The poor young ladies at Castle Howard* are as much alarmed as I am, being 'eft all alone, without any hopes of seeing their father again (though things should prove well) this eight or nine months. They have sent to desire me very earnestly to come to them, and bring my boy: 'tis the same thing as pensioning in a nunnery, for no mortal man ever enters the doors in the absence of their father, who is gone post. During this uncertainty, I think it will be a safe retreat; for Middlethorp stands exposed to plunderers, if there be any at all. I dare say, after the zeal the archbishop has showed, they 'll visit his house, and consequently this, in the first place. The archbishop made me many compliments on our near neighborhood, and said he should be overjoyed at the happiness of improving his acquaintance with you. I suppose you may now come in at Aldburgh, and I heartily wish you were in Parliament. I saw the archbishop's list of the lords regents appointed, and I perceive Lord W*** is not one of them; by which I guess the new scheme is not to make use of any man grossly infamous in either party; consequently, those that have been honest in regard to both will stand fairest for preferment. You understand these things much better than me; but I hope you will be persuaded by me and your other friends (who, I don't doubt, will be of my opinion) that 'tis necessary for the common good for an honest man to endeavor to be powerful, when he can be the one without losing the first more valuable title; and remember that money is the source of power. I hear that Parliament sits but six months: you know best whether 'tis worth any expense or bustle to be in it for so short a time.

* The daughters of the Earl of Carlisle.

LETTER XXIV.

No date.

You made me cry two hours last night. I can not imagine why you use me so ill ; for what reason you continue silent, when you know at any time your silence can not fail of giving me a great deal of pain ; and now to a higher degree because of the perplexity that I am in, without knowing where you are, what you are doing, or what to do with myself and my dear little boy. However (persuaded there can be no objection to it), I intend to go to-morrow to Castle Howard, and remain there with the young ladies, till I know when I shall see you, or what you would command. The archbishop and every body else are gone to London. We are alarmed with a story of a fleet being seen from the coasts of Scotland. An express went from thence through York to the Earl of Mar. I beg you would write to me. Till you do, I shall not have an easy minute. I am sure I do not deserve from you that you should make me uneasy. I find I am scolding—'tis better for me not to trouble you with it; but I can not help taking your silence very unkindly.

LETTER XXV.

1714.

Though I am very impatient to see you, I would not have you, by hastening to come down, lose any part of your interest. I am surprised you say nothing of where you stand. I had a letter from Mrs. Hewet last post, who said she heard you stood at Newark, and would be chose without opposition ; but I fear her intelligence is not at all to be depended on. I am glad you think of serving your friends ; I hope it will put you in mind of serving yourself. I need not enlarge upon the advantages of money ; every thing we see and every thing we hear, puts us in remembrance of it. If it were possible to restore liberty to your country, or limit the encroachments of the prerogative, by reducing yourself to a garret, I should be pleased to share so glorious a poverty with you ; but, as the world is and will be, 'tis a sort of duty to be rich, that it may be in one's power to do good ; riches being another word for power, toward the obtaining of which the first necessary qualification is impudence, and (as Demosthenes said of pronunciation in oratory) the second is impudence, and the third, still impudence. No modest man ever did or ever will make his fortune. Your friend Lord Halifax, R. Walpole, and all other remarkable instances of quick advancement, have been remarkably impudent. The ministry is like a play at court : there 's a little door to get in, and a great crowd without, shoving and trusting who shall be foremost ; people who knock others with their elbows, disregard a little kick of the shins, and still thrust heartily forward, are sure of a good place. Your modest man stands behind in the crowd, is shoved about by every body, his clothes torn, almost squeezed to death, and sees a thousand get in before him, that don't make so good a figure as himself.

I don't say it is impossible for an impudent man not to rise in the world ; but a moderate merit, with a large share of impudence, is more probable to be advanced, than the greatest qualifications without it.

If this letter is impertinent, it is founded upon an opinion of your merit, which, if it is a mistake, I would not be undeceived ; it is my interest to believe (as I do) that you deserve every thing, and are capable of every thing ; but nobody else will believe it, if they see you get nothing.

LETTER XXVI.

1714.

You do me wrong in imagining, as I perceive you do, that my reasons for being solicitous for your having that place.

was in view of spending more money than we do. You have no cause of fancying me capable of such a thought. I don't doubt but Lord Halifax will very soon have the staff, and it is my belief you will not be at all the richer: but I think it looks well, and may facilitate your election; and that is all the advantage I hope from it. When all your intimate acquaintance are preferred, I think you would have an ill air in having nothing: upon that account only, I am sorry so many considerable places are disposed of. I suppose, now, you will certainly be chosen somewhere or other; and I can not see why you should not pretend to be Speaker. I believe all the Whigs would be for you, and I fancy you have a considerable interest among the Tories, and for that reason would be very likely to carry it. 'Tis impossible for me to judge of this so well as you can do; but the reputation of being thoroughly of no party is, I think, of use in this affair, and I believe people generally esteem you impartial; and being chose by your coun try is more honorable than holding *any* place from *any* king.

LETTER XXVII.

No date.

I hope the child is better than he was, but I wish you would let Dr. Garth know he has a bigness in his joints, but not much; his ankles seem chiefly to have a weakness. I should be very glad of his advice upon it, and whether he approves rubbing them with spirits, which I am told is good for him.

I hope you are convinced I was not mistaken in my judgment of Lord Pelham; he is very silly, but very good-natured. I don't see how it can be improper for you to get it represented to him that he is obliged in honor to get you chose at Aldburgh, and may more easily get Mr. Jessop chose at another place. I can't believe but you may manage it in such a manner; Mr. Jessop himself would not be against it, nor would he have so much reason to take it ill, if he should not be chose, as you have after so much money fruitlessly spent. I dare say you may order it so that it may be so, if you talk to Lord Townshend, etc. I mention this, because I can not think you can stand at York, or any where else, without a great expense. Lord Morpeth is just now of age, but I know not whether he 'll think it worth while to return from travel upon that occasion. Lord Carlisle is in town; you may, if you think fit, make him a visit, and inquire concerning it. After all, I look upon Aldburgh to be the surest thing. Lord Pelham* is easily persuaded to any thing, and I am sure he may be told by Lord Townshend that he has used you ill; and I know that he 'll be desirous to do all things in his power to make it up. In my opinion, if you resolve upon an extraordinary expense to be in Parliament, you should resolve to have it turn to some account. Your father is very surprising if he persists in standing at Huntingdon; but there is nothing surprising in such a world as this.

LETTER XXVIII.

1714.

Your letter very much vexed me. I can not imagine why you should doubt being the better, for a place of that consideration, which it is in your power to lay down, whenever you dislike the measures that are taken. Supposing the commission lasts but a short time, I believe those that have acted in it will have the offer of some other considerable thing. I am perhaps the only woman in the world that would dissuade her husband (if he were inclined to it) from accepting the greatest place in England, upon the condition of his giving one vote disagreeing with his principles and the true interest of my country; but when it is possible to be of service to

---

* Lord Pelham was soon after created Duke of Newcastle, and was George the Second's minister

your country by going along with the ministry, I know not any reason for declining an honorable post. The world never believes it possible for people to act out of the common tract; and whoever is not employed by the public, may talk what they please of having refused or slighted great offers; but they are always looked upon either as neglected, or discontented because their pretensions have failed; and whatever efforts they make against the court are thought the effect of spleen and disappointment, or endeavors to get something they have set their heart on,—as now Sir T. H——* is represented, and I believe truly, as aiming at being secretary. No man can make a better figure than when he enjoys a considerable place. Being for the Place Bill, and if he finds the ministry in the wrong, withdrawing from them, when 'tis visible that he might still keep his places, if he had not chose to keep his integrity. I have sent you my thoughts of places in general, I solemnly protest, without any thought of any particular advantage to myself; and if I were your friend, and not your wife, I should speak in the same manner, which I really do without any consideration but that of your figure and reputation, which are a thousand times dearer to me than splendor, money, etc. I suppose this long letter might have been spared; for your resolution, I don't doubt, is already taken.

LETTER XXIX.

April.

I am extremely concerned at your illness. I have expected you all this day, and supposed you would be here by this time, if you had set out Saturday afternoon, as you say you intended. I hope you have left Wharncliffe; but, however, will continue to write till you let me know you have done so. Dr. Clarke has been spoke to, and excused himself from rec-

* Sir Thomas Hanmer.

ommending a chaplain, as not being acquainted with many orthodox divines. I don't doubt you know the death of Lord Sommers, which will for some time interrupt my commerce with Lady Jekyl. I have heard he is dead without a will; and I have heard he has made young Mr. Cox his heir: I can not tell which account is the truest. I beg you with the greatest earnestness that you would take the first care of your health—there can be nothing worth the least loss of it. I shall be, sincerely, very uneasy 'till I hear from you again; but I am not without hopes of seeing you to-morrow. Your son presents his duty to you, and improves every day in his conversation, which begins to be very entertaining to me. I directed a letter for you last post to Mr. B———. I can not conclude without once (*more*) recommending to you, if you have any sort of value for me, to take care of yourself. If there be any thing you would have me do, pray be particular in your directions. You say nothing positive about the liveries. Lord B.'s lace is silk, with very little silver in it, but for twenty liveries comes to £110. Adieu! Pray take care of your health.

LETTERS TO HER SISTER AND FRIENDS

DURING THE EMBASSY OF MR. WORTLEY.

FROM 1716 TO 1718.

LETTER I.*

Rotterdam, August 3, O. S., 1716.

I **FLATTER** myself, dear sister, that I shall give you some pleasure in letting you know that I have safely passed the sea, though we had the ill fortune of a storm.. We were persuaded by the captain of the yacht to set out in a calm, and he pretended there was nothing so easy as to tide it over; but, after two days slowly moving, the wind blew so hard that none of the sailors could keep their feet, and we were all Sunday night tossed very handsomely. I never saw a man more frighted than the captain.

For my part, I have been so lucky, neither to suffer from fear nor sea-sickness; though I confess I was so impatient to see myself once more upon dry land that I would not stay till the yacht could get to Rotterdam, but went in the long-boat to Helvoetsluys, where we had voitures to carry us to the Brill.

* Lady Frances Pierrepont, second daughter of Evelyn, first Duke of Kingston, married John Erskine, Earl of Mar, who was Secretary of State for Scotland in 1705, joined the Pretender in 1715, was attainted in 1716, and died at Aix-la-Chapelle in 1732. George I. confirmed to Lady Mar the jointure on Lord Mar's forfeited estate to which she was entitled by her marriage-settlement, with remainder to her daughter, Lady Frances Erskine. She resided many years at Paris.

I was charmed with the neatness of that little town; but my arrival at Rotterdam presented me a new scene of pleasure. All the streets are paved with broad stones, and before many of the meanest artificers' doors are placed seats of variously-colored marbles, so neatly kept, that I assure you I walked almost all over the town yesterday, *incognita*, in my slippers, without receiving one spot of dirt; and you may see the Dutch maids washing the pavement of the street with more application than ours do our bed-chambers. The town seems so full of people, with such busy faces, all in motion, that I can hardly fancy it is not some celebrated fair; but I see it is every day the same. 'Tis certain no town can be more advantageously situated for commerce. Here are seven large canals, on which the merchants' ships come up to the very doors of their houses. The shops and warehouses are of a surprising neatness and magnificence, filled with an incredible quantity of fine merchandise, and so much cheaper than what we see in England, that I have much ado to persuade myself I am still so near it. Here is neither dirt nor beggary to be seen. One is not shocked with those loathsome cripples so common in London, nor teased with the importunity of idle fellows and wenches that choose to be nasty and lazy. The common servants and little shopwomen here are more nicely clean than most of our ladies; and the great variety of neat dresses (every woman dressing her head after her own fashion) is an additional pleasure in seeing the town.

You see hitherto, dear sister, I make no complaints; and, if I continue to like traveling as well as I do at present, I shall not repent my project. It will go a great way in making me satisfied with it, if it affords me an opportunity of entertaining you. But it is not from Holland that you may expect a *disinterested* offer. I can write enough in the style of Rotterdam to tell you plainly, in one word, that I expect returns of all the London news. You see I have already learned to make a good bargain; and that it is not for nothing I will so much as tell you I am your affectionate sister.

LETTER II.

Vienna, September 8, O. S., 1716.

I am now, my dear sister, safely arrived at Vienna; and, I thank God, have not at all suffered in my health, nor (what is dearer to me) in that of *my child*,* by all our fatigues.

We traveled by water from Ratisbon, a journey perfectly agreeable, down the Danube, in one of those little vessels that they very properly call wooden houses, having in them all the conveniences of a palace—stoves in the chambers, kitchens, etc. They are rowed by twelve men each, and move with such incredible swiftness that in the same day you have the pleasure of a vast variety of prospects; and, within the space of a few hours, you have the pleasure of seeing a populous city adorned with magnificent palaces, and the most romantic solitudes, which appear distant from the commerce of mankind, the banks of the Danube being charmingly diversified with woods, rocks, mountains covered with vines, fields of corn, large cities, and ruins of ancient castles. I saw the great towns of Passau and Lintz, famous for the retreat of the imperial court when Vienna was besieged.

This town, which has the honor of being the emperor's residence, did not at all answer my ideas of it, being much less than I expected to find it: the streets are very close, and so narrow, one can not observe the fine fronts of the palaces, though many of them very well deserve observation, being truly magnificent. They are built of fine white stone, and are excessively high. For as the town is too little for the number of the people that desire to live in it, the builders seem to have projected to repair that misfortune by clapping one town on the top of another, most of the houses being of five, and some of them six stories. You may easily imagine that the streets being so narrow, the rooms are extremely dark; and, what is an inconvenience much more intolerable, in my opinion, there is no house that has so few as five or six families in

* Edward Wortley Montagu, her only son, was born 1713.

it. The apartments of the greatest ladies, and even of the ministers of state, are divided, but by a partition, from that of a tailor or shoemaker; and I know nobody that has above two floors in any house—one for their own use, and one higher for their servants. Those that have houses of their own, let out the rest of them to whoever will take them; and thus the great stairs (which are all of stone) are as common and as dirty as the street. 'Tis true, when you have once traveled through them, nothing can be more surprisingly magnificent than the apartments. They are commonly a suit of eight or ten large rooms, all inlaid, the doors and windows richly carved and gilt, and the furniture such as is seldom seen in the palaces of sovereign princes in other countries. Their apartments are adorned with hangings of the finest tapestry of Brussels, prodigious large looking-glasses in silver frames, fine japan tables, beds, chairs, canopies, and window-curtains of the richest Genoa damask or velvet, almost covered with gold lace or embroidery. The whole is made gay by pictures, and vast jars of Japan china, and in almost every room large lusters of rock crystal.

I have already had the honor of being invited to dinner by several of the first people of quality; and I must do them the justice to say, the good taste and magnificence of their tables very well answered to that of their furniture. I have been more than once entertained with fifty dishes of meat all served in silver, and well dressed; the dessert proportionable, served in the finest china. But the variety and richness of their wines is what appears the most surprising. The constant way is, to lay a list of their names upon the plates of the guests, along with the napkins; and I have counted several times to the number of eighteen different sorts, all exquisite in their kinds.

I was yesterday at Count Schœnbrunn,* the vice-chan-

* The palace of Schœnbrunn is distant about two miles from Vienna. It was designed by John Bernard Fischers, the Palladio of Germany, in 1696, and was afterward used as a hunting-seat by the emperor and his court.

cellor's garden, where I was invited to dinner. I must own I never saw a place so perfectly delightful as the faubourg of Vienna. It is very large, and almost wholly composed of delicious palaces. If the emperor found it proper to permit the gates of the town to be laid open, that the faubourg might be joined to it, he would have one of the largest and best built cities in Europe. Count Schœnbrunn's villa is one of the most magnificent; the furniture all rich brocades, so well fancied and fitted up, nothing can look more gay and splendid; not to speak of a gallery, full of rarities of coral, mother-of-pearl, etc., and, throughout the whole house, a profusion of gilding, carving, fine paintings, the most beautiful porcelain, statues of alabaster and ivory, and vast orange and lemon-trees in gilt pots. The dinner was perfectly fine and well ordered, and made still more agreeable by the good-humor of the count.

LETTER III.

PRAGUE, November 17, O. S., 1716.

I hope my dear sister wants no new proofs of my sincere affection for her: but I am sure, if you do, I could not give you a stronger than writing at this time, after three days, or, more properly speaking, three nights and days, hard post-traveling.

The kingdom of Bohemia is the most desert of any I have seen in Germany. The villages are so poor, and the post-houses so miserable, that clean straw and fair water are blessings not always to be met with, and better accommodation not to be hoped for. Though I carried my own bed with me, I could not sometimes find a place to set it up in; and I rather chose to travel all night, as cold as it is, wrapped up in my furs, than to go into the common stoves, which are filled with a mixture of all sorts of ill scents.

This town was once the royal seat of the Bohemian kings,

and is still the capital of the kingdom. There are yet some remains of its former splendor, being one of the largest towns in Germany, but, for the most part, old built, and thinly inhabited, which makes the houses very cheap. Those people of quality who can not easily bear the expense of Vienna, choose to reside here, where they have assemblies, music, and all other diversions (those of a court excepted), at very moderate rates, all things being here in great abundance, especially the best wild-fowl I ever tasted. I have already been visited by some of the most considerable ladies, whose relations I know at Vienna. They are dressed after the fashions there, after the manner that the people at Exeter imitate those of London: that is, their imitation is more excessive than the original. 'Tis not easy to describe what extraordinary figures they make. The person is so much lost between head-dress and petticoat, that they have as much occasion to write upon their backs, "*This is a Woman*," for the information of travelers, as ever sign-post painter had to write, "*This is a Bear.*"

LETTER IV.

VIENNA, January 16, O. S., 1717.

I am now, dear sister, to take leave of you for a long time, and of Vienna forever; designing to-morrow to begin my journey through Hungary, in spite of the excessive cold and deep snows, which are enough to damp a greater courage than I am mistress of. But my principles of *passive obedience* carry me through every thing.

I have had my audience of leave of the empress. His imperial majesty was pleased to be present when I waited on the reigning empress; and after a very obliging conversation, both their imperial majesties invited me to take Vienna in my road back; but I have no thoughts of enduring, over again, so great a fatigue. I delivered a letter from the Duchess of Blankenburg. I staid but a few days at that court, though her highness pressed me very much to stay ; and when I left her, engaged me to write to her.

I wrote you a long letter from thence, which I hope you have received, though you don't mention it ; but I believe I forgot to tell you one curiosity in all the German courts, which I can not forbear taking notice of : all the princes keep favorite dwarfs. The emperor and empress keep two of these little monsters, as ugly as devils, especially the female ; but they are all bedaubed with diamonds, and stand at her majesty's elbow, in all public places. The Duke of Wolfenbuttle has one, and the Duchess of Blankenburg is not without hers, but indeed the most proportionable I ever saw. I am told the King of Denmark has so far improved upon this fashion, that his dwarf is his chief minister. I can assign no reason for their fondness for these pieces of deformity, but the opinion all the absolute princes have, that it is below them to converse with the rest of mankind ; and, not to be quite alone, they are forced to seek their companions among the refuse of human nature, these creatures being the only part of their court privileged to talk freely to them.

I am at present confined to my chamber by a sore throat ; and am really glad of the excuse, to avoid seeing people that I love well enough to be very much mortified when I think I am going to part with them forever. It is true, the Austrians are not commonly the most polite people in the world, nor the most agreeable. But Vienna is inhabited by all nations, and I had formed to myself a little society of such as were perfectly to my own taste. And though the number was not very great, I could never pick up, in any other place, such a number of reasonable, agreeable people. We were almost always together, and you know I have ever been of opinion that a chosen conversation, composed of a few that one esteems, is the greatest happiness of life.

Here are some Spaniards of both sexes, that have all the vivacity and generosity of sentiments anciently ascribed to their nation ; and could I believe that the whole kingdom were like them, I would wish nothing more than to end my days there. The ladies of my acquaintance have so much goodness for me, they cry whenever they see me, since I have determined to undertake this journey. And, indeed, I am not very easy when I reflect on what I am going to suffer. Almost every body I see frights me with some new difficulty. Prince Eugene has been so good as to say all the things he could to persuade me to stay till the Danube is thawed, that I may have the conveniency of going by water; assuring me that the houses in Hungary are such as are no defense against the weather; and that I shall be obliged to travel three or four days between Buda and Essek, without finding any house at all, through desert plains covered with snow; where the cold is so violent, many have been killed by it. I own these terrors have made a very deep impression on my mind, because I believe he tells me things truly as they are, and nobody can be better informed of them.

Now I have named that great man, I am sure you expect I should say something particular of him, having the advantage of seeing him very often; but I am as unwilling to speak of him at Vienna as I should be to talk of Hercules in the court of Omphale, if I had seen him there. I don't know what comfort other people find in considering the weakness of great men (because, perhaps, it brings them nearer to their level), but 'tis always a mortification to me to observe that there is no perfection in humanity. The young Prince of Portugal is the admiration of the whole court; he is handsome and polite, with a great vivacity. All the officers tell wonders of his gallantry the last campaign. He is lodged at court with all the honors due to his rank. Adieu, dear sister: this is the last account you will have from me of Vienna. If I survive my journey, you shall hear from me again. I can say with great truth, in the words of Moneses, *I have long learned to hold myself as nothing;* but when I think of the fatigue my poor infant must suffer, I have all a mother's fondness in my eyes, and all her tender passions in my heart.

P.S.—I have written a letter to my Lady —— that I believe she won't like; and, upon cooler reflection, I think I had done better to have let it alone; but I was downright peevish at all her questions, and her ridiculous imagination that I have certainly seen abundance of wonders which I keep to myself out of mere malice. She is very angry that I won't lie like other travelers. I verily believe she expects I should tell her of the *Anthropophagi*, men whose heads grow below their shoulders: however, pray say something to pacify her.

LETTER V.

PETERWARADIN, Jan. 30, O. S., 1717.

At length, dear sister, I am safely arrived, with all my family, in good health, at Peterwaradin; having suffered so little from the rigor of the season (against which we were well provided by furs), and found such tolerable accommodation every where, by the care of sending before, that I can hardly forbear laughing, when I recollect all the frightful ideas that were given me of this journey. These, I see, were wholly owing to the tenderness of my Vienna friends, and their desire of keeping me with them for this winter.

Perhaps it will not be disagreeable to you to give a short journal of my journey, being through a country entirely unknown to you, and very little passed, even by the Hungarians themselves, who generally choose to take the conveniency of going down the Danube. We have had the blessing of being favored with finer weather than is common at this time of the year; though the snow was so deep we were obliged to have our own coaches fixed upon traineaus, which move so swift and so easily, 'tis by far the most agreeable manner of traveling post. We came to Raab (the second day from Vienna) on the seventeenth instant, where Mr. Wortley sending word of our arrival to the governor, the best house in the town was provided for us, the garrison put under arms, a guard ordered at our door, and all other honors paid to us. The governor, and all other officers, immediately waited on Mr. Wortley, to know if there was any thing to be done for his service. The Bishop of Temeswar came to visit us, with great civility, earnestly pressing us to dine with him next day ; which we refusing, as being resolved to pursue our journey, he sent us several baskets of winter fruit, and a great variety of Hungarian wines, with a young hind just killed. This is a prelate of great power in this country, of the ancient family of Nadasty, so considerable for many ages in this kingdom. He is a very polite, agreeable, cheerful old man, wearing the Hungarian habit, with a venerable white beard down to his girdle.

Raab is a strong town, well garrisoned and fortified, and was a long time the frontier town between the Turkish and German empires. It has its name from the river Rab, on which it is situated, just on its meeting with the Danube, in an open champaign country. It was first taken by the Turks, under the command of Pasha Sinan, in the reign of Sultan Amurath III., in the year fifteen hundred and ninety-four. The governor, being supposed to have betrayed it, was afterward beheaded by the emperor's command. The Counts of Swartzenburg and Palfi retook it by surprise, 1598 ; since which time it has remained in the hands of the Germans, though the Turks once more attempted to gain it by stratagem in 1642. The cathedral is large and well built, which is all I saw remarkable in the town.

Leaving Comora on the other side the river, we went the eighteenth to Nosmuhl, a small village, where, however, we made shift to find tolerable accommodation. We continued two days traveling between this place and Buda, through the finest plains in the world, as even as if they were paved, and extremely fruitful ; but for the most part desert and uncultivated, laid waste by the long wars between the Turk and the emperor, and the more cruel civil war occasioned by the barbarous persecution of the Protestant religion by the Emperor Leopold. That prince has left behind him the character of an extraordinary piety, and was naturally of a mild, merciful temper; but, putting his conscience into the hands of a Jesuit, he was more cruel and treacherous to his poor Hungarian subjects than ever the Turk has been to the Christians; breaking, without scruple, his coronation oath, and his faith, solemnly given in many public treaties. Indeed, nothing can be more melancholy than, in traveling through Hungary, to reflect on the former flourishing state of that kingdom, and to see such a noble spot of earth almost uninhabited. Such are also the present circumstances of Buda (where we arrived very early the twenty-second), once the royal seat of the Hungarian kings, whose palace was reckoned one of the most beautiful buildings of the age, now wholly destroyed, no part of the town having been repaired since the last siege, but the fortifications and the castle, which is the present residence of the Governor-general Ragule, an officer of great merit. He came immediately to see us, and carried us in his coach to his house, where I was received by his lady with all possible civility, and magnificently entertained.

This city is situated upon a little hill on the south side of the Danube. The castle is much higher than the town, and from it the prospect is very noble. Without the walls lie a vast number of little houses, or rather huts, that they call the Rascian town, being altogether inhabited by that people. The governor assured me it would furnish twelve thousand fighting men. These towns look very odd: their houses stand in rows, many thousands of them so close together that they appear, at a little distance, like old-fashioned thatched tents. They consist, every one of them, of one hovel above, and another under ground; these are their summer and winter apartments. Buda was first taken by Solyman the Magnificent, in 1526, and lost the following year to Ferdinand I., King of Bohemia. Solyman regained it by the treachery of the garrison, and voluntarily gave it into the hands of King John of Hungary; after whose death, his son being an infant, Ferdinand laid siege to it, and the queen-mother was forced to call Solyman to her aid. He indeed raised the siege, but left a Turkish garrison in the town, and commanded her to remove her court from thence, which she was forced to submit to, in 1541. It resisted afterward the sieges laid to it by the Marquis of Brandenburg, in the year 1542; Count Swartzenburg, in 1598; General Rosworm, in 1602; and the Duke of Lorrain, commander of the emperor's forces, in 1684, to whom it yielded, in 1686, after an obstinate defense; Apti Bassa, the governor, being killed, fighting in the breach with a Roman bravery. The loss of this town was so important, and so much resented by the Turks, that it occasioned the deposing of their emperor, Mohammed IV., the year following.

We did not proceed on our journey till the twenty-third, when we passed through Adam and Todowar, both considerable towns when in the hands of the Turks, but now quite ruined. The remains, however, of some Turkish towns show something of what they have been. This part of the country is very much overgrown with wood, and little frequented. 'Tis incredible what vast numbers of wild-fowl we saw, which often live here to a good old age—and, *undisturbed by guns, in quiet sleep.* We came the five-and-twentieth to Mohatch, and were shown the field near it, where Lewis, the young King of Hungary, lost his army and his life, being drowned in a ditch, trying to fly from Balybeus, general of Solyman the Magnificent. This battle opened the first passage for the Turks into the heart of Hungary. I don't name to you the little villages, of which I can say nothing remarkable; but I 'll assure you, I have always found a warm stove, and great plenty, particularly of wild boar, venison, and all kinds of *gibier.* The few people that inhabit Hungary live easily enough; they have no money, but the woods and plains afford them provision in great abundance: they were ordered to give us all things necessary, even what horses we pleased to demand, *gratis;* but Mr. Wortley would not oppress the poor country people, by making use of this order, and always paid them to the full worth of what he had. They were so surprised at this unexpected generosity, which they are very little used to, that they always pressed upon us, at parting, a dozen of fat pheasants, or something of that sort, for a present. Their dress is very primitive, being only a plain sheep's skin, and a cap and boots of the same stuff. You may easily imagine this lasts them many winters; and thus they have very little occasion for money.

The twenty-sixth we passed over the frozen Danube, with all our equipage and carriages. We met on the other side General Veterani, who invited us, with great civility, to pass the night at a little castle of his, a few miles off, assuring us we should have a very hard day's journey to reach Essek. This we found but too true, the woods being very dangerous, and scarcely passable, from the vast quantity of wolves that hoard in them. We came, however, safe, though late, to Essek, where we staid a day, to dispatch a courier with letters to the Pasha of Belgrade ; and I took that opportunity of seeing the town, which is not very large, but fair built, and well fortified. This was a town of great trade, very rich and populous, when in the hands of the Turks. It is situated on the Drave, which runs into the Danube. The bridge was esteemed one of the most extraordinary in the world, being eight thousand paces long, and all built of oak. It was burned and the city laid in ashes by Count Lesly, 1685, but was again repaired and fortified by the Turks, who, however, abandoned it in 1687. General Dunnewalt then took possession of it for the emperor, in whose hands it has remained ever since, and is esteemed one of the bulwarks of Hungary.

The twenty-eighth we went to Bocorwar, a very large Rascian town, all built after the manner I have described to you. We were met there by Colonel ——, who would not suffer us to go any where but to his quarters, where I found his wife, a very agreeable Hungarian lady, and his niece and daughter, two pretty young women, crowded into three or four Rascian houses cast into one, and made as neat and convenient as those places are capable of being made. The Hungarian ladies are much handsomer than those of Austria. All the Vienna beauties are of that country ; they are generally very fair and well-shaped, and their dress, I think, is extremely becoming. This lady was in a gown of scarlet velvet, lined and faced with sables, made exact to her shape, and the skirt falling to her feet. The sleeves are strait to their arms, and the stays buttoned before, with two rows of little buttons of gold, pearl, or diamonds. On their heads they wear a tassel of gold, that hangs low on one side, lined with sable, or some other fine fur. They gave us a handsome dinner, and I thought the conversation very polite and agreeable. They would accompany us part of our way.

The twenty-ninth we arrived here, where we were met by the commanding officer, at the head of all the officers of the garrison. We are lodged in the best apartment of the governor's house, and entertained in a very splendid manner by the emperor's order. We wait here till all points are adjusted concerning our reception on the Turkish frontiers. Mr. Wortley's courier, which he sent from Essek, returned this morning, with the pasha's answer in a purse of scarlet satin, which the interpreter here has translated. It is to promise him to be honorably received. I desired him to appoint where he would be met by the Turkish convoy. He has dispatched the courier back, naming Betsko, a village in the midway between Peterwaradin and Belgrade. We shall stay here till we receive his answer.

Thus, dear sister, I have given you a very particular, and, I am afraid you 'll think, a tedious, account of this part of my travels. It was not an affectation of showing my reading that has made me tell you some little scraps of the history of the towns I have passed through : I have always avoided any thing of that kind, when I spoke of places that I believe you knew the story of as well as myself. But Hungary being a part of the world which, I believe, is quite new to you, I thought you might read with some pleasure an account of it, which I have been very solicitous to get from the best hands. However, if you don't like it, 'tis in your power to forbear reading it.

I am promised to have this letter carefully sent to Vienna.

LETTER VI.

ADRIANOPLE, April 1, O. S. 1717.

I am now got into a new world, where every thing I see appears to me a change of scene; and I write to your ladyship with some content of mind, hoping, at least, that you will find the charms of novelty in my letters, and no longer reproach me that I tell you nothing extraordinary.

I won't trouble you with a relation of our tedious journey; but must not omit what I saw remarkable at Sophia, one of the most beautiful towns in the Turkish empire, and famous for its hot baths, that are resorted to both for diversion and health. I stopped here one day, on purpose to see them; and designing to go *incognita*, I hired a Turkish coach. These voitures are not at all like ours, but much more convenient for the country, the heat being so great that glasses would be very troublesome. They are made a good deal in the man ner of the Dutch stage-coaches, having wooden lattices painted and gilded; the inside being also painted with baskets and nosegays of flowers, intermixed commonly with little poetical mottos. They are covered all over with scarlet cloth, lined with silk, and very often richly embroidered and fringed. This covering entirely hides the persons in them, but may be thrown back at pleasure, and thus permits the ladies to peep through the lattices. They hold four people very conveniently, seated on cushions, but not raised.

In one of these covered wagons I went to the bagnio about ten o'clock. It was already full of women. It is built of stone, in the shape of a dome, with no windows but in the roof, which gives light enough. There were five of these domes joined together, the outmost being less than the rest, and serving only as a hall, where the portress stood at the door. Ladies of quality generally give this woman a crown or ten shillings; and I did not forget that ceremony. The next room is a very large one, paved with marble, and all round it are two raised sofas of marble, one above another. There were four fountains of cold water in this room, falling first into marble basins, and then running on the floor in little channels made for that purpose, which carried the streams into the next room, something less than this, with the same sort of marble sofas, but so hot with steams of sulphur proceeding from the baths joining to it, it was impossible to stay there with one's clothes on. The two other domes were the hot baths, one of which had cocks of cold water turning into it, to temper it to what degree of warmth the bathers pleased to have.

I was in my traveling-habit, which is a riding-dress, and certainly appeared very extraordinary to them. Yet there was not one of them that showed the least surprise or impertinent curiosity, but received me with all the obliging civility possible. I know no European court where the ladies would have behaved themselves in so polite a manner to such a stranger. I believe, upon the whole, there were two hundred women, and yet none of those disdainful smiles, and satirical whispers, that never fail in our assemblies, when any body appears that is not dressed exactly in the fashion. They repeated over and over to me—" Guzél, pék guzél," which is nothing but *Charming, very charming*. The first sofas were covered with cushions and rich carpets, on which sat the ladies; and on the second their slaves, behind them, but without any distinction of rank by their dress, all being in the state of nature, that is, in plain English, stark naked, without any beauty or defect concealed. Yet there was not the least wanton smile or immodest gesture among them. They walked and moved with the same majestic grace which Milton describes our general mother with. There were many among them as exactly proportioned as ever any goddess was drawn by the pencil of a Guido or Titian, and most of their skins shiningly white, only adorned by their beautiful hair, divided into many tresses, hanging on their shoulders, braided either with pearl or ribbon, perfectly representing the figures of the Graces.

I was here convinced of the truth of a reflection I have often made, *That if it were the fashion to go naked, the face would be hardly observed.* I perceived that the ladies of the most delicate skins and finest shapes had the greatest share of my admiration, though their faces were sometimes less beautiful than those of their companions. To tell you the truth, I had wickedness enough to wish secretly that Mr. Jervas* could have been there invisible. I fancy it would have very much improved his art, to see so many fine women naked, in different postures, some in conversation, some working, others drinking coffee or sherbet, and many negligently lying on their cushions, while their slaves (generally pretty girls of seventeen or eighteen) were employed in braiding their hair in several pretty fancies. In short, it is the women's coffee-house, where all the news of the town is told, scandal invented, etc. They generally take this diversion once a week. and stay there at least four or five hours, without getting cold by immediately coming out of the hot bath into the cold room, which was very surprising to me. The lady that seemed the most considerable among them entreated me to sit by her, and would fain have undressed me for the bath. I excused myself with some difficulty. They being, however, all so earnest in persuading me, I was at last forced to open my shirt and show them my stays, which satisfied them very well ; for I saw they believed I was locked up in that machine, and that it was not in my own power to open it,

---

* Charles Jervas was a pupil of Sir Godfrey Kneller. He was the friend of Pope, and much celebrated for his portraits of females. The beauties of his day were proud to be painted by his hand, after Pope had published his celebrated epistle to him, in which he is complimented as " selling a thousand years of bloom."

which contrivance they attributed to my husband. I was charmed with their civility and beauty, and should have been very glad to pass more time with them; but Mr. Wortley resolving to pursue his journey next morning, early, I was in haste to see the ruins of Justinian's church, which did not afford me so agreeable a prospect as I had left, being little more than a heap of stones.

Adieu, madam: I am sure I have now entertained you with an account of such a sight as you never saw in your life, and what no book of travels could inform you of, as it is no less than death for a man to be found in one of these places.*

LETTER VII.

ADRIANOPLE, April 1, O. S. 1717.

You see that I am very exact in keeping the promise you engaged me to make. I know not, however, whether your

---

* Dr. Russel, an author of great credit, in his History of Aleppo questions the truth of the account here given by Lady Mary Wortley, affirming that the native ladies of that city, with whom, as their physician, he had permission to converse through a lattice, denied to him the prevalence, and almost the existence of the custom she describes, and even seemed as much scandalized at hearing of it as if they had been born and bred in England. The writer of this note confesses to having entertained doubts upon this point, arising from the statement of Dr. Russel; but these doubts were removed by the testimony of a lady, who traveled some years ago in Turkey, and was several months an inmate of the English embassador's house in Pera, whose veracity no one who knew her could doubt, and whose word would have been taken before the oaths of a whole harem. That lady, having been prevented by circumstances from visiting the baths of Constantinople, had an opportunity of doing so at Athens, and there she found Lady Mary's account strictly correct in the main points, although the sight did not inspire her with the same degree of admiration. To use a trite metaphor, she found Lady Mary's outline faithful, but her coloring too vivid. It may, therefore, be fairly presumed that the Aleppo ladies, perceiving the doctor's opinion of the custom, thought fit to disclaim it, or that it really did not prevail in that particular city, and their knowledge went no further.

curiosity will be satisfied with the accounts I shall give you, though I can assure you the desire I have to oblige you to the utmost of my power has made me very diligent in my inquiries and observations. It is certain we have but very imperfect accounts of the manners and religion of these people; this part of the world being seldom visited, but by merchants, who mind little but their own affairs ; or travelers, who make too short a stay to be able to report any thing exactly of their own knowledge. The Turks are too proud to converse familiarly with merchants, who can only pick up some confused informations, which are generally false, and can give no better account of the ways here than a French refugee, lodging in a garret in Greek-street, could write of the court of England.

The journey we have made from Belgrade hither, can not possibly be passed by any out of a public character. The desert woods of Servia are the common refuge of thieves, who rob fifty in a company, so that we had need of all our guards to secure us ; and the villages are so poor that only force could extort from them necessary provisions. Indeed the janizaries had no mercy on their poverty, killing all the poultry and sheep they could find, without asking to whom they belonged ; while the wretched owners durst not put in their claim, for fear of being beaten. Lambs just fallen, geese and turkies big with egg, all massacred without distinction ! I fancied I heard the complaints of Melibeus for the hope of his flock. When the pashas travel, it is yet worse. These oppressors are not content with eating all that is to be eaten belonging to the peasants ; after they have crammed themselves and their numerous retinue, they have the impudence to exact what they call *teeth-money*, a contribution for the use of their teeth, worn with doing them the honor of devouring their meat. This is literally and exactly true, however extravagant it may seem ; and such is the natural corruption of a military government, their religion not allowing of this barbarity any more than ours does.

I had the advantage of lodging three weeks at Belgrade, with a principal effendi, that is to say, a scholar. This set of men are equally capable of preferments in the law or the church, these two sciences being cast into one, and a lawyer and a priest being the same word in the Turkish language. They are the only men really considerable in the empire : all the profitable employments and church revenues are in their hands. The grand-seignior, though general heir to his people, never presumes to touch their lands or money, which go, in an uninterrupted succession, to their children. It is true, they lose this privilege by accepting a place at court, or the title of pasha ; but there are few examples of such fools among them. You may easily judge of the power of these men who have engrossed all the learning and almost all the wealth of the empire. They are the real authors, though the soldiers are the actors, of revolutions. They deposed the late Sultan Mustapha ; and their power is so well known that it is the emperor's interest to flatter them.

This is a long digression. I was going to tell you that an intimate daily conversation with the Effendi Achmet-Bey gave me an opportunity of knowing their religion and morals in a more particular manner than perhaps any Christian ever did. I explained to him the difference between the religion of England and Rome ; and he was pleased to hear there were Christians that did not worship images, or adore the Virgin Mary. The ridicule of transubstantiation appeared very strong to him. Upon comparing our creeds together, I am convinced that if our friend Dr. —— had free liberty of preaching here, it would be very easy to persuade the generality to Christianity, whose notions are very little different from his. Mr. Whiston would make a very good apostle here. I don't doubt but his zeal will be much fired if you communicate this account to him ; but tell him he must first have the gift of tongues before he can be possibly of any use

Mohammedism is divided into as many sects as Christianity ; and the first institution is much neglected and obscured by interpretations. I can not here forbear reflecting on the natural inclination of mankind to make mysteries and novelties. The Zeidi, Kudi, Jabari, etc., put me in mind of the Catholics, Lutherans, and Calvinists, and are equally zealous against one another. But the most prevailing opinion, if you search into the secret of the effendis, is plain deism. This is indeed kept from the people, who are amused with a thousand different notions, according to the different interests of their preachers. There are very few among them (Achmet-Bey denied there were any) so absurd as to set up for wit by declaring they believe no God at all. And Sir Paul Rycaut is mistaken (as he commonly is) in calling the sect *muterin,** (*i. e. the secret with us*), atheists, they being deists, whose impiety consists in making a jest of their prophet. Achmet-Bey did not own to me that he was of this opinion, but made no scruple of deviating from some part of Mohammed's law, by drinking wine with the same freedom we did. When I asked him how he came to allow himself that liberty, he made answer, that all the creatures of God are good, and designed for the use of man; however, that the prohibition of wine was a very wise maxim, and meant for the common people, being the source of all disorders among them; but that the prophet never designed to confine those that knew how to use it with moderation; nevertheless, he said, that scandal ought to be avoided, and that he never drank it in public. This is the general way of thinking among them, and very few forbear drinking wine that are able to afford it. He assured me that if I understood Arabic, I should be very well pleased with reading the Alcoran, which is so far from the nonsense we charge it with, that it is the purest morality, delivered in the very best language. I have since heard impartial Christians speak of it in the same manner; and I don't doubt but that all our translations are from copies got from the Greek priests, who would

* See D'Ohsson, Tableau Général de l'Empire Otheman, 5 vols. 8vo., 1791, in which the religious code of the Mohammedans, and of each sect, is very satisfactorily detailed.

not fail to falsify it with the extremity of malice. No body of men ever were more ignorant, or more corrupt : yet they differ so little from the Romish Church, that, I confess, nothing gives me a greater abhorrence of the cruelty of your clergy, than the barbarous persecution of them whenever they have been their masters, for no other reason than their not acknowledging the Pope. The dissenting in that one article has got them the titles of heretics and schismatics ; and, what is worse, the same treatment. I found at Philippopolis a sect of Christians that call themselves Paulines. They show an old church, where, they say, St. Paul preached; and he is their favorite saint, after the manner that St. Peter is at Rome; neither do they forget to give him the same preference over the rest of the apostles.

But of all the religions I have seen, that of the Arnaöu's seems to me the most particular. They are natives of Arnaöutlich, the ancient Macedonia, and still retain the courage and hardiness, though they have lost the name of Macedonians, being the best militia in the Turkish empire, and the only check upon the janizaries. They are foot soldiers ; we had a guard of them, relieved in every considerable town we passed : they are all clothed and armed at their own expense, dressed in clean white coarse cloth, carrying guns of a prodigious length, which they run with upon their shouldiers as if they did not feel the weight of them, the leader singing a sort of rude tune, not unpleasant, and the rest making up the chorus. These people, living between Christians and Mohammedans, and not being skilled in controversy, declare that they are utterly unable to judge which religion is best ; but, to be certain of not entirely rejecting the truth, they very prudently follow both. They go to the mosque on Friday, and to the church on Sunday, saying for their excuse that at the day of judgment they are sure of protection from the true prophet ; but which that is, they are not able to determine in this world. I believe there is no other race of mankind who have so modest an opinion of their own capacity.

These are the remarks I have made on the diversity of religions I have seen. I don't ask your pardon for the liberty I have taken in speaking of the Roman. I know you equally condemn the quackery of all the churches as much as you revere the sacred truths, in which we both agree.

You will expect I should say something to you of the antiquities of this country; but there are few remains of ancient Greece. We passed near the piece of an arch, which is commonly called Trajan's Gate, from a supposition that he made it to shut up the passage over the mountains between Sophia and Philippopolis. But I rather believe it the remains of some triumphal arch (though I could not see any inscription); for if that passage had been shut up, there are many others that would serve for the march of an army; and, notwithstanding the story of Baldwin Earl of Flanders being overthrown in these straits, after he won Constantinople, I don't fancy the Germans would find themselves stopped by them at this day. It is true, the road is now made (with great industry) as commodious as possible for the march of the Turkish army; there is not one ditch or puddle between this place and Belgrade that has not a large strong bridge of planks built over it; but the precipices are not so terrible as I had heard them represented. At these mountains we lay at the little village Kiskoi, wholly inhabited by Christians, as all the peasants of Bulgaria are. Their houses are nothing but little huts, raised of dirt baked in the sun; and they leave them, and fly into the mountains, some months before the march of the Turkish army, who would else entirely ruin them, by driving away their whole flocks. This precaution secures them a sort of plenty; for such vast tracts of land lying in common, they have the liberty of sowing what they please, and are generally very industrious husbandmen. I drank here several sorts of delicious wine. The women dress themselves in a great variety of colored glass beads, and are not ugly, but of a tawny complexion.

I have now told you all that is worth telling you, and perhaps more, relating to my journey. When I am at Constantinople I'll try to pick up some curiosities, and then you shall hear from me again.

LETTER VIII.

ADRIANOPLE, April 1, O. S., 1717.

I wish, dear sister, that you were as regular in letting me know what passes on your side of the globe as I am careful in endeavoring to amuse you by the account of all I see here that I think worth your notice. You content yourself with telling me over and over, that the town is very dull: it may possibly be dull to you, when every day does not present you with something new; but for me, that am in arrears at least two months' news, all that seems very stale with you would be very fresh and sweet here. Pray let me into more particulars, and I will try to awaken your gratitude, by giving you a full and true relation of the novelties of this place, none of which would surprise you more than the sight of my person, as I am now in my Turkish habit, though I believe you would be of my opinion, that 'tis admirably becoming. I intend to send you my picture; in the mean time accept of it here.

The first part of my dress is a pair of drawers, very full, that reach to my shoes, and conceal the legs more modestly than your petticoats. They are of a thin rose-colored damask, brocaded with silver flowers. My shoes are of white kid leather, embroidered with gold. Over this hangs my smock, of a fine white silk gauze, edged with embroidery. This smock has wide sleeves, hanging half way down the arm, and is closed at the neck with a diamond button; but the shape and color of the bosom are very well to be distinguished through it. The *antery* is a waistcoat, made close to the shape, of white and gold damask, with very long sleeves falling back, and fringed with deep gold fringe, and should have diamond or pearl buttons. My *caftan*, of the same stuff with my drawers, is a robe exactly fitted to my shape, and reaching to my feet, with very long straight falling sleeves. Over this is my girdle, of about four fingers broad, which all that can afford it have entirely of diamonds or other precious stones; those who will not be at that expense, have it of exquisite embroidery on satin; but it must be fastened before with a clasp of diamonds. The *curdee* is a loose robe they throw off or put on according to the weather, being of a rich brocade (mine is green and gold), either lined with ermine or sables; the sleeves reach very little below the shoulders. The head-dress is composed of a cap, called *talpock*, which is in winter of fine velvet embroidered with pearls or diamonds, and in summer of a light shining silver stuff. This is fixed on one side of the head, hanging a little way down with a gold tassel, and bound on either with a circle of diamonds (as I have seen several) or a rich embroidered handkerchief. On the other side of the head the hair is laid flat; and here the ladies are at liberty to show their fancies: some putting flowers, others a plume of heron's feathers, and, in short, what they please; but the most general fashion is a large *bouquet* of jewels, made like natural flowers: that is, the buds, of pearl; the roses, of different colored rubies; the jasmins, of diamonds; the jonquils, of topazes, etc., so well set and enameled, 'tis hard to imagine any thing of that kind so beautiful. The hair hangs at its full length behind, divided into tresses braided with pearl or ribbon, which is always in great quantity.

I never saw in my life so many fine heads of hair. In one lady's, I have counted a hundred and ten of the tresses, all natural; but it must be owned that every kind of beauty is more common here than with us. 'Tis surprising to see a young woman that is not very handsome. They have naturally the most beautiful complexion in the world, and generally large black eyes. I can assure you with great truth, that the court of England (though I believe it is the fairest in

Christendom) does not contain so many beauties as are under our protection here. They generally shape their eyebrows, and both Greeks and Turks have a custom of putting round their eyes a black tincture, that, at a distance, or by candle-light, adds very much to the blackness of them. I fancy many of our ladies would be overjoyed to know this secret; but 'tis too visible by day. They dye their nails a rose-color; but, I own, I can not enough accustom myself to this fashion to find any beauty in it.

As to their morality or good conduct, I can say, like Harlequin, that 'tis just as it is with you; and the Turkish ladies don't commit one sin the less for not being Christians. Now that I am a little acquainted with their ways, I can not forbear admiring either the exemplary discretion or extreme stupidity of all the writers that have given accounts of them. 'Tis very easy to see they have in reality more liberty than we have. No woman, of what rank soever, is permitted to go into the streets without two *murlins;* one that covers her face all but her eyes, and another that hides the whole dress of her head, and hangs half way down her back. Their shapes are also wholly concealed by a thing they call a *ferigee,* which no woman of any sort appears without; this has straight sleeves, that reach to their finger-ends, and it laps all round them, not unlike a riding-hood. In winter 'tis of cloth, and in summer of plain stuff or silk. You may guess, then, how effectually this disguises them, so that there is no distinguishing the great lady from her slave. 'Tis impossible for the most jealous husband to know his wife when he meets her; and no man dare touch or follow a woman in the street.

This perpetual masquerade gives them entire liberty of following their inclinations without danger of discovery. The most usual method of intrigue is to send an appointment to the lover to meet the lady at a Jew's shop, which are as notoriously convenient as our Indian-houses; and yet, even those who don't make use of them, do not scruple to go to buy pennyworths, and tumble over rich goods, which are chiefly to be found among that sort of people. The great ladies seldom let their gallants know who they are ; and 'tis so difficult to find it out, that they can very seldom guess at her name, whom they have corresponded with for above half a year together. You may easily imagine the number of faithful wives very small in a country where they have nothing to fear from a lover's indiscretion, since we see so many have the courage to expose themselves to that in this world, and all the threatened punishment of the next, which is never preached to the Turkish damsels. Neither have they much to apprehend from the resentment of their husbands ; those ladies that are rich having all their money in their own hands.

Upon the whole, I look upon the Turkish women as the only free people in the empire: the very divan pays respect to them ; and the Grand-Seignior himself, when a pasha is executed, never violates the privileges of the *harem* (or women's apartment), which remains unsearched and entire to the widow. They are queens of their slaves, whom the husband has no permission so much as to look upon, except it be an old woman or two that his lady chooses. 'Tis true their law permits them four wives; but there is no instance of a man of quality that makes use of this liberty, or of a woman of rank that would suffer it.

LETTER IX.

ADRIANOPLE, April 18, O. S., 1717.

I wrote to you, dear sister, and to all my other English correspondents, by the last ship, and only Heaven can tell when I shall have another opportunity of sending to you ; but I can not forbear to write again, though perhaps my letter may lie upon my hands these two months. To confess the truth, my head is so full of my entertainment yesterday, that 'tis absolutely necessary for my own repose to give it some vent. Without further preface, I will then begin my story.

I was invited to dine with the Grand-Vizier's lady,* and it was with a great deal of pleasure I prepared myself for an entertainment which was never before given to any Christian. I thought I should very little satisfy her curiosity (which I did not doubt was a considerable motive to the invitation) by going in a dress she was used to see, and therefore dressed myself in the court habit of Vienna, which is much more magnificent than ours. However, I chose to go *incognita*, to avoid any disputes about ceremony, and went in a Turkish coach, only attended by my woman that held up my train, and the Greek lady who was my interpretress. I was met at the court door by her black eunuch, who helped me out of the coach with great respect, and conducted me through several rooms, where her she-slaves, finely dressed, were ranged on each side. In the innermost I found the lady sitting on her sofa, in a sable vest. She advanced to meet me, and presented me half a dozen of her friends with great civility. She seemed a very good-looking woman, near fifty years old. I was surprised to observe so little magnificence in her house, the furniture being all very moderate: and except the habits, and number of her slaves, nothing about her appeared expensive. She guessed at my thoughts, and told me she was no longer of an age to spend either her time or money in superfluities; that her whole expense was in charity, and her whole employment praying to God. There was no affectation in this speech; both she and her husband are entirely given up to devotion. He never looks upon any other woman; and, what is much more extraordinary, touches no bribes, notwithstanding the example of all his predecessors. He is so scrupulous on this point, he would not accept Mr. Wortley's present, till he had been assured over and over that it was a settled perquisite of his place at the entrance of every embassador.

She entertained me with all kind of civility till dinner came in, which was served, one dish at a time, to a vast number, all

* This was the Sultana Hafitén, the favorite and widow of the Sultan Mustapha II., who died in 1703.

finely dressed after their manner, which I don't think so bad as you have perhaps heard it represented. I am a very good judge of their eating, having lived three weeks in the house of an *effendi* at Belgrade, who gave us very magnificent dinners dressed by his own cooks. The first week they pleased me extremely; but I own I then began to grow weary of their table, and desired our own cook might add a dish or two after our manner. But I attribute this to custom, and am very much inclined to believe that an Indian, who had never tasted of either, would prefer their cookery to ours. Their sauces are very high, all the roast very much done. They use a great deal of very rich spice. The soup is served for the last dish; and they have at least as great a variety of ragouts as we have. I was very sorry I could not eat of as many as the good lady would have had me, who was very earnest in serving me of every thing. The treat concluded with coffee and perfumes, which is a high mark of respect; two slaves kneeling *censed* my hair, clothes, and handkerchief. After this ceremony, she commanded her slaves to play and dance, which they did with their guitars in their hands, and she excused to me their want of skill, saying she took no care to accomplish them in that art.

I returned her thanks, and soon after took my leave. I was conducted back in the same manner I entered, and would have gone straight to my own house; but the Greek lady with me earnestly solicited me to visit the *kiyaya's** lady, saying he was the second officer in the empire, and ought indeed to be looked upon as the first, the Grand-Vizier having only the name, while he exercised the authority. I had found so little diversion in the Vizier's *harem*,† that I had no mind to go into another. But her importunity prevailed with me, and I am extremely glad I was so complaisant.

All things here were with quite another air than at the

---

* Kyhaïá, lieutenant. The deputy to the Grand-Vizier.

† Harem, literally "The Forbidden," the apartment sacredly appropriate to females, into which every man in Turkey, but the master of the house, is interdicted from entering.

Grand-Vizier's; and the very house confessed the difference
between an old devotee and a young beauty. It was nicely
clean and magnificent. I was met at the door by two black
eunuchs, who led me through a long gallery between two ranks
of beautiful young girls, with their hair finely plaited, almost
hanging to their feet, all dressed in fine light damasks, brocaded
with silver. I was sorry that decency did not permit me to stop
to consider them nearer. But that thought was lost upon my
entrance into a large room, or rather pavillion, built round with
gilded sashes, which were most of them thrown up, and the
trees planted near them gave an agreeable shade, which hindered the sun from being troublesome. The jasmins and
honeysuckles that twisted round their trunks shed a soft perfume, increased by a white marble fountain playing sweet water
in the lower part of the room, which fell into three or four
basins with a pleasing sound. The roof was painted with all
sorts of flowers, falling out of gilded baskets, that seemed tumb-
ling down. On a sofa, raised three steps, and covered with
fine Persian carpets, sat the *kiyaya's* lady, leaning on cushions
of white satin, embroidered; and at her feet sat two young
girls about twelve years old, lovely as angels, dressed perfectly rich, and almost covered with jewels. But they were
hardly seen near the fair *Fatima* (for that is her name), so
much her beauty effaced every thing I have seen, nay, all that
has been called lovely either in England or Germany. I must
own that I never saw any thing so gloriously beautiful, nor can
I recollect a face that would have been taken notice of near
hers. She stood up to receive me, saluting me after their
fashion, putting her hand to her heart with a sweetness full of
majesty, that no court breeding could ever give. She ordered
cushions to be given me, and took care to place me in the
corner, which is the place of honor. I confess, though the
Greek lady had before given me a great opinion of her beauty,
I was so struck with admiration, that I could not for some time
speak to her, being wholly taken up in gazing. That surpris-
ng harmony of features! that charming result of the whole!

that exact proportion of body ! that lovely bloom of complexion
unsullied by art ! the unutterable enchantment of her smile !
But her eyes !—large and black, with all the soft languishment
of the blue ! every turn of her face discovering some new grace.

After my first surprise was over, I endeavored, by nicely
examining her face, to find out some imperfection, without any
fruit of my search but my being clearly convinced of the error
of that vulgar notion that a face exactly proportioned, and
perfectly beautiful, would not be agreeable ; nature having
done for her, with more success, what Apelles is said to have
essayed, by a collection of the most exact features, to form a
perfect face.   Add to all this a behavior so full of grace and
sweetness, such easy motions, with an air so majestic, yet free
from stiffness or affectation, that I am persuaded, could she be
suddenly transported upon the most polite throne of Europe,
nobody would think her other than born and bred to be a
queen, though educated in a country we call barbarous.   To
say all in a word, our most celebrated English beauties would
vanish near her.

When I took my leave, two maids brought in a fine silver
basket of embroidered handkerchiefs ; she begged I would
wear the richest for her sake, and gave the others to my
woman and interpretress.   I retired through the same ceremonies as before, and could not help thinking I had been some
time in Mohammed's paradise, so much was I charmed with
what I had seen.   I know not how the relation of it appears
to you.   I wish it may give you part of my pleasure ; for I
would have my dear sister share in all my diversions.

LETTER X.

ADRIANOPLE, May 17, O. S.

I am going to leave Adrianople, and I would not do it without giving you some account of all that is curious in it, which
I have taken a great deal of pains to see.

I will not trouble you with wise dissertations, whether or no this is the same city that was anciently called Orestesit, or Oreste, which you know better than I do. It is now called from the Emperor Adrian, and was the first European seat of the Turkish empire, and has been the favorite residence of many Sultans. Mohammed the Fourth, and Mustapha, the brother of the reigning Emperor, were so fond of it that they wholly abandoned Constantinople; which humor so far exasperated the janizaries, that it was a considerable motive to the rebellions that deposed them. Yet this man seems to love to keep his court here. I can give you no reason for this partiality. 'Tis true the situation is fine, and the country all around very beautiful; but the air is extremely bad, and the seraglio itself is not free from the ill effect of it. The town is said to be eight miles in compass; I suppose they reckon in the gardens. There are some good houses in it, I mean large ones; for the architecture of their palaces never makes any great show. It is now very full of people; but they are most of them such as follow the court or camp; and when they are removed, I am told 'tis no populous city. The river Maritza (anciently the Hebrus), on which it is situated, is dried up every summer, which contributes very much to make it unwholesome. It is now a very pleasant stream. There are two noble bridges built over it.

I had the curiosity to go to see the Exchange in my Turkish dress, which is disguise sufficient. Yet I own I was not very easy when I saw it crowded with janizaries; but they dare not be rude to a woman, and made way for me with as much respect as if I had been in my own figure. It is half a mile in length, the roof arched, and kept extremely neat. It holds three hundred and sixty-five shops, furnished with all sorts of rich goods, exposed to sale in the same manner as at the New Exchange* in London. But the the pavement is kept much neater; and the shops are all so clean they seem just new painted. Idle people of all sorts walk here for their di-

* Exeter 'Change.

version, or amuse themselves with drinking coffee, or sherbet, which is cried about as oranges and sweet-meats are in our play-houses.

I observed most of the rich tradesmen were Jews. That people are in incredible power in this country. They have many privileges above all the natural Turks themselves, and have formed a very considerable commonwealth here, being judged by their own laws. They have drawn the whole trade of the empire into their hands, partly by the firm union among themselves, and partly by the idle temper and want of industry in the Turks. Every pasha has his Jew, who is his *homme d'affaires ;* he is let into all his secrets, and does all his business. No bargain is made, no bribe received, no merchandise disposed of, but what passes through their hands. They are the physicians, the stewards, and the interpreters of all the great men.

You may judge how advantageous this is to a people who never fail to make use of the smallest advantages. They have found the secret of making themselves so necessary that they are certain of the protection of the court, whatever ministry is in power. Even the English, French, and Italian merchants, who are sensible of their artifices, are, however, forced to trust their affairs to their negotiation, nothing of trade being managed without them, and the meanest among them being too important to be disobliged, since the whole body take care of his interests with as much vigor as they would those of the most considerable of their members. There are many of them vastly rich, but take care to make little public show of it; though they live in their houses in the utmost luxury and magnificence. This copious subject has drawn me from my description of the exchange, founded by Ali Pasha, whose name it bears. Near it is the *tchartshi,* a street of a mile in length, full of shops of all kinds of fine merchandise, but excessively dear, nothing being made here. It is covered on the top with boards, to keep out the rain, that merchants may meet conveniently in all kinds of weathers. The *bessiten* near it is another exchange, built upon pillars, where all sorts of house-furniture are sold : glittering every where with gold, rich embroidery, and jewels, it makes a very agreeable show.

From this place I went, in my Turkish coach, to the camp, which is to move in a few days to the frontiers. The Sultan is already gone to his tents, and all his court ; the appearance of them is, indeed, very magnificent. Those of the great men are rather like palaces than tents, taking up a great compass of ground, and being divided into a vast number of apartments. They are all of green, and the *pashas of three tails* have those ensigns of their power placed in a very conspicuous manner before their tents, which are adorned on the top with gilded balls, more or less, according to their different ranks. The ladies go in coaches to see the camp, as eagerly as ours did to that of Hyde Park ; but it is very easy to observe that the soldiers do not begin the campaign with any great cheerfulness. The war is a general grievance upon the people, but particularly hard upon the tradesmen, now that the Grand-Signior is resolved to lead his army in person. Every company of them is obliged, upon this occasion, to make a present according to their ability.

I took the pains of rising at six in the morning to see the ceremony, which did not, however, begin till eight. The Grand-Seignior was at the seraglio window to see the procession, which passed through the principal streets. It was preceded by an *effendi*, mounted on a camel, richly furnished, reading aloud the Alcoran, finely bound, laid upon a cushion. He was surrounded by a parcel of boys, in white, singing some verses of it, followed by a man dressed in green boughs, representing a clean husbandman sowing seed. After him several reapers, with garlands of ears of corn, as Ceres is pictured, with scythes in their hands, seeming to mow. Then a little machine drawn by oxen, in which was a windmill, and boys employed in grinding corn, followed by another machine, drawn by buffaloes, carrying an oven, and two more boys, one employed in kneading the bread, and another in drawing it

out of the oven.   These boys threw little cakes on both sides
among the crowd, and were followed by the whole company
of bakers, marching on foot, two by two, in their best clothes,
with cakes, loaves, pastries, and pies of all sorts, on their heads,
and after them two buffoons, or jack-puddings, with their faces
and clothes smeared with meal, who diverted the mob with
their antic gestures.   In the same manner followed all the
companies of trade in the empire ; the nobler sort, such as
jewelers, mercers, etc., finely mounted, and· many of the pa-
geants that represent their trades, perfectly magnificent ;
among which, that of the furriers made one of the best figures, being a very large machine set round with the skins of
ermines, foxes, etc., so well stuffed that the animals seemed to
be alive, and followed by music and dancers.   I believe they
were, upon the whole, twenty thousand men, all ready to follow his highness if he commanded them.   The rear was closed
by the volunteers, who came to beg the honor of dying in his
service.   This part of the show seemed to me so barbarous
that I removed from the window upon the first appearance of
it.   They were all naked to the middle.   Some had their arms
pierced through with arrows, left sticking in them.   Others
had them sticking in their heads, the blood trickling down
their faces.   Some slashed their arms with sharp knives, making the blood spring out upon those that stood there ; and
this is looked upon as an expression of their zeal for glory.   I
am told that some make use of it to advance their love ; and
when they are near the window where their mistress stands
(all the women in town being vailed to see this spectacle), they
stick another arrow for her sake, who gives some sign of approbation and encouragement to this gallantry.   The whole
show lasted for near eight hours, to my great sorrow, who was
heartily tired, though I was in the house of the widow of the
captain-pasha (admiral), who refreshed me with coffee, sweet-
meats, sherbet, etc., with all possible civility.

I went two days after to see the mosque of Sultan Selim I.*

* The same Sultan, between the years 1552 and 1556, constructed

which is a building very well worth the curiosity of a traveler. I was dressed in my Turkish habit, and admitted without scruple ; though I believe they guessed who I was, by the extreme officiousness of the door-keeper to show me every part of it. It is situated very advantageously in the midst of the city, and in the highest part of it, making a very noble show. The first court has four gates, and the innermost three. They are both of them surrounded with cloisters, with marble pillars of the Ionic order, finely polished, and of very lively colors ; the whole pavement is of white marble, and the roof of the cloisters divided into several cupolas or domes, headed with gilt balls on the top. In the midst of each court are fine fountains of white marble ; and, before the great gate of the mosque, a portico, with green marble pillars, which has five gates, the body of the mosque being one prodigious dome.

I understand so little of architecture I dare not pretend to speak of the proportions. It seemed to me very regular ; this I am sure of, it is vastly high, and I thought it the noblest building I ever saw. It has two rows of marble galleries on pillars, with marble balusters ; the pavement is also marble, covered with Persian carpets. In my opinion, it is a great addition to its beauty that it is not divided into pews, and incumbered with forms and benches, like our churches ; nor the pillars, which are, most of them, red and white marble, disfigured by the little tawdry images and pictures that give Roman Catholic churches the air of toy-shops. The walls seemed to be inlaid with such very lively colors, in small flowers, that I could not imagine what stones had been made use of. But going nearer, I saw they were crusted with japan china, which has a very beautiful effect. In the midst hung a vast lamp of silver, gilt, besides which, I do verily believe, there were at least two thousand of a lesser size. This must look very glorious when they are all lighted ; but being at night,

another mosque at Constantinople, which bears his name. The architecture exactly resembles this, and forms a perfect square of seventy-five feet, with a flat cupola rising from the side walls.

no women are suffered to enter. Under the large lamp is a great pulpit of carved wood, gilt; and just by, a fountain to wash, which, you know, is an essential part of their devotion. In one corner is a little gallery, inclosed with gilded lattices, for the Grand-Seignior. At the upper end, a large niche, very like an altar, raised two steps, covered with gold brocade, and standing before it, two silver gilt candlesticks, the height of a man, and in them white wax candles, as thick as a man's waist. The outside of the mosque is adorned with towers, vastly high, gilt on the top, from whence the *imaums* call the people to prayers. I had the curiosity to go up one of them, which is contrived so artfully as to give surprise to all that see it. There is but one door, which leads to three different staircases, going to the three different stories of the tower, in such a manner that three priests may ascend, rounding, without ever meeting each other; a contrivance very much admired.

Behind the mosque is an exchange, full of shops, where poor artificers are lodged *gratis.* I saw several dervises at their prayers here. They are dressed in a plain piece of woolen, with their arms bare, and a woolen cap on their heads, like a high-crowned hat without brims. I went to see some other mosques, built much after the same manner, but not comparable in point of magnificence to this I have described, which is infinitely beyond any church in Germany or England; I won't talk of other countries I have not seen. The seraglio does not seem a very magnificent palace. But the gardens are very large, plentifully supplied with water, and full of trees; which is all I know of them, having never been in them.

I tell you nothing of the order of Mr. Wortley's entry, and his audience. These things are always the same, and have been so often described, I won't trouble you with the repetition. The young prince, about eleven years old, sits near his father when he gives audience: he is a handsome boy; but, probably, will not immediately succeed the Sultan, there

being two sons of Sultan Mustapha, his eldest brother, remaining; the eldest about twenty years old, on whom the
hopes of the people are fixed. This reign has been bloody and
avaricious. I am apt to believe they are very impatient to
see the end of it.

P. S.—I will write to you again from Constantinople.

LETTER XI.

CONSTANTINOPLE, May 29, O. S., 1717.

I have had the advantage of very fine weather all my journey; and, as the summer is now in its beauty, I enjoyed the
pleasure of fine prospects; and the meadows being full of all
sorts of garden flowers, and sweet herbs, my berlin perfumed
the air as it pressed them. The Grand Seignior furnished us
with thirty covered wagons for our baggage, and five coaches
of the country for our women. We found the road full of the
great spahis and their equipages coming out of Asia to the
war. They always travel with tents; but I chose to lie in
houses all the way.

I will not trouble you with the names of the villages we
passed, in which there was nothing remarkable, but at Tchiorlu,
where there was a *conac*, or little seraglio, built for the use of
the Grand Seignior when he goes this road. I had the curiosity to view all the apartments destined for the ladies of his
court. They were in the midst of a thick grove of trees, made
fresh by fountains; but I was most surprised to see the walls
almost covered with little distiches of Turkish verse, wrote
with pencils. I made my interpreter explain them to me, and
I found several of them very well turned; though I easily believed him, that they had lost much of their beauty in the
translation. One was literally thus in English:

We come into this world; we lodge, and we depart·
He never goes, that 's lodged within my heart.

The rest of our journey was through fine painted meadows, by the side of the sea of Marmora, the ancient Propontis. We lay the next night at Selivrea, anciently a noble town. It is now a good sea-port, and neatly built enough, and has a bridge of thirty-two arches. Here is a famous Greek church. I had given one of my coaches to a Greek lady, who desired the conveniency of traveling with me; she designed to pay her devotions, and I was glad of the opportunity of going with her. I found it an ill-built edifice, set out with the same sort of ornaments, but less rich, as the Roman Catholic churches. They showed me a saint's body, where I threw a piece of money; and a picture of the Virgin Mary, drawn by the hand of St. Luke, very little to the credit of his painting; but, however, the finest Madonna of Italy is not more famous for her miracles. The Greeks have a monstrous taste in their pictures, which, for more finery, are always drawn upon a gold ground. You may imagine what a good air this has; but they have no notion either of shade or proportion. They have a bishop here, who officiated in his purple robe, and sent me a candle almost as big as myself for a present, when I was at my lodging.

We lay that night at a town called Bujuk Checkmedji, or Great Bridge; and the night following, at Kujuk Checkmedji, or Little Bridge; in a very pleasant lodging, formerly a monastery of dervises, having before it a large court, encompassed with marble cloisters, with a good fountain in the middle. The prospect from this place, and the gardens round it, is the most agreeable I have seen; and shows that monks, of all religions, know how to choose their retirements. 'Tis now belonging to a *hogia* or schoolmaster, who teaches boys here. I asked him to show me his own apartment, and was surprised to see him point to a tall cypress-tree in the garden, on the top of which was a place for a bed for himself, and a little lower, one for his wife and two children, who slept there every night. I was so much diverted with the fancy, I resolved to examine his nest nearer; but, after going up fifty steps, I found I had still fifty to go up, and then I must climb from branch to branch, with some hazard of my neck. I thought it, therefore, the best way to come down again.

We arrived the next day at Constantinople; but I can yet tell you very little of it, all my time having been taken up with receiving visits, which are, at least, a very good entertainment to the eyes, the young women being all beauties, and their beauty highly improved by the high taste of their dress. Our palace is in Pera, which is no more a suburb of Constantinople than Westminster is a suburb to London. All the embassadors are lodged very near each other. One part of our house shows us the port, the city, and the seraglio, and the distant hills of Asia; perhaps, all together, the most beautiful prospect in the world.

A certain French author says, "Constantinople is twice as big as Paris." Mr. Wortley is unwilling to own it is bigger than London, though I confess it appears to me to be so; but I don't believe it is so populous. The burying-fields about it are certainly much larger than the whole city. It is surprising what a vast deal of land is lost this way in Turkey. Sometimes I have seen burying-places of several miles, belonging to very inconsiderable villages, which were formerly great towns, and retain no other mark of their ancient grandeur than this dismal one. On no occasion do they ever remove a stone that serves for a monument. Some of them are costly enough, being of very fine marble. They set up a pillar, with a carved turban on the top of it, to the memory of a man; and, as the turbans, by their different shapes, show the quality or profession, 'tis in a manner putting up the arms of the deceased; besides, the pillar commonly bears an inscription in gold letters. The ladies have a simple pillar, without other ornament, except those that die unmarried, who have a rose on the top of their monument. The sepulchers of particular families are railed in, and planted round with trees. Those of the sultans, and some great men, have lamps constantly burning in them.

When I spoke of their religion, I forgot to mention two particularities, one of which I have read of, but it seemed so odd to me, I could not believe it; yet 'tis certainly true: that when a man has divorced his wife in the most solemn manner, he can take her again, upon no other terms than permitting another man to pass a night with her; and there are some examples of those who have submitted to this law, rather than not have back their beloved. The other point of doctrine is very extraordinary. Any woman that dies unmarried is looked upon to die in a state of reprobation. To confirm this belief, they reason, that the end of the creation of woman is to increase and multiply; and that she is only properly employed in the works of her calling when she is bringing forth children, or taking care of them, which are all the virtues that God expects from her. And, indeed, their way of life, which shuts them out of all public commerce, does not permit them any other. Our vulgar notion, that they don't own women to have any souls, is a mistake. 'Tis true they say they are not of so elevated a kind, and therefore must not hope to be admitted into the paradise appointed for the men, who are to be entertained by celestial beauties. But there is a place of happiness destined for souls of the inferior order, where all good women are to be in eternal bliss. Many of them are very superstitious, and will not remain widows ten days, for fear of dying in the reprobate state of an useless creature. But those that like their liberty, and are not slaves to their religion, content themselves with marrying when they are afraid of dying. This is a piece of theology very different from that which teaches nothing to be more acceptable to God than a vow of perpetual virginity; which divinity is most rational, I leave you to determine.

I have already made some progress in a collection of Greek medals. Here are several professed antiquaries who are ready to serve any body that desires them. But you can not imagine how they stare in my face when I inquire about them, as if nobody was permitted to seek after medals till they were grown a piece of antiquity themselves. I have got some very valuable

ones of the Macedonian kings, particularly one of Perseus, s ›
lively, I fancy I can see all his ill qualities in his face. I have
a porphyry head finely cut, of the true Greek sculpture; but who
it represents is to be guessed at by the learned when I return.
For you are not to suppose these antiquaries (who are all
Greeks) know any thing. Their trade is only to sell; they have
correspondents at Aleppo, Grand Cairo, in Arabia, and Pales-
tine, who send them all they can find, and very often great
heaps that are only fit to melt into pans and kettles. They get
the best price they can for them, without knowing those that
are valuable from those that are not. Those that pretend to
skill, generally find out the image of some saint in the medals
of the Greek cities. One of them showing me the figure of a
Pallas, with a victory in her hand on a reverse, assured me it
was the Virgin holding a crucifix. The same man offered me
the head of a Socrates on a sardonyx; and, to enhance the
value, gave him the title of Saint Augustine.

I have bespoken a mummy, which I hope will come safe to
my hands, notwithstanding the misfortune that befell a very fine
one, designed for the King of Sweden. He gave a great price
for it, and the Turks took it into their heads that he must have
some considerable project depending upon it. They fancied it
the body of God knows who; and that the state of their empire
mystically depended on the conservation of it. Some old
prophecies were remembered upon this occasion, and the mummy was committed prisoner to the Seven Towers, where it has
remained under close confinement ever since: I dare not try
my interest in so considerable a point as the release of it; but
I hope mine will pass without examination.

LETTER XII.

BELGRADE VILLAGE, June 17, O. S.

I heartily beg your ladyship's pardon; but I really could
not forbear laughing heartily at your letter, and the commissions you are pleased to honor me with.

You desire me to buy you a Greek slave, who is to be mistress of a thousand good qualities. The Greeks are subjects, and not slaves. Those who are to be bought in that manner are either such as are taken in war, or stolen by the Tartars from Russia, Circassia, or Georgia, and are such miserable, awkward poor wretches, you would not think any of them worthy to be your house-maids. 'Tis true that many thousands were taken in the Morea; but they have been, most of them, redeemed by the charitable contributions of the Christians, or ransomed by their own relations at Venice. The fine slaves that wait upon the great ladies, or serve the pleasures of the great men, are all bought at the age of eight or nine years old, and educated with great care, to accomplish them in singing, dancing, embroidery, etc. They are commonly Circassians, and their patron never sells them, except it is as a punishment for some very great fault. If ever they grow weary of them, they either present them to a friend, or give them their freedom. Those that are exposed to sale at the markets are always either guilty of some crime, or so entirely worthless that they are of no use at all. I am afraid you will doubt the truth of this account, which I own is very different from our common notions in England; but it is no less truth for all that.

Your whole letter is full of mistakes from one end to the other. I see you have taken your ideas of Turkey from that worthy author Dumont, who has wrote with equal ignorance and confidence. 'Tis a particular pleasure to me here to read the voyages to the Levant, which are generally so far removed from truth, and so full of absurdities, I am very well diverted with them. They never fail giving you an account of the women, whom, 'tis certain, they never saw, and talking very wisely of the genius of the men, into whose company they are never admitted; and very often describe mosques, which they dare not even peep into. The Turks are very proud and will not converse with a stranger they are not assured is considerable in his own country. I speak of the men of distinction; for, as to the ordinary fellows, you may imagine what ideas their conversation can give of the general genius of the people.

As to the balm of Mecca, I will certainly send you some; but it is not so easily got as you suppose it, and I can not, in conscience, advise you to make use of it. I know not how it comes to have such universal applause. All the ladies of my acquaintance at London and Vienna have begged me to send pots of it to them. I have had a present of a small quantity (which, I 'll assure you, is very valuable) of the best sort, and with great joy applied it to my face, expecting some wonderful effect to my advantage. The next morning the change indeed was wonderful; my face was swelled to a very extraordinary size, and all over as red as my Lady H——'s. It remained in this lamentable state three days, during which you may be sure I passed my time very ill. I believed it would never be otherwise; and, to add to my mortification, Mr. Wortley reproached my indiscretion without ceasing. However, my face is since *in statu quo ;* nay, I am told by the ladies here, that it is much mended by the operation, which I confess I can not perceive in my looking-glass. Indeed, if one were to form an opinion of this balm from their faces, one should think very well of it. They all make use of it, and have the loveliest bloom in the world. For my part I never intend to endure the pain of it again; let my complexion take its natural course, and decay in its own due time. I have very little esteem for medicines of this nature; but do as you please, madam; only remember before you use it, that your face will not be such as you will care to show in the drawing-room for some days after.

LETTER XIII.

PERA, March 10, O. S, 1717.

l have not written to you, dear sister, these many months— a great piece of self-denial. But I know not where to direct;

or what part of the world you are in. I have received no
letter from you since that short note of April last, in which
you tell me that you are on the point of leaving England, and
promise me a direction for the place you stay in; but I have
in vain expected it till now: and now I only learn from the
gazette that you are returned, which induces me to venture
this letter to your house at London. I had rather ten of my
letters should be lost than you imagine I don't write; and I
think it is hard fortune if one in ten don't reach you. However, I am resolved to keep the copies as testimonies of my
inclination to give you, to the utmost of my power, all the
diverting parts of my travels, while you are exempt from all
the fatigues and inconveniences.

In the first place, then, I wish you joy of your niece; for I
was brought to bed of a daughter* five weeks ago. I don't
mention this as one of my diverting adventures; though I
must own that it is not half so mortifying here as in England;
there being as much difference as there is between a little cold
in the head, which sometimes happens here, and the consumption cough, so common in London. Nobody keeps their
house a month for lying-in; and I am not so fond of any of
our customs as to retain them when they are not necessary.
I returned my visits at three weeks' end ; and, about four days
ago, crossed the sea, which divides this place from Constantinople, to make a new one, where I had the good fortune to
pick up many curiosities.

I went to see the Sultana Hafiten, favorite of the late Emperor Mustapha, who, you know (or perhaps you don't know)
was deposed by his brother, the reigning Sultan, and died a
few weeks after, being poisoned, as it was generally believed.
This lady was, immediately after his death, saluted with an
absolute order to leave the seraglio, and choose herself a hus
band among the great men at the Porte. I suppose you may
imagine her overjoyed at this proposal. Quite the contrary.
These women, who are called, and esteem themselves, queens

* Mary, afterward married to John, Earl of Bute.

look upon this liberty as the greatest disgrace and affront that can happen to them. She threw herself at the Sultan's feet, and begged him to poniard her, rather than use his brother's widow with contempt. She represented to him, in agonies of sorrow, that she was privileged from this misfortune, by having brought five princes into the Ottoman family ; but all the boys being dead, and only one girl surviving, this excuse was not received, and she was compelled to make her choice. She chose Bekir Effendi, then secretary of state, and above fourscore years old, to convince the world that she firmly intended to keep the vow she had made, of never suffering a second husband to approach her bed ; and since she must honor some subject so far as to be called his wife, she would choose him as a mark of her gratitude, since it was he that had presented her, at the age of ten years, to her last lord. But she never permitted him to pay her one visit; though it is now fifteen years she has been in his house, where she passes her time in uninterrupted mourning, with a constancy very little known in Christendom, especially in a widow of one and twenty, for she is now but thirty-six. She has no black eunuchs for her guard, her husband being obliged to respect her as a queen, and not to inquire at all into what is done in her apartment.

I was led into a large room, with a sofa the whole length of it, adorned with white marble pillars like a *ruelle*, covered with pale-blue figured velvet on a silver ground, with cushions of the same, where I was desired to repose till the Sultana appeared, who had contrived this manner of reception to avoid rising up at my entrance, though she made me an inclination of her head when I rose up to her. I was very glad to observe a lady that had been distinguished by the favor of an emperor, to whom beauties were, every day, presented from all parts of the world. But she did not seem to me to have ever been half so beautiful as the fair Fatima I saw at Adrianople ; though she had the remains of a fine face, more decayed by sorrow than time. But her dress was something so

surprisingly rich that I can not forbear describing it to you.
She wore a vest called *donalma*, which differs from a *caftan*
by longer sleeves, and folding over at the bottom. It was of
purple cloth, strait to her shape, and thick set, on each side,
down to her feet, and round the sleeves, with pearls of the
best water, of the same size as their buttons commonly are.
You must not suppose that I mean as large as those of my
Lord ——, but about the bigness of a pea; and to these buttons large loops of diamonds, in the form of those gold loops
so common on birth-day coats. This habit was tied at the
waist with two large tassels of smaller pearls, and round the
arms embroidered with large diamonds. Her shift was fastened at the bottom with a great diamond, shaped like a loz-
enge; her girdle as broad as the broadest English ribbon,
entirely covered with diamonds. Round her neck she wore
three chains which reached to her knees : one of large pearl,
at the bottom of which hung a fine-colored emerald, as big as
a turkey-egg ; another, consisting of two hundred emeralds,
closely joined together, of the most lively green, perfectly
matched, every one as large as a half-crown piece, and as
thick as three crown pieces ; and another of small emeralds,
perfectly round. But her ear-rings eclipsed all the rest. They
were two diamonds, shaped exactly like pears, as large as a
big hazel-nut. Round her *kalpac* she had four strings of
pearl the whitest and the most perfect in the world, at least
enough to make four necklaces, every one as large as the
Duchess of Marlborough's, and of the same shape, fastened
with two roses, consisting of a large ruby for the middle
stone, and round them twenty drops of clean diamonds to
each. Besides this, her head-dress was covered with bodkins
of emeralds and diamonds. She wore large diamond brace-
lets, and had five rings on her fingers (except Mr. Pitt's) the
largest I ever saw in my life. It is for jewelers to compute
the value of these things ; but, according to the common estimation of jewels in our part of the world, her whole dress
must be worth a hundred thousand pounds sterling. This I

am sure of, that no European queen has half the quantity; and the empress's jewels, though very fine, would look very mean near hers.

She gave me a dinner of fifty dishes of meat, which (after their fashion) were placed on the table but one at a time, and was extremely tedious. But the magnificence of her table answered very well to that of her dress. The knives were of gold, and the hafts set with diamonds. But the piece of luxury which grieved my eyes, was the table-cloth and napkins, which were all tiffany, embroidered with silk and gold, in the finest manner, in natural flowers. It was with the utmost regret that I made use of these costly napkins, which were as finely wrought as the finest handkerchiefs that ever came out of this country. You may be sure that they were entirely spoiled before dinner was over. The sherbet (which is the liquor they drink at meals) was served in china bowls; but the covers and salvers massy gold. After dinner, water was brought in gold basins, and towels of the same kind with the napkins, which I very unwillingly wiped my hands upon; and coffee was served in china, with gold *soucoups*.*

The Sultana seemed in a very good humor, and talked to me with the utmost civility. I did not omit this opportunity of learning all that I possibly could of the seraglio, which is so entirely unknown among us. She assured me that the story of the sultan's *throwing a handkerchief* is altogether fabulous; and the manner, upon that occasion, no other than this: He sends the *kyslar aga*, to signify to the lady the honor he intends her. She is immediately complimented upon it by the others, and led to the bath, where she is perfumed and dressed in the most magnificent and becoming manner. The emperor precedes his visit by a royal present, and then comes into her apartment: neither is there any such thing as her creeping in at the bed's foot. She said, that the first he made choice of was always afterward the first in rank, and not the mother of the eldest son, as other writers would

* Saucers.

make us believe. Sometimes the sultan diverts himself in the company of all his ladies, who stand in a circle round him. And she confessed they were ready to die with envy and jealousy of the *happy she* that he distinguished by any appearance of preference. But this seemed to me neither better nor worse than the circles in most courts, where the glance of the monarch is watched, and every smile is waited for with impatience, and envied by those who can not obtain it.

She never mentioned the Sultan without tears in her eyes, yet she seemed very fond of the discourse. "My past happiness," said she, "appears a dream to me. Yet I can not forget that I was beloved by the greatest and most lovely of mankind. I was chosen from all the rest, to make all his campaigns with him; and I would not survive him, if I was not passionately fond of the princess my daughter. Yet all my tenderness for her was hardly enough to make me preserve my life. When I left him, I passed a whole twelvemonth without seeing the light. Time hath softened my despair; yet I now pass some days every week in tears, devoted to the memory of my Sultan."

There was no affectation in these words. It was easy to see she was in a deep melancholy, though her good humor made her willing to divert me.

She asked me to walk in her garden, and one of her slaves immediately brought her a *pellice* of rich brocade lined with sables. I waited on her into the garden, which had nothing in it remarkable but the fountains; and from thence she showed me all her apartments. In her bed-chamber her toilet was displayed, consisting of two looking-glasses, the frames covered with pearls, and her night *talpoche* set with bodkins of jewels, and near it three vests of fine sables, every one of which is, at least, worth a thousand dollars (two hundred pounds English money). I don't doubt but these rich habits were purposely placed in sight, though they seemed negligently thrown on the sofa. When I took my leave of her, I was complimented with perfumes, as at the Grand-Vizier's, and presented with a very fine embroidered handkerchief. Her slaves were to the number of thirty, besides ten little ones, the oldest not above seven years old. These were the most beautiful girls I ever saw, all richly dressed; and I observed that the Sultana took a great deal of pleasure in these lovely children, which is a vast expense; for there is not a handsome girl of that age to be bought under a hundred pounds sterling. They wore little garlands of flowers, and their own hair, braided, which was all their head-dress; but their habits were all of gold stuffs. These served her coffee, kneeling; brought water when she washed, etc. It is a great part of the work of the elder slaves to take care of these young girls, to learn them to embroider, and to serve them as carefully as if they were children of the family.

Now, do you imagine I have entertained you, all this while, with a relation that has, at least, received many embellishments from my hand? This, you will say, is but too like the Arabian Tales: these embroidered napkins, and a jewel as large as a turkey's egg:—You forget, dear sister, those very tales were written by an author of this country, and (excepting the enchantments) are a real representation of the manners here. We travelers are in very hard circumstances: if we say nothing but what has been said before us, *we are dull, and we have observed nothing;* if we tell any thing new, we are laughed at as *fabulous and romantic,* not allowing either for the difference of ranks, which affords difference of company, or more curiosity, or the change of customs, that happen every twenty years in every country. But the truth is, people judge of travelers, exactly with the same candor, good nature, and impartiality they judge of their neighbors upon all occasions. For my part, if I live to return among you, I am so well acquainted with the morals of all my dear friends and acquaintances, that I am resolved to tell them nothing at all, to avoid the imputation (which their charity would certainly incline them to) of my telling too much. But I depend upon your knowing me enough, to believe whatever I seriously assert for truth;

though I give you leave to be surprised at an account so new to you.

But what would you say if I told you that I have been in a harem, where the winter apartment was wainscoted with inlaid work of mother-of-pearl, ivory of different colors, and olive-wood, exactly like the little boxes you have seen brought out of this country; and in whose rooms designed for summer, the walls are all crusted with japan china, the roofs gilt, and the floors spread with the finest Persian carpets? Yet there is nothing more true; such is the palace of my lovely friend, the fair Fatima, whom I was acquainted with at Adrianople. I went to visit her yesterdey; and, if possible, she appeared to me handsomer than before. She met me at the door of her chamber, and, giving me her hand with the best grace in the world. "You Christian ladies," said she, with a smile that made her as beautiful as an angel, "have the reputation of in-constancy, and I did not expect, whatever goodness you ex-pressed for me at Adrianople, that I should ever see you again. But I am now convinced that I have really the happiness of pleasing you; and, if you knew how I speak of you among our ladies, you would be assured that you do me justice in making me your friend." She placed me in the corner of the sofa, and I spent the afternoon in her conversation, with the greatest pleasure in the world.

LETTER XIV.

PERA, March 16, O. S., 1717.

I am extremely pleased, my dear lady, that you have at length found a commission for me that I can answer without disappointing your expectations; though I must tell you that it is not so easy as perhaps you think it; and that if my curi-osity had not been more diligent than any other stranger's has ever yet been, I must have answered you with an excuse, as I was forced to do when you desired me to buy you a Greek slave. I have got for you, as you desire, a Turkish love-letter, which I have put into a little box, and ordered the captain of the Smyrniote to deliver it to you with this letter. The translation of it is literally as follows: The first piece you should pull out of the purse is a little pearl, which is in Turkish called *Ingi*, and must be understood in this manner:

Ingi,	Sensin Guzelern gingi.
Pearl,	*Fairest of the young.*
Caremfil,	Caremfilsen cararen yók.
Clove,	Conge gulsum timarin yók.
	Benseny chok than severim.
	Senin benden, haberin yók.
	You are as slender as the clove !
	You are an unblown rose !
	I have long loved you, and you have not known it !
Pul,	Derdime derman bul.
Jonquil,	*Have pity on my passion !*
Kihat,	Birlerum sahat sahat.
Paper,	*I faint every hour !*
Ermus,	Ver bixe bir umut.
Pear,	*Give me some hope.*
Jahun,	Derdinden oldum zabun.
Soap,	*I am sick with love.*
Chemur,	Ben oliyim size umur.
Coal,	*May I die, and all my years be yours !*
Gul,	Ben aglarum sen gul.
A rose,	*May you be pleased, and your sorrows mine !*
Hasir,	Oliim sana yazir.
A straw,	*Suffer me to be your slave.*
Jo ho,	Ustune bulunmaz pahu.
Cloth,	*Your price is not to be found.*
Tartsin,	Sen ghel ben chekeim senin hartsin.
Cinnamon,	*But my fortune is yours.*
Giro,	Esking-ilen oldum ghira.
A match,	*I burn, I burn ! my flame consumes me !*

Sirma,	Uzunu benden a yirmà.
Gold thread,	*Don't turn away your face from me.*

Satch,	Bazmazum tatch.
Hair;	*Crown of my head!*

Uzum,	Benim iki Guzum.
Grape,	*My two eyes!*

Til,	Ulugorum tez ghel.
Gold wire,	*I die—come quickly.*

And, by way of postscript:

Beber,	Bize bir dogm haber.
Pepper,	*Send me an answer.*

You see this letter is all in verse, and I can assure you there is as much fancy shown in the choice of them as in the most studied expressions of our letters; there being, I believe, a million of verses designed for this use. There is no color, no flower, no weed, no fruit, herb, pebble, or feather, that has not a verse belonging to it; and you may quarrel, reproach, or send letters of passion, friendship, or civility, or even of news, without ever inking your fingers.

I fancy you are now wondering at my profound learning; but, alas! dear madam, I am almost fallen into the misfortune so common to the ambitious; while they are employed on distant insignificant conquests abroad, a rebellion starts up at home: I am in great danger of losing my English. I find 'tis not half so easy to me to write in it as it was a twelvemonth ago. I am forced to study for expressions, and must leave off all other languages, and try to learn my mother tongue. Human understanding is as much limited as human power or human strength. The memory can retain but a certain number of images; and 'tis as impossible for one human creature to be perfect master of ten different languages as to have in perfect subjection ten different kingdoms, or to fight against ten men at a time. I am afraid I shall at last know none as I should do. I live in a place that very well represents the tower of Babel: in Pera they speak Turkish,

Greek, Hebrew, Armenian, Arabic, Persian, Russian, Sclavo-
nian, Wallachian, German, Dutch, French, English, Italian,
Hungarian; and, what is worse, there are ten of these languages spoken in my own family. My grooms are Arabs;
my footmen, French, English and Germans; my nurse an Armenian; my housemaids Russians; half a dozen other servants, Greeks; my steward, an Italian; my janizaries, Turks;
so that I live in the perpetual hearing of this medley of
sounds, which produces a very extraordinary effect upon the
people that are born here; for they learn all these languages
at the same time, and without knowing any of them well
enough to write or read in it. There are very few men,
women, or even children, here, that have not the same compass of words in five or six of them. I know myself of several infants of three or four years old, that speak Italian,
French, Greek, Turkish, and Russian, which last they learn of
their nurses, who are generally of that country. This seems
almost incredible to you, and is, in my mind, one of the most
curious things in this country, and takes off very much from
the merit of our ladies who set up for such extraordinary geniuses, upon the credit of some superficial knowledge of French
and Italian.

As I prefer English to all the rest, I am extremely mortified at the daily decay of it in my head, where I 'll assure you
(with grief of heart) it is reduced to such a small number
of words I can not recollect any tolerable phrase to conclude
my letter with, and am forced to tell your ladyship, very
bluntly, that I am, yours, etc.

LETTER XV.

TUNIS, July 31, O. S., 1718.

I left Constantinople the sixth of the last month, and this
is the first post from whence I could send a letter, though
I have often wished for the opportunity, that I might impart

some of the pleasure I found in this voyage through the most agreeable part of the world, where every scene presents me some poetical idea.

> Warm'd with poetic transport I survey
> The immortal islands, and the well-known sea.
> For here so oft the muse her harp has strung,
> That not a mountain rears its head unsung.

I beg your pardon for this sally, and will, if I can, continue the rest of my account in plain prose. The second day after we set sail we passed Gallipolis, a fair city, situated in the bay of Chersonesus, and much respected by the Turks, being the first town they took in Europe. At five the next morning we anchored in the Hellespont, between the castles of Sestos and Abydos, now called the Dardinelli. These are now two little ancient castles, but of no strength, being commanded by a rising ground behind them, which I confess I should never have taken notice of if I had not heard it observed by our captain and officers, my imagination being wholly employed by the tragic story that you are well acquainted with :

> The swimming lover, and the nightly bride,
> How Hero loved, and how Leander died.

Verse again !—I am certainly infected by the poetical air I have passed through. That of Abydos is undoubtedly very amorous, since that soft passion betrayed the castle into the hands of the Turks who besieged it in the reign of Orchanes. The governor's daughter imagining to have seen her future husband in a dream (though I don't find she had either slept upon bride-cake, or kept St. Agnes's fast), fancied she saw the dear figure in the form of one of her besiegers ; and, being willing to obey her destiny, tossed a note to him over the wall, with the offer of her person, and the delivery of the castle. He showed it to his general, who consented to try the sincerity of her intentions, and withdrew his army, ordering the young man to return with a select body of men at midnight. She admitted him at the appointed hour; he destroyed the garrison, took the father prisoner, and made her his wife. This town is in Asia, first founded by the Milesians. Sestos is in Europe, and was once the principal city of Chersonesus. Since I have seen this strait, I find nothing improbable in the adventure of Leander, or very wonderful in the bridge of boats of Xerxes. 'Tis so narrow 'tis not surprising a young lover should attempt to swim, or an ambitious king try to pass his army over it. But then, 'tis so subject to storms, 'tis no wonder the lover perished, and the bridge was broken. From hence we had a full view of Mount Ida,

> Where Juno once caress'd her am'rous Jove,
> And the world's master lay subdued by love.

Not many leagues' sail from hence, I saw the point of land where poor old Hecuba was buried; and about a league from that place is Cape Janizary, the famous promontory of Sigæum, where we anchored. My curiosity supplied me with strength to climb to the top of it to see the place where Achilles was buried, and where Alexander ran naked round his tomb in honor of him, which no doubt was a great comfort to his ghost. I saw there the ruins of a very large city, and found a stone, on which Mr. Wortley plainly distinguished the words of *ΣΙΓΑΙΑΝ ΠΟΛΙΝ*. We ordered this on board the ship; but were showed others much more curious by a Greek priest though a very ignorant fellow, that could give no tolerable account of any thing. On each side the door of this little church lie two large stones, about ten feet long each, five in breadth, and three in thickness. That on the right is a very fine white marble, the side of it beautifully carved in bas-relief; it represents a woman, who seems to be designed for some deity, sitting on a chair with a footstool, and before her another woman weeping, and presenting to her a young child that she has in her arms, followed by a procession of women with children in the same manner. This is certainly part of a very ancient tomb : but I dare not pretend to give the true explanation of it. On the stone, on the left side, is a very fair inscription ; but the Greek is too ancient for Mr. Wortley's interpretation. I am very sorry not to have the original in my possession, which might have been purchased of the poor inhabitants for a small sum of money. But our captain assured us that without having machines made on purpose, 'twas impossible to bear it to the sea-side ; and, when it was there, his long-boat would not be large enough to hold it.*

The ruins of this great city are now inhabited by poor Greek peasants, who wear the Sciote habit, the women being in short petticoats, fastened by straps round their shoulders, and large smock sleeves of white linen, with neat shoes and stockings, and on their heads a large piece of muslin, which falls in large folds on their shoulders. One of my countrymen, Mr. Sandys† (whose book I doubt not you have read, as one of the best of its kind), speaking of these ruins, supposes them to have been the foundation of a city begun by Constantine, before his building Byzautium ; but I see no good reason for that imagination, and am apt to believe them much more ancient.

We saw very plainly from this promontory the river Simois rolling from Mount Ida, and running through a very spacious valley. It is now a considerable river, and is called Simores ; it is joined in the vale by the Scamander, which appeared a small stream half choked with mud, but is perhaps large in the winter. This was Xanthus among the gods, as Homer tells

---

* The first-mentioned of these marbles is engraved in the Ionian Antiquities, published by the Dilettanti Society, and described by Dr. Chandler in his Tour in Asia Minor. The second bears the celebrated inscription so often referred to, in proof of the Βουστροφηδον, one of the most ancient forms of writing among the Greeks. For accurate accounts and engravings of these curiosities, see Chishull, Shuckforth, and Chandler, Inscript. Antiq. Knight on the Greek Alphabets, etc.

† George Sandys, one of the most valuable travelers into the Levant, whose work had reached four editions in the reign of Charles the First.

us; and 'tis by that heavenly name the nymph Oenone invokes it in her epistle to Paris. The Trojan virgins* used to offer their first favors to it, by the name of Scamander, till the adventure which Monsieur de la Fontaine has told so agreeably abolished that heathenish ceremony. When the stream is mingled with the Simois, they run together to the sea.

All that is now left of Troy is the ground on which it stood; for, I am firmly persuaded, whatever pieces of antiquity may be found round it are much more modern, and I think Strabo says the same thing. However, there is some pleasure in seeing the valley where I imagined the famous duel of Menelaus and Paris had been fought, and where the greatest city in the world was situated. 'Tis certainly the noblest situation that can be found for the head of a great empire, much to be preferred to that of Constantinople, the harbor here being always convenient for ships from all parts of the world, and that of Constantinople inaccessible almost six months in the year, while the north wind reigns.

North of the promontory of Sigéum we saw that of Rhæteum, famed for the sepulcher of Ajax. While I viewed these celebrated fields and rivers, I admired the exact geography of Homer, whom I had in my hand. Almost every epithet he gives to a mountain or plain is still just for it; and I spent several hours here in as agreeable cogitations as ever Don Quixote had on mount Montesinos. We sailed next night to the shore, where 'tis vulgarly reported Troy stood; and I took the pains of rising at two in the morning to view coolly those ruins which are commonly showéd to strangers, and which the Turks call *Eski Stamboul*,† *i. e.*, Old Constantinople. For

* For this curious story, Monsieur Bayle may be consulted in his Dictionary, article "Scamander." It appears in the Letters of Oschines, vol. i. pp. 125, 126, edit. Genev. 1607; also in Philostrates and Vigenerus.

† Alexandria Troas, which the early travelers have erroneously considered as the true site of ancient Troy. See Belon, Ch. vi. 4to. 1588, Viaggi di Pietro Della Valle, 4to. 1650. Gibbon (Rom. Hist. vol. iii. p. 10) remarks, that Wood, in his observations on the Troad, p. 140,

that reason, as well as some others, I conjecture them to be the remains of that city begun by Constantine. I hired an ass (the only voiture to be had here), that I might go some miles into the country, and take a tour round the ancient walls, which are of a vast extent. We found the remains of a castle on a hill, and of another in a valley, several broken pillars, and two pedestals, from which I took those Latin inscriptions:

1.

DIVI. AUG. COL.
ET COL. IUL. PHILIPPENSIS
EORUNDEM PRINCIPUM
COL. IUL. PARIANÆ. TRIBUN.
MILIT. COH. XXXII. VOLUNTAR.
TRIB. MILIT. LEG. XIII. GEM.
PRÆFECTO EQUIT. ALÆ. L
SCUBULORUM
VIC. VIII.

2.

DIVI. IULI. FLAMINI
C. ANTONIO. M. F.
VOLT. RUFO. FLAMIN.
DIV. AUG. COL· CL. APRENS.
ET COL. IUL. PHILIPPENSIS
EORUNDEM ET PRINCIP. ITEM
COL. IUL. PARIANÆ TRIB.
MILIT. COH. XXXII. VOLUNTARIOR
TRIB. MILIT. XIII.
GEM. PRÆF. EQUIT. ALÆ. L
SCUBULORUM
VIC. VII.

I do not doubt but the remains of a temple near this place are the ruins of one dedicated to Augustus; and I know not why Mr. Sandys calls it a Christian temple, since the Romans certainly built hereabouts. Here are many tombs of fine mar-

141, had confounded Ilium with Alexandria Troas, although sixteen miles distant from each other. In the Ionian Antiquities are some fine views of these ruins.

ble, and vast pieces of granite, which are daily lessened by the prodigious balls that the Turks make from them for their cannon. We passed that evening the isle of Tenedos, once under the patronage of Apollo, as he gave it in himself in the particulars of his estate when he courted Daphne. It is but ten miles in circuit, but in those days very rich and well-peopled, still famous for its excellent wine. I say nothing of Tennes, from whom it was called; but naming Mytilene, where we passed next, I can not forbear mentioning Lesbos, where Sappho sung, and Pittacus reigned, famous for the birth of Alcæus, Theophrastus, and Arion, those masters in poetry, philosophy, and music. This was one of the last islands that remained in the Christian dominion after the conquest of Constantinople by the Turks. But need I talk to you of Cantacuseni, etc., princes that you are as well acquainted with as I am? 'T was with regret I saw us sail from this island into the Egean sea, now the Archipelago, leaving Scio (the ancient Chios) on the left, which is the richest and most populous of these islands, fruitful in cotton, corn, and silk, planted with groves of orange and lemon-trees, and the Arvisian mountain, still celebrated for the nectar that Virgil mentions. Here is the best manufacture of silks in all Turkey. The town is well built, the women famous for their beauty, and show their faces as in Christendom. There are many rich families, though they confine their magnificence to the inside of their houses, to avoid the jealousy of the Turks, who have a pasha here: however, they enjoy a reasonable liberty, and indulge the genius of their country;

> And eat, and sing, and dance away their time,
> Fresh as their groves, and happy as their clime.

Their chains hang lightly on them, though 'tis not long since they were imposed, not being under the Turk till 1566. But perhaps 'tis as easy to obey the Grand-Seignior as the State of Genoa, to whom they were sold by the Greek Emperor. But I forget myself in these historical touches, which are very im-

pertinent when I write to you.   Passing the strait between the
islands of Andros and Achaia, now Libadia, we saw the promontory of Sunium, now called Cape Colonna, where are yet
standing the vast pillars of a temple of Minerva.   This venerable sight made me think, with double regret, on a beautiful
temple of Theseus, which, I am assured, was almost entire at
Athens till the last campaign in the Morea, that the Turks filled
it with powder, and it was accidentally blown up.   You may
believe I had a great mind to land on the famed Peloponnesus,
though it were only to look on the rivers of Æsopus, Peneus,
Inachus, and Eurotas, the fields of Arcadia, and other scenes
of ancient mythology.   But instead of demi-gods and heroes, I
was credibly informed 'tis now over-run by robbers, and that
I should run a great risk of falling into their hands by undertaking such a journey through a desert country, for which
however, I have so much respect that I have much ado to
hinder myself from troubling you with its whole history, from
the foundation of Nicana and Corinth, to the last campaign
there ; but I check the inclination as I did that of landing.
We sailed quietly by Cape Angelo, once Malea, where I saw no
remains of the famous temple of Apollo.   We came that evening in sight of Candia : it is very mountainous ; we easily distinguished that of Ida.   We have Virgil's authority, that here
were a hundred cities—

Centum urbes habitant magnas—

The chief of them—the scene of monstrous passions.   Metellus
first conquered this birth-place of his Jupiter ; it fell afterward
into the hands of—I am running on to the very siege of Candia ; and I am so angry with myself that I will pass by all the
other islands with this general reflection, that 'tis impossible to
imagine any thing more agreeable than this journey would have
been two or three thousand years since, when, after drinking
a dish of tea with Sappho, I might have gone the same evening to visit the temple of Homer in Chios, and passed this voy-

age in taking plans of magnificent temples, delineating the miracles of statuaries, and conversing with the most polite and most gay of mankind. Alas! art is extinct here; the wonders of nature alone remain; and it was with vast pleasure I observed those of Mount Etna, whose flame appears very bright in the night many leagues off at sea, and fills the head with a thousand conjectures. However, I honor philosophy too much to imagine it could turn that of Empedocles; and Lucian shall never make me believe such a scandal of a man, of whom Lucretius says:

Vix humana videtur stirpe creatus.

We passed Trinacria without hearing any of the syrens that Homer describes; and, being thrown on neither Scylla nor Charybdis, came safe to Malta, first called Melita, from the abundance of honey. It is a whole rock covered with very little earth. The Grand-Master lives here in the state of a sovereign prince; but his strength at sea now is very small. The fortifications are reckoned the best in the world, all cut in the solid rock with infinite expense and labor. Off this island we were tossed by a severe storm, and were very glad, after eight days, to be able to put into Porta Farine, on the African shore, where our ship now rides. At Tunis we were met by the English consul who resides there. I readily accepted of the offer of his house for some days, being very curious to see this part of the world, and particularly the ruins of Carthage. I set out in his chaise at nine at night, the moon being at full. I saw the prospect of the country almost as well as I could have done by daylight; and the heat of the sun is now so intolerable 'tis impossible to travel at any other time. The soil is for the most part sandy, but everywhere fruitful of date, olive, and fig-trees, which grow without art, yet afford the most delicious fruit in the world. Their vineyards and melon-fields are inclosed by hedges of that plant we call Indian fig, which is an admirable fence, no wild beast being able to pass it. It grows a great height, very thick, and the spikes or thorns are as long and as sharp as bodkins; it bears a fruit much eaten by the peasants, and which has no ill taste.

It being now the season of the Turkish *ramazan*, or Lent, and all here professing, at least, the Mohammedan religion, they fast till the going down of the sun, and spend the night in feasting. We saw under the trees companies of the country people, eating, singing, and dancing to their wild music. They are not quite black, but all mulattoes, and the most frightful creatures that can appear in a human figure. They are almost naked, only wearing a piece of coarse serge wrapped about them. But the women have their arms, to their very shoulders, and their necks and faces, adorned with flowers, stars, and various sorts of figures impressed by gunpowder; a considerable addition to their natural deformity; which is, however, esteemed very ornamental among them; and I believe they suffer a good deal of pain by it.

About six miles from Tunis we saw the remains of that noble aqueduct, which carried the water to Carthage over several high mountains, the length of forty miles. There are still many arches entire. We spent two hours viewing it with great attention, and Mr. Wortley assured me that of Rome is very much inferior to it. The stones are of a prodigious size, and yet all polished, and so exactly fitted to each other very little cement has been made use of to join them. Yet they may probably stand a thousand years longer, if art is not made use of to pull them down. Soon after daybreak I arrived at Tunis, a town fairly built of very white stone, but quite without gardens, which, they say, were all destroyed when the Turks first took it, none having been planted since. The dry sand gives a very disagreeable prospect to the eye; and the want of shade contributing to the natural heat of the climate, renders it so excessive that I have much ado to support it. 'Tis true here is every noon the refreshment of the sea-breeze, without which it would be impossible to live; but no fresh water but what is preserved in the cisterns of the rains that fall in the month of September. The women of the town go vailed from head to foot under a black crape; and, being mixed with a breed of renegadoes, are said to be many of them fair and handsome. This city was besieged in 1270, by Lewis, King of France, who died under the walls of it of a pestilential fever. After his death, Philip, his son, and our prince Edward, son of Henry III., raised the siege on honorable terms. It remained under its natural African kings, till betrayed into the hands of Barbarossa, admiral of Solyman the Magnificent. The Emperor Charles V. expelled Barbarossa, but it was recovered by the Turks, under the conduct of Sinan Pasha, in the reign of Selim II. From that time till now it has remained tributary to the Grand-Signior, governed by a *bey*, who suffers the name of subject to the Turk, but has renounced the subjection, being absolute, and very seldom paying any tribute. The great city of Bagdad is at this time in the same circumstances; and the Grand-Signior connives at the loss of these dominions, for fear of losing even the titles of them.

I went very early yesterday morning (after one night's repose) to see the ruins of Carthage. I was, however, half broiled in the sun, and overjoyed to be led into one of the subterranean apartments, which they called *The Stables of the Elephants*, but which I can not believe were ever designed for that use. I found in them many broken pieces of columns of fine marble, and some of porphyry. I can not think any body would take the insignificant pains of carrying them thither, and I can not imagine such fine pillars were designed for the use of stables. I am apt to believe they were summer apartments under their palaces, which the heat of the climate rendered necessary. They are now used as granaries by the country people. While I sat here, from the town of *Tents*, not far off, many of the women flocked in to see me, and we were equally entertained with viewing one another. Their posture in sitting, the color of their skin, their lank black hair falling on each side their faces, their features, and the shape of their limbs, differ so little from their country-people the baboons, 'tis hard to fancy them a distinct race; I could not help thinking there had been some ancient alliances between them.

When I was a little refreshed by rest, and some milk and exquisite fruit they brought me, I went up the little hill where once stood the castle of Byrsa, and from thence I had a distinct view of the situation of the famous city of Carthage, which stood on an isthmus, the sea coming on each side of it. 'Tis now a marshy ground on one side, where there are salt ponds. Strabo calls Carthage forty miles in circumference. There are now no remains of it but what I have described; and the history of it is too well known to want my abridgment of it. You see, sir, that I think you esteem obedience better than compliments. I have answered your letter, by giving you the accounts you desired, and have reserved my thanks to the conclusion. I intend to leave this place to-morrow, and continue my journey through Italy and France. In one of those places I hope to tell you, by word of mouth, that I am, Your humble servant, etc., etc.

LETTER XVI.

Genoa, August 28, O. S. 1718.

Genoa is situated in a very fine bay; and being built on a rising hill, intermixed with gardens, and beautified with the most excellent architecture, gives a very fine prospect off at sea; though it lost much of its beauty in my eyes, having been accustomed to that of Constantinople. The Genoese were once masters of several islands in the Archipelago, and all that part of Constantinople which is now called Galata. Their betraying the Christian cause by facilitating the taking of Constantinople by the Turk, deserved what has since happened to them, even the loss of all their conquests on that side to those infidels. They are at present far from rich, and are despised by the French, since their doge was forced by the late king to go in person to Paris, to ask pardon for such a trifle as the arms of France over the house of the envoy being spattered with dung in the night. This, I suppose, was done by some of the Spanish faction, which still makes up the majority here, though they dare not openly declare it. The ladies affect the French habit, and are more genteel than those they imitate. I do not doubt but the custom of cecisbeos has very much improved their airs. I know not whether you ever heard of those animals. Upon my word, nothing but my own eyes could have convinced me there were any such upon earth. The fashion began here, and is now received all over Italy, where the husbands are not such terrible creatures as we represent them. There are none among them such brutes as to pretend to find fault with a custom so well established, and so politically founded, since I am assured that it was an expedient first found out by the senate, to put an end to those family hatreds which tore their State to pieces, and to find employment for those young men who were forced to cut one another's throats *pour passer le temps ;* and it has succeeded so well, that, since the institution of cecisbei, there has been nothing but peace and good humor among them. These are gentlemen who devote themselves to the service of a particular lady (I mean a married one, for the virgins are all invisible, and confined to convents) : they are obliged to wait on her to all public places, such as the plays, the operas, and assemblies (which are here called *Conversations*), where they wait behind her chair, take care of her fan and gloves, if she play, have the privilege of whispers, etc. When she goes out they serve her instead of lacqueys, gravely trotting by her chair. 'Tis their business to prepare for her a present against any day of public appearance, not forgetting that of her own name :* in short, they are to spend all their time and money in her service, who rewards them accordingly (for opportunity they want none) ; but the husband is not to have the impudence to suppose this any other than pure Platonic friendship. 'Tis true, they endeavor to give her a cecisbeo of their own choosing ;

---

* That is, the day of the saint after whom she is called.

but when the lady happens not to be of the same taste, as that often happens, she never fails to bring it about to have one of her own fancy. In former times, one beauty used to have eight or ten of these humble admirers; but those days of plenty and humility are no more: men grow more scarce and saucy; and every lady is forced to content herself with one at a time.

You may see in this place the *glorious liberty* of a republic, or, more properly, an aristocracy, the common people being here as errant slaves as the French; but the old nobles pay little respect to the doge, who is but two years in his office, and whose wife, at that very time, assumes no rank above another noble lady. 'Tis true, the family of Andrea Doria (that great man, who restored them that liberty they enjoy) have some particular privileges: when the senate found it necessary to put a stop to the luxury of dress, forbidding the wearing of jewels and brocades, they left them at liberty to make what expense they pleased. I look with great pleasure on the statue of that hero, which is in the court belonging to the house of Duke Doria. This puts me in mind of their palaces, which I can never describe as I ought. Is it not enough that I say they are, most of them, the design of Palladio? The street called Strada Nova is perhaps the most beautiful line of building in the world. I must particularly mention the vast palaces of Durazzo; those of the two Balbi, joined together by a magnificent colonnade; that of the Imperiale at this village of St. Pierre d'Arena; and another of the Doria. The perfection of architecture, and the utmost profusion of rich furniture, are to be seen here, disposed with the most elegant taste and lavish magnificence. But I am charmed with nothing so much as the collection of pictures by the pencils of Raphael, Paulo Veronese, Titian, Caracci, Michael Angelo, Guido, and Correggio, which two I mention last as my particular favorites. I own I can find no pleasure in objects of horror; and, in my opinion, the more naturally a crucifix is represented, the more disagreeable it is. These, my beloved

painters, show nature, and show it in the most charming light.
I was particularly pleased with a Lucretia in the house of
Balbi : the expressive beauty of that face and bosom gives
all the expression of pity and admiration that could be raised
in the soul by the finest poem upon that subject. A Cleo-
patra of the same hand deserves to be mentioned ; and I
should say more of her, if Lucretia had not at first engaged
my eyes. Here are also some inestimable ancient bustos. The
Church of St. Lawrence is built of black and white marble,
where is kept that famous plate of a single emerald, which is
not now permitted to be handled, since a plot, which they say
was discovered to throw it on the pavement and break it—a
childish piece of malice, which they ascribe to the King of
Sicily, to be revenged for their refusing to sell it to him. The
Church of the Annunciation is finely lined with marble ; the
pillars are of red and white marble : that of St. Ambrose has
been very much adorned by the Jesuits : but I confess all the
churches appeared so mean to me, after that of Sancta Sophia,
I can hardly do them the honor of writing down their names.
But I hope you will own I have made good use of my time,
in seeing so much, since 'tis not many days that we have
been out of the quarantine, from which nobody is exempted
coming from the Levant. Ours, indeed, was very much shortened, and very agreeably passed in M. d'Avenant's company,
in the village of St. Pierre d'Arena, about a mile from Genoa,
in a house built by Palladio, so well designed, and so nobly
proportioned, 't was a pleasure to walk in it. We were visited
.here only by a few English, in the company of a noble Genoese, commissioned to see we did not touch one another. I
shall stay here some days longer, and could almost wish it
were for all my life; but mine, I fear, is not destined to so
much tranquillity.

Note.—Of the foregoing letters, the *sixth*, *twelfth*, and *fourteenth*
were addressed to Lady Rich; the *seventh*, *tenth* and *eleventh* to the
Abbot of ——; the *fifteenth* to the Abbé; and the others to her sister,
Lady Mar.—*Am. ed.*

LETTERS TO AND FROM ALEXANDER POPE.*

FROM 1716 TO 1718.

LETTER I.

TO LADY MARY WORTLEY MONTAGU.

TWICKENHAM, Aug. 18, O. S., 1716.

MADAM, I can say little to recommend the letters I am beginning to write to you but that they will be the most impartial representations of a free heart, and the truest copies you ever saw, though of a very mean original. Not a feature will be softened, or any advantageous light employed to make the ugly thing a little less hideous, but you shall find it in all respects most horribly-like. You will do me an injustice if you look upon any thing I shall say from this instant, as a compliment either to you or to myself: whatever I write will be the real thought of that hour, and I know you will no more expect it of me to persevere till death in every sentiment or

---

* This correspondence was held during the "Embassy;" but it seemed to me best to separate the letters from those written to the other "Friends" of Lady Mary, and give, consecutively, Mr. Pope's letters to her, as well as her answers. In this way, the friendship then subsisting between them can be best understood. It will be seen that he solicited the correspondence, and held the genius and character of Lady Mary in such regard as a devotee might have expressed for his patron saint. That he afterward became her most implacable enemy, was not her fault, but his; the meanness of wounded vanity prompted his bitter sarcasms on women in general and his wicked libels on Lady Mary in particular.—AM. ED.

notion I now set down, than you would imagine a man's face should never change after his picture was once drawn.

The freedom I shall use in this manner of thinking aloud (as somebody calls it) or talking upon paper, may indeed prove me a fool, but it will prove me one of the best sort of fools, the honest ones. And since what folly we have will infallibly buoy up at one time or other in spite of all our art to keep it down, it is almost foolish to take any pains to conceal it at all, and almost knavish to do it from those that are our friends. If Momus's project had taken of having windows in our breasts, I should be for carrying it further and making those windows casements : that while a man showed his heart to all the world, he might do something more for his friends, e'en take it out, and trust it to their handling. I think I love you as well as King Herod could Herodias (though I never had so much as one dance with you), and would as freely give you my heart in a dish as he did another's head. But since Jupiter will not have it so, I must be content to show my taste in life as I do my taste in painting—by loving to have as little drapery as possible, because it is good to use people to what they must be acquainted with ; and there will certainly come some day of judgment to uncover every soul of us. We shall then see how the prudes of this world owed all their fine figure only to their being a little straiter laced, and that they were naturally as arrant squabs as those that went more loose, nay, as those that never girded their loins at all.

But a particular reason to engage you to write your thoughts the more freely to me, is, that I am confident no one knows you better. For I find, when others express their opinion of you, it falls very short of mine, and I am sure, at the same time, theirs is such as you would think sufficiently in your favor.

You may easily imagine how desirous I must be of a correspondence with a person who had taught me long ago that it was as possible to esteem at first sight, as to love : and who has since ruined me for all the conversation of one sex, and almost all the friendship of the other. I am but too sensible, through your means, that the company of men wants a certain softness to recommend it, and that of women wants every thing else. How often have I been quietly going to take possession of that tranquillity and indolence I had so long found in the country, when one evening of your conversation has spoiled me for a solitaire too! Books have lost their effect upon me; and I was convinced since I saw you that there is something more powerful than philosophy, and, since I heard you, that there is one alive wiser than all the sages. A plague of female wisdom! it makes a man ten times more uneasy than his own! What is very strange, Virtue herself, when you have the dressing her, is too amiable for one's repose. What a world of good might you have done in your time, if you had allowed half the fine gentlemen who have seen you to have but conversed with you? They would have been strangely caught, while they thought only to fall in love with a fair face, and you had bewitched them with reason and virtue; two beauties, that the very fops pretend to no acquaintance with.

The unhappy distance at which we correspond, removes a great many of those punctilious restrictions and decorums that oftentimes in nearer conversation prejudice truth to save good breeding. I may now hear of my faults, and you of your good qualities, without a blush on either side. We converse upon such unfortunate generous terms as exclude the regards of fear, shame, or design in either of us. And methinks it would be as ungenerous a part to impose even in a single thought upon each other, in this state of separation, as for spirits of a different sphere, who have so little intercourse with us, to employ that little (as some would make us think they do) in putting tricks and delusions upon poor mortals.

Let me begin then, madam, by asking you a question, which may enable me to judge better of my own conduct than most instances of my life. In what manner did I behave the last hour I saw you ? What degree of concern did I discover when I felt a misfortune, which I hope you never will feel, that of parting from what one most esteems ? For if my parting looked but like that of your common acquaintance, I am the greatest of all the hypocrites that ever decency made.

I never since pass by the house but with the same sort of melancholy that we feel upon seeing the tomb of a friend, which only serves to put us in mind of what we have lost. I reflect upon the circumstances of your departure, your behavior in what I may call your last moments, and I indulge a gloomy kind of satisfaction in thinking you gave some of those last moments to me. I would fain imagine this was not accidental, but proceeded from a penetration which I know you have in finding out the truth of people's sentiments, and that you were not unwilling the last man that would have parted with you should be the last that did. I really looked upon you then, as the friends of Curtius might have done upon that hero in the instant he was devoting himself to glory, and running to be lost, out of generosity. I was obliged to admire your resolution in as great a degree as I deplored it; and could only wish that Heaven would reward so much merit as was to be taken from us with all the felicity it could enjoy elsewhere. May that person for whom you have left all the world be so just as to prefer you to all the world. I believe his good understanding has engaged him to do so hitherto, and I think his gratitude must for the future. May you continue to think him worthy of whatever you have done; may you ever look upon him with the eyes of a first lover, nay, if possible, with all the un-reasonable happy fondness of an unexperienced one, surrounded with all the enchantments and ideas of romance and poetry. In a word, may you receive from him as many pleasures and gratifications as even I think you can give. I wish this from my heart, and while I examine what passes there in regard to you, I can not but glory in my own heart that it is capable of so much generosity.

LETTER II.

TO MR. POPE.*

Vienna, Sept. 4, O. S., 1717.

Perhaps you 'll laugh at me for thanking you very gravely for all the obliging concern you express for me. 'Tis certain that I may, if I please, take the fine things you say to me for wit and raillery; and, it may be, it would be taking them right. But I never, in my life, was half so well disposed to believe you in earnest as I am at present; and that distance, which makes the continuation of your friendship improbable, has very much increased my faith in it.

I find that I have (as well as the rest of my sex), whatever face I set on't, a strong disposition to believe in miracles. Don't fancy, however, that I am infected by the air of these Popish countries; I have, indeed, so far wandered from the discipline of the Church of England, as to have been last Sunday at the Opera, which was performed in the garden of the Favorita; and I was so much pleased with it, I have not yet repented my seeing it. Nothing of that kind ever was more magnificent; and I can easily believe what I am told, that the decorations and habits cost the emperor thirty thousand pounds sterling. The stage was built over a very large canal, and, at the beginning of the second act, divided into two parts, discovering the water, on which there immediately came, from different parts, two fleets of little gilded vessels, that gave the representation of a naval fight. It is not easy to imagine the

---

* In the eighth volume of Pope's Works, are first published thirteen of his letters to Lady Mary Wortley Montagu communicated to Dr. Warton by the present Primate of Ireland. These MSS. are in the possession of the Marquis of Bute. As many are without date, the arrangement of them must be directed by circumstances; and as most of them were written to Lady Mary during her first absence from England, we shall advert to them, as making a part of this correspondence. The letter of Pope's, to which this is an answer, was first printed from the original MS. in Works of Lady Mary Wortley Montagu, 1803.

beauty of this scene, which I took particular notice of. But all the rest were perfectly fine in their kind. The story of the opera is the enchantment of Alcina, which gives opportunities for a great variety of machines, and changes of the scenes, which are performed with a surprising swiftness. The theater is so large that it is hard to carry the eye to the end of it, and the habits in the utmost magnificence, to the number of one hundred and eight. No house could hold such large decorations; but the ladies all sitting in the open air, exposes them to great inconveniences; for there is but one canopy for the imperial family; and, the first night it was represented, a shower of rain happening, the opera was broken off, and the company crowded away in such confusion that I was almost squeezed to death.

But if their operas are thus delightful, their comedies are in as high a degree ridiculous.. They have but one playhouse, where I had the curiosity to go to a German comedy, and was very glad it happened to be the story of Amphitryon. As that subject has been already handled by a Latin, French, and English poet, I was curious to see what an Austrian author would make of it. I understand enough of that language to comprehend the greatest part of it; and besides, I took with me a lady, who had the goodness to explain to me every word. The way is, to take a box, which holds four, for yourself and company. The fixed price is a gold ducat. I thought the house very low and dark; but I confess, the comedy admirably recompensed that defect. I never laughed so much in my life. It began with Jupiter's falling in love out of a peep-hole in the clouds, and ended with the birth of Hercules. But what was most pleasant, was the use Jupiter made of his metamorphosis; for you no sooner saw him under the figure of Amphitryon, but instead of flying to Alcmena, with the raptures Mr. Dryden puts into his mouth, he sends for Amphitryon's tailor, and cheats him of a laced coat, and his banker of a bag of money, a Jew of a diamond ring, and bespeaks a great supper in his name; and the greatest part of the comedy turns upon poor Amphitryon's being tormented by these people for their debts.   Mercury uses Sosia in the same manner.   But I could not easily pardon the liberty the poet has taken of larding his play with, not only indecent expressions, but such gross words as I don't think our mob would suffer from a mountebank. Besides, the two Sosias very fairly let down their breeches in the direct view of the boxes, which were full of people of the first rank, that seemed very well pleased with their entertainment, and assured me this was a celebrated piece.

I shall conclude my letter with this remarkable relation, very well worthy the serious consideration of Mr. Collier.*   I won't trouble you with farewell compliments, which I think generally as impertinent as courtesies at leaving the room, when the visit had been too long already.

LETTER III.

FROM MR. POPE.

Madam, I no more think I can have too many of your letters, than I would have too many writings to entitle me to the greatest estate in the world; which I think so valuable a friendship as yours is equal to.   I am angry at every scrap of paper lost as something that interrupts the history of my title; and though it is but an odd compliment to compare a fine lady to Sybil, your leaves, methinks, like hers, are too good to be committed to the winds; though I have no other way of receiving them but by those unfaithful messengers.   I have had but three, and I reckon in that short one from Dort, which was rather a dying ejaculation than a letter.   But I have so great an opinion of your goodness that, had I received none, I should

* Jeremy Collier, an English divine, eminent for his piety and wit. In 1698 he wrote "A short view of the Immorality and Profaneness of the English Stage, together with the sense of Antiquity on this subject," 8vo.   This tract excited the resentment of the wits, and engaged him in a controversy with Congreve and Vanbrugh.

not have accused you of neglect or insensibility. I am not so
wrong-headed as to quarrel with my friends the minute they
don't write, I'd as soon quarrel at the sun the minute he did
not shine, which he is hindered from by accidental causes, and
is in reality all that time performing the same course, and doing
the same good offices as ever.

You have contrived to say in your last, the two most pleasing things to me in nature; the first is, that whatever be the
fate of your letters, you will continue to write in the discharge
of your conscience. This is generous to the last degree, and
a virtue you ought to enjoy. Be assured, in return, my heart
shall be as ready to think you have done every good thing, as
yours can be to do it; so that you shall never be able to favor
your absent friend, before he has thought himself obliged to
you for the very favor you are then conferring.

The other is, the justice you do me in taking what I writ
to you in the serious manner it was meant : it is the point upon
which I can bear no suspicion, and in which, above all, I desire to be thought serious : it would be the most vexatious of
all tyranny, if you should pretend to take for raillery what is
the mere disguise of a discontented heart that is unwilling to
make you as melancholy as itself; and for wit what is really
only the natural overflowing and warmth of the same heart,
as it is improved and awakened by an esteem for you : but
since you tell me you believe me, I fancy my expressions have
not at least been entirely unfaithful to those thoughts, to which
I am sure they can never be equal. May God increase your
faith in all truths that any as great as this ; and depend upon it,
to whatever degree your belief may extend, you can never be
a bigot.

If you could see the heart I talk of, you would really think
it a foolish good kind of thing, with some qualities as well deserving to be half laughed at, and half esteemed, as any in the
world : its grand foible, in regard to you, is the most like
reason of any foible in nature. Upon my faith, this heart is
not, like a great warehouse, stored only with my own goods,

with vast empty spaces to be supplied as fast as interest or ambition can fill them up; but it is every inch of it let out into lodgings for its friends, and shall never want a corner at your service: where I dare affirm, madam, your idea lies as warm and as close as any idea in Christendom.

If I don't take care, I shall write myself all out to you; and if this correspondence continues on both sides at the free rate I would have it, we shall have very little curiosity to encourage our meeting at the day of judgment. I foresee that the further you go from me, the more freely I shall write; and if, as I earnestly wish, you would do the same, I can't guess where it will end: let us be like modest people, who, when they are close together, keep all decorums; but if they step a little aside, or get to the other end of a room, can untie garters or take off shifts without scruple.

If this distance, as you are so kind as to say, enlarges your belief of my friendship, I assure you it has so extended my notion of your value that I begin to be impious on our account and to wish that even slaughter, ruin, and desolation, might interpose between you and Turkey; I wish you restored to us at the expense of a whole people: I barely hope you will forgive me for saying this, but I fear God will scarcely forgive me for desiring it.

Make me less wicked then. Is there no other expedient to return you and your infant in peace to the bosom of your country? I hear you are going to Hanover; can there be no favorable planet at this conjuncture, or do you only come back so far to die twice? Is Eurydice once more snatched to the shades? If ever mortal had reason to hate the king, it is I; for it is my particular misfortune to be almost the only innocent man whom he has made to suffer, both by his government at home, and his negotiations abroad.

LETTER IV.

TO MR. POPE.

BELGRADE, Feb. 12, O. S. 1717.

I DID verily intend to write you a long letter from Peterwaradin, where I expected to stay three or four days; but the
pasha here was in such haste to see us, that he dispatched the
courier back, which Mr. Wortley had sent to know the time
he would send the convoy to meet us, without suffering him
to pull off his boots.

My letters were not thought important enough to stop our
journey; and we left Peterwaradin the next day, being waited
on by the chief officers of the garrison, and a considerable
convoy of Germans and Rascians. The emperor has several
regiments of these people; but, to say the truth, they are
rather plunderers than soldiers; having no pay, and being
obliged to furnish their own arms and horses; they rather
look like vagabond gipsies, or stout beggars, than regular
troops.

I can not forbear speaking a word of this race of creatures,
who are very numerous all over Hungary. They have a patriarch of their own at Grand Cairo, and are really of the
Greek Church; but their extreme ignorance gives their priests
occasion to impose several new notions upon them. These
fellows, letting their hair and beard grow inviolate, make exactly the figure of the Indian bramins. They are heirs-gen
eral to all the money of the laity, for which, in return, they
give them formal passports signed and sealed for heaven;
and the wives and children only inherit the house and cattle.
In most other points they follow the Greek Church.

This little digression has interrupted my telling you we
passed over the fields of Carlowitz, where the last great victory was obtained by Prince Eugene over the Turks. The
marks of that glorious bloody day are yet recent, the field
being yet strewed with the skulls and carcases of unburied

men, horses, and camels. I could not look without horror, on such numbers of mangled human bodies, nor without reflecting on the injustice of war, that makes murder not only necessary, but meritorious. Nothing seems to be a plainer proof of the *irrationality* of mankind, whatever fine claims we pretend to reason, than the rage with which they contest for a small spot of ground, when such vast parts of fruitful earth lie quite uninhabited. It is true, custom has now made it unavoidable; but can there be a greater demonstration of want of reason, than a custom being firmly established, so plainly contrary to the interest of man in general? I am a good deal inclined to believe Mr. Hobbes, that the *state of nature* is a *state of war ;* but thence I conclude human nature not rational, if the word reason means common sense, as I suppose it does. I have a great many admirable arguments to support this reflection; I won't, however, trouble you with them, but return, in a plain style, to the history of my travels.

We were met at Betsko (a village in the midway between Belgrade and Peterwaradin) by an aga of the janizaries, with a body of Turks, exceeding the Germans by one hundred men, though the pasha had engaged to send exactly the same number. You may judge by this of their fears. I am really persuaded that they hardly thought the odds of one hundred men set them even with the Germans; however, I was very uneasy till they were parted, fearing some quarrel might arise, notwithstanding the parole given.

We came late to Belgrade, the deep snows making the ascent to it very difficult. It seems a strong city, fortified on the east side by the Danube, and on the south by the river Save, and was formerly the barrier of Hungary. It was first taken by Solyman the Magnificent, and since by the emperor's forces, led by the Elector of Bavaria. The emperor held it only two years, it being retaken by the Grand-Vizier. It is now fortified with the utmost care and skill the Turks are capable of, and strengthened by a very numerous garrison of their bravest janizaries, commanded by a pasha seraskiér (*i. e.* general), though this last expression is not very just; for, to say truth, the seraskiér is commanded by the janizaries. These troops have an absolute authority here, and their conduct carries much more the aspect of rebellion than the appearance of subordination. You may judge of this by the following story, which, at the same time, will give you an idea of the *admirable* intelligence of the governor of Peterwaradin, though so few hours distant. We were told by him at Peterwaradin, that the garrison and inhabitants of Belgrade were so weary of the war they had killed their pasha, about two months ago, in a mutiny, because he had suffered himself to be prevailed upon, by a bribe of five purses (five hundred pounds sterling), to give permission to the Tartars to ravage the German frontiers. We were very well pleased to hear of such favorable dispositions in the people; but when we came hither, we found that the governor had been ill-informed, and the real truth of the story to be this: The late pasha fell under the displeasure of his soldiers for no other reason but restraining their incursions on the Germans. They took it into their heads, from that mildness, that he had intelligence with the enemy, and sent such information to the Grand Seignior at Adrianople; but redress not coming quick enough from thence, they assembled themselves in a tumultuous manner, and by force dragged their pasha before the cadi and mufti, and there demanded justice in a mutinous way; one crying out, Why he protected the infidels? Another, Why he squeezed them of their money? The pasha, easily guessing their purpose, calmly replied to them that they asked him too many questions, and that he had but one life, which must answer for all. They then immediately fell upon him with their cimeters, without waiting the sentence of their heads of the law, and in a few moments cut him in pieces. The present pasha has not dared to punish the murder; on the contrary, he affected to applaud the actors of it as brave fellows, that knew to do themselves justice. He takes all pretenses of throwing money among the garrison, and suffers them to make little excursions into Hungary, where they burn some poor Rascian houses.

You may imagine I can not be very easy in a town which is really under the government of an insolent soldiery. We expected to be immediately dismissed, after a night's lodging here; but the pasha detains us till he receives orders from Adrianople, which may, possibly, be a month a-coming. In the mean time, we are lodged in one of the best houses, belonging to a very considerable man among them, and have a whole chamber of janizaries to guard us. My only diversion is the conversation of our host, Achmet Bey, a title something like that of count in Germany. His father was a great pasha, and he has been educated in the most polite Eastern learning, being perfectly skilled in the Arabic and Persian languages, and an extraordinary scribe, which they call *effendi*. This accomplishment makes way to the greatest preferments; but he has had the good sense to prefer an easy, quiet, secure life, to all the dangerous honors of the Porte. He sups with us every night, and drinks wine very freely. You can not imagine how much he is delighted with the liberty of conversing with me. He has explained to me many pieces of Arabian poetry, which, I observe, are in numbers not unlike ours, generally of an alternate verse, and of a very musical sound. Their expressions of love are very passionate and lively. I am so much pleased with them, I really believe I should learn to read Arabic if I was to stay here a few months. He has a good library of their books of all kinds; and, as he tells me, spends the greatest part of his life there. I pass for a great scholar with him, by relating to him some of the Persian tales, which I find are genuine.* At first he

---

* The Persian Tales appeared first in Europe as a translation, by Monsieur Petit de la Croix; and what are called "The Arabian Nights," in a similar manner, by Monsier Galland. The Tales of the Genii, said in the title-page to have been translated by Sir Charles Morell, were, in fact, entirely composed by James Ridley, Esq.

believed I understood Persian. I have frequent disputes with him concerning the difference of our customs, particularly the confinement of women. He assures me there is nothing at all in it; only, says he, we have the advantage, that when our wives cheat us, nobody knows it. He has wit, and is more polite than many Christian men of quality. I am very much entertained with him. He has had the curiosity to make one of our servants set him an alphabet of our letters, and can already write a good Roman hand.

But these amusements do not hinder my wishing heartily to be out of this place; though the weather is colder than I believe it ever was any where but in Greenland. We have a very large stove constantly kept hot, and yet the windows of the room are frozen on the inside. God knows when I may have an opportunity of sending this letter; but I have written it, for the discharge of my own conscience; and you can not now reproach me, that one of yours makes ten of mine. Adieu.

LETTER V.

FROM MR. POPE.

Madam,—If to live in the memory of others have any thing desirable in it, 'tis what you possess with regard to me, in the highest sense of the words. There is not a day in which your figure does not appear before me; your conversations return to my thoughts, and every scene, place, or occasion, where I have enjoyed them, are as lively painted as an imagination equally warm and tender can be capable to represent them. Yet how little accrues to you from all this, when not only my wishes, but the very expressions of them, can hardly ever arrive to be known to you? I can not tell whether you have seen half the letters I have written; but if you had, I have not said in them half of what I designed to say; and you can have seen but a faint, slight, timorous eschantillon of what my spirit suggests, and my hand follows slowly and imperfectly, indeed unjustly, because discreetly and reservedly. When you told me there was no way left for our correspondence but by merchant ships, I watched ever since for any that set out, and this is the first I could learn of. I owe the knowledge of it to Mr. Congreve (whose letters, with my Lady Rich's, accompany this). However, I was impatient enough to venture two from Mr. Methuen's office : they have miscarried ; you have lost nothing but such words and wishes as I repeat every day in your memory, and for your welfare. I have had thoughts of causing what I write for the future to be transcribed, and to send copies by more ways than one, that one at least might have a chance to reach you. The letters themselves would be artless and natural enough to prove there could be no vanity in this practice, and to show it proceeded from the belief of their being welcome to you, not as they came from me, but from England. My eye-sight is grown so bad that I have left off all correspondence except with yourself; in which methinks I am like those people who abandon or abstract themselves from all that are about them (with whom they might have business and intercourse), to employ their addresses only to invisible and distant beings, whose good offices and favors can not reach them in a long time, if at all. If I hear from you, I look upon it as little less than a miracle, or extraordinary visitation from another world ; 'tis a sort of dream of an agreeable thing, which subsists no more to me; but, however, it is such a dream as exceeds most of the dull realities of my life. Indeed, what with ill-health and ill-fortune, I am grown so stupidly philosophical as to have no thought about me that deserves the name of warm or lively, but that which sometimes awakens me into an imagination that I may yet see you again. Compassionate a poet, who has lost all manner of romantic ideas ; except a few that hover about the Bosphorus and Hellespont, not so much for the fine sound of their names, as to raise up images of Leander, who was drowned in crossing the sea to kiss the hand of fair Hero. This were a destiny less to be lamented than what we are told of the poor Jew, one of your interpreters, who was beheaded at Belgrade as a spy. I confess such a death would have been a great disappointment to me ; and I believe that Jacob Tonson will hardly venture to visit you after this news.

You tell me the pleasure of being nearer the sun has a great effect upon your health and spirits. You have turned my affections so far eastward, that I could almost be one of his worshipers ; for I think the sun has more reason to be proud of raising your spirits than of raising all the plants, and ripening all the minerals, in the earth. It is my opinion a reasonable man might gladly travel three or four thousand leagues to see your nature and your wit in their full perfection. What may not we expect from a creature that went out the most perfect of this part of the world, and is every day improving by the sun in the other ! If you do not now write and speak the finest things imaginable, you must be content to be involved in the same imputation with the rest of the East, and be concluded to have abandoned yourself to extreme effeminacy, laziness, and lewdness of life.

I make not the least question but you could give me great eclaircissements upon many passages in Homer, since you have been enlightened by the same sun that inspired the father of poetry. You are now glowing under the climate that animated him ; you may see his images rising more boldly about you in the very scenes of his story and action ; you may lay the immortal work on some broken column of a hero's sepulcher ; and read the fall of Troy in the shade of a Trojan ruin. But if, to visit the tomb of so many heroes, you have not the heart to pass over that sea where once a lover perished, you may at least, at ease in your own window, contemplate the fields of Asia in such a dim and remote prospect as you have of Homer in my translation.

I send you, therefore, with this, the third volume of the Iliad, and as many other things as fill a wooden box, directed to Mr. Wortley.   Among the rest you have all I am worth, that is, my works: there are few things in them but what you have already seen, except the epistle of Eloisa to Abelard, in which you will find one passage, that I can not tell whether to wish you should understand or not.

The last I received from your hands was from Peterwaradin; it gave me the joy of thinking you in good health and humor: one or two expressions in it are too generous ever to be forgotten by me.   I writ a very melancholy one just before, which was sent to Mr. Stanyan, to be forwarded through Hungary.   It would have informed you how meanly I thought of the pleasures of Italy, without the qualification of your company, and that mere statues and pictures are not more cold to me than I to them.   I have had but four of your letters; I have sent several, and wish I knew how many you have received.   For God's sake, madam, send to me as often as you can, in the dependence that there is no man breathing more constantly or more anxiously mindful of you.   Tell me that you are well; tell me that your little son is well, tell me that your very dog (if you have one) is well.   Defraud me of no one thing that pleases you; for whatever that is, it will please me better than any thing else can do.

LETTER VI.

TO MR. POPE.

ADRIANOPLE, April 1, O. S., 1717.

I dare say you expect at least something very new in this letter, after I have gone a journey not undertaken by any Christian for some hundred years.   The most remarkable accident that happened to me, was my being very near overturned into the Hebrus; and, if I had much regard for the glories that one's name enjoys after death, I should certainly be sorry for having missed the romantic conclusion of swimming down the same river in which the musical head of Orpheus repeated verses so many ages since:

> Caput a cervice revulsum,
> Gurgite cum medio, portans Oeagrius Hebrus
> Volveret, Eurydicen vox ipsa, et frigida lingua,
> Ah! miseram Eurydicem! anima fugiente vocabat,
> Eurydicem toto referebant flumine ripæ.

Who knows but some of your bright wits might have found it a subject affording many poetical turns, and have told the world, in an heroic elegy, that,

> As equal were our souls, so equal were our fates?

I despair of ever hearing so many fine things said of me as so extraordinary a death would have given occasion for.

I am at this present moment writing in a house situated on the banks of the Hebrus, which runs under my chamber window. My garden is all full of cypress-trees, upon the branches of which several couple of true turtles are saying soft things to one another from morning till night. How naturally do *boughs* and *vows* come into my mind at this minute! and must not you confess, to my praise, that 'tis more than an ordinary discretion that can resist the wicked suggestions of poetry, in a place where truth, for once, furnishes all the ideas of pastoral. The summer is already far advanced in this part of the world; and for some miles round Adrianople, the whole ground is laid out in gardens, and the banks of the rivers are set with rows of fruit-trees, under which all the most considerable Turks divert themselves every evening; not with walking, that is not one of their pleasures, but a set party of them choose out a green spot, where the shade is very thick, and there they spread a carpet, on which they sit drinking their coffee, and are generally attended by some slave with a fine voice, or that plays on some instrument. Every twenty paces you may see one of these little companies listening to the dashing of the river; and this taste is so universal that the very gardeners are not without it. I have often seen them and their children sitting on the banks of the river, and playing on a rural instrument, perfectly answering the description of the ancient *fistula*, being composed of unequal reeds, with a simple but agreeable softness in the sound.

Mr. Addison might here make the experiment he speaks of in his travels; there not being one instrument of music among the Greek or Roman statues, that is not to be found in the hands of the people of this country. The young lads generally divert themselves with making garlands for their favorite lambs, which I have often seen painted and adorned with flowers lying at their feet while they sung or played. It is not that they ever read romances, but these are the ancient amusements here, and as natural to them as cudgel-playing and foot-ball to our British swains; the softness and warmth of the climate forbidding all rough exercises, which were never so much as heard of among them, and naturally inspiring a laziness and aversion to labor, which the great plenty indulges. These gardeners are the only happy race of country people in Turkey. They furnish all the city with fruits and herbs, and seem to live very easily. They are most of them Greeks, and have little houses in the midst of their gardens, where their wives and daughters take a liberty not permitted in the town, I mean, to go unvailed. These wenches are very neat and handsome, and pass their time at their looms under the shade of the trees.

I no longer look upon Theocritus as a romantic writer; he has only given a plain image of the way of the life among the peasants of his country; who, before oppression had reduced them to want, were, I suppose, all employed as the better sort of them are now. I don't doubt, had he been born a Briton, but his *Idylliums* had been filled with descriptions of thrashing and churning, both which are unknown here, the corn being all trodden out by oxen; and butter, I speak it with sorrow, unheard of.

I read over your Homer here with an infinite pleasure, and

find several little passages explained that I did not before entirely comprehend the beauty of; many of the customs, and much of the dress then in fashion, being yet retained. I don't wonder to find more remains here of an age so distant than is to be found in any other country, the Turks not taking that pains to introduce their own manners as has been generally practiced by other nations, that imagine themselves more polite. It would be too tedious to you to point out all the passages that relate to present customs. But I can assure you that the princesses and great ladies pass their time at their looms, embroidering vails and robes, surrounded by their maids, which are always very numerous, in the same manner as we find Andromache and Helen described. The description of the belt of Menelaus exactly resembles those that are now worn by the great men, fastened before with broad golden clasps, and embroidered round with rich work. The snowy vail that Helen throws over her face, is still fashionable; and I never see half a dozen of old bashaws (as I do very often), with their reverend beards, sitting basking in the sun, but I recollect good King Priam and his counselors. Their manner of dancing is certainly the same that Diana is sung to have danced on the banks of Eurotas. The great lady still leads the dance, and is followed by a troop of young girls, who imitate her steps, and, if she sing, make up the chorus. The tunes are extremely gay and lively, yet with something in them wonderfully soft. The steps are varied according to the pleasure of her that leads the dance, but always in exact time, and infinitely more agreeable than any of our dances, at least in my opinion. I sometimes make one in the train, but am not skillful enough to lead; these are the Grecian dances, the Turkish being very different.

I should have told you, in the first place, that the Eastern manner gives a great light into many Scripture passages that appear odd to us, their phrases being commonly what we should call Scripture language. The vulgar Turk is very different from what is spoken at court, or among the people of figure, who always mix so much Arabic and Persian in their discourse, that it may very well be called another language. And 'tis as ridiculous to make use of the expressions commonly used, in speaking to a great man or lady, as it would be to speak broad Yorkshire or Somersetshire in the drawing-room. Besides this distinction, they have what they call the *sublime*, that is, a style proper for poetry, and which is the exact Scripture style. I believe you will be pleased to see a genuine example of this; and I am very glad I have it in my power to satisfy your curiosity, by sending you a faithful copy of the verses that Ibrahim Pasha, the reigning favorite, has made for the young princess, his contracted wife, whom he is not yet permitted to visit without witnesses, though she is gone home to his house. He is a man of wit and learning; and whether or no he is capable of writing good verse, you may be sure that, on such an occasion, he would not want the assistance of the best poets in the empire. Thus the verses may be looked upon as a sample of their finest poetry; and I don't doubt you'll be of my mind, that it is most wonderfully resembling *The Song of Solomon*, which was also addressed to a royal bride.

TURKISH VERSES ADDRESSED TO THE SULTANA,

ELDEST DAUGHTER OF ACHMET III.

STANZA I.

1. The nightingale now wanders in the vines:
   Her passion is to seek roses.

2. I went down to admire the beauty of the vines:
   The sweetness of your charms has ravished my soul.

3. Your eyes are black and lovely,
   . But wild and disdainful as those of a stag.*

---

* Sir W. Jones, in the preface to his Persian Grammar, objects to this translation. The expression is merely analogous to the " Βουῶπις " of Homer.

STANZA II.

1. The wished possession is delayed from day to day;
The cruel Sultan Achmet will not permit me
To see those cheeks, more vermillion than roses.

2. I dare not snatch one of your kisses:
The sweetness of your charms has ravished my soul.

8. Your eyes are black and lovely,
But wild and disdainful as those of a stag.

STANZA III.

1. The wretched Ibrahim sighs in these verses:
One dart from your eyes has pierced thro' my heart.

2. Ah! when will the hour of possession arrive?
Must I yet wait a long time?
The sweetness of your charms has ravish'd my soul.

3. Ah, Sultana! stag-eyed—an angel among angels!
I desire—and my desire remains unsatisfied—
Can you take delight to prey upon my heart?

STANZA IV.

1. My cries pierce the heavens!
My eyes are without sleep!
Turn to me, Sultana—let me gaze on thy beauty.

2. Adieu—I go down to the grave.
If you call me—I return.
My heart is hot as sulphur; sigh, and it will flame.

3. Crown of my life! fair light of my eyes!
My Sultana! my princess?
I rub my face against the earth—I am drowned in scalding tears—
I rave!
Have you no compassion? Will you not turn to look upon me?

I have taken abundance of pains to get these verses a literal
translation; and if you were acquainted with my interpreters,
I might spare myself the trouble of assuring you that they
have received no poetical touches from their hands. In my

opinion, allowing for the inevitable faults of a prose translation into a language so very different, there is a good deal of
beauty in them. The epithet of *stag-eyed*, though the sound
is not very agreeable in English, pleases me extremely ; and I
think it a very lively image of the fire and indifference in his
mistress's eyes. Monsieur Boileau has very justly observed,
that we are never to judge of the elevation of an expression of
an ancient author by the sound it carries with us ; since it may
be extremely fine with them, when, at the same time, it appears
low or uncouth to us. You are so well acquainted with Homer,
you can not but have observed the same thing, and you must
have the same indulgence for all Oriental poetry.

The repetitions at the end of the two first stanzas are meant
for a sort of chorus, and are agreeable to the ancient manner
of writing. The music of the verses apparently changes in
the third stanza, where the burthen is altered ; and I think he
very artfully seems more passionate at the conclusion, as 'tis
natural for people to warm themselves by their own discourse,
especially on a subject in which one is deeply concerned ; 'tis
certainly far more touching than our modern custom of concluding a song of passion with a turn which is inconsistent with
it. The first verse is a description of the season of the year ;
all the country now being full of nightingales, whose amours
with roses is an Arabian fable, as well known here as any part
of Ovid among us, and is much the same as if an English
poem should begin by saying—" *Now Philomela sings.*" Or
what if I turned the whole in to the style of English poetry, to
see how it would look ?

STANZA I.

Now Philomel renews her tender strain,
Indulging all the night her pleasing pain :

I sought the groves to hear the wanton sing,
There saw a face more beauteous than the spring.

Your large stag-eyes, where thousand glories play,
As bright, as lively, but as wild as they.

STANZA II.

In vain I 'm promised such a heav'nly prize ;
Ah! cruel Sultan! who delay'st my joys!

While piercing charms transfix my am'rous heart,
I dare not snatch one kiss to ease the smart.

Those eyes! like, etc.

STANZA III.

Your wretched lover in these lines complains;
From those dear beauties rise his killing pains.

When will the hour of wished-for bliss arrive ?
Must I wait longer?   Can I wait and live?

Ah! bright Sultana! maid divinely fair!
Can you, unpitying, see the pains I bear?

STANZA IV.

The heavens relenting, hear my piercing cries,
I loathe the light, and sleep forsakes my eyes;
Turn thee, Sultana, ere thy lover dies:

Sinking to earth, I sigh the last adieu;
Call me, my goddess, and my life renew.

My queen! my angel! my fond heart's desire!
I rave—my bosom burns with heavenly fire!
Pity that passion which thy charms inspire.

I have taken the liberty, in the second verse, of following what I suppose the true sense of the author, though not literally expressed. By his saying, *He went down to admire the beauty of the vines, and her charms ravished his soul*, I understand a poetical fiction, of having first seen her in a garden, where he was admiring the beauty of the spring.   But I could not forbear retaining the comparison of her eyes with those of a stag, though, perhaps, the novelty of it may give it a burlesque sound in our language.   I can not determine upon the whole how well I have succeeded in the translation, neither do I think our English proper to express such violence of passion, which is very seldom felt among us. We want also those compound words which are very frequent and strong in the Turkish language.

You see I am pretty far gone in Oriental learning; and to say truth, I study very hard. I wish my studies may give me an occasion of entertaining your curiosity, which will be the utmost advantage hoped for from them by   Yours, etc.

LETTER VII.

TO MR. POPE.

BELGRADE VILLAGE, June 17, O. S. 1717

I hope before this time you have received two or three of my letters. I had yours but yesterday, though dated the third of February, in which you suppose me to be dead and buried. I have already let you know that I am still alive; but, to say truth, I look upon my present circumstances to be exactly the same with those of departed spirits.

The heats of Constantinople have driven me to this place, which perfectly answers the description of the Elysian fields. I am in the middle of a wood, consisting chiefly of fruit-trees, watered by a vast number of fountains, famous for the excellency of their water, and divided into many shady walks, upon short grass, that seems to me artificial; but, I am assured, is the pure work of nature, and within view of the Black Sea, from whence we perpetually enjoy the refreshment of cool breezes, that make us insensible of the heat of the summer. The village is only inhabited by the richest among the Christians, who meet every night at a fountain, forty paces from my house, to sing and dance. The beauty and dress of the women exactly resemble the ideas of the ancient nymphs, as they are given us by the representations of the poets and painters. But what persuades me more fully of my decease, is the situation of my own mind, the profound ig-norance I am in of what passes among the living (which only comes to me by chance), and the great calmness with which I receive it. Yet I have still a hankering after my friends and acquaintances left in the world, according to the authority of that admirable author,

> That spirits departed are wondrous kind
> To friends and relations left behind :
>> Which nobody can deny.

Of which solemn truth I am a *dead* instance. I think Virgil is of the same opinion, that in human souls there will still be some remains of human passions.

> —— Curæ non ipsæ in morte relinquunt.

And 'tis very necessary, to make a perfect Elysium, that there should be a river Lethe, which I am not so happy as to find.

To say truth, I am sometimes very weary of the singing and dancing, and sunshine, and wish for the smoke and impertinencies in which you toil, though I endeavor to persuade myself that I live in a more agreeable variety than you do ; and that Monday, setting of partridges—Tuesday, reading English—Wednesday, studying in the Turkish language (in which, by the way, I am already very learned)—Thursday, classical authors—Friday, spent in writing—Saturday, at my needle—and Sunday, admitting of visits, and hearing of music, is a better way of disposing of the week than—Monday, at the drawing-room—Tuesday, Lady Mohun's—Wednesday, at the opera—Thursday, the play—Friday, Mrs. Chetwynd's, etc., a perpetual round of hearing the same scandal, and seeing the same follies acted over and over, which here affect me no more than they do other dead people. I can now hear of displeasing things with pity, and without indignation. The reflection on the great gulf between you and me, cools all news that come hither. I can neither be sensibly touched with joy nor grief, when I consider that possibly the cause of either is removed before the letter comes to my hands. But (as I said before) this indolence does not extend to my few friendships; I am still warmly sensible of yours and Mr. Congreve's, and desire to live in your remembrance, though dead to all the world beside.

LETTER VIII.

FROM MR. POPE.

Madam,—I could quarrel with you quite through this paper, upon a period in yours, which bids me remember you if possibly I can. You would have shown more knowledge both of yourself and of me, had you bid me forget you if possibly I could. When I do, may this hand (as the Scripture says) forget its cunning, and this heart its—folly, I was going to say—but I mean its reason, and the most rational sensation it ever had—that of your merit.

The poetical manner in which you paint some of the scenes about you, makes me despise my native country, and sets me on fire to fall into the dance about your fountain in Belgrade village. I fancy myself, in my romantic thoughts and distant admiration of you, not unlike the man in the Alchymist, that has a passion for the queen of the fairies; I lie dreaming of you in moonshiny nights, exactly in the posture of Endymion gaping for Cynthia in a picture; and with just such a surprise and rapture should I awake, if, after your long revolutions were accomplished, you should at last come rolling back again, smiling with all that gentleness and serenity peculiar to the moon and you, and gilding the same mountains from which you first set out on your solemn, melancholy journey. I am told that fortune (more just to us than your virtue) will restore the most precious thing it ever robbed us of. Some think it will be the only equivalent the world affords for Pitt's diamond, so lately sent out of our country; which, after you were gone, was accounted the most valuable thing here. Adieu to that toy! let the costly bauble be hung about the neck of the baby-king it belongs to, so England does but recover that jewel which was the wish of all her sensible hearts, and the joy of all her discerning eyes. I can keep no measures in speaking of this subject. I see you already coming; I feel you as you draw nearer; my heart leaps at your arrival. Let us have you from the East, and the sun is at her service.

I write as if I were drunk; the pleasure I take in thinking of your return transports me beyond the bounds of common sense and decency. You believe me, madam, if there be any circumstance of chagrin in the occasion of that return, if there be any public or private ill-fortune that may give you a displeasure, I must still be ready to feel a part of it, notwithstanding the joy I now express.

I have been mad enough to make all the inquiry I could at what time you set out, and what route you were to take. If Italy run yet in your thoughts, I hope you'll see it in your return. If I but knew you intended it, I'd meet you there, and travel back with you. I would fain behold the best and brightest thing I know, in the scene of ancient virtue and glory: I would fain see how you look on the very spot where Curtius sacrificed himself for his country; and observe what difference there would be in your eyes when you ogled the statue of Julius Cæsar, and Marcus Aurelius. Allow me but to sneak after you in your train, to fill my pockets with coins, or to lug an old busto behind you, and I shall be proud beyond expression. Let people think, if they will, that I did all this for the pleasure of treading on classic ground; I would whisper other reasons in your ear. The joy of following your footsteps would as soon carry me to Mecca as to Rome; and let me tell you as a friend, if you are really disposed to embrace the Mohammedan religion, I'll fly on pilgrimage with you thither, with as good a heart and as sound devotion as ever Jeffery Rudel, the Provençal poet, went after the fine Countess of Tripoli to Jerusalem. If you never heard of this Jeffery, I'll assure you he deserves your acquaintance. He lived in our Richard the First's time; put on a pilgrim's weed, took his voyage, and when he got ashore was just upon the point of expiring. The Countess of Tripoli came to the ship, took him by the hand; he lifted up his eyes, said he had been blest with a sight of her, he was satisfied, and so departed this life. What did the Countess of Tripoli upon this? She made him a splendid funeral; built him a tomb of porphyry; put his epitaph upon it in Arabic verse; had his sonnets curiously copied out, and illumined with letters of gold; was taken with melancholy, and turned nun. All this, madam, you may depend upon for a truth, and I send it to you in the very words of my author.

I don't expect all this should be punctually copied on either side, but methinks something like it is done already. The letters of gold, and the curious illumining of the sonnets, was not a greater token of respect than I have paid to your eclogues: they lie inclosed in a monument of red Turkey, written in my fairest hand; the gilded leaves are opened with no less veneration than the pages of the sibyls; like them, locked up and concealed from all profane eyes; none but my own have beheld these sacred remains of yourself, and I should think it as great a wickedness to divulge them as to scatter abroad the ashes of my ancestors. As for the rest, if I have not followed you to the ends of the earth, 'tis not my fault; if I had, I might possibly have died as gloriously as Jeffery Rudel; and if I had so died, you might probably have done every thing for me that the Countess of Tripoli did, except turning nun.

But since our romance is like to have a more fortunate conclusion, I desire you to take another course to express your favor toward me; I mean by bringing over the fair Circassian we used to talk of. I was serious in that request, and will prove it by paying for her, if you will lay out my money so well for me. The thing shall be as secret as you please, and the lady made another half of me, that is, both my mistress and my servant, as I am both my own servant and my own master. But I beg you to look oftener than you used to do

in your glass, in order to choose me one I may like. If you
have any regard to my happiness, let there be something as
near as possible to that face; but, if you please, the colors a
little less vivid, the eyes a little less bright (such as reflection
will show 'em); in short, let her be such a one as you seem
in your own eyes, that is, a good deal less amiable than you
are. Take care of this, if you have any regard to my quiet;
for otherwise, instead of being her master, I must be only her
slave.

LETTER IX.

FROM MR. POPE.

September 1.

MADAM,—I have been (what I never was till now) in debt
to you for a letter some weeks. I was informed you were at
sea, and that 't was to no purpose to write till some news had
been heard of your arriving somewhere or other. Besides, I
have had a second dangerous illness, from which I was more
diligent to be recovered than from the first, having now some
hopes of seeing you again. If you make any tour in Italy, I
shall not easily forgive you for not acquainting me soon
enough to have met you there. I am very certain I can never
be polite unless I travel with you: and it is never to be repaired, the loss that Homer has sustained, for want of my
translating him in Asia. You will come hither full of criticisms against a man who wanted nothing to be in the right
but to have kept you company; you have no way of making
me amends but by continuing an Asiatic when you return to
me, whatever English airs you may put on to other people.

I prodigiously long for your sonnets, your remarks, your
Oriental learning; but I long for nothing so much as your
Oriental self. You must of necessity be *advanced* so far *back*
into true nature and simplicity of manners by these three
years' residence in the east, that I shall look upon you as so

many years younger than you were, so much nearer innocence (that is, truth) and infancy (that is, openness). I expect to see your soul as much thinner dressed as your body; and that you have left off, as unwieldy and cumbersome, a great many European habits. Without offense to your modesty be it spoken, I have a burning desire to see your soul stark naked, for I am confident 'tis the prettiest kind of white soul in the universe. But I forget whom I am talking to; you may possibly by this time believe, according to the prophet, that you have none; if so, show me that which comes next to a soul; you may easily put it upon a poor ignorant Christian for a soul, and please him as well with it; I mean your heart; Mohammed, I think, allows you hearts; which (together with fine eyes and other agreeable equivalents) are worth all the souls on this side the world. But if I must be content with seeing your body only, God send it to come quickly: I honor it more than the diamond casket that held Homer's Iliads; for in the very twinkle of one eye of it there is more wit, and in the very dimple of one cheek of it there is more meaning than all the souls that ever were casually put into women since men had the making of them.

I have a mind to fill the rest of this paper with an accident that happened just under my eyes, and has made a great impression upon me. I have just passed part of this summer at an old romantic seat of my Lord Harcourt's, which he lent me.* It overlooks a common-field, where, under the shade of a hay-cock, sat two lovers, as constant as ever were found in romance, beneath a spreading beech. The name of the one (let it sound as it will) was John Hewet, of the other Sarah Drew. John was a well-set man about five and twenty; Sarah a brown woman of eighteen. John had for several months borne the labor of the day in the same field with Sarah; when she milked, it was his morning and evening charge to bring the cows to her pail. Their love was the talk, but not the scandal, of the whole neighborhood; for all they

* At Stanton-Harcourt, in Oxfordshire.

aimed at was the blameless possession of each other in marriage. It was but this very morning that he had obtained her parents' consent, and it was but till the next week that they were to wait to be happy. Perhaps this very day, in the intervals of their work, they were talking of their wedding-clothes; and John was now matching several kinds of poppies and field-flowers to her complexion, to make her a present of knots for the day. While they were thus employed (it was on the last of July), a terrible storm of thunder and lightning arose, and drove the laborers to what shelter the trees or hedges afforded. Sarah, frightened and out of breath, sunk on a hay-cock, and John (who never separated from her) sat by her side, having raked two or three heaps together to secure her. Immediately there was heard so loud a crack as if Heaven had burst asunder. The laborers, all solicitous for each other's safety, called to one another: those that were nearest our lovers, hearing no answer, stepped to the place where they lay. They first saw a little smoke, and after, this faithful pair—John, with one arm about his Sarah's neck, and the other held over her face, as if to screen her from the lightning. They were struck dead, and already grown stiff and cold in this tender posture. There was no mark or discoloring on their bodies, only that Sarah's eye-brow was a little singed, and a small spot between her breasts. They were buried the next day in one grave, in the parish of Stanton-Harcourt, in Oxfordshire, where my Lord Harcourt, at my request, has erected a monument over them. Of the following epitaphs which I made, the critics have chosen the godly one. I like neither, but wish you had been in England to have done this office better; I think 't was what you could not have refused me on so moving an occasion:

> When Eastern lovers feed the fun'ral fire,
> On the same pile their faithful fair expire;
> Here pitying Heav'n that virtue mutual found,
> And blasted both, that it might neither wound.
> Hearts so sincere th' Almighty saw well pleased,
> Sent his own lightning, and the victims seized.

I.

Think not, by rig'rous judgment seized,
    A pair so faithful could expire ;
Victims so pure Heav'n saw, well pleased,
    And snatched them in celestial fire.

II.

Live well, and fear no sudden fate :
    When God calls virtue to the grave,
Alike 'tis justice, soon or late,
    Mercy alike to kill or save.
Virtue unmoved can hear the call,
And face the flash that melts the ball.

Upon the whole, I can't think these people unhappy. The greatest happiness, next to living as they would have done, was to die as they did. The greatest honor people of this low degree could have was to be remembered on a little monument ; unless you will give them another—that of being honored with a tear from the finest eyes in the world. I know you have tenderness ; you must have it ; it is the very emanation of good sense and virtue ; the finest minds, like the finest metals, dissolve the easiest.

But when you are reflecting upon objects of pity, pray do not forget one who had no sooner found out an object of the highest esteem, than he was separated from it ; and who is so very unhappy as not to be susceptible of consolation from others, by being so miserably in the right as to think other women what they really are. Such a one can't but be desperately fond of any creature that is quite different from these. If the Circassian be utterly void of such honor as these have, and such virtue as these boast of, I am content. I have detested the sound of *honest woman*, and *loving spouse*, ever since I heard the pretty name of Odaliche.

LETTER X.

DOVER, November 1, O. S., 1718.

I have this minute received a letter of yours, sent me from Paris. I believe and hope I shall very soon see both you and Mr. Congreve; but as I am here in an inn, where we stay to regulate our march to London, bag and baggage, I shall employ some of my leisure time in answering that part of yours that seems to require an answer.

I must applaud your good-nature in supposing that your pastoral lovers (vulgarly called haymakers) would have lived in everlasting joy and harmony, if the lightning had not interrupted their scheme of happiness. I see no reason to imagine that John Hughes and Sarah Drew were either wiser or more virtuous than their neighbors. That a well-set man of twenty-five should have a fancy to marry a brown woman of eighteen, is nothing marvelous; and I can not help thinking that, had they married, their lives would have passed in the common track with their fellow-parishioners. His endeavoring to shield her from a storm, was a natural action, and what he would have certainly done for his horse, if he had been in the same situation. Neither am I of opinion that their sudden death was a reward of their mutual virtue. You know the Jews were reproved for thinking a village destroyed by fire more wicked than those that had escaped the thunder. Time and chance happen to all men. Since you desire me to try my skill in an epitaph, I think the following lines perhaps more just, though not so poetical as yours.

> Here lie John Hughes and Sarah Drew;
> Perhaps you 'll say, what 's that to you?
> Believe me, friend, much may be said
> On this poor couple that are dead.
> On Sunday next they should have married;
> But see how oddly things are carried!

On Thursday last it rained and lighten'd;
These tender lovers sadly frighten'd,
Shelter'd beneath the cocking hay,
In hopes to pass the time away;
But the bold thunder found them out
(Commission'd for that end no doubt),
And, seizing on their trembling breath,
Consign'd them to the shades of death.
Who knows if 't was not kindly done?
For had they seen the next year's sun,
A beaten wife and cuckold swain
Had jointly cursed the marriage chain:
Now they are happy in their doom,
For Pope has wrote upon their tomb.

I confess, these sentiments are not altogether so heroic as yours; but I hope you will forgive them in favor of the two last lines. You see how much I esteem the honor you have done them, though I am not very impatient to have the same; and had rather continue to be your stupid *living* humble servant, than be *celebrated* by all the pens in Europe.

I would write to Congreve, but suppose you will read this to him if he inquires after me.

LETTER XI.

TO MR. POPE.

September 1, 1717.

When I wrote to you last, Belgrade was in the hands of the Turks; but at this present moment, it has changed masters, and is in the hands of the Imperialists. A janizary, who, in nine days, and yet without any wings but what a panic terror seems to have furnished, arrived at Constantinople from the army of the Turks before Belgrade, brought Mr. Wortley the news of a complete victory obtained by the Imperialists, commanded by Prince Eugene over the Ottoman troops. It is said the Prince has discovered great conduct and valor in this action, and I am particularly glad that the voice of glory and duty has called him from the—(*here several words of the manuscript art effaced.*) Two days after the battle the town surrendered. The consternation which this defeat has occasioned here, is inexpressible ; and the Sultan apprehending a revolution from the resentment and indignation of the people, fomented by certain leaders, has begun his precautions, after the goodly fashion of this blessed government, by ordering several persons to be strangled who were the objects of his royal suspicion. He has also ordered his treasurer to advance some months' pay to the janizaries, which seems the less necessary, as their conduct has been bad in this campaign, and their licentious ferocity seems pretty well tamed by the public contempt. Such of them as return in straggling and fugitive parties to the metropolis, have not spirit nor credit enough to defend themselves from the insults of the mob; the very children taunt them, and the populace spit in their faces as they pass. They refused during the battle to lend their assistance to save the baggage and the military chest, which, however, were defended by the bashaws and their retinue, while the janizaries and spahis were nobly employed in plundering their own camp.

You see here that I give you a very handsome return for your obliging letter. You entertain me with a most agreeable account of your amiable connections with men of letters and taste, and of the delicious moments you pass in their society under the rural shade ; and I exhibit to you in return, the barbarous spectacle of Turks and Germans cutting one another's throats. But what can you expect from such a country as this, from which the Muses have fled, from which letters seem eternally banished, and in which you see, in private scenes, nothing pursued as happiness but the refinements of an indolent voluptuousness, and where those who act upon the public theater live in uncertainty, suspicion, and terror ! Here pleasure, to which I am no enemy, when it is properly seasoned and of a good composition, is surely of the cloying kind. Veins of wit, elegant conversation, easy commerce, are unknown among the Turks; and yet they seem capable of all these, if the vile spirit of their government did not stifle genius, damp curiosity, and suppress a hundred passions, that embellish and render life agreeable. The luscious passion of the seraglio is the only one almost that is gratified here to the full, but it is blended so with the surly spirit of despotism in one of the parties, and with the dejection and anxiety which this spirit produces in the other, that to one of my way of thinking it can not appear otherwise than as a very mixed kind of enjoyment. The women here are not, indeed so closely confined as many have related; they enjoy a high degree of liberty, even in the bosom _of servitude, and they have methods of evasion and disguise that are very favorable to gallantry; but after all, they are still under uneasy apprehensions of being discovered; and a discovery exposes them to the most merciless rage of jealousy, which is here a monster that can not be satiated but with blood. The magnificence and riches that reign in the apartments of the ladies of fashion here seem to be one of their chief pleasures, joined with their retinue of female slaves, whose music, dancing and dress amuse them highly: but there is such an air of form and stiffness amid this grandeur, as hinders it from pleasing me at long run, however I was dazzled with it at first sight. This stiffness and formality of manners are peculiar to the Turkish ladies; for the Grecian belles are of quite another character and complexion; with them pleasure appears in more engaging forms, and their persons, manners, conversation, and amusements, are very far from being destitute of elegance and ease.

I received the news of Mr. Addison's being declared Secretary of State with the less surprise in that I know that post was almost offered to him before. At that time he declined it, and I really believe that he would have done well to have declined it now. Such a post as that, and such a wife as the Countess, do not seem to be, in prudence, eligible for a man that is asthmatic, and we may see the day when he will be heartily glad to resign them both. It is well that he laid aside the thoughts of the voluminous dictionary, of which I have heard you or somebody else frequently make mention. But no more on that subject ; I would not have said so much were I not assured that this letter will come safe and unopened to hand. I long much to tread upon English ground, that I may see you and Mr. Congreve, who render that ground classic ground ; nor will you refuse our present secretary a part of that merit, whatever reasons you may have to be dissatisfied with him in other respects. You are the three happiest poets I ever heard of; one a Secretary of State, the other enjoying leisure with dignity in two lucrative employments ; and you, though your religious profession is an obstacle to court promotion, and disqualifies you from filling civil employments, have found the philosopher's stone, since by making the Iliad pass through your poetical crucible into an English form, without losing aught of its original beauty, you have drawn the golden current of Pactolus to Twickenham. I call this finding the philosopher's stone, since you alone found out the secret, and nobody else has got into it. Addison and Tickell tried it, but their experiments failed ; and they lost, if not their money, at least a certain portion of their fame in the trial—while you touched the mantle of the divine bard, and imbibed his spirit. I hope we shall have the Odyssey soon from your happy hand, and I think I shall follow with singular pleasure the traveler Ulysses, who was an observer of men and manners, when he travels in your harmonious numbers. I love him much better than the hot-headed son of Peleus, who bullied his general, cried for his mistress, and so on. It is true, the excellence of the Iliad does not depend upon his merit or dignity, but I wish, nevertheless, that Homer had chosen a hero somewhat less pettish and less fantastic : a perfect hero is chimerical and unnatural, and consequently uninstructive ; but it is also true that while the epic hero ought to be drawn with the infirmities that are the lot of humanity, he ought never to be represented as extremely absurd. But it becomes me ill to play the critic ; so I take my leave of you for this time, and desire you will believe me, with the highest esteem,   Yours, etc.

LETTER XII.

TO MR. POPE.

1718.

I have been running about Paris at a strange rate with my sister, and strange sights have we seen. They are, at least, strange sights to me, for after having been accustomed to the gravity of the Turks, I can scarcely look with an easy and familiar aspect at the levity and agility of the airy phantoms that are dancing about me here, and I often think that I am at a puppet-show amid the representations of real life. I stare prodigiously, but nobody remarks it, for every body stares here ; staring is à la mode—there is a stare of attention and *intérêt*, a stare of curiosity, a stare of expectation, a stare of surprise, and it would greatly amuse you to see what trifling objects excite all this staring. This staring would have rather a solemn kind of air, were it not alleviated by grinning, for at the end of a stare there comes always a grin, and very commonly the entrance of a gentleman or a lady into a room is accompanied with a grin, which is designed to express complacence and social pleasure, but really shows nothing more than a certain contortion of muscles that must make a stranger laugh really, as they laugh artificially. The French grin is equally remote from the cheerful serenity of a smile, and the cordial mirth of an honest English horse-laugh. I shall not perhaps stay here long enough to form a just idea of French manners and characters, though this, I believe, would require but little study, as there is no real depth in either. It appears on a superficial view, to be a frivolous. restless, and agreeable people. The Abbot is my guide, and I could not easily light upon a better ; he tells me that here the women form the character of the men, and I am convinced in the persuasion of this by every company into which I enter. There seems here to be no intermediate state between infancy and manhood; for as soon as the boy has cut his leading-strings, he is set agog in the world; the ladies are his tutors, they make the first impressions, which generally remain, and they render the men ridiculous by the imitation of their humors and graces, so that dignity in manners is a rare thing here before the age of sixty. Does not King David say somewhere, that *Man walketh in a vain show?* I think he does, and I am sure this is peculiarly so of the Frenchman—but he walks merrily and seems to enjoy the vision, and may he not therefore be esteemed more happy than many of our solid thinkers, whose brows are furrowed by deep reflection, and whose wisdom is so often clothed with a rusty mantle of spleen and vapors?

What delights me most here is a view of the magnificence, often accompanied with taste, that reigns in the king's palaces and gardens; for though I don't admire much the architecture, in which there is great irregularity and want of proportion, yet the statues, paintings, and other decorations afford me high entertainment. One of the pieces of antiquity that struck me most in the gardens of Versailles, was the famous colossean statue of Jupiter, the workmanship of Myron, which Mark Antony carried away from Samos, and Augustus ordered to be placed in the Capitol. It is of Parian marble, and though it has suffered in the ruin of time, it still preserves striking lines of majesty. But surely, if marble could feel, the god would frown with a generous indignation to see himself transported from the Capitol into a French garden; and after having received the homage of the Roman Emperors, who laid their laurels at his feet when they returned from their conquests, to behold now nothing but the frizzled beaus passing by him with indifference.

I propose setting out soon from this place, so that you are to expect no more letters from this side of the water; besides,

I am hurried to death, and my head swims with that vast variety of objects which I am obliged to view with such rapidity, the shortness of my time not allowing me to examine them at my leisure. There is here an excessive prodigality of ornaments and decorations, that is just the opposite extreme to what appears in our royal gardens; this prodigality is owing to the levity and inconstancy of the French taste, which always pants after something new, and thus heaps ornament upon ornament without end or measure. It is time, however, that I should put an end to my letter; so I wish you good night, and am, etc.

LETTERS TO THE COUNTESS OF MAR,

AT PARIS.

FROM 1720 TO 1727.

LETTER I.

TWICKENHAM, 1720.

I HAVE had no answer, dear sister, to a long letter that I wrote to you a month ago ; however, I shall continue letting you know, *de temps en temps*, what passes in this corner of the world 'till you tell me 'tis disagreeable. I shall say little of the death of our great minister, because the papers say so much.* I suppose that the same faithful historians give you regular accounts of the growth and spreading of the inoculation for the small pox, which is become almost a general practice, attended with great success. I pass my time in a small snug set of dear intimates, and go very little into the *grand monde*, which has always had my hearty contempt. I see sometimes Mr. Congreve, and very seldom Mr. Pope, who continues to embellish his house at Twickenham. He has made a subterranean grotto, which he has furnished with looking-glasses, and *they tell me* it has a very good effect. I here send you some verses addressed to Mr. Gay, who wrote him a congratulatory letter on the finishing his house. I stifled them here, and I beg they may die the same death at Paris, and never go further than your closet :

* James Craggs, Esq., Secretary of State, died February 15, 1720, aged 35.

    ' Ah, friend, 'tis true—this truth you lovers know—
    In vain my structures rise, my gardens grow,
    In vain fair Thames reflects the double scenes
    Of hanging mountains, and of sloping greens:
    Joy lives not here; to happier seats it flies,
    And only dwells where Wortley casts her eyes.

    " What are the gay parterre, the checker'd shade,
    The morning bower, the ev'ning colonnade,
    But soft recesses of uneasy minds,
    To sigh unheard in, to the passing winds?
    So the struck deer in some sequester'd part
    Lies down to die, the arrow at his heart;
    There, stretch'd unseen in coverts hid from day,
    Bleeds drop by drop, and pants his life away."*

My paper is done, and I beg you to send my lutestring of what color you please.

LETTER II.

1722.

Dear Sister,—I am surprised at your silence, which has been very long, and I am sure it is very tedious to me. I have writ three times; one of my letters I know you received long since, for Charles Churchill told me so at the opera. At this instant I am at Twickenham; Mr. Wortley has purchased the small habitation where you saw me. We propose to make some small alterations. That and the education of my daughter are my chief amusements. I hope yours is well, *et ne fait que croître et embellir.* I beg you would let me hear soon from you; and particularly if the approaching coronation at Paris raises the price of diamonds. I have some to sell, and can not dispose of them here. I am afraid you have quite forgot my plain lutestring, which I am in

* In Pope's Works the last eight lines only are published as a fragment. After his quarrel with Lady Mary Wortley Montagu, he disingenuously suppressed the compliment conveyed in the preceding.

great want of, and I can hardly think you miss of opportunities to send it. At this dead season 'tis impossible to entertain you with news; and yet more impossible (with my dullness) to entertain you without it. The kindest thing I can do is to bring my letter to a speedy conclusion. I wish I had some better way of showing you how sincerely I am yours. I am sure I never will slip any occasion of convincing you of it.

LETTER III.

TWICKENHAM, 1723.

I do verily believe, my dear sister, that this is the twelfth if not the thirteenth letter I have written since I had the pleasure of hearing from you. It is an uncomfortable thing to have precious time spent, and one's wit neglected in this manner. Sometimes I think you are fallen into that utter indifference for all things on this side the water, that you have no more curiosity for the affairs of London than for those of Pekin; and if that be the case, 'tis downright impertinence to trouble you with news. But I can not cast off the affectionate concern I have for you, and consequently must put you in mind of me whenever I have any opportunity. The bearer of this epistle is our cousin,* and a consummate puppy, as you will perceive at first sight; his shoulder-knot last birthday made many a pretty gentleman's heart ache with envy, and his addresses have made Miss Howard the happiest of her highness's honorable virgins;† besides the glory of thrusting the Earl of Deloraine from the post he held in her affections. But his relations are so ill-bred as to be quite insensible of the honor arising from this conquest, and fearing that so much gallantry may conclude in captivity for life, pack him

---

* This cousin probably was Lord Fielding.

† Miss Howard was daughter of Colonel Philip Howard, and was married, in 1726, to Henry Scott Earl of Deloraine, third son of James Duke of Monmouth.

off to you, where 'tis to be hoped there is no such killing fair
as Miss Howard.

LETTER IV.

CAVENDISH SQUARE, 1723.

DEAR SISTER,—I have written to you twice since I received
yours in answer to that I sent by Mr. De Caylus, but I believe
none of what I send by the post ever come to your hands, nor
ever will while they are directed to Mr. Waters, for reasons
that you may easily guess. I wish you would give me a safer
direction; it is very seldom I can have the opportunity of a
private messenger, and it is very often that I have a mind to
write to my dear sister. If you have not heard of the Duchess
of Montagu's intended journey, you will be surprised at your
manner of receiving this, since I send it by one of her servants;
she does not design to see any body nor any thing in Paris,
and talks of going from Montpelier to Italy. I have a tender
esteem for her, and am heartily concerned to lose her conversation, yet I can not condemn her resolution. I am yet in this
wicked town, but propose to leave it as soon as the Parliament
rises. Mrs. Murray and all her satellites have so seldom fallen
in my way, I can say little about them. Your old friend Mrs.
Lowther is still fair and young, and in pale pink every night in
the parks; but, after being highly in favor, poor I am in utter
disgrace, without my being able to guess wherefore, except
she fancied me the author or abettor of two vile ballads written
on her dying adventure, which I am so innocent of that I never
saw it.* *A propos* of ballads, a most delightful one is said or
sung in most houses about our dearly-beloved plot, which has
been laid first to Pope and secondly to me, when God knows
we have neither of us wit enough to make it. Poets increase
and multiply to that stupendous degree, you see them at every
turn, even in embroidered coats and pink-colored top-knots;

* Mrs. Lowther was a respectable woman, single, and, as it appears by
the text, not willing to own herself middle-aged.

making verses is become almost as common as taking snuff, and who can tell what miserable stuff people carry about in their pockets, and offer to all their acquaintances, and you know one can not refuse reading and taking a pinch. This is a very great grievance and so particularly shocking to me, that I think our wise lawgivers should take it into consideration, and appoint a fast-day to beseech Heaven to put a stop to this epidemical disease, as they did last year for the plague with great success.

Dear sister, adieu. I have been very free in this letter, because I think I am sure of its going safe. I wish my night-gown may do the same: I only choose that as most convenient to you; but if it was equally so, I had rather the money was laid out in plain lutestring, if you could send me eight yards at a time of different colors, designing it for linings; but if this scheme is impracticable, send me a night-gown *à la mode.*

LETTER V.

TWICKENHAM, Oct. 20, 1723.

I am heartily sorry to have the pleasure of hearing from you lessened by your complaints of uneasiness, which I wish with all my soul I was capable of relieving, either by my letters or any other way. My life passes in a kind of indolence which is now and then awakened by agreeable moments; but pleasures are transitory, and the ground work of every thing in England stupidity, which is certainly owing to the coldness of this vile climate. I envy you the serene air of Paris, as well as many other conveniences there: what between the things one can not do, and the things one must not do, the time but dully lingers on, though I make as good a shift as many of my neighbors. To my great grief, some of my best friends have been extremely ill; and, in general, death and sickness have never been more frequent than now. You may imagine poor gallantry droops; and, except in the elysian shades of Richmond, there is no such thing as love or pleasure. It is said there is a fair lady retired for having taken too much of it : for my part they are not at all cooked to my taste ; and I have very little share in the diversions there, which, except seasoned with wit, or at least vivacity, will not go down with me who have not altogether so voracious an appetite as I once had : I intend, however, to shine and be fine on the birth-night, and review the figures there.

I desire you would say something very pretty to your daughter in my name ; notwithstanding the great gulf that is at present between us, I hope to wait on her to an opera one time or other.   I suppose you know our uncle Fielding * is dead.   I regret him prodigiously.

LETTER VI.

Oct. 31, 1723.

I write to you at this time piping hot from the birth-night ; my brain warmed with all the agreeable ideas that fine clothes, fine gentlemen, brisk tunes, and lively dances, can raise there. It is to be hoped that my letter will entertain you : at least you will certainly have the freshest account of all passages on that glorious day.   First you must know that I led up the ball, which you'll stare at ; but what is more, I believe in my conscience I made one of the best figures there ; to say truth, people are grown so extravagantly ugly that we old beauties are forced to come out on show-days, to keep the court in countenance.   I saw Mrs. Murray there, through whose hands this epistle will be conveyed ; I do not know whether she will make the same complaint to you that I do.   Mrs. West was with her, who is a great prude, having but two lovers at a time ; I think those are Lord Haddington and Mr. Lindsay ; the one for use, the other for show.

---

* William Fielding, Esq., second son of William, Earl of Denbigh, Gentleman of the Bed-chamber and Deputy-Comptroller of the Household, died in September, 1723.

The world improves in one virtue to a violent degree, I mean plain-dealing. Hypocrisy being, as the Scripture declares, a damnable sin, I hope our publicans and sinners will be saved by the open profession of the contrary virtue. I was told by a very good author, who is deep in the secret, that at this very minute, there is a bill cooping up at a hunting-seat in Norfolk,* to have not taken out of the commandments and clapped into the creed, the ensuing session of Parliament. This bold attempt for the liberty of the subject is wholly projected by Mr. Walpole, who proposed it to the secret committee in his parlor. William Young † seconded it, and answered for all his acquaintance voting right to a man: Doddington ‡ very gravely objected that the obstinacy of human nature was such that he feared when they had positive commandments to do so, perhaps people would not commit adultery and bear false witness against their neighbors with the readiness and cheerfulness they do at present. This objection seemed to sink deep into the minds of the greatest politicians at the board, and I don't know whether the bill won't be dropped, though it is certain it might be carried on with great ease, the world being entirely "*revenue du bagatelle*," and honor, virtue, reputation, etc. which we used to hear of in our nursery, is as much laid aside and forgotten as crumpled ribbons.

LETTER VII.

CAVENDISH SQUARE, 1724.

DEAR SISTER—I can not positively fix a time for my waiting on you at Paris; but I do verily believe I shall make a trip thither, sooner or later. This town improves in gayety every day; the young people are younger than they used to be, and all the old are growing young. Nothing is talked of but en-

* Houghton; Mr. (afterward Sir Robert) Walpole's, then prime-minister.

† Sir William Young.

‡ George Bubb Doddington, afterward Lord Melcomb-Regis, whose Diary has been published.

tertainments of gallantry by land and water, and we insensibly begin to taste all the joys of arbitrary power. Politics are no more; nobo ly pretends to wince or kick under their burdens; but we go on cheerfully with our bells at our ears, ornamented with ribbons, and highly contented with our present condition. So much for the general state of the nation. The last pleasure that fell in my way was Madame Sévigné's Letters; very pretty they are, but I assert, without the least vanity, that mine will be full as entertaining forty years hence. I advise you, therefore, to put none of them to the use of waste paper. You say nothing to me of the change of your ministry; I thank you for your silence upon that subject; I don't remember myself ever child enough to be concerned who reigned ir any part of the earth.

LETTER VIII.

TWICKENHAM, Jan. 1726.

DEAR SISTER—Having a few momentary spirits, I take pen in hand, though 'tis impossible to have tenderness for you, without having the spleen upon reading your letter, which will, I hope, be received as a lawful excuse for the dullness of the following lines; and I plead (as I believe I have on different occasions), that I should please you better if I loved you less. My Lord Carleton* has left this transitory world, and disposed of his estate as he did of his time, between Lady C——† and the Duchess of Q——y.‡ Jewels to a great value he has given, as he did his affections, first to the mother and then to the daughter. He was taken ill in my company at a concert at the Duchess of Marlborough's, and died two days after, holding the fair Duchess by the hand, and being fed at the

---

* Henry Boyle, fifth son of Richard Earl of Orrery, was Secretary of State to Queen Anne. Created Baron Carlton in 1714, and died in 1725.

† Clarendon.   † Queensberry.

same time with a fine fat chicken; thus dying as he had lived, indulging his pleasures. Your friend Lady A. Bateman (every body being acquainted with her affair) is grown discreet; and nobody talks of it now but his family, who are violently piqued at his refusing a great fortune. Lady Gainsborough* has stolen poor Lord Shaftesbury, *aged fourteen*, and chained him for life to her daughter, upon pretence of having been in love with her several years. But Lady Hervey† makes the top figure in town, and is so good as *to show* twice a week at the drawing-room, and twice more at the opera, for the entertainment of the public. As for myself, having nothing to say, I say nothing. I insensibly dwindle into a spectatress, and lead a kind of—as it were. I wish you here every day; and see, in the mean time, Lady Stafford and the Duchess of Montagu and Miss Skerret, and really speak to almost nobody else, though I walk about every where. Adieu, dear sister; if my letters could be any consolation to you, I should think my time best spent in writing.

When you buy the trifles that I desired of you, I fancy Mr. Walpole will be so good as to give you opportunity of sending them without trouble, if you make it your request and tell him they are for me.

LETTER IX.

1726

I received yours, dear sister, this minute, and am very sorry both for your past illness and affliction; though, *au bout du compte*, I don't know why filial piety should exceed fatherly

---

* Lady Gainsborough was Lady Dorothy Manners, second daughter of John first Duke of Rutland. Her daughter, Lady Susanna, was the first wife of Anthony fourth Earl of Shaftesbury. This marriage took place in 1725.

† Mary, Daughter of Brigadier-general Nicholas Le Pel, formerly Maid of Honor to the Princess of Wales, and Mistress of the Robes to her Majesty Queen Caroline. Married Oct. 25, 1720.

fondness. So much by way of consolation. As to the management at the time—I do verily believe, if my good aunt and
sister had been less fools, and my dear mother-in-law less mercenary, things might have had a turn more to your advantage
and mine too ; when we meet, I will tell you many circumstances which would be tedious in a letter. I could not get
my sister Gower to join to act with me, and mamma and I
were in an actual scold when my poor father expired ; she has
shown a hardness of heart upon this occasion that would appear incredible to any body not capable of it themselves.
The addition to her jointure is, one way or other, £2000 per
annum ; so her good grace remains a passable rich widow,
and is already presented by the town with a variety of young
husbands ; but I believe her constitution is not good enough
to let her amorous inclinations get the better of her covetous.
* * * * * * * * * *

All I had to say to you was that my father expressed a
great deal of kindness to me at last, and even a desire of talking with me, which my lady duchess would not permit ; nor
my aunt and sister show any thing but a servile complaisance
to her. This is the abstract of what you desire to know, and
is now quite useless.

LETTER X.

CAVENDISH SQUARE, 1726.

I am very sorry for your ill health, dear sister, but hope it is
so entirely past, that you have by this time forgot it. I never
was better in my life, nor ever passed my hours more agreeably ;
I ride between London and Twickenham perpetually, and
have little societies quite to my taste, and that is saying every
thing. I leave the great world to girls that know no better,
and do not think one bit the worse of myself for having outlived a certain giddiness, which is sometimes excusable, but
never pleasing. Depend upon it, 'tis only the spleen that

gives you those ideas; you may have many delightful days to come, and there is nothing more silly than to be too wise to be happy:

> If to be sad is to be wise,
> I do most heartily despise
> Whatever Socrates has said,
> Or Tully writ, or Montaigne read.

So much for philosophy. What do you say to Pelham's marriage?* There's flame! There's constancy! If I could not employ my time better, I would write the history of their loves in twelve tomes: Lord Hervey should die in her arms like the poor King of Assyria, she should be sometimes carried off by troops of Masques, and at other times blocked up in the strong castles of the Bagnio; but her honor should always remain inviolate by the strength of her own virtue, and the friendship of the enchantress Mrs. Murray, till her happy nuptials with her faithful Cyrus; 'tis a thousand pities I have not time for these vivacities. Here is a book come out† that all our people of taste run mad about; 'tis no less than the united work of a dignified clergyman, an eminent physician, and the first poet of the age ;‡ and very wonderful it is!— great eloquence have they employed to prove themselves beasts, and show such a veneration for horses, that since the Essex Quaker, nobody has appeared so passionately devoted to that species; and to say truth, they talk of a stable with so much warmth and affection I can not help suspecting some very powerful motive at the bottom of it.

* Henry Pelham, only brother to his grace the Duke of Newcastle, was married Oct. 17, 1726, to Lady Catherine, eldest daughter of John second Duke of Rutland, by Catherine second daughter of William Lord Russell, and sister to Wriothesly Duke of Bedford.

† The Travels of Captain Lemuel Gulliver.

‡ Swift, Arbuthnot, and Pope.

LETTER XI.

CAVENDISH SQUARE, 1727.

This is a vile world, dear sister, and I can easily comprehend, that whether one is at Paris or London, one is stifled with a certain mixture of fool and knave, that most people are composed of. I would have patience with a parcel of polite rogues, or your downright honest fools; but father Adam shines through his whole progeny. So much for our inside —then our outward is so liable to ugliness and distempers that we are perpetually plagued with feeling our own decays and seeing those of other people. Yet, sixpennyworth of common sense divided among a whole nation, would make our lives roll away glibly enough; but then we make laws, and we follow customs. By the first we cut off our own pleasures, and by the second we are answerable for the faults and extravagances of others. All these things, and five hundred more, convince me (as I have the most profound veneration for the Author of nature) that we are here in an actual state of punishment; I am satisfied I have been one of *the condemned* ever since I was born; and in submission to the divine justice I don't at all doubt but I deserved it in some pre-existent state. I will still hope that I am only in purgatory; and that after whining and grunting a certain number of years, I shall be translated to some more happy sphere, where virtue will be natural, and custom reasonable; that is, in short, where common sense will reign. I grow very devout, as you see, and place all my hopes in the next life, being totally persuaded of the nothingness of this. Don't you remember how miserable we were in the little parlor at Thoresby? we then thought marrying would put us at once into possession of all we wanted. Then came being with child, etc., and you see what comes of being with child. Though, after all, I am still of opinion that it is extremely silly to submit to ill fortune. One should pluck a spirit, and live upon cordials when one can have no other nourishment. These are my present endeavors, and I run about, though I have five thousand pins and needles running into my heart. I try to console myself with a small damsel,* who is at present every thing I like—but, alas! she is yet in a white frock. At fourteen, she may run away with the butler: there 's one of the blessed consequences of great disappointments; you are not only hurt by the thing present, but it cuts off all future hopes, and makes your very expectations melancholy. *Quelle vie ! ! !*

LETTER XII.

CAVENDISH SQUARE, 1727.

I can not deny but that I was very well diverted on the coronation day. I saw the procession much at my ease, in a house which I filled with my own company, and then got into Westminster Hall without trouble, where it was very entertaining to observe the variety of airs that all meant the same thing. The business of every walker there was to conceal vanity and gain admiration. For these purposes some languished and others strutted; but a visible satisfaction was diffused over every countenance, as soon as the coronet was clapped on the head. But she that drew the greatest number of eyes, was indisputably Lady Orkney.† She exposed behind a mixture of fat and wrinkles; and before, a very considerable protuberance which preceded her. Add to this, the inimitable roll of her eyes, and her gray hairs which by good fortune stood directly upright, and 'tis impossible to imagine a more delightful spectacle. She had embellished all this with considerable magnificence, which made her look as big again as

---

* Her daughter, afterward Countess of Bute.

† Lady Orkney, whom Swift calls the wisest woman he ever knew, must have been pretty old at the time of George the Second's coronation, since, in spite of her ugliness, also commemorated by Swift, she was King William's declared mistress after the death of Queen Mary. Mrs. Villiers originally, she married Lord Orkney, one of the sons of the Duke and Duchess of Hamilton.

usual; and I should have thought her one of the largest
things of God's making if my Lady St. J——n* had not displayed all her charms in honor of the day. The poor Duchess
of M——se† crept along with a dozen of black snakes playing round her face, and my Lady P——‡ and (who is fallen
away since her dismission from court) represented very finely
an Egyptian mummy embroidered over with hieroglyphics.
In general, I could not perceive but that the old were as well
pleased as the young; and I, who dread growing wise more
than any thing in the world, was overjoyed to find that one
can never outlive one's vanity. I have never received the
long letter you talk of, and am afraid that you have only
fancied that you wrote it. Adieu, dear sister.

LETTER XIII.

CAVENDISH SQUARE, 1727.

My Lady Stafford § set out toward France this morning, and
has carried half the pleasures of my life along with her; I am

---

* St. John.   † Montrose.

‡ Portland, a Temple by birth, widow of Lord Berkeley of Stratton,
and secondly of Earl of Portland. She was his second wife, and had
by him two sons, who settled in Holland, and from whom descends the
Dutch branch of the Bentincks. George I. appointed her governess of
his grandchildren, when he took them away from their parent, upon
coming to an open breach with his son. The prince and princess one
day going to visit them, and the latter desiring to see her daughter;
Lady Portland, with many expressions of respect, lamented that she
could not permit it, having his Majesty's strict orders to the contrary.
Upon this, the prince flew into such a rage that he would literally
and truly have actually kicked her out of the room, if the princess
had not thrown herself between them. Of course he made haste to
dismiss her as soon as he came to the crown.

§ Claude Charlotte, daughter of Philibert, Count of Grammont, (author of the celebrated Memoirs), and "La Belle Hamilton," eldest
daughter of Sir George Hamilton, Bart., was married to Henry Stafford
Howard, Earl of Stafford, at St. Germain-en-Laye, 1694.

more stupid than I can describe, and am as full of moral reflections as either Cambray or Pascal. I think of nothing but
the nothingness of the good things of this world, the transito-
riness of its joys, the pungency of its sorrows, and many discoveries that have been made these three thousand years, and
committed to print ever since the first erecting of presses. I
advise you, as the best thing you can do that day, let it happen as it will, to visit Lady Stafford ; she has the goodness to
carry with her a true-born Englishwoman, who is neither good
nor bad, nor capable of being either; Lady Phil. Pratt by
name, of the Hamilton family, and who will be glad of your
acquaintance, and you can never be sorry for hers.*

Peace or war, cross or pile, makes all the conversation ; this
town never was fuller, and, God be praised, some people *brille*
in it who *brilled* twenty years ago. My cousin Buller is of
that number, who is just what she was in all respects when
she inhabited Bond-street. The sprouts of this age are such
green withered things, 'tis a great comfort to us grown up
people ; I except my own daughter, who is to be the ornament
of the ensuing court. I beg you will exact from Lady Stafford a particular of her perfections, which would sound suspected from my hand ; at the same time I must do justice to
a little twig belonging to my sister Gower. Miss Jenny is
like the Duchess of Queensberry both in face and spirit. *A
propos* of family affairs : I had almost forgot our dear and
amiable cousin Lady Denbigh, who has blazed out all this
winter ; she has brought with her from Paris cart-loads of
ribbon, surprising fashion, and of a complexion of the last
edition, which naturally attracts all the she and he fools
in London ; and accordingly she is surrounded with a little
court of both, and keeps a Sunday assembly to show she has
learned to play at cards on that day. Lady Frances Fielding†

† Lady Philippa Hamilton, daughter of James Earl of Abercorn, and
wife of Dr. Pratt, Dean of Downe.

* Youngest daughter of Basil fourth Earl of Denbigh; married to
Daniel seventh Earl of Winchelsea; died Sept. 17, 1734.

is really the prettiest woman in town, and has sense enough
to make one's heart ache to see her surrounded with such fools
as her relations are. The man in England that gives the greatest pleasure, and the greatest pain, is a youth of royal blood,
with all his grandmother's beauty, wit, and good qualities. In
short, he is Nell Gwyn in person, with the sex altered, and
occasions such fracas among the ladies of gallantry that it
passes description. You'll stare to hear of her Grace of
Cleveland at the head of them.* If I was poetical I would
tell you—

The god of love, enraged to see
   The nymph despise his flame,
At dice and cards misspend her nights,
   And slight a nobler game;

For the neglect of offers past
   And pride in days of yore,
He kindles up a fire at last,
   That burns her at threescore.

A polish'd wile is smoothly spread
   Where whilome wrinkles lay;
And glowing with an artful red,
   She ogles at the play.

Along the Mall she softly sails,
   In white and silver drest;
Her neck exposed to Eastern gales,
   And jewels on her breast.

Her children banish'd, age forgot,
   Lord Sidney is her care;
And, what is much a happier lot,
   Has hopes to be her *heir*.

This is all true history, though it is doggrel rhyme; in good
earnest she has turned Lady D——† and family out of doors

* Anne, daughter of Sir W. Pulteney of Misterton, in the county of
Stafford; remarried to Philip Southcote, Esq. Died in 1746.

† Lady Grace Fitzroy, third daughter of Charles Duke of Cleveland;
married in 1725, to Henry first Earl of Darlington.

to make room for him, and there he lies like leaf-gold upon a
pill; there never was so violent and so indiscreet a passion.
Lady Stafford says nothing was ever like it, since Phædra and
Hippolytus. "Lord ha' mercy upon us. See what we may
all come to!"

LETTER XIV.

No date.

I am always pleased to hear from you, dear sister, particularly when you tell me you are well. I believe you will find
upon the whole my sense is right; that air, exercise, and company are the best medicines, and physic and retirement good
for nothing but to break hearts and spoil constitutions. I was
glad to hear Mr. Remond's history from you, though the newspapers had given it me *en gros*, and my Lady Stafford in detail, some time before. I will tell you in return as well as I
can what happens among our acquaintances here. To begin
with family affairs; the Duchess of Kingston grunts on as
usual, and I fear will put us in black bombazine soon, which
is a real grief to me. My aunt Cheyne makes all the money
she can of Lady Frances, and I fear will carry on those politics
to the last point, though the girl is such a fool 'tis no great
matter; I am going within this half-hour to call her to court.
Our poor cousins, the Fieldings, are grown yet poorer by the
loss of all the money they had, which in their infinite wisdom
they put into the hands of a roguish broker, who has fairly
walked off with it.

LETTER XV.

1727.

My cousin is going to Paris, and I will not let her go without a letter for you, my dear sister, though I never was in a worse humor for writing. I am vexed to the blood by my young rogue of a son, who has contrived at his age to make himself the talk of the whole nation. He has gone knight-erranting, God knows where; and hitherto 'tis impossible to find him. You may judge of my uneasiness by what your own would be if dear Lady Fanny was lost. Nothing that ever happened to me has troubled me so much; I can hardly speak or write of it with tolerable temper, and I own it has changed mine to that degree I have a mind to cross the water, to try what effect a new heaven and a new earth will have upon my spirit. If I take this resolution, you shall hear in a few posts. There can be no situation in life in which the conversation of my dear sister will not administer some comfort to me.

LETTERS

FROM

LADY MARY TO MR. WORTLEY,

DURING HER SECOND RESIDENCE ABROAD.

FROM 1739 TO 1761.

LETTERS FROM LADY MARY TO MR. WORTLEY.*

DURING HER SECOND RESIDENCE ABROAD.

FROM 1739 TO 1761.

LETTER I.

CALAIS, July 27, 1739.

I AM safely arrived at Calais, and found myself better on
shipboard than I have been these six months; not in the least
sick, though we had a very high sea, as you may imagine,
since we came over in two hours and three-quarters. My
servants behaved very well; and Mary not in the least afraid,
but said she would be drowned very willingly with my ladyship. They ask me here extravagant prices for chaises, of
which there are great choice, both French and Italian: I have
at last bought one for fourteen guineas, of a man whom Mr.
Hall recommended to me. My things have been examined
and sealed at the Custom-house : they took from me a pound
of snuff, but did not open my-jewel boxes, which they let pass

* These letters to her husband show Lady Mary's wifely character
in a very agreeable light. That she had a warm esteem for his virtues
and reverenced his character, is evident in her letters to her daughter
as well as in this correspondence. Nor does it appear there was any
estrangement between Mr. Wortley and herself, which caused her to
go abroad. Her letters prove her regard for him, and all she writes
indicate her confidence in his esteem for her, though his cold tempera
ment and cautious wisdom made her confine her expressions of affection to her daughter and sister.—AM. ED.

on my word, being things belonging to my dress. I set out early to-morrow. I am very impatient to hear from you : I could not stay for the post at Dover for fear of losing the tide. I beg you would be so good as to order Mr. Kent to pack up my side-saddle, and all the tackle belonging to it, in a box, to be sent with my other things : if (as I hope) I recover my health abroad so much as to ride, I can get none I shall like so well.

———

LETTER II.

Dijon, August 18, N. S., 1739.

I am at length arrived here very safely, and without any bad accident; and so much mended in my health that I am surprised at it. France is so much improved, it would not be known to be the same country we passed through twenty years ago. Every thing I see speaks in praise of Cardinal Fleury: the roads are all mended, and the greater part of them paved as well as the streets of Paris, planted on both sides like the roads in Holland; and such good care taken against robbers that you may cross the country with your purse in your hand : but as to traveling *incognita*, I may as well walk *incognita* in the Pall Mall. There is not any town in France where there are not English, Scotch, or Irish families established; and I have met with people that have seen me (though often such as I do not remember to have seen) in every town I have passed through ; and I think the further I go, the more acquaintances I meet. Here are in this town no less than sixteen English families of fashion. Lord Mansel lodges in the house with me, and a daughter of Lord Bathurst's (Mrs. Whitshed) is in the same street. The Duke of Rutland is gone from hence some time ago, as Lady Peterborough told me at St. Omer's; which was one reason that determined me to come here, thinking to be quiet ; but I find it impossible, and that will make me leave the place, after the return of this post. The French are more changed than their roads; instead of pale, yellow faces, wrapped up in blankets, as we saw them, the villages are all filled with fresh-colored lusty peasants, in good clothes and clean linen. It is incredible what an air of plenty and content is over the whole country. I hope to hear, as soon as possible, that you are in good health.

LETTER III.

VENICE, Sept. 25, 1739.

I am at length happily arrived here, I thank God; I wish it had been my original plan, which would have saved me some money and fatigue; though I have not much reason to regret the last, since I am convinced it has greatly contributed to the restoration of my health. I met nothing disagreeable on my journey but too much company. I find (contrary to the rest of the world) I did not think myself so considerable as I am; for I verily believe, if one of the pyramids of Egypt had traveled it could not have been more followed; and if I had received all the visits that have been intended me, I should have stopped at least two years in every town I came through. I liked Milan so well that if I had not desired all my letters to be directed hither, I think I should have been tempted to stay there. One of the pleasures I found there was the Borromean library, where all strangers have free access; and not only so, but liberty, on giving a note for it, to take any printed book home with them. I saw several curious manuscripts there; and as a proof of my recovery, I went up to the very top of the dome of the great church without any assistance. I am now in a lodging on the Great Canal. Lady Pomfret * is not yet arrived, but I expect her very soon; and

* Henrietta Louisa, daughter and heir of Lord Chancellor Jeffries, wife of Thomas Earl of Pomfret. She resided chiefly at Rome, where she wrote the life of Vandyck. A part of the collection of marbles made by Thomas, Earl of Arundel, having been purchased by William Earl of Pomfret, was given by her to the University of Oxford, in 1758.

if the air does not disagree with me, I intend seeing the carnival here. I hope your health continues, and that I shall hear from you very soon.

LETTER IV.

VENICE, Dec. 25, O. S. 1739.

I received yours yesterday, dated December 7. I find my health very well here, notwithstanding the cold, which is very sharp, but the sun shines as clear as at midsummer. I am treated here with more distinction than I could possibly expect. I went to see the ceremony of high mass celebrated by the Doge, on Christmas eve. He appointed a gallery for me and the Prince of Wolsembatch, where no other person was admitted but those of our company. A greater compliment could not have been paid me if I had been a sovereign princess. The Doge's niece (he having no lady) met me at the palace-gate, and led me through the palace to the Church of St. Mark, where the ceremony was performed in the pomp you know, and we were not obliged to any act of adoration. The Electoral Prince of Saxony is here in public, and makes a prodigious expense. His governor is Count Wackerbart, son to that Madame Wackerbart with whom I was so intimate at Vienna; on which account he shows me particular civilities, and obliges his pupil to do the same. I was last night at an entertainment made for him by the Signora Pisani Mocenigo, which was one of the finest I ever saw, and he desired me to sit next him in a great chair; in short I have all the reason that can be, to be satisfied with my treatment in this town; and I am glad I met Lord Carlisle, who directed me hither.

I have so little correspondence at London, I should be pleased to hear from you whatever happens among my acquaintance. I am sorry for Mr. Pelham's misfortune;* though 'tis long

* The death of his two sons on two following days, November 26, 28, 1739.

since that I have looked on the hopes of continuing a family
as one of the vainest of mortal prospects.

Tho' Solomon, with a thousand wives,
To get a wise successor strives;
But one, and he a fool, survives.

LETTER V.

VENICE, June 1, 1740.

I wrote you a long letter yesterday, which I sent by a
private hand, who will see it safely delivered. It is impossible to be better treated, I may even say more courted, than
I am here. I am very glad of your good fortune at London.
You may remember I have always told you it is in your
power to make the first figure in the House of Commons. As
to the bill, I perfectly remember the paying of it, which you
may easily believe when you inquire, that all auction bills
are paid at furthest within eight days after the sale : the date
of this is March 1, and I did not leave London till July 25 ;
and in that time have been at many other auctions, particularly Lord Halifax's, which was a short time before my journey. This is not the first of Cock's mistakes ; he is famous
for making them, which are (he says) the fault of his servants. You seem to mention the regatta in a manner as if
you would be pleased with a description of it. It is a race
of boats: they are accompanied by vessels which they call
piotes or bichones, that have a mind to display their magnificence ; they are a sort of machines adorned with all that
sculpture and gilding can do to make a shining appearance.
Several of them cost one thousand pounds sterling, and I believe none less than five hundred ; they are rowed by gondoliers dressed in rich habits, suitable to what they represent.
There were enough of them to look like a little fleet, and I
own I never saw a finer sight. It would be too long to describe every one in particular, I shall only name the princi-

pal: the Signora Pisani Mocenigo's represented the Chariot of the Night, drawn by four sea-horses, and showing the rising of the moon, accompanied with stars, the statues on each side representing the hours to the number of twenty-four, rowed by gondoliers in rich liveries, which were changed three times, all of equal richness, and the decorations changed also to the dawn of Aurora and the mid-day sun, the statues being new dressed every time, the first in green, the second time red, and the last blue, all equally laced with silver, there being three races. Signor Soranto represented the kingdom of Poland, with all the provinces and rivers in that dominion, with a concert of the best instrumental music in rich Polish habits; the painting and gilding were exquisite in their kinds. Signor Contarini's piote showed the liberal arts; Apollo was seated on the stern upon Mount Parnassus, Pegasus behind, and the Muses seated round him: opposite was a figure representing Painting, with Fame blowing her trumpet; and on each side Sculpture and Music in their proper dresses. The Procurator Foscarini's was the chariot of Flora guided by Cupids, and adorned with all sorts of flowers, rose-trees etc. Signor Julio Contarini's represented the triumphs of Valor; Victory was on the stern, and all the ornaments warlike trophies of every kind. Signor Correri's was the Adriatic Sea receiving into her arms the Hope of Saxony. Signor Alvisio Moncenigo's was the garden of Hesperides; the whole fable was represented by different statues. Signor Querini had the chariot of Venus drawn by doves, so well done, they seemed ready to fly upon the water; the Loves and Graces attended her. Signor Paul Doria had the chariot of Diana, who appeared hunting in a large wood; the trees, hounds, stag, and nymphs, all done naturally: the gondoliers dressed like peasants attending the chase; and Endymion, lying under a large tree, gazing on the goddess. Signor Angelo Labbia represented Poland crowning Saxony, waited on by the Virtues and subject Provinces. Signor Angelo Molino was Neptune, waited on by the Rivers. Signor Vicenzo Morosini's piote showed the triumphs of Peace; Discord being chained at her feet, and she surrounded with the Pleasures, etc.

LETTER VI.

FLORENCE, August 11, 1740.

This is a very fine town, and I am much amused with visiting the gallery, which I do not doubt you remember too well to need any description of. Lord and Lady Pomfret take pains to make the place agreeable to me, and I have been visited by the greatest part of the people of quality. Here is an opera which I have heard twice, but it is not so fine either for voices or decorations as that at Venice. I am very willing to be at Leghorn when my things arrive, which I fear will hinder my visiting Rome this season, except they come sooner than is generally expected. If I could go from thence by sea to Naples with safety, I should prefer it to a land journey, which I am told is very difficult; and that it is impossible I should stay there long, the people being entirely unsociable. I do not desire much company, but would not confine myself to a place where I could see none. I have written to your daughter, directed to Scotland, this post.

LETTER VII.

ROME, October 24, 1740.

I arrived here in good health three days ago, and this is the first post-day. I have taken a lodging for a month, which is (as they tell me) but a short time to take a view of all the antiquities, etc., that are to be seen. From hence I purpose to set out for Naples. I am told by every body that I shall not find it agreeable to reside in. I expect Lady Pomfret here in a few days. It is summer here, and I left winter at Florence; the snows having begun to fall on the mountains. I shall probably see the new ceremony of the Pope's taking possession of the Vatican, which is said to be the finest that is ever performed at Rome. I have no news to send from hence. If you would have me speak to any particular point, I beg you will let me know it, and I will give you the best information I am able.

LETTER VIII.

ROME, November 1, N. S., 1740.

I have now been here a week, and am very well diverted with viewing the fine buildings, paintings, and antiquities. I have neither made nor received one visit, nor sent word to any body of my arrival, on purpose to avoid interruptions of that sort. The weather is so fine that I walk every evening in a different beautiful garden; and I own I am charmed with what I see of this town, though there yet remains a great deal more to be seen. I purpose making a stay of a month, which shall be entirely taken up in that employment, and then I will remove to Naples, to avoid, if possible, feeling the winter. I do not trouble you with any descriptions, since you have been here, and I suppose very well remember every thing that is worth remembering; but (as I mentioned in my last) if you would have me speak to any particular point, I will give you the best information in my power. Direct your next letter to Monsieur Belloni, Banquier, à Rome. He will take care to deliver it to me, either here or at Naples. Letters are very apt to miscarry, especially those to this place.

LETTER IX.

NAPLES, November 23, N. S., 1740.

I arrived here last night, after a very disagreeable journey. I would not in my last give you any account of the present state of Rome, knowing all letters are opened there; but I can

not help mentioning what is more curious than all the antiquities, which is, that there is literally no money in the whole
town, where they follow Mr. Law's scheme, and live wholly
upon paper.

Belloni, who is the greatest banker not only of Rome but
all Italy, furnished me with fifty sequins, which he solemnly
swore was all the money he had in the house. They go to
market with paper, pay the lodgings with paper, and, in short,
there is no specie to be seen, which raises the price of every
thing to the utmost extravagance, nobody knowing what to
ask for their goods. It is said the present Pope (who has a
very good character) has declared he will endeavor a remedy,
though it is very difficult to find one. He was bred a lawyer, and has passed the greatest part of his life in that profession ; and is so sensible of the misery of the state that he is
reported to have said that he never thought himself in want
till his elevation. He has no relations that he takes any notice of; but the country belonging to him, which I have
passed, is almost uninhabited, and in a poverty beyond any
thing I ever saw. The kingdom of Naples appears gay and
flourishing, and the town so crowded with people that I have
with great difficulty got a very sorry lodging.

LETTER X.

NAPLES, Dec. 6, 1740.

I heard last night the good news of the arrival of the ship
on which my things are loaded, at Leghorn : it would be easy
to have them conveyed hither : I like the climate extremely,
which is now so soft that I am actually sitting without any want
of a fire. I do not find the people so savage as they were represented to me. I have received visits from several of the
principal ladies ; and I think I could meet with as much company here as I desire; but here is one article both disagreeable
and incommodious, which is the grandeur of the equipages.

Two coaches, two running footmen, four other footmen, a gentleman usher, and two pages, are as necessary here as the attendance of a single servant is at London. All the Spanish customs are observed very rigorously. I could content myself with all of them, except this : but I see plainly, from my own observation as well as intelligence, that it is not to be dispensed with, which I am heartily vexed at.

The affairs of Europe are now so uncertain that it appears reasonable to me to wait a little, before I fix my residence, that I may not find myself in the theater of war, which is threatened on all sides. I hope you have the continuation of your health ; mine is very well established at present. The town lately d'scovered is at Portici, about three miles from this place. Since the first discovery, no care has been taken, and the ground fallen in, so that the present passage to it is, as I am told by every body, extremely dangerous, and for some time, nobody ventures into it. I have been assured by some English gentlemen, who were let down into it the last year, that the whole account given in the newspapers is literally true. Probably great curiosities might be found there ; but there has been no expense made, either by propping the ground or clearing away into it ; and as the earth falls in daily, it will possibly be soon stopped up as it was before. I wrote to you last post a particular account of my reasons for not choosing my residence here, though the air is very agreeable to me, and I see I could have as much company as I desire ; but I am persuaded the climate is much changed since you knew it. The weather is now very moist and misty, and has been so for a long time ; however it is much softer than in any other place I know. I desire you would direct to Monsieur Belloni, banker, at Rome : he will forward your letters wherever I am ; the present uncertain situation of affairs all over Europe makes every correspondence precarious.

LETTER XI.

Rome, Jan. 13, N. S., 1740–1.

I returned hither last night, after six weeks' stay at Naples; great part of that time was vainly taken up in endeavoring to satisfy your curiosity and my own, in relation to the late discovered town of Herculaneum. I waited eight days in hopes of permission to see the pictures and other rarities taken from thence, which are preserved in the king's palace at Portici; but I found it was to no purpose, his majesty keeping the key in his own cabinet, which he would not part with, though the Prince de Zathia (who is one of his favorites) I believe very sincerely tried his interest to obtain it for me. He is son to the Spanish embassador I knew at Venice, and both he and his lady loaded me with civilities at Naples. The court in general is more barbarous than any of the ancient Goths. One proof of it, among many others, was melting down a beautiful copper statue of a vestal found in this new ruin, to make medallions, for the late solemn christening. The whole court follow the Spanish customs and politics. I could say a good deal on this subject if I thought my letter would come safe to your hands; the apprehension it may not, hinders my answering another inquiry you make, concerning a family here, of which indeed I can say little; avoiding all commerce with those that frequent it. Here are some young English travelers; among them Lord Strafford* behaves himself really very modestly and genteelly, and has lost the pertness he acquired in his mother's assembly. Lord Lincoln appears to have spirit and sense, and professes great abhorrence of all measures destructive to the liberty of

---

* William Wentworth, the fourth Earl of Strafford, married Lady Anne, second daughter of John Duke of Argyll, sister of Lady Mary Coke and Lady Betty Mackenzie. He built the south front of Wentworth Castle, in Yorkshire, and was eminently skilled in architecture and virtue. He enjoyed an intimate friendship with the last Lord Orford, in the fifth volume of whose works his correspondence is published from 1756 to 1790.

his country. I do not know how far the young men may be corrupted on their return, but the majority of those I have seen have seemed strongly in the same sentiment. Lady Newburgh's eldest daughter, whom I believe you may have seen at Lord Westmoreland's, is married to Count Mahony, who is in great figure at Naples: she was extremely obliging to me; they made a fine entertainment for me, carried me to the opera, and were civil to me to the utmost of their power. If you should happen to see Mrs. Bulkely, I wish you would make her some compliment upon it. I received this day yours of the 20th and 28th of November.

LETTER XII.

LEGHORN, Feb. 25, N. S., 1740-1.

I arrived here last night, and have received this morning the bill of seven hundred and five dollars, odd money.

I shall be a little more particular in my accounts from hence than I durst be from Rome, where all the letters are opened and often stopped. I hope you had mine, relating to the antiquities in Naples. I shall now say something of the court of Rome. The first minister, Cardinal Valenti, has one of the best characters I ever heard of, though of no great birth, and has made his fortune by an attachment to the Duchess of Salviah. The present Pope is very much beloved, and seems desirous to ease the people, and deliver them out of the miserable poverty they are reduced to. I will send you the history of his elevation, as I had it from a very good hand, if it will be any amusement to you. The English travelers at Rome behaved in general very discreetly. I have reason to speak well of them, since they were all exceedingly obliging to me. It may sound a little vain to say it, but they really paid a regular court to me, as if I had been their queen, and their governess told me that the desire of my approbation had a very great influence on their conduct. While I staid there was neither gaming nor any sort of extravagance. I used to preach to them very freely, and they all thanked me for it. I shall stay some time in this town, where I expect Lady Pomfret. I think I have answered every particular you seemed curious about. If there be any other point you would have me speak of, I will be as exact as I can.

LETTER XIII.

Tubin, April 11, 1741.

The English politics are the general jest of all the nations I have passed through ; and even those who profit by our folly can not help laughing at our notorious blunders ; though they are all persuaded that the minister does not act from weakness but corruption, and that the Spanish gold influences his measures. I had a long discourse with Count Mahony on this subject, who said, very freely, that half the ships sent to the coast of Naples, that have lain idle in our ports last summer, would have frightened the Queen of Spain into a submission to whatever terms we thought proper to impose. The people, who are loaded with taxes, hate the Spanish government, of which I had daily proofs, hearing them curse the English for bringing their king to them, whenever they saw any of our nation ; but I am not much surprised at the ignorance of our ministers, after seeing what creatures they employ to send them intelligence. Except Mr. Villette, at this court, there is not one that has common sense ; I say this without prejudice, all of them having been as civil and serviceable to me as they could. I was told at Rome, and convinced of it by circumstances, that there have been great endeavors to raise up a sham plot ; the person who told it me was an English antiquarian, who said he had been offered any money to send accusations. The truth is, he carried a letter, written by Mr. Mann,* from Florence to that purpose to him, which he showed in the English palace ; however, I believe he is a spy, and

* Sir Horace Mann.

made use of that stratagem to gain credit. This court makes great preparations for war; the king is certainly no bright genius, but has great natural humanity ; his minister, who has absolute power, is generally allowed to have sense ; as a proof of it, he is not hated as the generality of ministers are. I have seen neither of them, not going to court, because I will not be at the trouble and expense of the dress, which is the same as at Vienna. I sent my excuse by Mr. Villette, as I hear is commonly practiced by ladies that are only passengers. I have had a great number of visitors ; the nobility piquing themselves on civility to strangers. The weather is still exceedingly cold, and I do not intend to move till I have the prospect of a pleasant journey.

LETTER XIV.

GENOA, July 15, 1741.

It is so long since I have heard from you, that though I hope your silence is occasioned by your being in the country, yet I can not help being very uneasy, and in some apprehension that you are indisposed. I wrote you word, some time ago, that I have taken a house here for the remainder of the summer, and desired you would direct, *recommandé à Monsieur Birtles, Consul de S. M. Britannique.* I saw in the last newspapers (which he sends me) the death of Lord Orford. I am vexed at it, for the reasons you know, and recollect what I've often heard you say, that it is impossible to judge what is best for ourselves. I received yesterday the bill for ——, for which I return you thanks. If I wrote you all the political stories I hear, I should have a great deal to say. A great part is not true, and what I think so, I dare not mention, in consideration of the various hands this paper must pass through before it reaches you. Lord Lincoln* and Mr. Wal-

* Henry Clinton, Earl of Lincoln, married Catherine, daughter of Henry Pelham, and was afterward Duke of Newcastle.

pole* (youngest son to Sir Robert) left this place two days
ago; they visited me during their short stay; they are gone to
Marseilles, and design passing some months in the south of
France. I have had a particular account of Lord Orford's
death† from a very good hand, which he advanced by choice,
refusing all remedies till it was too late to make use of them.
There was a will found, dated 1728, in which he gave every
thing to my lady; ‡ which has affected her very much. Notwithstanding the many reasons she had to complain of him, I
always thought there was more weakness than dishonesty in
his actions, and is a confirmation of the truth of that maxim
of Mr. Rochefoucault, *un sot n'a pas assez d'étoffe pour être
honnête homme.*

LETTER XV.

GENOA, Aug. 25, N. S., 1741.

I received yours of the 27th July this morning. I had that
of March 19, which I answered very particularly the following
post, with many thanks for the increase of my allowance. It
appears to me that the letters I wrote between the 11th of
April and the 31st of May were lost, which I am not surprised
at. I was then at Turin, and that court in a very great confusion, and extremely jealous of me, thinking I came to examine their conduct. I have some proof of this, which I do not
repeat, lest this should be stopped also.

The manners of Italy are so much changed since we were
here last, the alteration is scarcely credible. They say it has
been by the last war. The French, being masters, introduced

---

* Honorable Horace Walpole, the last Earl of Orford, then on his
travels.

† Robert, the second Earl of Orford, died in June 1741.

‡ Margaret, daughter and sole heir of Samuel Rolle of Haynton, in
the county of Dorset, who married secondly the Hon. Sewallis Shirley,
fourth son of the first Earl Ferrers by his second wife Selina, daughter
of George Finch, of the City of London, Esq.

all their customs, which were eagerly embraced by the ladies, and I believe will never be laid aside; yet the different governments make different manners in every state. You know, though the republic is not rich, here are many private families vastly so, and live at a great superfluous expense: all the people of the first quality keep coaches as fine as the Speaker's, and some of them two or three, though the streets are too narrow to use them in the town; but they take the air in them, and their chairs carry them to the gates. Their liveries are all plain: gold or silver being forbidden to be worn within the walls, the habits are all obliged to be black, but they wear exceedingly fine lace and linen; and in their country-houses, which are generally in the faubourg, they dress very richly, and have extremely fine jewels. Here is nothing cheap but houses. A palace fit for a prince may be hired for fifty pounds per annum: I mean unfurnished. All games of chance are strictly prohibited, and it seems to me the only law they do not try to evade: they play at quadrille, picquet, etc., but not high. Here are no regular public assemblies. I have been visited by all of the first rank, and invited to several fine dinners, particularly to the wedding of one of the House of Spinola, where there were ninety-six sat down to table, and I think the entertainment one of the finest I ever saw. There was the night following a ball and supper for the same company, with the same profusion. They tell me that all their great marriages are kept in the same public manner. Nobody keeps more than two horses, all their journeys being post; the expense of them, including the coach man, is (I am told) fifty pounds per annum. A chair is very nearly as much; I give eighteen francs a-week for mine. The senators can converse with no strangers during the time of their magistracy, which lasts two years. The number of servants is regulated, and almost every lady has the same, which is two footmen, a gentleman-usher, and a page, who follow her chair.

9*

LETTER XVI.

GENEVA, Oct. 12, 1741.

I arrived here last night, where I find every thing quite different from what it was represented to me: it is not the first time it has so happened to me on my travels. Every thing is as dear as it is at London. 'Tis true, as all equipages are forbidden, that expense is entirely retrenched. I have been visited this morning by some of the chiefs of the town, who seem extremely good sort of people, which is their general character; very desirous of attracting strangers to inhabit with them, and consequently very officious in all they imagine can please them. The way of living is absolutely the reverse of that in Italy. Here is no show, and a great deal of eating; there is all the magnificence imaginable, and no dinners but on particular occasions; yet the difference of the prices renders the total expense very nearly equal. As I am not yet determined whether I shall make any considerable stay, I desire not to have the money you intended me, till I ask for it. If you have any curiosity for the present condition of any of the states of Italy, I believe I can give you a truer account than perhaps any other traveler can do, having always had the good fortune of a sort of intimacy with the first persons in the governments where I resided, and they not guarding themselves against the observations of a woman, as they would have done from those of a man.

LETTER XVII.

CHAMBERY, Nov. 30, N. S., 1741.

I received this morning yours of October 26, which has taken me out of the uneasiness of fearing for your health. I suppose you know before this the Spaniards are landed at different ports in Italy, etc. When I received early information of the design, I had the charity to mention it to the English consul (without naming my informer); he laughed, and answered it was impossible. This may serve for a small specimen of the general good intelligence our wise ministry have of all foreign affairs. If you were acquainted with the people whom they employ, you would not be surprised at it. Except Mr. Villette at Turin (who is a very reasonable man), there is not one of them who knows any thing more of the country they inhabit than that they eat and sleep in it. I have wrote you word that I left Geneva on the sharpness of the air, which much disagreed with me. I find myself better here, though the weather is very cold at present. Yet this situation is not subject to those terrible winds which reign at Geneva. I dare write you no news, though I hear a great deal. Direct to me at Chambery *en Savoye, par Paris.*

LETTER XVIII.

FROM MR. WORTLEY TO LADY MARY.

22d March, 1741–2.

Our son embarked at Harwich on the 10th, after having been in England about three months. I hear he avoided the sharpers, and is grówn a good manager of his money. But his weakness is such that Mr. Gibson with much difficulty prevailed with him to go back; and he writ a letter as if he was afraid he should come hither again unless he was soon advised what to do. He declares as if he wanted to be in the army, unless something more for his advantage is proposed, and I have said to Mr. G. I will not oppose his going into the army as a volunteer, but that I believe he may take some course more to his advantage. I hear my Lord Carteret, with whom he has been more than once, speaks well of his behavior. But his obstinacy in staying here, and what he writes, inclines me to think it will not be easy to persuade him to follow good advice. I can not imagine any body is so likely as yourself to give an impartial account of him. Under this difficulty, I can think of no better expedient than to advise him to apply to you for leave to come to some place where you may converse with him. If you appoint him to be at a place twenty miles or further from that where you choose to reside, and order him to go by a feigned name, you may easily reach him in a post-chaise, and come back. after you have passed a week where he is. And this you may do more than once, to make a full trial of him. And I wish he might stay within a certain distance of you, till you have given an account of him, and have agreed to what is fixed. between him and you.

He declares he sets his heart on being in England, but then he should give me such proofs as I require that he is able to persevere in behaving like a reasonable man. These proofs may be agreed on between you and me, and I believe I shall readily agree to what you shall think right.

I think you should say nothing to him but in the most calm and gentle way possible, that he may be invited to open himself to you freely. He seems, I hear, shocked at your letter, in which you complained of his not regarding the truth, though I believe you made no mistake in it, unless your saying his marriage could not be dissolved. He knows very well it may by act of Parliament, which is what he means when he writes he wants to be quit of his wife. He denies that he knew Birtles to be nephew to Henshaw who lent the £200. As he is commended by several here, and by more in Holland (who perhaps flatter him), it may be wrong to speak to him with any show of warmth or anger.

I incline to think he has been made an enthusiast in Holland, and you would do well to try thoroughly whether he is in earnest, and likely to continue so. If he is, I need not mention how much caution should be used in speaking to him. I think, whatever his notions are, you would do well to say nothing to him but what you would say before any company.

I shall advise him by Mr. G. to go to Langres, or some place near it, where he may wait for your answer to such letter as he writes for leave to come to any place you shall appoint him.

I shall give you fuller instructions about him in a post or two, if not by this. I hope this affair will not be very troublesome to you, as you can retire from him whenever you please. He shall not have much more money than is sufficient to carry him to you. When you have furnished him with any, it shall be made good to you.

To tell you fully what I judge of him from the variety of accounts I have had, I incline to think he will for the future avoid thieves, and be no ill manager of his money. These, you will say, are great amendments. But I believe he will always appear a weak man. The single question seems to be whether he will be one of those weak men that will follow the advice of those who wish them well, or be governed by his own fancies, or companions that will make a prey of him. In Holland he seems to have followed the advice of Captain Leutslager and other persons of good credit. I believe he has been in no company here this last time but men of good credit, and I hear he values himself upon it. I have not heard so much as I hope I shall in a week, of the opinion of those who conversed with him. If you have patience to pass away hours with him, you will know him better than any one.

I need not recommend to you the discoursing with him fully upon his patience, and his observing his promises strictly.

Mr. Gibson says his whole deportment and conversation is entirely different from what it was when he was here above four years ago, and that he seems another man.

To give you all the light I can into him, I send you letters writ to him by Captain Leutslager and others. I also send you extracts of his own letters, to show you how he has acted contrary to his professions. I doubt you will find him quite obstinate for going into the army, unless he may be quite certain of mending his circumstances some other way. He may perhaps speak of promises I made him by Mr. G.; but I made none, but that I would let him know by Mr. G. what I advised him to do as preferable to his going to the army. What I meant was his discoursing with you, if you allowed him, and his following your advice.

That you may have the state of the case more fully, I send you his letter to Mr. G., which came by the last mail, and a copy of that which Mr. G. will send him to-morrow.

Mr. G. told me our son thought it hard usage that orders should be given to confine him in Holland, and told Mr. G. that whenever he kept much company it would be right to get him confined, to prevent his going to the pillory or to the gallows.

As he excuses his coming over by the uneasiness he was under, I gave Mr. G. these words:

"The excuse of the uneasiness you should be under in doing right, is the same excuse which is constantly used by all murderers and robbers, and seems to have been taught you by the infamous company by which you were influenced when you were here above four years ago."

Mr. G. said these words were too strong for him to write, and changed them for a paragraph of his own, by which he says he means the same thing. He agreed it would be quite right in you to use these strong words; but you may do it in a gentle way.

He may have more cunning than is imagined to gain his points, and perhaps is *not* made uneasy by being abroad, and may have little or no inclination to go into the army, but thinks, to prevent it, I may give him some considerable advantage. If you seem not at all averse to his going, perhaps he will of himself quit that scheme, and go into some other that you may like better.

If you think it best he should make a campaign, you will take care not to detain him too long. Perhaps you may recommend him to our minister at Turin, that he may serve in the Sardinian forces, where, if he should do wrong, it will be less known than if he did it in Flanders.

Perhaps, by another name, he might meet you unobserved at Lyons, or Pont Beauvoisin. I need not mention that whatever money you put into his hands shall be repaid you at demand. If he goes back to Holland, I suppose £20 is enough for his charges.

I have yours of the 24th February. Lord and Lady Bute seem to live well together. They lost their son (who was above a year old) on the 16th; he had fits and a fever. The surgeons say his brains were too large, and occasioned the fits.

LETTER XIX.

FROM LADY MARY TO MR. WORTLEY.

Lyons, April 13, N. S., 1742.

I have this minute received four letters from you, dated February 1, February 22, March 22, March 29th. I fancy their lying so long in the post-office may proceed from your forgetting to frank them, which I am informed is quite necessary. I am very glad you have been prevailed on to let our son take a commission; if you had prevented it, he would have always said, and perhaps thought, and persuaded other people, you had hindered his rising in the world; though I am fully persuaded that he can never make a tolerable figure in any station of life. When he was at Morins, on his first leaving France, I then tried to prevail with him to serve the emperor as volunteer; and represented to him that a handsome behavior one campaign might go a great way in retrieving his character; and offered to use my influence with you (which I said I had no doubt would succeed) to furnish him with a handsome equipage. He then answered, he supposed I wished him killed out of the way. I am afraid his pretended reformation is not very sincere. I wish time may prove me in the wrong. I here inclose the last letter I received from him; I answered it the following post, in these words:

" I am very glad you resolve to continue obedient to your father, and are sensible of his goodness toward you. Mr. Birtles showed me your letter to him, in which you inclosed yours to me, where you speak to him as your friend, subscribing yourself his faithful humble servant. He was at Genoa in his uncle's house when you were there, and well acquainted with you ; though you seem ignorant of every thing relating to him. I wish you would not make such sort of apologies for any errors you may commit. I pray God your future behavior may redeem the past, which will be a great blessing to your affectionate mother."

I have not since heard from him ; I suppose he knew not what to say to so plain a detected falsehood. It is very disagreeable to me to converse with one from whom I do not expect to hear a word of truth, and who, I am very sure, will repeat many things that never passed in our conversation. You see the most solemn assurances are not binding from him, since he could come to London in opposition to your commands, after having so frequently protested he would not move a step but by your order. However, as you insist on my seeing him, I will do it, and think Valence the properest town for that interview ; it is but two days' journey from this place, it is in Dauphiné. I arrived here Friday night, having left Chambery on the report of the French designing to come soon thither. So far is certain, that the governor had given command for repairing the walls, etc. ; on which men were actually employed when I came away. But the Court of Turin is so politic and mysterious it is hard to judge ; and I am apt to believe their designs change according to circumstances.

I shall stay here till I have an answer to this letter. If you order your son to go to Valence, I desire you would give him a strict command of going by a feigned name. I do not doubt your returning me whatever money I may give him ; but as I believe if he receives money from me, he will be making me frequent visits, it is clearly my opinion that I should give him none. Whatever you may think proper for his journey you may remit him.

I am very sorry for my daughter's loss, being sensible how much it may affect her. I suppose it will be soon repaired. It is a great pleasure to me when I hear she is happy. I wrote to her last post, and will write again the next.

Since I wrote, I have looked every where for my son's letter, which I find has been mislaid in the journey. There is nothing more in it than long professions of doing nothing but by your command; and a positive assertion that he was ignorant of Mr. Birtles's relation to the late consul.

Direct your next, *recommandé à Mr. Imbert, Banquier, à Lyons.*

LETTER XX.

LYONS, April 25, N. S., 1742.

On recollection (however inconvenient it may be to me), I am not sorry to converse with my son. I shall at least have the satisfaction of making a clear judgment of his behavior and temper, which I shall deliver to you in the most sincere and unprejudiced manner. You need not apprehend that I shall speak to him in passion. I do not know that I ever did in my life. I am not apt to be overheated in discourse, and am so far prepared, even for the worst on his side, that I think nothing he can say can alter the resolution I have taken of treating him with calmness. Both reason and interest (were I inclined to follow blindly the dictates of either) would determine me to wish him your heir rather than a stranger; but I think myself obliged both by honor and by conscience, and my regard for you, no way to deceive you; and I confess, hitherto I see nothing but falsehood and weakness through his whole conduct. It is possible his person may be altered since I saw him, but his figure then was very agreeable, and his manner insinuating. I very well remember the professions he made to me, and do not doubt he is lavish of them to other people. Perhaps Lord Carteret may think him no ill match for an ugly girl that sticks on his hands. The project of breaking his marriage shows, at least, his devotion counterfeit, since I am sensible it can not be done but by false witness. — *His wife is not young enough to get gallants, nor rich enough to buy them.*

I made choice of Valence for our meeting as a town where we are not likely to find any English, and he may, if he pleases, be quite unknown, which is hardly possible to be in any capital town either of France or Italy. Here are many English of the trading sort of people, who are more likely to be inquisitive and talkative than any other. Near Chambery there is a little colony of English, who have undertaken the working the mines in Savoy, in which they find very pure silver, of which I have seen several cakes of about eighty ounces each.

LETTER XXI.

AVIGNON, June 10, N. S., 1742.

I am just returned from passing two days with our son, of whom I will give you the most exact account I am capable of. He is so much altered in person, I should scarcely have known him. He has entirely lost his beauty, and looks at least seven years older than he did; and the wildness that he always had in his eyes is so much increased it is downright shocking, and I am afraid will end fatally. He is grown fat, but he is still genteel, and has an air of politeness that is agreeable. He speaks French like a Frenchman, and has got all the fashionable expressions of that language, and a volubility of words which he always had, and which I do not wonder should pass for wit, with inconsiderate people. His behavior is perfectly civil, and I found him very submissive; but in the main, no way really improved in his understanding, which is exceedingly weak; and I am convinced he will always be led by the person he converses with either right or wrong, not being capable of forming any fixed judgment of his own. As to his enthusiasm, if he had it, I suppose he has already lost it; since I could perceive no turn of it in all his conversation. But with his head I believe it is possible to make him a monk one day and a Turk three days after. He has a flattering, insinuating manner, which naturally prejudices strangers in his favor. He began to talk to me in the usual silly cant I have so often heard from him, which I shortened by telling him I desired not to be troubled with it; that professions were of no use where actions were expected; and that the only thing could give me hopes of a good conduct was regularity and truth. He very readily agreed to all I said (as indeed he has always done when he has not been hot-headed). I endeavored to convince him how favorably he has been dealt with, his allowance being much more than, had I been his father, I would have given in the same case. The Prince of Hesse, who is now married to the Princess of England, lived some years at Geneva on £500 per annum. Lord Hervey sent his son at sixteen thither, and to travel afterward, on no larger pension than £200; and, though without a governor, he had reason enough, not only to live within the compass of it, but carried home little presents to his father and mother, which he showed me at Turin. In short, I know there is no place so expensive but a prudent single man may live in it on £300 per annum, and an extravagant one may run out ten thousand in the cheapest. Had you (said I to him) thought rightly, or would have regarded the advice I gave you in all my letters, while in the little town of Islestein, you would have laid up £150 per annum; you would now have had £750 in your pocket, which would have almost paid your debts, and such a management would have gained you the esteem of the reasonable part of the world. I perceived this reflection, which he had never made himself, had a very great weight with him. He would have excused part of his follies, by saying Mr. G.

had told him it became Mr. W.'s son to live handsomely. I answered, that whether Mr. G. had said so or no, the good sense of the thing was no way altered by it; that the true figure of a man was the opinion the world had of his sense and probity, and not the idle expenses, which were only respected by foolish and ignorant people; that his case was particular, he had but too publicly shown his inclination to vanities, and the most becoming part he could now act would be owning the ill use he had made of his father's indulgence, and professing to endeavor to be no further expense to him, instead of scandalous complaints, and being always at his last shirt and last guinea, which any man of spirit would be ashamed to own. I prevailed so far with him that he seemed very willing to follow this advice; and I gave him a paragraph to write to G., which I suppose you will easily distinguish from the rest of his letter. He asked me whether you had settled your estate. I made answer that I did not doubt (like all other wise men) you always had a will by you; but that you had certainly not put any thing out of your power to change. On that he began to insinuate that if I could prevail on you to settle the estate on him, I might expect any thing from his gratitude. I made him a very clear and positive answer in these words: "I hope your father will outlive me, and if I should be so unfortunate to have it otherwise, I do not believe he will leave me in your power. But was I sure of the contrary, no interest, nor no necessity, shall ever make me act against my honor and conscience; and I plainly tell you that I will never persuade your father to do any thing for you till I think you deserve it." He answered by great promises of good behavior, and economy. He is highly delighted with the prospect of going into the army; and mightily pleased with the good reception he had from Lord Stair: though I find it amounts to no more than telling him he was sorry he had already named his aides-de-camp, and otherwise should have been glad of him in that post. He says Lord Carteret has confirmed to him his promise of a commission.

The rest of his conversation was extremely gay. The various things he has seen has given him a superficial universal knowledge. He really knows most of the modern languages, and if I could believe him, can read Arabic, and has read the Bible in Hebrew. He said it was impossible for him to avoid going back to Paris; but he promised me to lie but one night there, and to go to a town six posts from thence on the Flanders road, where he would wait your orders, and go by the name of Mons. du Durand, a Dutch officer; under which name I saw him. These are the most material passages, and my eyes are so much tired I can write no more at this time. I gave him 240 livres for his journey.

LETTER XXII.

Oct. 18, 1743.

I received yours of September 21, O. S., this day, October 18, N. S., and am always glad to hear of your health. I can never be surprised at any sort of folly or extravagance of my son. Immediately on leaving me at Orange, after the most solemn promises of reformation, he went to Montelimart, which is but one day's post from thence, where he behaved himself with as much vanity and indiscretion as ever. I had my intelligence from people who did not know my relation to him; and I do not trouble you with the particulars, thinking it needless to expose his character to you, who are so well acquainted with it. I am persuaded whoever protects him will be very soon convinced of the impossibility of his behaving like a rational creature.

LETTER XXIII.

AVIGNON, Dec. 20, 1743

I received yours of the 24th of November, O. S., yesterday. You may, perhaps, hear of a trifle which makes a great noise

iu this part of the world, which is that I am building; but the
whole expense which I have contracted for is but twenty-six
pounds.   You know the situation of this town is on the meeting of the Rhone and Durance.   On the one side of it within
the walls, was formerly a fortress built on a very high rock;
they say it was destroyed by lightning: one of the towers was
left partly standing, the walls being a yard in thickness: this
was made use of for some time as a public mill, but the height
making it inconvenient for the carriage of meal, it has stood
useless many years.   Last summer, in the hot evenings, I
walked often thither, where I always found a fresh breeze,
and the most beautiful land prospect I ever saw (except
Wharncliffe), being a view of the windings of two great
rivers, and overlooking the whole country, with part of Lan-
guedoc and Provence.   I was so much charmed with it that I
said in company that if that old mill were mine I would turn
it into a belvidere; my words were repeated, and the two con-
suls waited on me soon after, with a donation from the town
of the mill and the land about it; I have added a dome to it,
and made it a little rotunda for the aforesaid sum.   I have
also amused myself with patching up an inscription, which I
have communicated to the archbishop, who is much delighted
with it; but it is not placed, and perhaps never will be.

* Hic, viator! sub Lare parvulo,
Maria hic est condita, hic jacet,
Defuncta humani laboris
Sorte, supervacuaque vitâ.
Non indecorâ pauperie nitens,
Et non inerti nobilis otio,
Vanoque dilectis popello
Divitiis animosus hostis.
Possis et illam dicere mortuam,
En terra jam nunc quantula sufficit!

---

* Lady Mary had the merit of applying Cowley's "Epitaphium
vivi auctoris," published in his works, of which this is a copy, with
grammatical alterations where necessary.

Exempta sit curis, viator,
Terra sit illa levis, precare!
Hic sparge flores, sparge breves rosas:
Nam vita gaudet mortua floribus:
Herbisque odoratis corona
Vatis adhuc cinerem calentem.

LETTER XXIV.

Avignon Feb. 17, 1743–4.

I am sorry you have given yourself so much trouble about the inscription. I find I expressed myself ill, if you understood by my letter that it was already placed; I never intended it without your approbation, and then would have put it in the inside of the dome. The word " pauperie" is meant, as is shown by the whole line,

Non indecorâ pauperie nitens,

to be a life rather distant from ostentation than in poverty; and which very well answers to my way of living, which, though decent, is far from the show which many families make here.

LETTER XXV.

Avignon, June 8, 1745.

I have this day yours of the 8th of April, O. S., and at the same time one from Lady Oxford, who has not received (as she says) any from me since November, though I have written several times.

I perfectly remember carrying back the manuscript you mention, and delivering it to Lord Oxford. I never failed returning to himself all the books he lent me. It is true, I showed it to the Duchess of Montagu, but we read it together, and I did not even leave it with her. I am not surprised that in that vast quantity of manuscripts some should be lost or mislaid, particularly knowing Lord Oxford to be careless of them, easily lending, and as easily forgetting he had done it. I remember I carried him once one finely illuminated, that, when I delivered, he did not recollect he had lent to me, though it was but a few days before. Wherever this is, I think you need be in no pain about it. The verses are too bad to be printed, excepting from malice, and since the death of Pope I know nobody that is an enemy to either of us. I will write to my son the first opportunity I have of doing it. By the post it is impossible at this time. I have seen the French list of the dead and wounded, in which he is not mentioned: so that I suppose he has escaped. All letters, even directed to Holland, are opened; and I believe those to the army would be stopped.

I know so little of English affairs, I am surprised to hear Lord Granville* has lost his power.

LETTER XXVI.

BRESCIA, Aug. 25, N. S., 1746.

You will be surprised at the date of this letter, but Avignon has been long disagreeable to me on many accounts, and now more than ever, from the increase of Scotch and Irish rebels, that chose it for their refuge, and are so highly protected by the Vice-legate that it is impossible to go into any company without hearing a conversation that is improper to be listened to, and dangerous to contradict. The war with France hindered my settling there for reasons I have already told you; and the difficulty of passing into Italy confined me, though I

* John Carteret, Earl Granville, was Secretary of State in 1720, Lord-lieutenant of Ireland from 1724 to 1730; in 1742 Secretary of State, which office he resigned in 1744. He was a third time appointed Secretary of State in February 1746, and removed on the 14th of the same month, to which circumstance this letter alludes.

was always watching an opportunity of returning thither. Fortune at length presented me one.

I believe I wrote you word, when I was at Venice, that I saw there the Count of Wacherbarth, who was governor to the Prince of Saxony, and is a favorite of the King of Poland, and the many civilities I received from him, as an old friend of his mother's. About a month since, a gentleman of the Bedchamber of the prince, who is a man of the first quality in this province, I believe charged with some private commission from the Polish court, brought me a letter of recommendation from Count Wacherbarth, which engaged me to show him what civilities lay in my power. In conversation I lamented to him the impossibility of my attempting a journey to Italy where he was going. He offered me his protection, and represented to me that if I would permit him to wait on me, I might pass under the notion of a Venetian lady. In · short, I ventured upon it, which has succeeded very well, though I met with more impediments in my journey than I expected. We went by sea to Genoa, where I made a very short stay, and saw nobody, having no passport from that State, and fearing to be stopped if I were known. We took post-chaise from thence the 16th of this month, and were very much surprised to meet, on the Briletta, the baggage of the Spanish army, with a prodigious number of sick and wounded soldiers and officers, who marched in a very great hurry.

The Count of Palazzo ordered his servants to say we were in haste for the service of Don Philip, and without further examination they gave us place every where : notwithstanding which the multitude of carriages and loaded mules which we met in these narrow roads made it impossible for us to reach Scravalli till it was near night. Our surprise was great to find, coming out of that town, a large body of troops surrounding a body of guards, in the midst of which was Don Philip in person, going a very round trot, looking down, and pale as ashes. The army was in too much confusion to take notice of us, and the night favoring us, we got into the town, but when we came there, it was impossible to find any lodging, all the inns being filled with wounded Spaniards. The Count went to the governor, and asked a chamber for a Venetian lady, which he granted very readily; but there was nothing in it but the bare walls, and in less than a quarter of an hour after the whole house was empty both of furniture and people, the governor flying into the citadel, and carrying with him all his goods and family. We were forced to pass the night without beds, or supper. About day-break the victorious Germans entered the town. The Count went to wait on the generals, to whom, I believe he had a commission. He told them my name, and there was no sort of honor or civility they did not pay me. They immediately ordered me a guard of hussars (which was very necessary in the present disorder), and sent me refreshments of all kinds. Next day I was visited by the Prince of Baden Dourlach, the Prince Louestein, and all the principal officers, with whom I passed .for a heroine, showing no uneasiness though the cannon of the citadel (where was a Spanish garrison) played very briskly. I was forced to stay there two days for want of post-horses, the post-master having fled, with all his servants, and the Spaniards having levied all the horses they could find. At length I set out from thence the 19th instant, with a strong escort of hussars, meeting with no further accident on the road, except at the little town of Vogherra, where they refused post-horses, till the hussars drew their sabers. The 30th I arrived safe here. It is a very pretty place, where I intend to repose myself at least during the remainder of the summer. This journey has been very expensive; but I am very glad I have made it. I am now in a neutral country, under the protection of Venice. The Doge is our old friend Grimani, and I do not doubt meeting with all sort of civility. When I set out I had so bad a fluxion on my eyes, I was really afraid of losing them : they are now quite recovered, and my health better than it has been for some time. I hope yours continues good, and that you will always take care of it. Direct for me at Brescia by way of Venice.

LETTER XXVII.

BRESCIA, September 24, N. S., 1746.

I can no longer resist the desire I have to know what is become of ———.* I have long suppressed it from a belief that
if there was any thing of good to be told, you would not fail
to give me the pleasure of hearing it. I find it now grows so
much upon me, that whatever I am to know, I think it would
be easier for me to support than the anxiety I suffer from my
doubts. I beg to be informed, and prepare myself for the
worst, with all the philosophy I have. At my time of life I
ought to be detached from a world which I am soon to leave ;
to be totally so is a vain endeavor, and perhaps there is vanity
in the endeavor : while we are human we must submit to
human infirmities, and suffer them in mind as well as body.
All that reflection and experience can do is to mitigate, we can
never extinguish, our passions. I call by that name every sentiment that is not founded upon reason, and own I can not justify to mine the concern I feel for one who never gave me any
view of satisfaction.

This is too melancholy a subject to dwell upon. You compliment me on the continuation of my spirits : 'tis true I try to
maintain them by every act I can, being sensible of the terrible
consequences of losing them. Young people are too apt to let
them sink on any disappointment. I have wrote to my daughter all the considerations I could think to lessen her affliction.

LETTER XXVIII.

LOUVERE, ———, 1747.

Yours of the 1st of December, O. S., came to me this morning, Feb. 2, N. S. I hope your health continues good, since
you say nothing to the contrary.

* Her son.

The new opera at Brescia, I hear, is much applauded, and I intend to see it before the end of the carnival. The people of this province are much at their ease during the miseries the war occasions their neighbors, and employ all their time in diversions.

We have hitherto had no winter, to the great sorrow of the people here, who are in fear of wanting ice in the summer, which is as necessary as bread. They also attribute a malignant fever, which has carried off great numbers in the neighboring towns, to the uncommon warmth of the air. It has not infected this village, which they say has ever been free from any contagious distemper. The method of treating the physician here, I think, should be the same every where : they make it his interest that the whole parish should be in good health, giving him a stated pension, which is collected by a tax on every house, on condition that he neither demands any fees, nor ever refuses a visit either to rich or poor. This last article would be very hard, if we had as many vaporish ladies as in England ; but those imaginary ills are entirely unknown among us, and the eager pursuit after every new piece of quackery that is introduced. I can not help thinking that there is a fund of credulity in mankind that must be employed somewhere, and the money formerly given to the monks for the health of the soul, is now thrown to doctors for the health of the body, and generally with as little prospect of success.

LETTER XXIX.

LOUVERE, July 17, N. S., 1748.

Yours of June 7, O. S., came to my hands but yesterday. I am very much vexed and surprised at the miscarriage of my letters. I have never failed answering both yours and my daughter's the very next post after I received them. I began to suspect my servants put the franking money in their pockets, and threw away the letters. I have been in the country this year and a half, though I continued to date from Brescia, as the place to which I would have directed, being, though not the nearest, the safest post-town. I send all my packets thither, and will for the future inclose them to a banker, who, I hope, will be more careful in forwarding them.

I am glad my daughter's conduct satisfies the opinion I always had of her understanding. I do not wonder at her being well received in sets of company different from one another, having myself preserved a long intimacy with the Duchesses of Marlborough and Montagu, though they were at open war, and perpetually talking of their complaints. I believe they were both sensible I never betrayed either, each of them giving me the strongest proofs of confidence in the last conversations I had with them, which were the last I had in England. What I think extraordinary, is my daughter's continuing so many years agreeable to Lord Bute, Mr. Mackensie telling me, the last time I saw him, that his brother frequently said among his companions that he was still as much in love with his wife as before he married her. If the Princess's favor lasts, it may be of use to her family. I have often been dubious if the seeming indifference of her highness's behavior was owing to very good sense, or great insensibility. Should it be the first, she will get the better of all her rivals, and probably one day have a large share of power.

I am very much pleased that you accustom yourself to tea, being persuaded that the moderate use of it is generally wholesome. I have planted a great deal in my garden, which is a fashion lately introduced in this country, and has succeeded very well. I can not say it is as strong as the Indian, but it has the advantage of being fresher, and, at least, unmixed.

I thank you for the copies of Sir Charles Hanbury's poetry, which extremely entertained me. I find tar-water has succeeded to Ward's drop; it is possible by this time that some other quackery has taken the place of that; the English are easier than any other nation infatuated by the prospect of universal medicines ; nor is there any country in the world where the doctors raise such immense fortunes. I attribute it to the fund of credulity which is in all mankind. We have no longer faith in miracles and relics, and, therefore, with the same fury, run after recipes and physicians. The same money which, three hundred years ago, was given for the health of the soul, is now given for the health of the body, and by the same sort of people, women and half-witted men. In the country where they have shrines and images, quacks are despised, and monks and confessors find their account in managing the fear and hope which rule the actions of the multitude.

LETTER XXX.

PADUA, September 16, 1748.

I am informed that your health and sight are perfectly good, which gives me courage to trouble you with a letter of congratulation on a blessing that is equal to us both : I mean the great and good character I hear from every body of Lord Bute. It is a satisfaction I never hoped to have—a son that does honor to his family. I am persuaded you are of my opinion, and had rather be related to him than to any silly duke in Christendom. Indeed, money (however considerable the sum) in the hands of a fool, is as useless as if presented to a monkey, and will as surely be scattered in the street. I need not quote examples. My daughter is also generally esteemed, and I can not help communicating to you the pleasure I receive whenever I hear her commended. I am afraid my letter may be too long. This subject runs away with me. I wish you many years' continuance of the health and spirits I am told you now enjoy.

LETTER XXXI.

VENICE, Dec. 25, N. S., 1748.

I hope I have now regulated our correspondence in a manner more safe than by Holland. I have sent a large collection of letters to you and my daughter, which have all miscarried; neither have I one line from either for some months.

I was surprised not many days ago by a very extraordinary visit: it was from the Duchess of Guastalla, who you know is a princess of the house d'Armstadt, and reported to be near marriage with the King of Sardinia. I confess it was an honor I could easily have spared, she coming attended with the greatest part of her court: her grand-master, who is brother to Cardinal Valenti, the first lady of her bed-chamber, four pages, and a long et cetera of inferior servants, beside her guards. She entered with an easy French air, and told me, since I would not oblige her by coming to her court, she was resolved to come to me, and eat a salad of my raising, having heard much fame of my gardening. You may imagine I gave her as good a supper as I could. She was (or seemed to be) extremely pleased with an English sack-posset of my ordering. I owned to her fairly that my house was much at her service; but it was impossible for me to find beds for all her suite. She said she intended to return when the moon rose, which was an hour after midnight. In the mean time I sent for the violins to entertain her attendants, who were very well pleased to dance, while she and her grand-master and I played at picquet. She pressed me extremely to return with her to her jointure-house, where she now resides (all the furniture of Guastalla being sold). I excused myself on not daring to venture in the cold night fifteen miles, but promised I would not fail to pay her my acknowledgments for the great honor her highness had done me, in a very short time, and we parted very good friends. She said she intended this spring to retire into her native country. I did not take the liberty of mentioning to her the report of her being in treaty with the King of Sardinia, though it has been in the newspaper of Mantua; but I found an opportunity of hinting it to Signor Gonzago, her grand-master, who told me the duchess would not have been pleased to talk of it, since, perhaps, there was nothing in it more than a friendship that had long been between them, and since her widowhood the king sends her an express every day.

I believe you 'll wish this long story much shorter; but I think you seemed to desire me to lengthen my letters, and I can have no greater pleasure than endeavoring to amuse you.

LETTER XXXII.

Gotolengo, April 24, 1749.

C. Mutius Sext: F.
P. Papilius, M. F.
Q. Mutius P. F.
M. Cornelius P. F.
IIII vir. Turrim Ex D D.
Ad augendam Locavêre.
Idemque Probavêre.

This is a very fair inscription, in large characters, on a large stone found in the pavement of the old church, and makes now a part of the wall of the new one, which is now building. The people here, who are as ignorant as their oxen, and live like them on the product of their land, without any curiosity for the history of it, would infer from thence that this town is of Roman foundation, though the walls, which are yet the greatest part standing (only the towers and battlements demolished), are very plainly Gothic, and not one brick to be found any where of Roman fabric, which is very easily distinguished. I can easily believe their tradition, that the old church, which was pulled down two years ago, being ready to drop, was a pagan temple, and do not doubt it was a considerable town, founded by the Goths, when they overran Italy. The fortifications were strong for that age: the ditch still remaining within the walls being very broad and deep, in which ran the little river that is now before my house, and the moat turned 'nto gardens for the use of the town, the name of which being Gotolengo, is a confirmation of my conjecture. The castle, which certainly stood on the spot where my house does, being on an eminence in the midst of the town, was probably destroyed by fire. When I ordered the court to be leveled, which was grown uneven by long neglect, there was found such quantities of burnt bricks, that plainly showed the remains of a considerable fire; but whether by the enemy, or accidental, I could get no information. They have no records, or parish books, beyond the time of their coming under the Venetian dominion, which is not much above three hundred years ago, at which time they were, as they now are, a large village, being two miles in circuit, and contains at present (as the curate told me) two thousand communicants. The ladies of this neighborhood that had given themselves the trouble and expense of going to see Don Philip's entry into Parma, are returned, according to the French saying, *avec un pied de nez*. As they had none of them ever seen a court before, they had figured to themselves prodigious scenes of gallantry and magnificence.

If I did not write by the post, I would tell you several particulars, that I believe would make you laugh. He is retired into the country till the arrival of his princess, who is expected in May next. I take the liberty of inclosing this to Lord Bute, not knowing where to direct to him in London.

LETTER XXXIII.

LOUVERE, Oct. 19, N. S., 1753.

I think I know why our correspondence is so miserably interrupted, and so many letters lost to and from England.

An old priest made me a visit as I was folding my last packet to my daughter. Observing it to be large, he told me I had done a great deal of business that morning. I made

answer that I had done no business at all; I had only wrote
to my daughter on family affairs, or such trifles as make up
women's conversation. He said gravely, "People like your
excellenza do not write long letters upon trifles." I assured
him that if he understood English I would let him read my
letter. He replied, with a mysterious smile—"If I did under·
stand English, I should not understand what you have written,
except you would give me the key, which I durst not presume
to ask." "What key?" said I, staring—"there is not one
cipher besides the date." He answered—"Ciphers were only
used by novices in politics, and it was very easy to write intel-
ligibly, under feigned names of persons and places, to a correspondent, in such a manner as should be almost impossible to
be understood by any body else."

Thus I suppose my innocent epistles are severely scrutinized:
and when I talk of my grand-children, they are fancied to represent all the potentates of Europe. This is very provoking.
I confess there are good reasons for extraordinary caution at
this juncture; but it is very hard I can not pass for being as
insignificant as I really am.

I heartily congratulate you on the recovery of your sight.
It is a blessing I prefer to life, and will seek for glasses whenever I am in a place where they are sold.

LETTER XXXIV.

LOUVERE, Dec. 19, N. S., 1754.

I received yours of October 6, yesterday, which gave me
great pleasure. I am flattered by finding that our sentiments
are the same in regard to Lord Bolingbroke's writings, as you
will see more clearly, if you ever have the long letter I have
wrote to you on that subject. I believe he never read Horace,
or any other author, with a design of instructing himself, thinking he was born to give precepts, and not to follow them: at
least if he was not mad enough to have this opinion, he endeavored to impose it on the rest of the world. All his works,

being well considered, are little more than a panegyric on his own universal genius; many of his pretensions are as preposterously inconsistent as if Sir Isaac Newton had aimed at being a critic in fashions, and wrote for the information of tailors and mantua makers. I am of opinion that he never looked into half the authors he quotes, and am much mistaken if he is not obliged to M. Bayle for the generality of his criticisms; for which reason he affects to despise him, that he may steal from him with the less suspicion. A diffuse style (though admired as florid by all half-witted readers) is commonly obscure, and always trifling. Horace has told us that where words abound, sense is thinly spread; as trees overcharged with leaves bear little fruit.

You do not mention Lord Orrery, or perhaps would not throw away time in perusing that extraordinary work, addressed to a son, whom he educates with an intention that he should be a first minister, and promises to pray to God for him if ever he plays the knave in that station. I perceive that he has already been honored with five editions. I wish that encouragement may prevail with him to give the world more memoirs. I am resolved to read them all, though they should multiply to as many tomes as Erasmus.

Here are no newspapers to be had but those printed under this government; consequently I never learn the births or deaths of private persons. I was ignorant of that of my poor friend the Duchess of Bolton, when my daughter's last letter told me the death of the duke,* and the jointure he has left his second duchess.

I am very glad your health is so good. May that and every other blessing be ever yours.

* He died August 26, 1754. His second wife was Lavinia Fenton, the celebrated Polly Peachum in Gay's Beggar's Opera, whom he married in 1751.

LETTER XXXV.

VENICE, December 11, 1758.

I assure you I live as agreeably here as any stranger in my
circumstances possibly can do; and, indeed, a repetition of
all the civilities I have received here would sound more like
vanity than truth. I am sensible that I owe a great part of
them to Grimani, who is in the first esteem and authority in
this republic; and, as he takes pains to appear my friend, his
relations and allies, of both sexes (who are the most considerable people here), endeavor to oblige me in all sorts of ways.
The carnival is expected to be more brilliant than common,
from the great concourse of noble strangers. The Princess
of Holstein and the Prince of Wolfenbuttle (nephew of the
empress) are already arrived, and the Electoral Prince of Saxony is expected next week. If my age and humor would permit me much pleasure in public amusements, here are a great
variety of them. I take as little share of them as I can.

> Frui paratis et valido mihi
> Latoe dones, et precor integrâ
> Cum mente, nec turpem senectam
> Degere, nec citharâ carentem.
>
> HORACE, ODES, L. 1, O. 31.

You see I have got a Horace, which is borrowed of the
consul, who is a good scholar; but I am very impatient for
my own books. I could wish you to send me the cushions
that were used at Constantinople; they would be very useful
to me here. As to what regards ——, I have long since fixed
my opinion concerning him. Indeed, I am not insensible of
the misfortune, but I look upon it as the loss of a limb, which
should cease to give solicitude by being irretrievable.

Lord Brudenel* is here, and appears to be in an extremely
bad state of health, and unwilling to return to England, being

---

* John Lord Brudenel, eldest son of George Earl of Cardigan.

apprehensive of the air. I fear his friends will have the affliction of losing him, as he seems highly disposed, if not actually fallen into a consumption. I have had a letter from Mr. Mackensie, who is excessively liked at Turin. I can not contrive to go there, but heartily wish I could contrive to see him and Lady Betty in some other place. I am determined, on account of my health, to take some little jaunt next spring; perhaps on the side of the Tyrol, which I have never seen, but hear it is an exceedingly fine country. To say truth, I am tempted by the letters of Lady F. Stewart and Sir James. I never knew people more to my taste. They reside in a little town, only two days' journey from Padoua, where it will be asy to find a lodging for the summer months, and I am sure of being pleased in their company. I have found, wherever I have traveled, that the pleasantest spots of ground have been in the valleys, which are encompassed with high mountains.

LETTER XXXVI.

VENICE, February 24, 1759.

I return you many thanks for yours of the 5th instant. I never have received any in so short a time from England. I am very sincerely, heartily, glad to hear of your health, but will not trouble you with reading a long letter, which may be uneasy to you, when I write so often and fully to our daughter. I have not heard from her for some time; I hope her silence is not occasioned by any indisposition. I hear her and her family praised very much by every Briton that arrives here. I need not say what comfort I receive from it. It is now finer weather than I ever saw in the season (Naples excepted): the sun shines with as much warmth as in May. I walk in my little garden every morning. I hope you do the same at Bath.

The carnival is now over, and we have no more ridotto or

theatrical amusements.   Diversions have taken a more private, perhaps a more agreeable, turn here.   It is the fashion to have little houses of retreat, where the lady goes every evening, at seven or eight o'clock, and is visited by all her intimates of both sexes, which commonly amount to seventy or eighty persons, where they have play, concerts of music, sometimes dancing, and always a handsome collation.   I believe you will think these little assemblies very pleasing; they really are so.   Whoever is well acquainted with Venice must own that it is the center of pleasure; not so noisy, and, in my opinion, more refined than Paris.

LETTER XXXVII.*

TO LADY MARY PIERREPONT.

Saturday morning.—1712.

Every time you see me, gives me a fresh proof of your not caring for me: yet I beg you will meet me once more.   How could you pay me that great compliment of your loving the country for life, when you would not stay with me a few minutes longer?   Who is the happy man you went to?   I agree with you, I am often so dull, I can not explain my meaning; but will not own that the expression was so very obscure, when I said if I had you, I should act against my opinion.   Why need I add, I see what is best for me, I condemn what I do, and yet I fear I must do it.   If you can't find it out, that

---

* It was my intention to include the two following letters in the Biography of Lady Mary, as giving the clearest notion of the idiosyn crasies of the lovers—those peculiarities that may be traced in their intercourse as husband and wife—which can now be obtained.   For this reason the letters were omitted in the first part of the volume.   After that was stereotyped, I found the Biographical Sketch would be too long for the space reserved; therefore these letters are placed here to draw more particular attention.   The reader can easily find their proper place in the first correspondence, between the Letters VIII. and IX., page 31.—AM. ED.

you are going to be unhappy, ask your sister, who agrees with you in every thing else, and she will convince you of your rashness in this. She knows you don't care for me, and that you will like me less and less every year; perhaps every day of your life. You may, with a little care, please another as well, and make him less timorous. It is possible I too may please some of those that have but little acquaintance ; and if I should be preferred by a woman, for being the first among her companions, it would give me as much pleasure as if I were the first man in the world. Think again, and prevent a misfortune from falling on both of us.

When you are at leisure, I shall be as ready to end all, as I was last night, when I disobliged one, that will do me hurt, by crossing his desires, rather than fail of meeting you. Had I imagined you could have left me, without finishing, I had not seen you. Now you have been so free before Mrs. Steele,* you may call upon her, or send for her, to-morrow, or next day. Let her dine with you, or go to visit shops, Hyde Park, or other diversions. You may bring her home. I can be in the house, reading, as I often am, though the master is abroad. If you will have her visit you first, I will get her to go to-morrow. I think a man, or a woman, is under no engagement till the writings are sealed ; but it looks like indiscretion even to begin a treaty, without a probability of concluding it. When you hear of all my objections to you, and to myself, you will resolve against me. Last night you were much upon the reserve : I see you can never be thoroughly intimate with me ; 'tis because you have no pleasure in it. You can be easy, and complaisant, as you have sometimes told me ; but never think that enough to make me easy, unless you refuse me.

Write a line this evening, or early to-morrow. If I don't speak plain, do you understand what I write ? Tell me how to mend the style, if the fault is in that. If the characters are not plain, I can easily mend them. I always comprehend

* The wife of Mr. (afterward Sir Richard) Steele.

your expressions, but would give a great deal to know what passes in your heart.

In you I might possess youth, beauty, and all things that can charm. It is possible that they may strike me less after a time; but I may then consider I have once enjoyed them in perfection; that they would have decayed as soon in any other. You see this is not your case. You will think you might have been happier. Never engage with a man, unless you propose to yourself the highest satisfaction from him and none other. E. W. MONTAGU.

LETTER XXXVIII.
(THE ANSWER)
TO E. W. MONTAGU, ESQ.

Tuesday night.

I received both your Monday letters before I writ the inclosed, which, however, I send you. The kind letter was writ and sent Friday morning, and I did not receive yours till Saturday noon. To speak truth, you would never have had it, there were so many things in yours to put me out of humor. Thus, you see, it was on no design to repair any thing that offended you. You only show me how industrious you are to find faults in me;—why will you not suffer me to be pleased with you?

I would see you if I could (though perhaps it may be wrong); but, in the way that I am here, 'tis impossible. I can't come to town, but in company with my sister-in-law; I can carry her nowhere but where she pleases; or, if I could, I would trust her with nothing. I could not walk out alone, without giving suspicion to the whole family; should I be watched, and seen to meet a man—judge of the consequences!

You speak of treating with my father, as if you believed he would come to terms afterward. I will not suffer you to remain in the thought, however advantageous it might be to me; I will deceive you in nothing. I am fully persuaded he will never hear of terms afterward. You may say, 'tis talking oddly of him. I can't answer to that; but 'tis my real opinion, and I think I know him. You talk to me of estates, as if I was the most interested woman in the world. Whatever faults I may have shown in my life, I know not one action of it that ever proved me mercenary. I think there can not be a greater proof to the contrary than my treating with you, where I am to depend entirely upon your generosity, at the same time that I may have settled on me £500 per annum pin-money, and a considerable jointure, in another place; not to reckon that I may have by his temper what command of his estate I please; and with you I have nothing to pretend to. I do not, however, make a merit to you; money is very little to me, because all beyond necessaries I do not value, that is to be purchased by it. If the man proposed to me had £10,000 per annum, and I was sure to dispose of it all, I should act just as I do. I have in my life known a good deal of show, and never found myself the happier for it.

In proposing to you to follow the scheme proposed by that friend, I think 'tis absolutely necessary for both our sakes. I would have you want no pleasure which a single life would afford you. You own you think nothing so agreeable. A woman that adds nothing to a man's fortune ought not to take from his happiness. If possible, I would add to it; but I will not take from you any satisfaction you could enjoy without me. On my own side, I endeavor to form as right a judgment of the temper of human nature, and of my own in particular, as I am capable of. I would throw off all partiality and passion, and be calm in my opinion. Almost all people are apt to run into a mistake, that when they once feel or give a passion, there needs nothing to entertain it. If we marry, our happiness must consist in loving one another; 'tis principally my concern to think of the most probable method of making that love eternal. You object against living in London; I am not fond of it myself, and readily give it up to you; though I am assured there needs more art to keep a fondness alive in solitude, where it generally preys upon itself.

There is one article absolutely necessary—to be ever beloved, one must be ever agreeable. There is no such thing as being agreeable, without a thorough good humor, a natural sweetness of temper, enlivened by cheerfulness. Whatever natural funds of gayety one is born with, 'tis necessary to be entertained with agreeable objects. Any body, capable of tasting pleasure, when they confine themselves to one place, should take care 'tis the place in the world the most agreeable. Whatever you may now think (now, perhaps, you have some fondness for me), though your love should continue in its full force, there are hours when the most beloved mistress would be troublesome. People are not forever (nor is it in human nature that they should be) disposed to be fond ; you would be glad to find in me the friend and the companion. To be agreeably the last, it is necessary to be gay and entertaining. A perpetual solitude, in a place where you see nothing to raise your spirits, at length wears them out, and conversation insensibly falls into dull and insipid. When I have no more to say to you, you will like me no longer. How dreadful is that view ! You will reflect for my sake you have abandoned the conversation of a friend that you liked, and your situation in a country where all things would have contributed to make your life pass in (the true *volupté*) a smooth tranquillity. *I* shall lose the vivacity which should entertain you, and *you* will have nothing to recompense you for what you have lost. Very few people that have settled entirely in the country, but have grown at length weary of one another. The lady's conversation generally falls into a thousand impertinent effects of idleness ; and the gentleman falls *in* love with his dogs and his horses, and *out* of love with every thing else. I am not now arguing in favor of the town ; you have answered me as to that point. In respect of your health, 'tis the first thing to be considered, and I shall never ask you to do any thing injurious to that. But 'tis my opinion, 'tis necessary, to be happy, that we neither of us think any place more agreeable than that where we can live together.   M. P.

LETTERS TO THE COUNTESS OF BUTE.*

FROM 1794 TO 1761.

LETTER I.

LOUVERE, Nov. 29, 1749.

MY DEAR CHILD—I received your agreeable letter of September 21, yesterday, November 29, and am very glad our daughter (for I think she belongs to us both) turns out so much to your satisfaction ; may she ever do so. I hope she has by this time received my token. You please me extremely in saying my letters are of any entertainment to you.

LETTER II.

LOUVERE, Dec. 17, N. S., 1749.

DEAR CHILD—I received yours of October 14 but yesterday : the negligence of the post is very disagreeable. I have

* Mary, Countess of Bute, only daughter of her parents, was born in Constantinople, 1715, during Mr. Wortley's embassy. This darling daughter seems to have deserved the devoted affection her mother always manifested for her. Her marriage, which took place in 1736, was highly gratifying to both her parents. Lady Mary was proud of her son-in-law, John, third Earl of Bute (afterward minister of George III.); and her heart had its fondest resting-place, and sweetest hopes in the family of her grandchildren. The Countess of Bute died in 1794, cherishing to the last, as her dearest inheritance, the memory of her gifted mother.—AM. ED.

at length had a letter from Lady Oxford, by which I find mine to her has miscarried, and perhaps the answer which I have now wrote may have the same fate.

I wish you joy of your young son : may he live to be a blessing to you. I find I amuse myself here in the same manner as if at London, according to your account of it; that is, I play whist every night with some old priests that I have taught it to, and are my only companions. To say truth, the decay of my sight will no longer suffer me to read by candlelight, and the evenings are now long and dark. I believe you 'll be persuaded my gaming makes nobody uneasy, when I tell you that we play only a penny per corner. 'Tis now a year that I have lived wholly in the country, and have no design of quitting it. I am entirely given up to rural amusements, and have forgot there are any such things as wits or fine ladies in the world. However, I am pleased to hear what happens to my acquaintance. I wish you would inform me what is become of the Pomfret family, and who Sir Francis Dashwood* has married. I knew him at Florence : he seemed so nice in the choice of a wife, I have some curiosity to know who it is that has had charms enough to make him enter into an engagement he used to speak of with fear and trembling.

LETTER III.

Louvere, December 14, 1750.

Dear Child—I received yours of October the 28th this morning, December 24th, N. S. I am afraid a letter of two sheets of paper that I sent you from Salo never came to your hands, which I am very sorry for : it would have been, perhaps, some entertainment, being the description of places that I am sure you have not found in any book of travels. I also made my hearty congratulations to Lord Bute and yourself,

---

* He married Sarah, daughter and co-heir of Thomas Gould, Esq., of Ivor, Bucks, and widow of Sir Richard Ellis, Bart.

on his place, which I hope is an earnest of future advantages.
I desired you would send me all the books of which you gave
a catalogue, except H. Fielding's and his sister's, which I have
already. I thank God my taste still continues for the gay
part of reading.* Wiser people may think it trifling, but it
serves to sweeten life to me, and is at worst better than the
generality of conversation. I am extremely pleased with the
account you give me of your father's health: his life is the
greatest blessing that can happen to his family. I am very
sincerely touched with the Duchess of Montagu's misfortune,†
though I think it no reasonable cause for locking herself up.
Age and ugliness are as inseparable as heat and fire, and I
think it all one in what shape one's figure grows disagreeable.
I remember the Princess of Moldavia at Constantinople made
a party of pleasure the next day after losing one of her eyes;
and when I wondered at her philosophy, said she had more
reason to divert herself than she had before. 'Tis true our
climate is apt to inspire more melancholy ideas: the enliven-
ing heat of the sun continues the cheerfulness of youth to the
grave with most people. I received a visit not long since
from a fair young lady, that had new lain-in of her nineteenth
child: in reality she is but thirty-seven, and has so well preserved her fine shape and complexion, she appears little past
twenty. I wish you the same good fortune, though not quite
so numerous a posterity. Every happiness is ardently desired
for you by, dear child, your most affectionate mother.

P. S.—My compliments to Lord Bute, and blessings to all
your little ones. I am ashamed not to have sent my token to
my god-daughter; I hope to do it in a short time.

---

* In Spencer's Anecdotes, by Singer, there is an observation of
Lady Oxford in these words: "I wonder how any body can find pleasure in reading the books which are that lady's chief favorites." Here
we have Lady Mary's confession of her liking to works of imagination, and her defense of her taste.

† Lady Mary Churchill, youngest daughter of John Duke of Marlborough, wife of John Duke of Montagu, died May 4, 1751.

LETTER IV.

April 15, N. S., 1751.

MY DEAR CHILD—I received yours of Feb. 10th with great pleasure, as it brought me the news of your health, and that of your family. I can not guess who you mean by Lord Montfort,* there being no such title when I left England, nor any Lord Hertford,† who I hear is named embassador to France: these are all new people to me. I wish you would give me some information concerning them: none can be so agreeable as the continuation of your father's health; you see in him the good effect of a strict abstinence, and regular exercise. I am much pleased (but not at all surprised) at his kindness to you: I know him to be more capable of a generous action than any man I ever knew. I have never heard one word of the books that you told me were packed up last June. These things are very provoking, but fretting mends nothing. I will continue to write on, though the uncertainty of your receiving my letters is a strong abatement of my pleasure in writing, and will be of heavy consequence to my style. I feel at this minute the spirit of dullness chill my heart, and I am ready to break out into alacks and alases, with many murmurs against my cruel destiny, that will not even permit this distant conversation between us, without such allaying circumstances. However, I beg you not to be discouraged. I am persuaded, from the goodness of your heart, that you are willing to give me happiness; and I can have none here so great as a letter from you. You can never want subjects; and I can assure you that your eldest daughter can not be more delighted with a birth-day suit, or your youngest with a paper of sugar-plums, than I am at the sight of your hand. You seem very anxious on the account of your children's education. I have said all I have to say on that head; and am still of the same opinion, that learning is necessary to the happiness of women, and ignorance the com-

---

* Henry Bromley, created Baron Montfort, 1741.
† Francis Seymour Conway, created Earl of Hertford, 1750.

mon foundation of their errors, both in morals and conduct. I was well acquainted with a lady (the Duchess of M———r*) who, I am persuaded, owed all her misfortunes to the want of instruction in her youth. You know another, who, if she had had her natural good understanding cultivated by letters, would never have mistaken Johnny Gay for a wit, and much less have printed that he took the liberty of calling her his Laura.†

I am pleasingly interrupted by the welcome information from Lord Bute that you are safely delivered of a son. I am never in pain for any of that sex. If they have any merit, there are so many roads for them to meet good fortune, they can no way fail but by not deserving it. We have but one of establishing ours, and that surrounded with precipices, and perhaps after all better missed than found. I have already told you I look on my grand-daughters as lay nuns. Lady Mary‡ might avoid that destiny, if religion was not a bar to her being disposed of in this country. You will laugh to hear it, but it is really true, I had proposed to me a young man of quality, with a good estate: his parents are both dead: she would find a fine palace, and neither want jewels nor equipage; and her name (with a present from me) be thought a sufficient fortune.

I shall write to Lord Bute this post. My blessing to you and yours is sincerely sent from your most affectionate mother.

LETTER V.

LOUVERE, June 19, N. S., 1751.

MY DEAR CHILD—I am much obliged to Lord Bute for thinking of me so kindly: to say truth, I am as fond of baubles as ever, and am so far from being ashamed of it, that it is a taste I endeavor to keep up with all the art I am mistress of.

* Manchester.   † The Duchess of Queensberry.
‡ Lady Mary Stuart, afterward Countess of Lonsdale.

I should have despised them at twenty for the same reason that I would not eat tarts or cheesecakes at twelve years old, as being too childish for one capable of more solid pleasures. I now know (and alas! have long known) all things in this world are almost equally trifling, and our most serious projects have scarce more foundation than those edifices that your little ones raise in cards. You see to what period the vast fortunes of the Duke and Duchess of Marlborough, and Sir Robert Walpole are soon arrived. I believe as you do, that Lady Orford is a joyful widow, but am persuaded she has as much reason to weep for her husband as ever any women has had, from Andromache to this day. I never saw any second marriage that did not appear to me very ridiculous: hers is accompanied with circumstances that render the folly complete.

Sicknesses have been very fatal in this country, as well as England. I should be glad to know the names of those you say are deceased: I believe I am ignorant of half of them, the Dutch news being forbid here. I would not have you give yourself the trouble, but order one of your servants to transcribe the catalogue. You will perhaps laugh at this curiosity. If you ever return to Bute, you will find that what happens in the world is a considerable amusement in solitude. The people I see here make no more impression on my mind than the figures in the tapestry, while they are directly before my eyes. I know one is clothed in blue, and another in red; but out of sight, they are so entirely out of memory, I hardly remember whether they are tall or short. I sometimes call myself to account for this insensibility, which has something of ingratitude in it, this little town thinking themselves highly honored and obliged by my residence: they intended me an extraordinary mark of it, having determined to set up my statue in the most conspicuous place: the marble was bespoke, and the sculptor bargained with, before I knew any thing of the matter; and it would have been erected without my knowledge, if it had not been necessary for him to see me to take the resemblance. I thanked them very much for the intention; but utterly refused complying with it, fearing it would be reported (at least in England) that I had set up my own statue. They were so obstinate in the design, I was forced to tell them my religion would not permit it. I seriously believe it would have been worshiped, when I was forgotten, under the name of some saint or other, since I was to have been represented with a book in my hand, which would have passed for a proof of canonization. This compliment was certainly founded on reasons not unlike those that first famed goddesses, I mean being useful to them, in which I am second to Ceres. If it be true she taught the art of sowing wheat, it is certain I have learned them to make bread, in which they continued in the same ignorance Misson complains of (as you may see in his letter from Padnor). I have introduced French rolls, custards, minced pies, and plum-pudding, which they are very fond of. 'Tis impossible to bring them to conform to sillabub, which is so unnatural a mixture in their eyes, they are even shocked to see me eat it: but I expect immortality from the science of butter making, in which they are become so skillful from my instructions. I can assure you here is as good as in any part of Great Britain.

LETTER VI.

LOUVERE, Dec. 8, N. S., 1751.

This town is at present in a general stare, or, to use their own expression, *sotto sopra;* and not only this town, but the capital, Bergamo, the whole province, the neighboring Brescian, and perhaps all the Venetian dominion, occasioned by an adventure exactly resembling, and I believe copied from, Pamela. I know not under what constellation that foolish stuff was wrote, but it has been translated into more languages than any modern performance I ever heard of. No proof of its influence was ever stronger than this present story, which, in Richardson's hands, would serve very well to furnish out seven or eight volumes. I shall make it as short as I can.

Here is a gentleman's family, consisting of an old bachelor and his sister, who have fortune enough to live with great elegance, though without any magnificence, possessed of the esteem of all their acquaintance, he being distinguished by his probity, and she by her virtue. They are not only suffered but sought after by all the best company, and indeed are the most conversable and reasonable people in this place. She is an excellent housewife, and particularly remarkable for keeping her pretty house as neat as any in Holland. She appears no longer in public, being past fifty, and passes her time chiefly at home with her work, receiving few visitants. This Signora Diana, about ten years since, saw, at a monastery, a girl of eight years old, who came thither to beg alms for her mother. Her beauty, though covered with rags, was very observable, and gave great compassion to the charitable lady, who thought it meritorious to rescue such a modest sweetness as appeared in her face from the ruin to which her wretched circumstances exposed her. She asked some questions, to which she answered with a natural civility that seemed surprising ; and finding the head of her family (her brother) to be a cobbler, who could hardly live by that trade, she bid the child follow her home; and sending for her parent, proposed to her to breed the little Octavia for her servant. This was joyfully accepted, the old woman dismissed with a piece of money, and the girl remained with the Signora Diana, who bought her decent clothes, and took pleasure in teaching her whatever she was capable of learning. She learned to read, write, and cast accounts, with uncommon facility; and had such a genius for work, that she excelled her mistress in embroidery, point, and every operation of the needle. She grew perfectly skilled in confectionary, had a good insight into cookery, and was a great proficient in distillery. To these accomplishments she was so handy, well-bred, humble, and modest, that not only her master and mistress, but every body that frequented the house took notice of her. She lived thus near nine years, never going out but to church. However, beauty is as difficult to

conceal as light; hers begun to make a great noise. Signora
Diana told me she observed an unusual concourse of peddling
women that came on pretext to sell pennyworths of lace,
china, etc., and several young gentlemen, very well powdered,
that were perpetually walking before her door, and looking up
at the windows. These prognostics alarmed her prudence,
and she listened very willingly to some honorable proposals
that were made by many honest thriving tradesmen. She
communicated this to Octavia, and told her that though she
was sorry to lose so good a servant, yet she thought it right
to advise her to choose a husband. The girl answered modestly that it was her duty to obey all her commands, but she
found no inclination to marriage; and if she would permit her
to live single, she would think it a greater obligation than any
other she could bestow. Signora Diana was too conscientious
to force her into a state from which she could not free her, and
left her to her own disposal. However, they parted soon
after: whether (as the neighbors say) Signor Aurelio Ardinghi, her brother, looked with too much attention on the young
woman, or that she herself (as Diana says) desired to seek a
place of more profit, she removed to Bergamo, where she soon
found preferment, being strongly recommended by the Ardinghi family. She was advanced to be first waiting-woman to
an old countess, who was so well pleased with her service,
she desired, on her death-bed, Count Jeronimo Losi, her son,
to be kind to her. He found no repugnance to this act of obedience, having distinguished the beautiful Octavia, from his first
sight of her; and during the six months that she had served
in the house, had tried every art of a fine gentleman accustomed to victories of that sort, to vanquish the virtue of this
fair virgin. He has a handsome figure, and has had an education uncommon in this country, having made the tour of
Europe, and brought from Paris all the improvements that are
to be picked up there, being celebrated for his grace in dancing, and skill in fencing and riding, by which he is a favorite
among the ladies, and respected by the men. Thus qualified

for conquest, you may judge of his surprise at the firm yet
modest resistance of this country girl, who was neither to be
moved by address, nor gained by liberality, nor on any terms
would be prevailed on to stay as his housekeeper, after the
death of his mother. She took that post in the house of an
old judge, where she continued to be solicited by the emissa-
ries of the Count's passion, and found a new persecutor in her
master, who after three months' endeavor to corrupt her,
offered her marriage. She chose to return to her former ob-
scurity, and escaped from his pursuit, without asking any
wages, and privately returned to the Signora Diana. She
threw herself at her feet, and, kissing her hands, begged her
with tears to conceal her, at least some time, if she would not
accept her service. She protested she had never been happy
since she left it. While she was making these submissions,
Signor Aurelio entered. She entreated his intercession on her
knees, who was easily persuaded to consent she should stay
with them, though his sister blamed her highly for her precipi-
tate flight, having no reason, from the age and character of
her master, to fear any violence, and wondered at her declining the honor he offered her. Octavia confessed that perhaps
she had been too rash in her proceedings, but said that he
seemed to resent her refusal in such a manner as frightened
her; she hoped that after a few days' search he would think
no more of her; and that she scrupled entering into the holy
bands of matrimony, where her heart did not sincerely accompany all the words of the ceremony. Signora Diana had
nothing to say in contradiction to this pious sentiment; and
her brother applauded the honesty which could not be per-
verted by any interest whatever. She remained concealed
in their house, where she helped in the kitchen, cleaned the
rooms, and redoubled her usual diligence and officiousness.
Her old master came to Louvere on pretense of adjusting a
law-suit, three days after, and made private inquiry after her;
but hearing from her mother and brother (who knew nothing
of her being here) that they had never heard of her, he con-.

cluded she had taken another route, and returned to Bergamo; and she continued in this retirement near a fortnight.

Last Sunday, as soon as the day was closed, arrived at Signor Aurelio's door, a handsome equipage in a large coach, attended by four well-armed servants on horseback. An old priest stepped out of it, and desiring to speak with Signora Diana, informed her he came from the Count Jeronimo Losi, to demand Octavia: that the Count waited for her at a village four miles from hence, where he intended to marry her; and had sent him, who was engaged to perform the divine rite, that Signora Diana might resign her to his care without any difficulty. The young damsel was called for, who entreated she might be permitted the company of another priest with whom she was acquainted: this was readily granted; and she sent for a young man that visits me very often, being remarkable for his sobriety and learning. Meanwhile a valet-de-chambre presented her with a box, in which was a complete genteel undress for a lady. Her laced linen and fine night-gown were soon put on, and away they marched, leaving the family in a surprise not to be described.

Signor Aurelio came to drink coffee with me next morning; his first words were, he had brought me the history of Pamela. I said, laughing, I had been tired with it long since. He explained himself by relating this story, mixed with great resentment for Octavia's conduct. Count Jeronimo's father had been his ancient friend and patron; and this escape from his house (he said) would lay him under a suspicion of having abetted the young man's folly, and perhaps expose him to the anger of all his relations, for contriving an action he would rather have died than suffered, if he had known how to prevent it. I easily believed him, there appearing a latent jealousy under his affliction, that showed me he envied the bridegroom's happiness, at the same time he condemned his extravagance.

Yesterday noon, being Saturday, Don Joseph returned, who has got the name of Parson Williams by this expedition. He relates, that when the bark which carried the coach and train arrived, they found the amorous count waiting for his bride on the bank of the lake. He would have proceeded immediately to the church; but she utterly refused it, till they had each of them been at confession; after which the happy knot was tied by the parish priest. They continued their journey, and came to their palace at Bergamo in a few hours, where every thing was prepared for their reception. They received the communion next morning, and the count declares that the lovely Octavia has brought him an inestimable portion, since he owes to her the salvation of his soul. He has renounced play, at which he had lost a great deal of time and money. She has already retrenched several superfluous servants, and put his family into an exact method of economy, preserving all the splendor necessary to his rank. He has sent a letter in his own hand to her mother, inviting her to reside with them, and subscribing himself her dutiful son; but the countess has sent another privately by Don Joseph, in which she advises the old woman to stay at Louvere, promising to take care she shall want nothing, accompanied with a token of twenty sequins,* which is at least nineteen more than ever she saw in her life.

I forgot to tell you that from Octavia's first serving the old lady, there came frequent charities in her name to her poor parent, which nobody was surprised at, the lady being celebrated for pious works, and Octavia known to be a great favorite with her. It is now discovered that they were all sent by the generous lover, who has presented Don Joseph very handsomely, but he has brought neither letter nor message to the house of Ardinghi, which affords much speculation.

I am afraid you are heartily tired with this tedious tale. I will not lengthen it with reflections, as I fancy yours will be the same as mine.

With mine all these adventures proceed from artifice on one side, and weakness on the other. An honest, tender mind

* About ten guineas English.

is often betrayed to ruin by the charms that make the fortune
of a designing head, which, when joined with a beautiful
face, can never fail of advancement, except barred by a wise
mother, who locks up her daughters from view till nobody
cares to look on them. My poor friend the Duchess of Bolton* was educated in solitude, with some choice of books, by
a saint-like governess: crammed with virtue and good qualities, she thought it impossible not to find gratitude, though
she failed to give passion; and upon this plan threw away
her estate, was despised by her husband, and laughed at by
the public. Polly, bred in an ale-house, and produced on
the stage, has obtained wealth and title, and found the way
to be esteemed. So useful is early experience—without it
half of life is dissipated in correcting the errors that we have
been taught to receive as indisputable truths.

LETTER VII.

LOUVERE, January 21, 1752.

MY DEAR CHILD—I am extremely concerned to hear you
complain of ill health, at a time of life when you ought to
be in the flower of your strength. I hope I need not recommend to you to take care of it: the tenderness you have for
your children is sufficient to enforce you to the utmost regard
for the preservation of a life so necessary to their well-being.
I do not doubt your prudence in their education; neither can
I say any thing particular relating to it at this distance, different tempers requiring different management. In general,
never attempt to govern them (as most people do) by deceit:
if they find themselves cheated, even in trifles, it will so far
lessen the authority of their instructor as to make them neg-

* Lady Anne Vaughan, daughter and heir of John Earl of Carberry,
married Charles Duke of Bolton in 1713, and died in 1751. The Duke
of Bolton afterward married Lavinia Fenton, the celebrated *Polly* in
Gay's *Beggar's Opera.*

lect all their future admonitions ; and, if possible, breed them free from prejudices; those contracted in the nursery often influence the whole life after, of which I have seen many melancholy examples. I shall say no more of this subject, nor would have said this little if you had not asked my advice: 'tis much easier to give rules than to practice them. I am sensible my own natural temper is too indulgent: I think it the least dangerous error, yet still it is an error. I can only say with truth that I do not know in my whole life having ever endeavored to impose on you, or give a false color to any thing that I represented to you. If your daughters are inclined to love reading, do not check their inclination by hindering them of the diverting part of it; it is as necessary for the amusement of women as the reputation of men ; but teach them not to expect or desire any applause from it. Let their brothers shine, and let them content themselves with making their lives easier by it, which I experimentally know is more effectually done by study than any other way. Ignorance is as much the fountain of vice as idleness, and, indeed, generally produces it. People that do not read or work for a livelihood, have many hours they know not how to employ, especially women, who commonly fall into vapors, or something worse. I am afraid you'll think this letter very tedious: forgive it as coming from your most affectionate mother.

LETTER VIII.

1752.

DEAR CHILD—I received yesterday, February 15, N. S., the case of books you were so good to send me. The entertainment they have already given me has recompensed me for the long time I expected them. I began, by your direction, with Peregrine Pickle. I think Lady Vane's memoirs contain more truth and less malice than any I ever read in my life. When she speaks of her own being disinterested, I am apt to believe she really thinks so herself, as many highwaymen, after having no possibility of retrieving the character of honesty, please themselves with that of being generous, because whatever they get on the road they always spend at the next ale-house, and are still as beggarly as ever. Her history, rightly considered, would be more instructive to young women than any sermon I know. They may see there what mortifications and variety of misery are the unavoidable consequences of gallantry. I think there is no rational creature that would not prefer the life of the strictest Carmelite to the round of hurry and misfortune she has gone through. Her style is clear and concise, with some strokes of humor, which appear to me so much above her, I can't help being of opinion the whole has been modeled by the author of the book in which it is inserted, who is some subaltern admirer of hers. I may judge wrong, she being no acquaintance of mine, though she has married two of my relations. Her first wedding was attended with circumstances that made me think a visit not at all necessary, though I disobliged Lady Susan by neglecting it; and her second, which happened soon after, made her so near a neighbor that I rather chose to stay the whole summer in town than partake of her balls and parties of pleasure, to which I did not think it proper to introduce you; and had no other way of avoiding it without incurring the censure of a most unnatural mother for denying you diversions that the pious Lady Ferrers permitted to her exemplary daughters. Mr. Shirley has had uncommon fortune in making the conquest of two such extraordinary ladies, equal in their heroic contempt of shame, and eminent above their sex, the one for beauty, and the other wealth, both which attract the pursuit of all mankind, and have been thrown into his arms with the same unlimited fondness. He appeared to me gentle, wellbred, well-shaped, and sensible; but the charms of his face and eyes, which Lady Vane describes with so much warmth, were, I confess, always invisible to me, and the artificial part

11*

of his character very glaring, which I think her story shows in a strong light.

The next book I laid my hand on was the Parish Girl, which interested me enough not to be able to quit it till it was read over, though the author has fallen into the common mistake of romance-writers; intending a virtuous character, and not knowing how to draw it; the first step of his heroine (leaving her patroness's house) being altogther absurd and ridiculous, justly entitling her to all the misfortunes she met with. Candles came (and my eyes grown weary), I took up the next book, merely because I supposed from the title it could not engage me long. It was Pompey the Little, which has really diverted me more than any of the others, and it was impossible to go to bed till it was finished. It is a real and exact representation of life, as it is now acted in London, as it was in my time, and as it will be, I do not doubt, a hundred years hence, with some little variation of dress, and perhaps of government. I found there many of my acquaintance. Lady T. and Lady O. are so well painted, I fancied I heard them talk, and have heard them say the very things there repeated. I also saw myself (as I now am) in the character of Mrs. Qualmsick. You will be surprised at this, no Englishwoman being so free from vapors, having never in my life complained of low spirits, or weak nerves; but our resemblance is very strong in the fancied loss of appetite, which I have been silly enough to be persuaded into by the physician of this place. He visits me frequently, as being one of the most considerable men in the parish, and is a grave, sober, thinking, great fool, whose solemn appearance and deliberate way of delivering his sentiments, gives them an air of good sense, though they are often the most injudicious that ever were pronounced. By perpetual telling me I eat so little, he is amazed I am able to subsist. He had brought me to be of his opinion; and I began to be seriously uneasy at it. This useful treatise has roused me into a recollection of what I eat yesterday, and do almost every day the same. I wake generally about seven,

and drink half a pint of warm asses' milk, after which I sleep
two hours; as soon as I am risen, I constantly take three cups
of milk coffee, and two hours after that a large cup of milk
chocolate: two hours more brings my dinner, where I never
fail swallowing a good dish (I don't mean plate) of gravy
soup, with all the bread, roots, etc., belonging to it. I then
eat a wing and the whole body of a large fat capon, and a veal
sweetbread, concluding with a competent quantity of custard,
and some roasted chestnuts. At five in the afternoon I take
another dose of asses' milk; and for supper twelve chestnuts
(which would weigh two of those in London), one new laid
egg, and a handsome porringer of white bread and milk.
With this diet, notwithstanding the menaces of my wise doctor, I am now convinced I am in no danger of starving; and
am obliged to Little Pompey for this discovery.

I opened my eyes this morning on Leonora, from which I
defy the greatest chemist in morals to extract any instruction.
The style is most affectedly florid and naturally insipid, with
such a confused heap of admirable characters, that never are,
or can be, in human nature. I flung it aside after fifty pages,
and laid hold of Mrs. Philips, where I expected to find, at
least probable if not true facts, and was not disappointed.
There is a great similitude in the genius and adventures (the
one being productive of the other) between Madam Constantia and Lady Vane: the first mentioned has the advantage in
birth, and, if I am not mistaken, in understanding: they have
both had scandalous law-suits with their husbands, and are
endowed with the same intrepid assurance. Constantia seems
to value herself also on her generosity, and has given the same
proofs of it. The parallel might be drawn out to be as long
as any of Plutarch's; but I dare swear you are already heartily
weary of my remarks, and wish I had not read so much in so
short a time, that you might not be troubled with my com-
ments; but you must suffer me to say something of the polite
Mr. S——, whose name I should never have guessed by the
rapturous description his mistress makes of his person, having

always looked upon him as one of the most disagreeable fellows about town, as odious in his outside as stupid in his conversation, and I should as soon have expected to hear of his conquests at the head of an army as among women ; yet he has been, it seems, the darling favorite of the most experienced of the sex, which shows me I am a very bad judge of merit.   But I agree with Mrs. Philips, that however profligate she may have been, she is infinitely his superior in virtue ; and if her penitence is as sincere as she says, she may expect their future fate to be like that of Dives and Lazarus.

This letter is of a most immoderate length.   It will find you at Caenwood ; your solitude there will permit you to peruse, and even to forgive, all the impertinence of your most affectionate mother.

LETTER IX.

LOUVERE, June 23, N. S., 1752.

Soon after I wrote my last letter to my dear child, I was seized with so violent a fever, accompanied with so many bad symptoms, my life was despaired of by the physician of Gottolengo, and I prepared myself for death with as much resignation as that circumstance admits : some of my neighbors, without my knowledge, sent express for the doctor of this place, whom I have mentioned to you formerly as having uncommon secrets.   I was surprised to see him at my bedside. He declared me in great danger, but did not doubt my recovery, if I was wholly under his care : and his first prescription was transporting me hither : the other physician asserted positively I should die on the road.   It has always been my opinion that it is a matter of the utmost indifference where we expire, and I consented to be removed.   My bed was placed on a brancard ; my servants followed in chaises ; and in this equipage I set out.   I bore the first day's journey of fifteen miles without any visible alteration.   The doctor said as I was not worse I was certainly better; and the next day proceeded twenty miles to Isco, which is at the head of this lake. I lay each night at noblemen's houses, which were empty. My cook, with my physician, always preceded two or three hours, and I found my chamber and all necessaries ready prepared with the exactest attention. I was put into a bark in my litter-bed, and in three hours arrived here. My spirits were not at all wasted (I think rather raised) by the fatigue of my journey. I drank the water next morning, and, with a few doses of my physician's prescription, in three days found myself in perfect health, which appeared almost a miracle to all that saw me. You may imagine I am willing to submit to the orders of one that I must acknowledge the instrument in saving my life, though they are not entirely conformable to my will and pleasure. He has sentenced me to a long continuance here, which, he says, is absolutely necessary to the confirmation of my health, and would persuade me that my illness has been wholly owing to my omission of drinking the waters these two years past. I dare not contradict him, and must own he deserves (from the various surprising cures I have seen) the name given him in this country, of the "miraculous man." Both his character and practice are so singular I can not forbear giving you some account of them. He will not permit his patients to have either surgeon or apothecary : he performs all the operations of the first with great dexterity, and whatever compounds he gives, he makes in his own house ; those are very few : juice of herbs and these waters, being commonly his sole prescriptions. He has very little learning, and professes drawing all his knowledge from experience, which he possesses, perhaps, in a greater degree than any other mortal, being the seventh doctor of his family, in a direct line. His forefathers have all of them left journals and registers solely for the use of their posterity, none of them having published any thing ; and he has recourse to these manuscripts on every difficult case, the veracity of which, at least, is unquestionable. His vivacity is prodigious, and he is indefatigable in his industry ;

but what most distinguishes him is a disinterestedness I never saw in any other: he is as regular in his attendance on the poorest peasant from whom he never can receive one farthing, as on the richest of the nobility; and whenever he is wanted, will climb three or four miles on the mountains, in the hottest sun, or heaviest rain, where a horse can not go, to arrive at a cottage, where, if their condition requires it, he does not only give them advice and medicines gratis, but bread, wine, and whatever is needful. There never passes a week without one or more of these expeditions. His last visit is generally to me. I often see him as dirty and tired as a foot post, having eat nothing all day but a roll or two that he carries in his pocket, yet blessed with such a perpetual flow of spirits he is always gay to a degree above cheerfulness. There is a peculiarity in this character that I hope will incline you to forgive my drawing it.

I have already described to you this extraordinary spot of land, which is almost unknown to the rest of the world, and indeed does not seem to be destined by nature to be inhabited by human creatures, and I believe would never have been so without the cruel civil war between the Guelphs and Ghibellines. Before that time here were only the huts of a few fishermen, who came at certain seasons on account of the fine fish with which this lake abounds, particularly trouts, as large and red as salmon. The lake itself is different from any other I ever saw or read of, being the color of the sea, rather deeper tinged with green, which convinces me that the surrounding mountains are full of minerals, and it may be rich in mines yet undiscovered, as well as quarries of marble, from whence the churches and houses are ornamented, and even the streets paved, which, if polished and laid with art, would look like the finest mosaic work, being a variety of beautiful colors. I ought to retract the honorable title of street, none of them being broader than an alley, and impassable for any wheel-carriage, except a wheel-barrow. This town, which is the largest of twenty-five that are built on the banks of the lake of Isco, is near two miles long, and the figure of a semicircle, and situated at the northern extremity. If it was a regular range of building, it would appear magnificent; but being founded accidentally by those who sought a refuge from the violence of those times, it is a mixture of shops and palaces, gardens and houses, which ascend a mile high, in a confusion which is not disagreeable. After this salutary water was found, and the purity of the air experienced, many people of quality chose it for their summer residence, and embellished it with several fine edifices. It was populous and flourishing till that fatal plague, which overran all Europe in the year 1626. It made a terrible ravage in this place: the poor were almost destroyed, and the rich deserted it. Since that time it has never recovered its former splendor; few of the nobility returned; it is now only frequented during the water-drinking season. Several of the ancient palaces are degraded into lodging-houses, and others stand empty in a ruinous condition: one of these I have bought. I see you lift up your eyes in wonder at my indiscretion. I beg you to hear my reasons before you condemn me. In my infirm state of health the unavoidable noise of a public lodging is very disagreeable ; and here is no private one : secondly, and chiefly, the whole purchase is but one hundred pounds, with a very pretty garden in terraces down to the water, and a court behind the house. It is founded on a rock, and the walls so thick they will probably remain as long as the earth. It is true the apartments are in most tattered circumstances, without doors or windows. The beauty of the great saloon gained my affection : it is forty-two feet in length by twenty-five, proportionably high, opening into a balcony of the same length, with a marble balluster: the ceiling and flooring are in good repair, but I have been forced to the expense of covering the wall with new stucco; and the carpenter is at this minute taking measure of the windows in order to make frames for sashes. The great stairs are in such a declining way it would be a very hazardous exploit to mount them : I never intend to attempt it. The state bed-chamber shall also remain for the sole use of the spiders that have taken possession of it, along with the grand cabinet, and some other pieces of magnificence quite useless to me, and which would cost a great deal to make habitable. I have fitted up six rooms with lodgings for five servants, which are all I ever will have in this place : and I am persuaded that I could make a profit if I would part with my purchase, having been very much favored in the sale, which was by auction, the owner having died without children, and I believe he had never seen this mansion in his life, it having stood empty from the death of his grandfather. The governor bid for me, and nobody would bid against him. Thus I am become a citizen of Louvere, to the great joy of the inhabitants, not (as they would pretend) from their respect for my person, but I perceive they fancy I shall attract all the traveling English ; and, to say truth, the singularity of the place is well worth their curiosity ; but, as I have no correspondents, I may be buried here thirty years, and nobody know any thing of the matter.

I received the books you were so kind to send me, five days ago, but not the china, which I would not venture among the precipices that lead hither. I have only had time to read Lord Orrery's work, which has extremely entertained, and not at all surprised me, having the honor of being acquainted with him, and know him for one of those danglers after wit, who, like those after beauty, spend their time in humbly admiring, and are happy in being permitted to attend, though they are laughed at and only encouraged to gratify the insatiate vanity of those professed wits and beauties who aim at being publicly distinguished in those characters. Dean Swift, by his lordship's own account, was so intoxicated with the love of flattery, he sought it among the lowest of people, and the silliest of women ; and was never so well pleased with any companions as those that worshiped him, while he insulted them. It is a wonderful condescension in a man of quality to offer his incense in such a crowd, and think it an honor to share a friendship with Sheridan,* etc., especially being himself endowed with such universal merit as he displays in these Letters, where he shows that he is a poet, a patriot, a philosopher, a physician, a critic, a complete scholar, and most excellent moralist; shining in private life as a submissive son, a tender father, and zealous friend. His only error has been that love of learned ease which he has indulged in a solitude, which has prevented the world from being blessed with such a general, minister, or admiral, being equal to any of these employments, if he would have turned his talents to the use of the public. Heaven be praised, he has now drawn his pen in its service, and given an example to mankind, that the most villainous actions, nay the most arrant nonsense, are only small blemishes in a great genius. I happen to think quite contrary, weak woman as I am. I have always avoided the conversation of those who endeavor to raise an opinion of their understanding by ridiculing what both law and decency obliges them to revere; but whenever I have met with any of those bright spirits, who would be smart on sacred subjects, I have ever cut short their discourse by asking them if they had any lights and revelations by which they would propose new articles of faith? Nobody can deny but religion is a comfort to the distressed, a cordial to the sick, and sometimes a restraint on the wicked; therefore, whoever would argue or laugh it out of the world, without giving some equivalent for it, ought to be treated as a common enemy: but, when this language comes from a churchman, who enjoys large benefices and dignities from that very Church he openly despises, it is an object of horror for which I want a name, and can only be excused by madness, which I think the Dean was always strongly touched with. His character seems to me a parallel with that of Caligula; and had he had the same power, would have made the same use of it. That emperor erected a temple to himself, where he was his own high-priest, preferred his horse to

* Dr. Thomas Sheridan, the grandfather of R. Brinsley Sheridan, Esq.

the highest honors in the state, professed enmity to the human race, and at last lost his life by a nasty jest on one of his inferiors, which I dare swear Swift would have made in his place. There can be no worse picture made of the Doctor's morals than he has given us himself in the letters printed by Pope. We see him vain, trifling, ungrateful to the memory of his patron, that of Lord Oxford, making a servile court where he had any interested views, and meanly abusive where they were disappointed, and, as he says (in his own phrase) flying in the face of mankind, in company with his adorer Pope. It is pleasant to consider, that had it not been for the good nature of these very mortals they contemn, these two superior beings were entitled, by their birth and hereditary fortune, to be only a couple of link-boys. I am of opinion their friendship would have continued, though they had remained in the same kingdom : it had a very strong foundation—the love of flattery on one side, and the love of money on the other. Pope courted with the utmost assiduity all the old men from whom he could hope a legacy, the Duke of Buckingham, Lord Peterborough, Sir G. Kneller, Lord Bolingbroke, Mr. Wycherly, Mr. Congreve, Lord Harcourt, etc., and I do not doubt projected to sweep the Dean's whole inheritance, if he could have persuaded him to throw up his deanery, and come to die in his house ; and his general preaching against money was meant to induce people to throw it away, that he might pick it up. There can not be a stronger proof of his being capable of any action for the sake of gain than publishing his literary correspondence, which lays open such a mixture of dullness and iniquity that one would imagine it visible even to his most passionate admirers, if Lord Orrery did not show that smooth lines have as much influence over some people as the authority of the Church in these countries, where it can not only excuse, but sanctify any absurdity of villainy whatever. It is remarkable that his lordship's family have been smatterers in wit and learning for three generations: his grandfather has left monuments of his good taste in several rhyming tragedies, and the romance of Parthenissa. His father began the world by giving his name to a treatise wrote by Atterbury and his club, which gave him great reputation; but (like Sir Martin Marall, who would fumble with his lute when the music was over) he published soon after a sad comedy of his own, and, what was worse, a *dismal* tragedy he had found among the first Earl of Orrery's papers. People could easier forgive his being partial to his own silly works, as a common frailty, than the want of judgment in producing a piece that dishonored his father's memory.

Thus fell into dust a fame that had made a blaze by borrowed fire. To do justice to the present lord, I do not doubt this fine performance is all his own, and is a public benefit, if every reader has been as well diverted with it as myself. I verily believe it has contributed to the establishment of my health.

I wrote two long letters to your father, to which I have had no answer. I hope he is well. The prosperity of you and yours is the warmest wish of, my dear child, your most affectionate mother.

This letter is of a horrible length; I dare not read it over. I should have told you (to justify my folly as far as I can), here is no ground-rent to be paid, taxes for Church and poor, or any imposition whatever, on houses. I desire, in the next parcel, you would send me Lady Frail, the Adventures of G. Edwards, and the Life of Lord Stair, which I suppose very superficial, and partly fictitious; but as he was my acquaintance, I have some curiosity to see how he is represented.

LETTER X.

March 1, N. S., 1752.

DEAR CHILD—I have now finished your books, and I believe you will think I have made quick dispatch. To say truth, I have read night and day. Mr. Loveill gave me some entertainment, though there is but one character in it that I can find out. I do not doubt Mr. Depy is designed for Sir J. R. The adventure mentioned at Rome really happened to him, with this addition, that after he was got quit of his fear of being suspected in the interest of the P., he endeavored to manifest his loyalty by railing at him in all companies, with all the warmth imaginable, on which his companions persuaded him that his death was absolutely determined by that court; and he durst not stir out for some time, for fear of being assassinated; nor eat, for fear of being poisoned. I saw him at Venice, where, on hearing it said I had been at Constantinople, he asked Lord Mansel by what accident I made that journey. He answered, Mr. Wortley had been embassador to the Porte. Sir J. replied, to what port? the port of Leghorn! I could relate many speeches of his of equal beauty, but I believe you are already tired of hearing of him, as much as I was with the memoirs of Miss H. Stewart;* who, being intended for an example of wit and virtue, is a jilt and a fool in every page. But while I was indolently perusing the marvelous figures she exhibits, no more resembling any thing in human nature than the wooden cut in the Seven Champions, I was roused into great surprise and indignation by the monstrous abuse of one of the very few women I have a real value for; I mean Lady B. Finch;† who is not only clearly meant by the mention of her library (she being the only lady at court that has one), but her very name at length; she being christened Cæcilia Isabella, though she chooses to be called by the latter. I always thought her conduct, in every light, so irreproachable, I did not think she had an enemy upon earth; I now see 'tis impossible to avoid them, especially in her situation. It is one

* "Harriet Stewart" was the first novel written by Mrs. Charlotte Lennox, and certainly a very indifferent one.

† Lady Belle Finch, one of the many daughters of Lord Nottingham (Swift's "Dismal"), who before his death succeeded to the older title of Winchelsea. She was sister to the Duchess of Roxburgh, the Duchess of Cleveland, Lady Mansfield, Lady Rockingham, etc.; and was Lady of the Bedchamber to the Princess Amelia.

of the misfortunes of a supposed court interest (perhaps you may know it by experience), even the people you have obliged hate you, if they do not think you have served to the utmost extent of a power that they fancy you are possessed of; which it may be is only imaginary.

On the other hand, I forgive Jo. Thompson two volumes of absurdities, for the sake of justice he has done to the memory of the Duke of Montagu; who really had (in my opinion) one of the most humane dispositions that ever appeared in the world. I was such an old fool as to weep over Clarissa Harlowe, like any milkmaid of sixteen over the ballad of the Lady's Fall. To say truth, the first volume softened me by a near resemblance of my maiden days; but on the whole 'tis most miserable stuff. Miss How, who is called a young lady of sense and honor, is not only extreme silly, but a more vicious character than Sally Martin; whose crimes are owing at first to seduction, and afterward to necessity: while this virtuous damsel, without any reason, insults her mother at home, and ridicules her abroad: abuses the man she marries, and is impertinent and impudent with great applause. Even that model of perfection Clarissa is so faulty in her behavior as to deserve little compassion. Any girl that runs away with a young fellow, without intending to marry him, should be carried to Bridewell or to Bedlam the next day. Yet the circumstances are so laid as to inspire tenderness, notwithstanding the low style and absurd incidents; and I look upon this and Pamela to be two books that will do more general mischief than the works of Lord Rochester. There is something humorous in R. Random that makes me believe that the author is H. Fielding. I am horribly afraid, I guess too well the writer of those abominable insipidities of Cornelia, Leonora, and the Ladies' Drawing Room. I fancy you are now saying, 'tis a sad thing to grow old; what does my poor mamma mean by troubling me with criticisms on books, that nobody but herself will ever read? You must allow something to my solitude. I have a pleasure n writing to my dear child, and not many subjects to write upon. The adventures of people here would not at all amuse you, having no acquaintance with the persons concerned; and an account of myself would hardly gain credit, after having fairly owned to you how deplorably I was misled in regard to my own health; though I have all my life been on my guard against the information by the sense of hearing; it being one of my earliest observations, the universal inclination of human-kind is to be led by the ears; and I am sometimes apt to imagine that they are given to men, as they are to pitchers, purposely that they may be carried about by them. This consideration should abate my wonder to see (as I do here) the most astonishing legends embraced as the most sacred truths, by those who have always heard them asserted, and never contradicted; they even place a merit in complying, in direct opposition to the evidence of all their other senses.

I am very much pleased with the account you give me of your father's health. I hope your own, and that of your family, is perfect; give my blessing to your little ones, and my compliments to Lord Bute.

LETTER XI.

LOUVERE, Aug. 20, 1752.

MY DEAR CHILD—'Tis impossible to tell you to what degree I share with you in the misfortune that has happened. I do not doubt your own reason will suggest to you all the alleviations that can serve on so sad an occasion, and will not trouble you with the common-place topics that are used, generally to no purpose, in letters of consolation. Disappointments ought to be less sensibly felt at my age than yours; yet I own I am so far affected by this that I have need of all my philosophy to support it. However, let me beg of you not to indulge a useless grief, to the prejudice of your health, which is so necessary to your family. Every thing may turn out better than you expect. We see so darkly into futurity, we never know when we have real cause to rejoice or lament. The worst appearances have often happy consequences, as the best lead many times into the greatest misfortunes. Human prudence is very straitly bounded. What is most in our power, though little so, is the disposition of our own minds. Do not give way to melancholy; seek amusements; be willing to be diverted, and insensibly you will become so. Weak people only place a merit in affliction. A grateful remembrance, and whatever honor we can pay to their memory, is all that is owing to the dead. Tears and sorrow are no duties to them, and make us incapable of those we owe to the living.

I give you thanks for your care of my books. I yet retain, and carefully cherish, my taste for reading. If relays of eyes were to be hired like posthorses, I would never admit any but silent companions: they afford a constant variety of entertainment, which is almost the only one pleasing in the enjoyment, and inoffensive in the consequence.

LETTER XII.

BRESCIA, October 10, 1752.

This letter will be very dull or very peevish (perhaps both). I am at present much out of humor, being on the edge of a quarrel with my friend and patron, the Cardinal Querini.* He is really a good-natured and generous man, and spends his vast revenue in (what he thinks) the service of his country, besides contributing largely to the building a new cathedral, which, when finished, will stand in the first rank of fine churches (where he has already the comfort of seeing his own busto, finely done both within and without). He has founded a magnificent college for one hundred scholars, which I don't doubt he will endow very nobly, and greatly enlarged and em-

----

* Cardinal Angelo Maria Querini. He published the works of St. Ephrem Syrus, in six volumes, folio, 1732; and the Life of Pope Paul II., quarto, 1740. See de Bure, Bibliographie Instructive, etc.

bellished his episcopal palace. He has joined to it a public library, which, when I saw it, was a very beautiful room : it is now finished, furnished, and open twice in a week with proper attendance. Yesterday here arrived one of his chief chaplains, with a long compliment, which concluded with desiring I would send him my works ; having dedicated one of his cases to English books, he intended my labors should appear in the most conspicuous place. I was struck dumb for some time with this astonishing request ; when I recovered my vexatious surprise (foreseeing the consequence), I made answer I was highly sensible of the honor designed me, but, upon my word, I had never printed a single line in my life. I was answered in a cold tone, that his Eminence could send for them to England, but they would be a long time coming, and with some hazard ; and that he had flattered himself I would not refuse him such a favor, and I need not be ashamed of seeing my name in a collection where he admitted none but the most eminent authors. It was to no purpose to endeavor to convince him. He would not stay dinner, though earnestly invited ; and went away with the air of one that thought he had reason to be offended. I know his master will have the same sentiments, and I shall pass in his opinion for a monster of ingratitude, while it is the blackest of vices, in my opinion, and of which I am utterly incapable—I really could cry for vexation.

Sure nobody ever had such various provocations to print as myself. I have seen things I have wrote so mangled and falsified I have scarce known them. I have seen poems I never read published with my name at length ; and others, that were truly and singly wrote by me, printed under the names of others. I have made myself easy under all these mortifications by the reflection I did not deserve them, having never aimed at the vanity of popular applause ; but I own my philosophy is not proof against losing a friend, and it may be making an enemy of one to whom I am obliged.

I confess I have often been complimented, since I have been in Italy, on the books I have given the public. I used at first to deny it with some warmth; but finding I persuaded nobody, I have of late contented myself with laughing whenever I heard it mentioned, knowing the character of a learned woman is far from being ridiculous in this country, the greatest families being proud of having produced female writers; and a Milanese lady being now professor of mathematics in the University of Bologna, invited thither by a most obliging letter, wrote by the present Pope, who desired her to accept of the chair, not as a recompense for her merit, but to do honor to a town which is under his protection. To say truth, there is no part of the world where our sex is treated with so much contempt as in England. I do not complain of men for having engrossed the government; in excluding from us all degrees of power, they preserve us from many fatigues, many dangers, and perhaps many crimes. The small proportion of authority that has fallen to my share (only over a few children and servants) has always been a burden, and never a pleasure, and I believe every one finds it so, who acts from a maxim (I think an indispensable duty) that whoever is under my power is under my protection. Those who find a joy in inflicting hardships, and seeing objects of misery, may have other sensations; but I have always thought corrections, even when necessary, as painful to the giver as to the sufferer, and am therefore very well satisfied with the state of subjection we are placed in: but I think it the highest injustice to be debarred the entertainment of my closet, and that the same studies which raise the character of a man should hurt that of a woman. We are educated in the grossest ignorance, and no art omitted to stifle our natural reason; if some few get above their nurse's instructions, our knowledge must rest concealed, and be as useless to the world as gold in the mine. I am now speaking according to our English notions, which may wear out, some ages hence, along with others equally absurd. It appears to me the strongest proof of a clear understanding in Longinus (in every light acknowledged one of the greatest men among the ancients), when I find him so far superior to vulgar prejudices as to choose his two examples of fine writing from a Jew (at that time the most despised people upon earth) and a woman. Our modern wits would be so far from quoting, they would scarce own they had read the works of such contemptible creatures, though perhaps they would condescend to steal from them, at the same time they declared they were below their notice : this subject is apt to run away with me ; I will trouble you with no more of it.

LETTER XIII.

LOUVERE, Oct. 20, N. S., 1752.

DEAR CHILD—I have now read over Richardson—he sinks horribly in his third volume (he does so in his story of Clarissa). When he talks of Italy, it is plain he is no better acquainted with it than he is with the kingdom of Mancomingo. He might have made his Sir Charles's amour with Clementina begin in a convent, where the pensioners sometimes take great liberties ; but that such familiarity should be permitted in her father's house, is as repugnant to custom as it would be in London for a young lady of quality to dance on the ropes at Bartholomew fair : neither does his hero behave to her in a manner suitable to his nice notions. It was impossible a discerning man should not see her passion early enough to check it, if he had really designed it. His conduct puts me in mind of some ladies I have known, who could never find out a man to be in love with them, let him do or say what he would, till he made a direct attempt, and then they were so surprised, I warrant you ! nor do I approve Sir Charles's offered compromise (as he calls it). There must be a great indifference as to religion on both sides, to make so strict a union as marriage tolerable between people of such distinct persuasions. He seems to think women have no souls, by agreeing so easy that his daughters should be educated in bigotry and idolatry. You will perhaps think this last a hard word ; yet it is not difficult to prove that either the papists are guilty of idolatry, or the pagans never were so.

You may see, in Lucian (in his vindication of his images), that they did not take their statues to be real gods, but only the representation of them. The same doctrine may be found in Plutarch; and it is all the modern priests have to say in excuse for their worshiping wood and stone, though they can not deny at the same time that the vulgar are apt to confound that distinction. I always, if possible, avoid controversial disputes: whenever I can not do it, they are very short. I ask my adversary if he believes the Scripture; when that is answered affirmatively, their Church may be proved by a child of ten years old contradictory to it, in their most important points. My second question is, if they think St. Peter and St. Paul knew the true Christian religion? The constant reply is, O yes. Then, say I, purgatory, transubstantiation, invocation of saints, adoration of the Virgin, relics (of which they might have had a cart-load), and observation of Lent, is no part of it, since they neither taught nor practiced any of these things. Vows of celibacy are not more contrary to nature than to the positive precept of St. Paul. He mentions a very common case, in which people are obliged, by conscience, to marry. No mortals can promise that case shall never be theirs, which depends on the disposition of the body as much as a fever; and 'tis as reasonable to engage never to feel the one as the other. He tells us, the marks of the Holy Spirit are charity, humility, truth, and long-suffering. Can any thing be more uncharitable than damning eternally so many millions for not believing what they never heard? or prouder than calling their head a Vice-God? Pious frauds are avowedly permitted, and persecution applauded. These maxims can not be dictated by the spirit of peace, which is so warmly preached in the Gospel. The creeds of the apostles, and Council of Nice, do not speak of the mass, or real presence, as articles of belief; and Athanasius asserts, whosoever believes according to them shall be saved. Jesus Christ, in answer to the lawyer bids him love God above all things, and his neighbor as himself, as all that is necessary to salvation. When he describes the

last judgment, he does not examine what sect, or what Church
men were of, but how far they had been beneficial to mankind.
Faith can not determine reward or punishment, being involuntary, and only the consequence of conviction. We do not
believe what we please, but what appears to us with the face
of truth. As I do not mistake exclamation, invective, or ridicule, for argument, I never recriminate on the lives of their
popes and cardinals, when they urge the character of Henry
the Eighth ; I only answer, good actions are often done by
ill men through interested motives, and 'tis the common
method of Providence to bring good out of evil : history,
both sacred and profane, furnishes many examples of it.
When they tell me I have forsook the worship of my ancestors, I say I have had more ancestors heathen than Christian,
and my faith is certainly ancienter than theirs, since I have
added nothing to the practice of the primitive professors of
Christianity. As to the prosperity or extent of the dominion
of their Church, which Cardinal Bellarmin counts among the
proofs of its orthodoxy, the Mohammedans, who have larger
empires, and have made a quicker progress, have a better plea
for the visible protection of heaven. If the fopperies of their
religion were only fopperies, they ought to be complied with
whenever it is established, like any ridiculous dress in fashion ; but I think them impieties ; their devotions are a scandal to humanity from their nonsense ; the mercenary deceits,
and barbarous tyranny of their ecclesiastics, inconsistent with
moral honesty. If they object to the diversity of our sects
as a mark of reprobation, I desire them to consider that objection has equal force against Christianity in general. When
they thunder with the names of fathers and councils, they
are surprised to find me as well (often better) acquainted with
them than themselves. I show them the variety of their doc-
trines, their violent contests, and various factions, instead of
that union they boast of. I have never been attacked a second time in any of the towns where I have resided, and perhaps shall never be so again after my last battle, which was

with an old priest, a learned man, particularly esteemed as a mathematician, and who has a head and heart as warm as poor Whiston's. When I first came here, he visited me every day, and talked of me every where with such violent praise that, had we been young people, God knows what would have been said. I have always the advantage of being quite calm on a subject which they can not talk of without heat. He desired I would put on paper what I had said. I immediately wrote one side of a sheet, leaving the other for his answer. He carried it with him, promising to bring it the next day, since which time I have never seen it, though I have often demanded it, being ashamed of my defective Italian. I fancy he sent it to his friend the Archbishop of Milan. I have given over asking for it, as a desperate debt. He still visits me, but seldom, and in a cold sort of a way. When I have found disputants I less respected, I have sometimes taken pleasure in raising their hopes by my concessions: they are charmed when I agree with them in the number of the sacraments; but are horribly disappointed when I explain myself by saying the word sacrament is not to be found either in Old or New Testament; and one must be very ignorant not to know it is taken from the 'listing oath of the Roman soldiers, and means nothing more than a solemn, irrevocable engagement. Parents vow, in infant baptism, to educate their children in the Christian religion, which they take upon themselves by confirmation; the Lord's Supper is frequently renewing the same oath. Ordination and matrimony are solemn vows of a different kind: confession includes a vow of revealing all we know, and reforming what is amiss: extreme unction, the last vow, that we have lived in the faith we were baptized. In this sense they are all sacraments. As to the mysteries preached since, they were all invented long after, and some of them repugnant to the primitive institution. This digression has carried me far from my criticism. You will laugh at my making any on a work below examination. It may be of use to my grand-daughters. I am persuaded he is a favorite author in all the nurseries in England, and has done much harm in the boarding schools, therefore ought to have his absurdities detected. You will think me angry with him for repeating a saying of mine, accompanied with a description of my person, which resembles me as much as one of the giants in Guildhall, and plainly shows he never saw me in his life. Indeed, I think, after being so many years dead and buried, I might be suffered to enjoy the right of the departed, and rest in peace. I can not guess how I can possibly have incurred his indignation, except he takes for truth the literary correspondence between me and the Mrs. Argens, whom I never saw, and who, with many high compliments, have attributed to me sentiments that never came into my head, and among them a criticism on Pamela, who is, however, more favorably treated than she deserves.

The book of letters I mention never came to my hands till some time after it was printed, accidentally at Toulouse. I have need of all my philosophy on these occasions ; though, they happen so often, I ought to be accustomed to them. When I print, I submit to be answered, and criticized ; but as I never did, 'tis hard to be abused for other people's follies. A light thing said in gay company should not be called upon for a serious defense, especially when it injures nobody. It is certain there are as many marriages as ever. Richardson is so eager for the multiplication of them, I suppose he is some parish curate, whose chief profit depends on weddings and christenings. He is not a man-midwife ; for he would be better skilled in physic than to think fits and madness any ornament to the characters of his heroines : though this Sir Charles had no thoughts of marrying Clementine till she had lost her wits, and the divine Clarissa never acted prudently till she was in the same condition, and then very wisely desired to be carried to Bedlam, which is really all that is to be done in that case. Madness is as much a corporal distemper as the gout or asthma, never occasioned by affliction, or to be cured by the enjoyment of extravagant wishes. Passion may indeed bring on a fit, but the disease is lodged in the blood, and it is not more ridiculous to attempt to relieve the gout by an embroidered slipper than to restore reason by the gratification of wild desires.

Richardson is as ignorant in morality as he is in anatomy, when he declares abusing an obliging husband, or an indulgent parent, to be an innocent recreation. His Anna How and Charlotte Grandison are recommended as patterns of charming pleasantry, and applauded by his saint-like dames, who mistake folly for wit and humor, and impudence and ill-nature for spirit and fire. Charlotte behaves like a humorsome child, and should have been used like one, and well whipped in the presence of her friendly confidante Harriet. Lord Halifax very justly tells his daughter that a husband's kindness is to be received by a wife, even when he is drunk, and though it is wrapped up in never so much impertinence. Charlotte acts with an ingratitude that I think too black for human nature, with such coarse jokes and low expressions as are only to be heard among the lowest class of people. Women of that rank often plead a right to beat their husbands, when they don't cuckold them: and I believe this author was never admitted into higher company, and should confine his pen to the amours of housemaids, and the conversation at the steward's table, where I imagine he has sometimes intruded, though oftener in the servants' hall: yet, if the title be not a puff, this work has passed three editions. I do not forgive him his disrespect of old china, which is below nobody's taste, since it has been the Duke of Argyll's, whose understanding has never been doubted either by his friends or enemies.

Richardson never had probably money enough to purchase any, or even a ticket for a masquerade, which gives him such an aversion to them ; though his intended satire against them is very absurd on the account of his Harriet, since she might have been carried off in the same manner if she had been going from supper with her grandam. Her whole behavior, which he designs to be exemplary, is equally blamable and ridiculous. She follows the maxim of Clarissa, of declaring all she thinks to all the people she sees, without reflecting that in this mortal state of imperfection, fig-leaves are as necessary for our minds as our bodies, and 'tis as indecent to show all we think as all we have. He has no idea of the manners of high life : his old Lord M. talks in the style of a country justice, and his virtuous young ladies romp like the wenches round a May-pole. Such liberties as pass between Mr. Lovelace and his cousins, are not to be excused by the relation. I should have been much astonished if Lord Denbigh should have offered to kiss me; and I dare swear Lord Treatham never attempted such an impertinence to you.

With all my contempt I will take notice of one good thing; I mean his project of an English monastery. It was a favorite scheme of mine when I was fifteen; and had I then been mistress of an independent fortune, would certainly have executed it, and elected myself lady abbess. There would you and your ten children have been lost forever. Yet such was the disposition of my early youth : so much was I unlike those girls that declare, if they had been born of the male kind they should have been great rakes, which is owning they have strong inclinations to —— and drinking, and want only opportunity and impunity to exert them vigorously.

This tedious miscellany of a letter is promised to be delivered into your own hand ; nay further, that I shall have an account how you look, how you are dressed, and in what manner your room is furnished. Nothing relating to you is indifferent to me; and if the performance answers the engagement, it will be a vast pleasure to your most affectionate mother.

LETTER XIV.

Louvere, January 28, N. S., 1753.

Dear Child—You have given me a great deal of satisfaction by your account of your eldest daughter. I am particularly pleased to hear she is a good arithmetician ; it is the best proof of understanding : the knowledge of numbers is one of the chief distinctions between us and brutes. If there is any thing in blood, you may reasonably expect your children should be endowed with an uncommon share of good sense. Mr. Wortley's family and mine have both produced some of the greatest men that have been born in England : I mean Admiral Sandwich, and my grandfather, who was distinguished by the name of Wise William.* I have heard Lord Bute's father mentioned as an extraordinary genius, though he had not many opportunities of showing it ; and his uncle, the present Duke of Argyll† has one of the best heads I ever knew. I will therefore speak to you as supposing Lady Mary not only capable, but desirous of learning : in that case let her by all means be indulged in it. You will tell me I did not make it a part of your education : your prospect was very different from hers. As you had much in your circumstances to attract the highest offers, it seemed your business to learn how to live in the world, as it is hers to know how to be easy out of it. It is the common error of builders and parents to follow some plan they think beautiful (and perhaps is so), without considering that nothing is beautiful which is displaced. Hence we see so many edifices raised that the raisers can never inhabit, being too large for their fortunes. Vistas are laid open over barren heaths, and apartments contrived for a coolness very agreeable in Italy, but killing in the north of Britain : thus every woman endeavors to breed her daughter a fine lady, qualifying her for a station in which she will never appear, and at the same time incapacitating her for that retirement to which she is destined. Learning, if she has a real taste for it, will not

* William Pierrepont, second son of Robert Earl of Kingston, died 1679, aged 71.

† The Duke of Argyll here mentioned was Archibald, who, before he succeeded his brother John Duke of Argyll in the dukedom, was Earl of Islay.

only make her contented, but happy in it. No entertainment
is so cheap as reading, nor any pleasure so lasting. She will
not want new fashions, nor regret the loss of expensive diversions, or variety of company, if she can be amused with an
author, in her closet. To render this amusement complete,
she should be permitted to learn the languages. I have heard
it lamented that boys lose so many years in mere learning of
words. This is no objection to a girl, whose time is not so
precious. She can not advance herself in any profession, and
has, therefore, more hours to spare; and as you say her
memory is good, she will be very agreeably employed in this
way. There are two cautions to be given on this subject:
first, not to think herself learned when she can read Latin, or
even Greek. Languages are more properly to be called vehi-
cles of learning than learning itself, as may be observed in
many schoolmasters, who, though perhaps critics in grammar, are the most ignorant fellows upon earth. True knowledge consists in knowing things, not words. I would no further wish her a linguist than to enable her to read books in
their originals, that are often corrupted, and are always injured by translations. Two hours' application every morning
will bring this about much sooner than you can imagine,
and she will have leisure enough beside to run over the English poetry, which is a more important part of a woman's
education than it is generally supposed. Many a young
damsel has been ruined by a fine copy of verses, which she
would have laughed at if she had known it had been stolen
from Mr. Waller. I remember, when I was a girl, I saved
one of my companions from destruction who communicated
to me an epistle she was quite charmed with. As she had
naturally a good taste, she observed the lines were not so
smooth as Prior's or Pope's, but had more thought and spirit
than any of theirs. She was wonderfully delighted with such
a demonstration of her lover's sense and passion, and not a
little pleased with her own charms, that had force enough to
inspire such elegancies. In the midst of this triumph I

showed her that they were taken from Randolph's poems, and the unfortunate transcriber was dismissed with the scorn he deserved. To say truth, the poor plagiary was very unlucky to fall into my hands; that author being no longer in fashion, would have escaped any one of less universal reading than myself. You should encourage your daughter to talk over with you what she reads; and as you are very capable of distinguishing, take care she does not mistake pert folly for wit and humor, or rhyme for poetry, which are the common errors of young people, and have a train of ill consequences. The second caution to be given her (and which is most absolutely necessary) is to conceal whatever learning she attains with as much solicitude as she would hide crookedness or lameness. The parade of it can only serve to draw on her the envy, and consequently the most inveterate hatred, of all he and she fools, which will certainly be at least three parts in four of her acquaintance. The use of knowledge in our sex, beside the amusement of solitude, is to moderate the passions, and learn to be contented with a small expense which are the certain effects of a studious life; and it may be preferable even to that fame which men have engrossed to themselves, and will not suffer us to share. You will tell me I have not observed this rule myself; but you are mistaken: it is only inevitable accident that has given me any reputation that way. I have always carefully avoided it, and ever thought it a misfortune. The explanation of this paragraph would occasion a long digression, which I will not trouble you with, it being my present design only to say what I think useful for the instruction of my granddaughter, which I have much at heart. If she has the same inclination (I should say passion) for learning that I was born with, history, geography, and philosophy, will furnish her with materials to pass away cheerfully a longer life than is allotted to mortals. I believe there are few heads capable of making Sir Isaac Newton's calculations, but the result of them is not difficult to be understood by a moderate capacity. Do not fear this should make her affect the character of Lady ——, or Lady ——, or Mrs.——; those women are ridiculous, not because they have learning, but because they have it not. One thinks herself a complete historian, after reading Echard's Roman History; another a profound philosopher, having got by heart some of Pope's *unintelligible* essays; and a third an able divine on the strength of Whitfield's sermons. Thus you hear them screaming politics and controversy.

It is a saying of Thucydides, that ignorance is bold, and knowledge reserved. Indeed it is impossible to be far advanced in it, without being more humbled by a conviction of human ignorance than elated by learning. At the same time I recommend books, I neither exclude work nor drawing. I think it as scandalous for a woman not to know how to use a needle, as for a man not to know how to use a sword. I was once extremely fond of my pencil, and it was a great mortification to me when my father turned off my master, having made a considerable progress for the short time I learned. My over-eagerness in the pursuit of it had brought a weakness in my eyes, that made it necessary to leave off; and all the advantage I got was the improvement of my hand. I see, by hers, that practice will make her a ready writer; she may attain it by serving you for a secretary, when your health or affairs make it troublesome to you to write yourself; and custom will make it an agreeable amusement to her. She can not have too many for that station of life which will probably be her fate. The ultimate end of your education was to make you a good wife (and I have the comfort to hear that you are one); hers ought to be, to make her happy in a virgin state. I will not say it is happier; but it is undoubtedly safer than any marriage. In a lottery, where there is (at the lowest computation) ten thousand blanks to a prize, it is the most prudent choice not to venture. I have always been so thoroughly persuaded of this truth, that, notwithstanding the flattering views I had for you (as I never intended you a sacrifice to my vanity), I thought I owed you the justice to lay before you all the hazards attending matrimony : you may recollect I did so in the strongest manner. Perhaps you may have more success in the instructing your daughter: she has so much company at home, she will not need seeking it abroad, and will more readily take the notions you think fit to give her. As you were alone in my family, it would have been thought a great cruelty to suffer you no companions of your own age, especially having so many near relations, and I do not wonder their opinions influenced yours. I was not sorry to see you not determined on a single life, knowing it was not your father's intention, and contented myself with endeavoring to make your home so easy that you might not be in haste to leave it.

I am afraid you will think this a very long insignificant letter, I hope the kindness of the design will excuse it, being willing to give you every proof in my power that I am your most affectionate mother.

LETTER XV.

LOUVERE, Feb. 19, N. S., 1753.

MY DEAR CHILD—I gave you some general thoughts on the education of your children in my last letter ; but fearing you should think I neglected your request, by answering it with too much conciseness, I am resolved to add to it what little I know on that subject, and which may perhaps be useful to you in a concern with which you seem so nearly affected.

People commonly educate their children as they build their houses, according to some plan they think beautiful, without considering whether it is suited to the purposes for which they are designed. Almost all girls of quality are educated as if they were to be great ladies, which is often as little to be expected as an immoderate heat of the sun in the north of Scotland. You should teach yours to confine their desires to probabilities, to be as useful as is possible to themselves, and to think privacy (as it is) the happiest state of life. I do not doubt your giving them all the instructions necessary to form them to a virtuous life; but 'tis a fatal mistake to do this without proper restrictions. Vices are often hid under the name of virtues, and the practice of them followed by the worst of consequences. Sincerity, friendship, piety, disinterestedness, and generosity, are all great virtues; but pursued without discretion become criminal. I have seen ladies indulge their own ill-humor by being very rude and impertinent, and think they deserved approbation, by saying I love to speak truth. One of your acquaintances made a ball the next day after her mother died, to show she was sincere. I believe your own reflections will furnish you with but too many examples of the ill effects of the rest of the sentiments I have mentioned, when too warmly embraced. They are generally recommended to young people without limits or distinction, and this prejudice hurries them into great misfortunes, while they are applauding themselves in the noble practice (as they fancy) of very eminent virtues.

I can not help adding (out of my real affection for you) that I wish you would moderate that fondness you have for your children. I do not mean you should abate any part of your care, or not do your duty to them in its utmost extent; but I would have you early prepare yourself for disappointments, which are heavy in proportion to their being surprising. It is hardly possible in such a number that none should be unhappy; prepare yourself against a misfortune of that kind. I confess there is hardly any more difficult to support; yet, it is certain imagination has a great share in the pain of it, and it is more in our power—than it is commonly believed—to soften whatever ills are founded or augmented by fancy. Strictly speaking, there is but one real evil, I mean, acute pain; all other complaints are so considerably diminished by time that it is plain the grief is owing to our passion, since the sensation of it vanishes when that is over.

There is another mistake, I forgot to mention, usual in mothers; if any of their daughters are beauties, they take great pains to persuade them that they are ugly, or at least, that they think so, which the young woman never fails to believe springs from envy, and is perhaps not so much in the wrong. I would, if possible, give them a just notion of their figure, and show them how far it is valuable. Every advantage has its price, and may be over or undervalued. It is the common doctrine of (what are called) good books, to inspire a contempt for beauty, riches, greatness, etc., which has done as much mischief among the young of our sex as an over eager desire of them. Why they should not look on those things as blessings where they are bestowed, though not necessaries that it is impossible to be happy without, I can not conceive. I am persuaded the ruin of Lady F—— M—— was in a great measure owing to the notions given her by the good people that had the care of her. 'Tis true, her circumstances and your daughters' are very different: they should be taught to be content with privacy, and yet not neglect good fortune, if it should be offered them.

I am afraid I have tired you with my instructions. I do not give them as believing my age has furnished me with superior wisdom, but in compliance with your desire, and being fond of every opportunity that gives a proof of the tenderness with which I am ever your affectionate mother.

I should be glad if you sent me the third volume of Campbell's Architecture, and with it any other entertaining books. I have seen the Duchess of Marlborough's Memoirs, but should be glad of the Apology for a late resignation. As to the ale, 'tis now so late in the year, it is impossible it should come good. You do not mention your father; my last letter from him told he intended soon for England.

LETTER XVI.

LOUVERE, March 6, 1753.

I can not help writing a sort of apology for my last letter foreseeing that you will think it wrong, or at least Lord Bute will be extremely shocked, at the proposal of a learned education for daughters, which the generality of men believe to be as great a profanation as the clergy would do if the laity should presume to exercise the functions of the priesthood. I desire you would take notice, I would not have learning enjoined them as a task, but permitted as a pleasure, if their genius leads them naturally to it. I look upon my granddaughters as a sort of lay nuns: destiny may have laid up other things for them, but they have no reason to expect to pass their time otherwise than their aunts do at present; and I know, by experience, it is in the power of study not only to make solitude tolerable, but agreeable. I have now lived almost seven years in a stricter retirement than yours in the Isle of Bute, and can assure you I have never had half an hour heavy on my hands for want of something to do. Whoever will cultivate their own mind will find full employment. Every virtue does not only require great care in the planting, but as much daily solicitude in cherishing, as exotic fruits and flowers. The vices and passions (which I am afraid are the natural product of the soil) demand perpetual weeding. Add to this the search after knowledge (every branch of which is entertaining,) and the longest life is too short for the pursuit of it; which, though in some regard confined to very strait limits, leaves still a vast variety of amusements to those capable of tasting them, which is utterly impossible to be attained by those that are blinded by prejudice, the certain effect of an ignorant education. My own was one of the worst in the world, being exactly the same as Clarissa Harlowe's; her pious Mrs. Norton so perfectly resembling my governess, who had been nurse to my mother I could almost fancy the author was acquainted with her, she took so much pains, from my infancy, to fill my head with superstitious tales and false notions. It was none of her fault that I am not at this day afraid of witches and hob-goblins, or turned Methodist. Almost all girls are bred after this manner. I believe you are the only woman (perhaps I might say, person) that never was either frighted or cheated into any thing by your parents. I can truly affirm I never deceived any body in my life, excepting (which I confess has often happened undesigned) by speaking plainly ; as Earl Stanhope used to say (during his ministry) he always imposed on the foreign ministers by telling them the naked truth, which, as they thought *impossible* to come from the mouth of a statesman, they never failed to write information to their re-spective courts directly contrary to the assurances he gave them. Most people confound the ideas of sense and cunning, though there are really no two things in nature more opposite : it is, in part, from this false reasoning, the unjust custom pre-vails of debarring our sex from the advantages of learning, the men fancying the improvement of our understandings would only furnish us with more art to deceive them, which is di-rectly contrary to the truth. Fools are always enterprising, not seeing the difficulties of deceit, or the ill consequences of detection. I could give many examples of ladies whose ill conduct has been very notorious, which has been owing to that ignorance which has exposed them to idleness, which is justly called the mother of mishief. There is nothing so like the education of a woman of quality as that of a prince : they are taught to dance, and the exterior part of what is called good breeding, which, if they attain, they are extraordinary crea-tures in their kind, and have all the accomplishments required by their directors. The same characters are formed by the same lessons, which inclines me to think (if I dare say it) that nature has not placed us in an inferior rank to men, no more than the females of other animals, where we see no distinction of capacity ; though, I am persuaded, if there was a common-wealth of rational horses (as Doctor Swift has supposed), it would be an established maxim among them that a mare could

not be taught to pace.   I could add a great deal on this subject, but I am not now endeavoring to remove the prejudices
of mankind : my only design is to point out to my grand-
daughters the method of being contented with that retreat to
which unforseen circumstances may oblige them, and which is
perhaps preferable to all the show of public life.   It has always
been my inclination.   Lady Stafford (who knew me better than
any body else in the world, both from her own just discern-
ment, and my heart being ever as open to her as myself) used
to tell me, my true vocation was a monastery ; and I now find,
by experience, more sincere pleasures with my books and garden than all the flutter of a court could give me.

If you follow my advice in relation to Lady Mary, my correspondence may be of use to her; and I shall very willingly
give her those instructions that may be necessary in the pursuit
of her studies.   Before her age, I was in the most regular commerce with my grandmother, though the difference of our time
of life was much greater, she being past forty-five when she
married my grandfather.   She died at ninety-six, retaining, to
the last, the vivacity and clearness of her understanding, which
was very uncommon.

<hr>

LETTER XVII.

LOUVERE, June 3, N. S., 1753.

MY DEAR CHILD—You see I was not mistaken in supposing
we should have disputes concerning your daughters, if we
were together, since we can differ even at this distance.   The
sort of learning that I recommended is not so expensive, either
of time or money, as dancing, and in my opinion likely to be
of much more use to Lady ——, if her memory and apprehension are what you represented them to me.   However, every
one has a right to educate their children after their own way,
and I shall speak no more on that subject.   I was so much
pleased with the character you gave her, that had there been

any possibility of her undertaking so long a journey, I should certainly have asked for her; and I think out of such a number you might have spared her. I own my affection prevailed over my judgment in this thought, since nothing can be more imprudent than undertaking the management of another's child. I verily believe that had I carried six daughters out of England with me, I could have disposed of them all advantageously. The winter I passed at Rome there was an unusual concourse of English, many of them with great estates, and their own masters: as they had no admittance to the Roman ladies, nor understood the language, they had no way of passing their evenings but in my apartment, where I had always a full drawing-room. Their governors encouraged their assiduities as much as they could, finding I gave them lessons of economy and good conduct; and my authority was so great, it was a common threat among them, I'll tell Lady Mary what you say. I was judge of all their disputes, and my decisions always submitted to. While I staid, there was neither gaming, drinking, quarreling, or keeping. The Abbé Grant (a very honest good-natured North Briton, who has resided several years at Rome) was so much amazed at this uncommon regularity, he would have made me believe I was bound in conscience to pass my life there, for the good of my countrymen. I can assure you my vanity was not at all raised by this influence over them, knowing very well that had Lady Charlotte de Roussi been in my place, it would have been the same thing. There is that general emulation in mankind, I am fully persuaded if a dozen young fellows bred a bear among them, and saw no other creature, they would every day fall out for the bear's favors, and be extremely flattered by any mark of distinction shown by that ugly animal. Since my last return to Italy, which is now near seven years, I have lived in a solitude not unlike that of Robinson Crusoe, excepting my short trips to Louvere: my whole time is spent in my closet and garden, without regretting any conversation but that of my own family. The study of simples is a new amusement to me. I have no correspondence with any body at London but yourself and your father, whom I have not heard from a long time. My best wishes attend you and yours.

LETTER XVIII.

LOUVERE, July 10, 1753.

I have been these six weeks, and still am, at my dairy-house, which joins to my garden. I believe I have already told you it is a long mile from the castle, which is situate in the midst of a very large village, once a considerable town, part of the walls still remaining, and has not vacant ground enough about it to make a garden, which is my greatest amusement, it being now troublesome to walk, or even go in the chaise till the evening. I have fitted up in this farm-house a room for myself, that is to say, strewed the floor with rushes, covered the chimney with moss and branches, and adorned the room with basons of earthen-ware (which is made here to great perfection) filled with flowers, and put in some straw chairs, and a couch bed, which is my whole furniture. This spot of ground is so beautiful, I am afraid you will scarce credit the description, which, however, I can assure you shall be very literal, without any embellishment from imagination. It is on a bank, forming a kind of peninsula, raised from the river Oglio fifty feet, to which you may descend by easy stairs cut in the turf, and either take the air on the river, which is as large as the Thames at Richmond, or by walking an avenue two hundred yards on the side of it, you find a wood of a hundred acres, which was all ready cut into walks and ridings when I took it. I have only added fifteen bowers in different views, with seats of turf. They were easily made, here being a large quantity of underwood, and a great number of wild vines, which twist to the top of the highest trees, and from which they make a very good sort of wine they call *brusco*. I am now writing to you in one of these arbors, which is so thick shaded the sun

is not troublesome, even at noon. Another is on the side of
the river, where I have made a camp kitchen, that I may take
the fish, dress, and eat it immediately, and at the same time see
the barks, which ascend or descend every day to or from
Mantua, Guastalla, or Pont de Vie, all considerable towns.
This little wood is carpeted, in their succeeding seasons, with
violets and strawberries, inhabited by a nation of nightingales,
and filled with game of all kinds, excepting deer and wild boar,
the first being unknown here, and not being large enough for
the other.

My garden was a plain vineyard when it came into my hands
not two years ago, and it is, with a small expense, turned into
a garden that (apart from the advantage of the climate) I like
better than that of Kensington. The Italian vineyards are not
planted like those in France, but in clumps, fastened to trees
planted in equal ranks (commonly fruit trees), and continued
in festoons from one to another, which I have turned into covered galleries of shade, that I can walk in the heat without
being incommoded by it. I have made a dining-room of ver-
dure, capable of holding a table of twenty covers; the whole
ground is three hundred and seventeen feet in length, and two
hundred in breadth. You see it is far from large; but so pret-
tily disposed (though I say it), that I never saw a more agreeable rustic garden, abounding with all sorts of fruit, and producing a variety of wines. I would send you a pipe, if I did
not fear the customs would make you pay too dear for it. I
believe my description gives you but an imperfect idea of my
garden. Perhaps I shall succeed better in describing my manner of life, which is as regular as that of any monastery. I
generally rise at six, and as soon as I have breakfasted, put
myself at the head of my needle-women and work with them
till nine. I then inspect my dairy, and take a turn among my
poultry, which is a very large inquiry. I have, at present, two
hundred chickens, besides turkeys, geese, ducks, and peacocks.
All things have hitherto prospered under my care; my bees
and silk-worms are doubled, and I am told that, without acci-

dents, my capital will be so in two years' time. At eleven o'clock I retire to my books, I dare not indulge myself in that pleasure above an hour. At twelve I constantly dine, and sleep after dinner till about three. I then send for some of my old priests, and either play at piquet or whist, till 'tis cool enough to go out. One evening I walk in my wood, where I often sup, take the air on horseback the next, and go on the water the third. The fishery of this part of the river belongs to me; and my fisherman's little boat (to which I have a green lutestring awning) serves me for a barge. He and his son are my rowers without any expense, he being very well paid by the profit of the fish, which I give him on condition of having every day one dish for my table. Here is plenty of every sort of fresh water fish (excepting salmon); but we have a large trout so like it that I who have almost forgot the taste, do not distinguish it.

We are both placed properly in regard to our different times of life: you amid the fair, the gallant, and the gay; I, in a retreat, where I enjoy every amusement that solitude can afford. I confess I sometimes wish for a little conversation; but I reflect that the commerce of the world gives more uneasiness than pleasure, and quiet is all the hope that can reasonably be indulged at my age.

LETTER XIX.

LOUVERE, Nov. 27, N. S., 1753.

DEAR CHILD—By the account you give me of London, I think it very much reformed; at least you have one sin the less, and it was a very reigning one in my time, I mean scandal: it must be literally reduced to a whisper, since the custom of living all together. I hope it has also banished the fashion of talking all at once, which was very prevailing when I was in town, and may perhaps contribute to brotherly love and unity, which was so much declined in my memory that it was hard to invite six people that would not, by cold looks, or piquing reflections, affront one another. I suppose parties are at an end, though I fear it is the consequence of the old almanac prophecy, " Poverty brings peace ;" and I fancy you really follow the French mode, and the lady keeps an assembly, that the assembly may keep the lady, and card money pay for clothes and equipage, as well as cards and candles. I find I should be as solitary in London as I am here in the country, it being impossible for me to submit to live in a *drum*, which I think so far from a cure of uneasiness, that it is, in my opinion, adding one more to the heap. There are so many attached to humanity, 'tis impossible to fly from them all; but experience has confirmed to me (what I always thought) that the pursuit of pleasure will be ever attended with pain, and the study of ease be most certainly accompanied with pleasures. I have had this morning as much delight in a walk in the sun as ever I felt formerly in the crowded mall, even when I imagined I had my share of the admiration of the place, which was generally soured, before I slept, by the informations of my female friends, who seldom failed to tell me it was observed that I showed an inch above my shoe-heels, or some other criticism of equal weight, which was construed affectation, and utterly destroyed all the satisfaction *my* vanity had given me. I have now no other but in my little housewifery, which is easily gratified in this country, where, by the help of my recipe-book, I make a very shining figure among my neighbors, by the introduction of custards, cheesecakes, and mince-pies, which were entirely unknown to these parts, and are received with universal applause, and have reason to believe will preserve my memory even to future ages, particularly by the art of butter-making, in which I have so improved them that they now make as good as in any part of England.

LETTER XX.

LOUVERE, Dec. 13, 1753.

DEAR CHILD—I have wrote you so many letters without any return, that if I loved you at all less than I do, I should certainly give over writing. I received a kind letter last post from Lady Oxford, which gives me hopes I shall at length receive yours, being persuaded you have not neglected our correspondence, though I am not so happy to have the pleasure of it.

I have little to say from this solitude, having already sent you a description of my garden, which, with my books, takes up all my time. I made a small excursion last week to visit a nunnery, twelve miles from hence, which is the only institution of the kind in all Italy. It is in a town in the state of Mantua, founded by a princess of the house of Gonzaga, one of whom (now very old) is the present abbess: they are dressed in black, and wear a thin cypress vail at the back of their heads, excepting which, they have no mark of a religious habit, being set out in their hair, and having no guimpe, but wearing *des collets montés*, for which I have no name in English, but you may have seen them in very old pictures, being in fashion before and after ruffs. Their house is a very large handsome building, though not regular, every sister having liberty to build her own apartment to her taste, which consists of as many rooms as she pleases: they have each a separate kitchen, and keep cooks and what other servants they think proper, though there is a very fine public refectory: they are permitted to dine in private whenever they please. Their garden is very large, and the most adorned of any in these parts. They have no grates, and make what visits they will, always two together, and receive those of the men as well as ladies. I was accompanied, when I went, with all the nobility of the town, and they showed me all the house, without excluding the gentlemen: but what I think the most remarkable privilege is a country-house, which belongs to them, three miles from the town, where they pass every vintage, and at any time any four of them may take their pleasure there for as many days as they choose. They seem to differ from the *chanoinesse* of Flanders only in their vow of celibacy. They take pensioners, but only those of quality. I saw here a niece of General Brown. Those that profess are obliged to prove a descent as noble as the Knights of Malta. Upon the whole, I think it the most agreeable community I have seen, and their behavior more decent than that of the cloistered nuns, who I have heard say themselves, that the grate permits all liberty of speech since it leaves them no other, and indeed, they generally talk as if they thought so. I went to a monastery, which gave me occasion to know a great deal of their conduct, which (though the convent of the best reputation in that town where it is) was such as I would as soon put a girl in a play-house for education as send her among them.

My paper is at an end, and hardly leaves room for my compliments to Lord Bute, blessing to my grandchildren, and assurance to yourself of being your most affectionate mother.

LETTER XXI.

13th May, 1754.

It was with great pleasure I received my dear child's letter of April 15, this day, May 13. Do not imagine that I have had hard thoughts of you when I lamented your silence; I think I know your good heart too well to suspect you of any unkindness to me; in your circumstances many unavoidable accidents may hinder your writing, but having not heard from you for many months, my fears for your health made me very uneasy. I am surprised I am not oftener low-spirited, considering the vexations I am exposed to by the folly of Murray; I suppose he attributes to me some of the marks of contempt he is treated with ; without remembering that he was in no higher esteem before I came. I confess I have received great civilities from some friends that I made here so long ago as the year '40, but upon my honor have never named his name, or heard him mentioned by any noble Venetian whatever ; nor have in any shape given him the least provocation to all the low malice he has shown me, which I have overlooked as below my notice, and would not trouble you with any part of it at present if he had not invented a new persecution which may be productive of ill consequences. Here arrived, a few days ago, Sir James Stuart with his lady ; that name was sufficient to make me fly to wait on her. I was charmed to find a man of uncommon sense and learning, and a lady that without beauty is more amiable than the fairest of her sex. I offered them all the little good offices in my power, and invited them to supper ; upon which our wise minister has discovered that I am in the interest of popery and slavery. As he has often said the same thing of Mr. Pitt, it would give me no mortification, if I did not apprehend that his fertile imagination may support this wise idea by such circumstances as may influence those that do not know me. It is very remarkable that, after having suffered all the rage of that party at Avignon, for my attachment to the present reigning family, I should be accused here of favoring rebellion, when I hoped all our odious divisions were forgotten.

I return you many thanks, my dear child, for your kind intention of sending me another set of books. I am still in your debt nine shillings, and send you inclosed a note on Child to pay for whatever you buy ; but no more duplicates ; as well as I love nonsense, I do not desire to have it twice over in the same words ; no translations ; no periodical papers, though, I confess, some of the World entertained me very much, particularly Lord Chesterfield and Harry Walpole, whom I knew at Florence ; but whenever I met Dodsley I wished him out of the World with all my heart. The title was a very lucky one, being as you see productive of puns world without end ; which is all the species of wit some people can either practice or understand. I beg you would direct the next box to me, without passing through the hands of Smith ;* he makes so much merit of giving himself the trouble of asking for it that I am quite weary of him ; beside that he imposes upon me in every thing. He has lately married Murray's† sister, a beauteous virgin of forty, who after having refused all the peers in England, because the nicety of her conscience would not permit her to give her hand when her heart was untouched, she remained without a husband till the charms of that fine gentleman Mr. Smith, who is only eighty-two, determined her to change her condition. In short, they are (as Lord Orrery says of Swift and company) an illustrious group, but with that I have nothing to do. I should be sorry to ruin any body, or offend a man of such strict honor as Lord Holderness, who, like a great politician, has provided for a worthless relation without any expense. It has long been a maxim not to consider if a man is fit for a place, but if the place is fit for him, and we see the fruit of these Machiavellian proceedings. All I desire is, that Mr. Pitt would require of this noble minister to behave civilly to me, the contrary conduct being very disagreeable. I will talk further on this subject in another letter, if this arrives safely. Let me have an answer as soon as possible, and think of me as your most affectionate mother.

My compliments to Lord Bute, and blessing to all yours, who are very near my heart.

LETTER XXII.

LOUVERE, June 23, 1754.

MY DEAR CHILD—I have promised you some remarks on all the books I have received. I believe you would easily forgive

* Joseph Smith, Esq., Consul at Venice. He made a large collection of paintings and gems, which were purchased by King George the Third for £20,000. The Dactyliotheca Smithiana, in two vols. quarto was published in 1765.

† Mr. Murray was afterward embassador at the Porte, and died in the Lazaretto at Venice in 1777, upon his return to England.

me not keeping my word; however, I shall go on. The Ram-
bler is certainly a strong misnomer; he always plods in the
beaten road of his predecessors, following the Spectator (with
the same pace a pack-horse would do a hunter) in the style that
is proper to lengthen a paper. These writers, may, perhaps,
be of service to the public, which is saying a great deal in their
favor. There are numbers of both sexes who never read any-
thing but such productions, and can not spare time, from doing
nothing, to go through a sixpenny pamphlet. Such gentle
readers may be improved by a moral hint, which, though repeated over and over, from generation to generation, they never
heard in their lives. I should be glad to know the name of this
laborious author. H. Fielding has given a true picture of himself and his first wife, in the characters of Mr. and Mrs. Booth,
some compliments to his own figure excepted; and, I am persuaded, several of the incidents he mentions are real matters
of fact. I wonder he does not perceive Tom Jones and Mr.
Booth are sorry scoundrels. All this sort of books have the
same fault, which I can not easily pardon, being very mischiev-
ous. They place a merit in extravagant passions, and encourage young people to hope for impossible events, to draw them
out of the misery they choose to plunge themselves into, expecting legacies from unknown relations, and generous ben-
efactors to distressed virtue, as much out of nature as fairy
treasures. Fielding has really a fund of true humor, and
was to be pitied at his first entrance into the world, having
no choice, as he said himself, but to be a hackney writer, or
a hackney coachman. His genius deserved a better fate;
but I can not help blaming that continued indiscretion, to
give it the softest name, that has run through his life, and I
am afraid still remains. I guessed R. Random to be his,
though without his name. I can not think Ferdinand Fathom
wrote by the same hand, it is every way so much below it.
Sally Fielding has mended her style in her last volume of
David Simple, which conveys a useful moral, though she does
not seem to have intended it: I mean, shows the ill conse-

quences of not providing against casual losses, which happen to almost every body. Mr. Orgueil's character is well drawn, and is frequently to be met with. The Art of Tormenting, the Female Quixote, and Sir C. Goodville, are all sale work. I suppose they proceed from her pen, and I heartily pity her, constrained by her circumstances to seek her bread by a method, I do not doubt, she despises. Tell me who is that accomplished countess she celebrates. I left no such person in London ; nor can I imagine who is meant by the English Sappho mentioned in Betsy Thoughtless, whose adventures, and those of Jemmy Jessamy, gave me some amusement. I was better entertained by the valet, who very fairly represents how you are bought and sold by your servants. I am now so accustomed to another manner of treatment, it would be difficult to me to suffer them. His adventures have the uncommon merit of ending in a surprising manner. The general want of invention which reigns among our writers, inclines me to think it is not the natural growth of our island, which has not sun enough to warm the imagination. The press is loaded by the servile flock of imitators. Lord Bolingbroke would have quoted Horace in this place. Since I was born, no original has appeared excepting Congreve and Fielding, who would, I believe, have approached nearer to his excellencies, if not forced by necessity to publish without correction, and throw many productions into the world he would have thrown into the fire, if meat could have been got without money, or money without scribbling. The greatest virtue, justice, and the most distinguishing prerogative of mankind, writing, when duly executed, do honor to human nature ; but when degenerated into trades, are the most contemptible ways of getting bread. I am sorry not to see any more of Peregrine Pickle's performances ; I wish you would tell me his name.

I can't forbear saying something in relation to my granddaughters, who are very near my heart. If any of them are fond of reading, I would not advise you to hinder them (chiefly because it is impossible) seeing poetry, plays, or romances; but accustom them to talk over what they read, and point out to them, as you are very capable of doing, the absurdity often concealed under fine expressions, where the sound is apt to engage the admiration of young people. I was so much charmed, at fourteen, with the dialogue of Henry and Emma, I can say it by heart to this day, without reflecting on the monstrous folly of the story in plain prose, where a young heiress to a fond father is represented falling in love with a fellow she had only seen as a huntsman, a falconer, and a beggar, and who confesses, without any circumstances of excuse, that he is obliged to run his country, having newly committed a murder. She ought reasonably to have supposed him, at best, a highwayman; yet the virtuous virgin resolves to run away with him, to live among the banditti, and wait upon his trollop, if she had no other way of enjoying his company. This senseless tale is, however, so well varnished with melody of words, and pomp of sentiments, I am convinced it has hurt more girls than ever were injured by the worst poems extant.

I fear this counsel has been repeated to you before; but I have lost so many letters designed for you, I know not which you have received. If you would have me avoid this fault, you must take notice of those that arrive, which you very seldom do. My dear child, God bless you and yours.

LETTER XXIII.

LOUVERE, July 24, 1754.

It is always a great pleasure to me, my dear child, to hear of your health, and that of your family. This year has been fatal to the literati of Italy. The Marquis Maffei soon followed Cardinal Querini. He was in England when you were married. Perhaps you may remember his coming to see your father's Greek inscription :* he was then an old man, and con-

* Presented by Mr. Wortley to Trinity College, Cambridge.

sequently now a great age; but preserved his memory and senses in their first vigor. After having made the tour of Europe in the search of antiquities, he fixed his residence in his native town of Verona, where he erected himself a little empire, from the general esteem, and a conversation (so they call an assembly) which he established in his palace, which is one of the largest in that place, and so luckily situated that it is between the theater and the ancient amphitheater. He made piazzas leading to each of them, filled with shops, where were sold coffee, tea, chocolate, all sorts of sweetmeats, and in the midst, a court well kept, and sanded, for the use of those young gentlemen who would exercise their managed horses, or show their mistresses their skill in riding. His gallery was open every evening at five o'clock, where he had a fine collection of antiquities, and two large cabinets of medals, intaglios, and cameos, arranged in exact order. His library joined to it; and on the other side a suit of five rooms, the first of which was destined to dancing, the second to cards (but all games of hazard excluded), and the others (where he himself presided in an easy chair) sacred to conversation, which always turned upon some point of learning, either historical or poetical. Controversy and politics being utterly prohibited, he generally proposed the subject, and took great delight in instructing the young people, who were obliged to seek the medal, or explain the inscription, that illustrated any fact they discoursed of. Those who chose the diversion of the public walks, or theater, went thither, but never failed returning to give an account of the drama, which produced a critical dissertation on that subject, the marquis having given shining proofs of his skill in that art. His tragedy of Merope, which is much injured by Voltaire's translation, being esteemed a master-piece; and his comedy of the Ceremonies, being a just ridicule of those formal fopperies, it has gone a great way in helping to banish them out of Italy. The walkers contributed to the entertainment by an account of some herb, or flower, which led the way to a botanical conversation; or, if they were such inaccurate observers as to have nothing of that kind to offer, they repeated some pastoral description. One day in the week was set apart for music, vocal and instrumental, but no mercenaries were admitted to the concert. Thus, at very little expense (his fortune not permitting a large one), he had the happiness of giving his countrymen a taste of polite pleasure, and showing the youth how to pass their time agreeably without debauchery; and if I durst say it) in so doing, has been a greater benefactor to his country than the cardinal, with all his magnificent foundations, and voluminous writings, to support superstition, and create disputes on things, for the most part, in their own nature indifferent. The Veronese nobility, having no road open to advancement, are not tormented with ambition, or its child, faction; and having learned to make the best of the health and fortune allotted them, terminate all their views in elegant pleasure. They say God has reserved glory to himself, and permitted pleasure to the pursuit of man. In the autumn, which is here the pleasanest season of the year, a band of about thirty join their hunting equipages, and, carrying with them a portable theater and a set of music, make a progress in the neighboring provinces, where they hunt every morning, perform an opera every Sunday, and other plays the rest of the week, to the entertainment of all the neighborhood. I have had many honorable invitations from my old friend Maffei* to make one of this society; but some accident or other has always prevented me. You that are accustomed to hear of deep political schemes and wise harangues, will despise, perhaps, this trifling life. I look upon them in another light; as a sect of rational philosophers,

> Who sing and dance, and laugh away their time,
> Fresh as their groves, and happy as their clime.

---

* The Marquis Scipione Maffei, the author of the "Verona Illustrata," 1733, folio, and the "Museum Veronese," 1749, folio, was very highly esteemed in the literary world as an antiquary and virtuoso.

LETTER XXIV.

LOUVERE, Sep. 20, 1754.

MY DEAR CHILD—I am extremely delighted by your last letter. Your pleasure in your daughter's company is exactly what I have felt in yours, and recalls to me many tender ideas perhaps better forgot. You observe very justly, that my affection, which was confined to one, must be still more intense than yours, which is divided among so many. I can not help being anxious for their future welfare, though thoroughly convinced of the folly of being so. Human prudence is so short-sighted that it is common to see the wisest schemes disappointed, and things often take a more favorable turn than there is any apparent reason to expect. My poor sister Gower, I really think, shortened her life by fretting at the disagreeable prospect of a numerous family, slenderly provided for; yet you see how well fortune has disposed of them. You may be as lucky as Lady Selina Bathurst.* I wish Lady Mary's destiny may lead her to a young gentleman I saw this spring.† He is son to Judge Hervey, but takes the name of Desbouverie, on inheriting a very large estate from his mother. He will not charm at first sight; but I never saw a young man of better understanding with the strictest notions of honor and morality, and, in my opinion, a peculiar sweetness of temper. Our acquaintance was short, he being summoned to England on the death of his younger brother. I am persuaded he will never marry for money, nor even for beauty. Your daughter's character perfectly answers the description of what he wished for his bride. Our conversation happened on the subject of matri-

* Lady Selina Shirley, daughter of Robert Earl Ferrers, wife of Peter Bathurst, Esq., of Clarendon Park, Wilts.

† The gentleman referred to was the son of John Hervey of Beachworth, Esq., one of the Welsh judges, by Anne eldest daughter of Christopher Desbouvries by Elizabeth his wife, daughter and sole heir of Ralph Foreman, Esq., of Beachworth in Surrey. This Christopher was the youngest son of Sir Edward Desbouvries, knighted in 1694, one of the ancestors of the Earl of Radnor.

13*

mony, in his last visit, his mind being much perplexed on that subject, supposing his father, who is old and infirm, had sent for him with some view of that sort.

You will laugh at the castles I build in relation to my grandchildren ; and will scarcely think it possible that those I have never seen should so much employ my thoughts. I can assure you that they are, next to yourself, the objects of my tenderest concern ; and it is not from custom, but my heart, when I send them my blessing, and say that I am your most affectionate mother.

LETTER XXV.

LOUVERE, 1754.

MY DEAR CHILD—I received yours of September 15, this morning, October 9, and am exceedingly glad of the health of you and your family. I am fond of your little Louisa : to say truth, I was afraid of a Bess, a Peg, or a Suky, which all give me the ideas of washing tubs and scowering of kettles.

I am much obliged to Mr. Hamilton, which is according to the academy of compliments ; more his goodness than my de-serts : I saw him but twice, and both times in mixed company, but am surprised you have never mentioned Lord Roseberry,* by whom I sent a packet to you, and took some pains to show him civilities : he breakfasted with me at Padua : I gave him bread and butter of my own manufacture, which is the admiration of all the English. He promised to give you full information of myself, and all my employments. He seemed delighted with my house and gardens, and perhaps has forgot he ever saw me, or any thing that belonged to me. We have had many English here. Mr. G——le,† his lady, and her

----

* James Primerose, Earl of Roseberry, died November 28, 1755.

† Greville. Of the book in question, Horace Walpole, in a letter to General Conway, speaks thus: "A wonderful book, by a more won-derful author, Greville. It is called Maxims and Characters ; several of

suite of adorers, deserve particular mention : he was so good to present me with his curious book : since the days of the Honorable Mr. Edward, nothing has ever been published like it. I told him the age wanted an Earl of Dorset to celebrate it properly ; and he was so well pleased with that speech that he visited me every day, to the great comfort of madame, who was entertained, meanwhile, with parties of pleasure of another kind, though I fear I lost his esteem at last by refusing to correspond with him. However, I qualified my denial by complaining of my bad eyes not permitting me to multiply my correspondents. I could give you the characters of many other travelers, if I thought it would be of any use to you. It is melancholy to see the pains our pious minister takes to debauch the younger sort of them : but, as you say, all is melancholy that relates to Great Britain. I have a high value for Mr. Pitt's* probity and understanding, without having the honor of being acquainted with him. I am persuaded he is able to do whatever is within the bounds of possibility ; but there is an Augæan stable to be cleaned, and several other labors that I doubt if Hercules himself would be equal to.

LETTER XXVI.

LOUVERE, March 1, 1755.

I pity Lady Mary Coke† extremely. You will be surprised at this sentiment, when she is the present envy of her sex, in the possession of youth, health, wealth, wit, beauty, and liberty. All these seeming advantages will prove snares to

the former are pretty; all the latter so absurd, that one in particular which at the beginning you take for the character of a man, turns out to be the character of a post-chaise.

* The first Earl of Chatham.

† Lady Mary Coke, the fifth daughter of John Duke of Argyll, was married to Edward Lord Viscount Coke, eldest son of the Earl of Leicester, who died in 1755. The title became extinct in that family in 1759.

her. She appears to me, as I observed in a former instance, to be walking blindfolded, upon stilts, amid precipices. She is at a dangerous time of life, when the passions are in full vigor, and, we are apt to flatter ourselves, the understanding arrived at maturity. People are never so near playing the fool as when they think themselves wise : they lay aside that distrust which is the surest guard against indiscretion, and venture on many steps they would have trembled at at fifteen; and, like children, are never so much exposed to falling as when they first leave off leading-strings. I think nothing but a miracle, or the support of a guardian angel, can protect her. It is true (except I am much mistaken), nature has furnished her with one very good defense. I took particular notice of her, both from my own liking her, and her uncommonly obliging behavior to me. She was then of an age not capable of much disguise, and I thought she had a great turn to economy : it is an admirable shield against the most fatal weaknesses. Those who have the good fortune to be born with that inclination seldom ruin themselves, and are early aware of the designs laid against them. Yet, with all that precaution, she will have so many plots contrived for her destruction that she will find it very difficult to escape ; and if she is a second time unhappily engaged, it will make her much more miserable than the first; as all misfortunes, brought on by our own imprudence, are the most wounding to a sensible heart. The most certain security would be that diffidence which naturally arises from an impartial self-examination. But this is the hardest of all tasks, requiring great reflection, long retirement, and is strongly repugnant to our own vanity, which very unwillingly reveals, even to ourselves, our common frailty, though it is every way a useful study. Mr. Locke, who has made a more exact dissection of the human mind than any man before him, declares that he gained all his knowledge from the consideration of himself. It is indeed necessary to judge of others. You condemn Lord Cornbury without knowing what he could say in his justification. I am persuaded he thought he performed an act of rigid justice, in excluding the Duchess of Queensberry from an inheritance to which she had no natural, though a legal, right; especially having had a large portion from her real father. I have heard him talk on that subject without naming names, and call it a robbery within the law. He carried that notion to a great height. I agreed with him, that a woman who produced a false child into a family, incurred the highest degree of guilt (being irreparable); but I could not be of his opinion, that it was the duty of the child, in such a case, to renounce the fortune the law entitled it to. You see he has acted by a maxim he imagined just. Lady E——x* being, inside and out, resembling Lord Clarendon; and whoever remembers Lord Carleton's eyes, must confess they now shine in the Duchess's face. I am not bribed, by Lord Cornbery's behavior to me, to find excuses for him; but I have always endeavored to look on the conduct of my acquaintance without any regard to their way of acting toward me. I can say, with truth, I have strictly adhered to this principle whenever I have been injured; but I own, to my shame be it spoken, the love of flattery has sometimes prevailed on me, under the mask of gratitude, to think better of people than they deserved, when they have professed more value for me than I was conscious of meriting. I slide insensibly into talking of myself, though I always resolve against it. I will rescue you from so dull a subject by concluding my letter with my compliments to Lord Bute, my blessing to my grandchildren, and the assurance of my being ever your most affectionate mother.

LETTER XXVII.

April 1, 1755.

My Dear Child—I have this minute received yours of February 1. I had one before (which I have answered), in which you mention some changes among your ministerial subalterns.

* Essex.

I see the motion of the puppets, but not the master that directs them; nor can guess at him. By the help of some miserable newspapers, with my own reflections, I can form such a dim telescope as serves astronomers to survey the moon. I can discern spots and inequalities, but your beauties (if you have any) are invisible to me: your provinces of politics, gallantry, and literature, all *terra incognita.* The merchant, who undertook to deliver my ring to Lady Jane, assures me it is delivered, though I have no advice of it either from her or you. Here are two new fortunes far superior to Miss Crawley's. They are become so by an accident which would be very extraordinary in London. Their father was a Greek, and had been several years chief farmer of the customs at Venice. About ten days ago, a creditor, who had a demand of five hundred crowns, was very importunate with him. He answered he was not satisfied it was due to him, and would examine his accounts. After much pressing without being able to obtain any other reply, the fellow drew his stiletto, and in one stroke stabbed him to the heart. The noise of his fall brought in his servants; the resolute assassin drew a pistol from his pocket and shot himself through the head. The merchant has left no will, and is said to have been worth four millions of sequins, all of which will be divided between two daughters. If it be only half as much, they are (I believe) the greatest heiresses in Europe. It is certain he has died immensely rich. The eldest lady is but eighteen; and both of them are reputed to be very beautiful. I hear they declare they will choose husbands of their own country and religion, and refuse any other prospects. If they keep their resolution I shall admire them much. Since they are destined to be a prey, 'tis a sort of patriotism to enrich their own country with their spoils. You put me out of patience when you complain you want subjects to entertain me. You need not go out of your own walls for that purpose. You have within them ten strangers to me, whose characters interest me **extremely.** I should be glad to know something of them inside and out. What provision of wit and beauty has Heaven allotted them ? I shall be sorry if all the talents have fallen into the male part of your family. Do not forget, among the books, Fielding's Posthumous Works, his Journey to the Next World, and Jon. Wild's Memoirs; also those of a Young Lady, and the History of London. I have said this already, but am afraid the letter is lost among many others.

LETTER XXVIII.

LOUVERE, July 20, N. S., 1755.

My DEAR- CHILD—I have now read over the books you were so good to send, and intend to say something of them all, though some are not worth speaking of. I shall begin, in respect to his dignity, with Lord Bolingbroke, who is a glaring proof how far vanity can blind a man, and how easy it is to varnish over to one's self the most criminal conduct. He declares he always loved his country, though he confesses he endeavored to betray her to popery and slavery ; and loved his friends, though he abandoned them in distress, with all the blackest circumstances of treachery. His account of the peace of Utrecht is almost equally unfair or partial : I shall allow that, perhaps, the views of the Whigs, at that time, were too vast, and the nation, dazzled by military glory, had hopes too sanguine; but surely the same terms that the French consented to, at the treaty of Gertruydenberg, might have been obtained; or if the displacing of the Duke of Marlborough raised the spirits of our enemies to a degree of refusing what they had before offered, how can he excuse the guilt of removing him from the head of a victorious army, and exposing us to submit to any articles of peace, being unable to continue the war? I agree with him that the idea of conquering France is a wild extravagant notion, and would, if possible, be impolitic ; but she might have been reduced to such a state as would have rendered her incapable of being terrible to her neighbors for some ages : nor should we have been obliged, as we have done almost ever since, to bribe the French ministers to let us live in quiet. So much for his political reasonings, which, I confess, are delivered in a florid, easy style ; but I can not be of Lord Orrery's opinion, that he is one of the best English writers. Well turned periods, or smooth lines, are not the perfection either of prose or verse; they may serve to adorn, but can never stand in the place of good sense. Copiousness of words, however ranged, is always false eloquence, though it will ever impose on some sort of understandings. How many readers and admirers has Madame de Sévigné, who only gives us, in a lively manner, and fashionable phrases, mean sentiments, vulgar prejudices, and endless repetitions ? Sometimes the tittle-tattle of a fine lady, sometimes that of an old nurse, always tittle-tattle; yet so well gilt over by airy expressions, and a flowing style, she will always please the same people to whom Lord Bolingbroke will shine as a first-rate author. She is so far to be excused as her letters were not intended for the press ; while he labors to display to posterity all the wit and learning he is master of and sometimes spoils a good argument by a profusion of words, running out into several pages a thought that might have been more clearly expressed in a few lines, and, what is worse, often falls into contradiction and repetitions, which are almost unavoidable to all voluminous writers, and can only be forgiven to those retailers whose necessity compels them to diurnal scribbling, who load their meaning with epithets, and run into digressions, because (in the jockey phrase) it rids ground, that is, covers a certain quantity of paper, to answer the demand of the day. A great part of Lord Bolingbroke's letters are designed to show his reading, which, indeed, appears to have been very extensive ; but I can not perceive that such a minute account of it can be of any use to the pupil he pretends to instruct; nor can I help thinking he is far below either Tillotson or Addison, even in style, though the latter was sometimes more diffuse than his judgment approved, to furnish out the length of a daily Spectator. I own I have small regard for Lord Bolingbroke as an author, and the highest contempt for him as a man. He came into the world greatly favored both by nature and fortune, blessed with a noble birth, heir to a large estate, endowed with a strong constitution, and, as I have heard, a beautiful figure, high spirits, a good memory, and a lively apprehension, which was cultivated by a learned education: all these glorious advantages being left to the direction of a judgment stifled by unbounded vanity, he dishonored his birth, lost his estate, ruined his reputation, and destroyed his health, by a wild pursuit of eminence even in vice and trifles.

I am far from making misfortune a matter of reproach. I know there are accidental occurrences not to be foreseen or avoided by human prudence, by which a character may be injured, wealth dissipated, or a constitution impaired: but I think I may reasonably despise the understanding of one who conducts himself in such a manner as naturally produces such lamentable consequences, and continues in the same destructive paths to the end of a long life, ostentatiously boasting of morals and philosophy in print, and with equal ostentation bragging of the scenes of low debauchery in public conversation, though deplorably weak both in mind and body, and his virtue and his vigor in a state of non-existence. His confederacy with Swift and Pope puts me in mind of that of Bessus and his swordmen, in the King and No King, who endeavor to support themselves by giving certificates of each other's merit. Pope has triumphantly declared that they may do and say whatever silly things they please, they will still be the greatest geniuses nature ever exhibited. I am delighted with the comparison given of their benevolence, which is indeed most amply figured by a circle in the water, which widens till it comes to nothing at all; but I am provoked at Lord Bolingbroke's misrepresentation of my favorite Atticus, who seems to have been the only Roman that, from good sense, had a true notion of the times in which he lived, in which the republic was inevitably perishing, and the two factions, who pretended to support it, equally endeavoring to gratify their ambition in its ruin. A wise man, in that case, would certainly declare for neither, and try to save himself and family from the general wreck, which could not be done but by a superiority of understanding acknowledged on both sides. I see no glory in losing life or fortune by being the dupe of either, and very much applaud that conduct which could preserve a universal esteem amid the fury of opposite parties. We are obliged to act vigorously, where action can do any good; but in a storm, when it is impossible to work with success, the best hands and ablest pilots may laudably gain the shore if they can. Atticus could be a friend to men, without awakening their resentment, and be satisfied with his own virtue without seeking popular fame. He had the reward of his wisdom in his tranquillity, and will ever stand among the few examples of true philosophy, either ancient or modern.

You must forgive this tedious dissertation. I hope you read in the same spirit I write, and take as proof of affection whatever is sent you by your truly affectionate mother.

I must add a few words on the Essay on Exile, which I read with attention, as a subject that touched me. I found the most abject dejection under a pretended fortitude. That the author felt it, can be no doubt to one who knows (as I do) the mean submissions and solemn promises he made to obtain a return, flattering himself (I suppose) he must of course appear to be at the head of the administration, as every ensign of sixteen fancies he is in a fair way to be a general, on the first sight of his commission.

You will think I have been too long on the character of Atticus. I own I took pleasure in explaining it. Pope thought himself covertly very severe on Addison, by giving him that name; and I feel indignation whenever he is abused, both from his own merit, and because he was ever your father's friend; besides that, it is naturally disgusting to see him lampooned after his death by the same man who paid him the most servile court while he lived, and was, besides highly obliged by him.

LETTER XXIX.

LOUVERE, September 22, 1755.

MY DEAR CHILD—I received, two days ago, the box of books you were so kind to send; but I can scarce say whether my pleasure or disappointment was the greater. I was much pleased to see before me a fund of amusement, but heartily vexed to find your letter consisting only of three lines and a half. Why will you not employ ·Lady Mary as secretary, if it is troublesome to you to write? I have told you over and over you may at the same time oblige your mother and improve your daughter, both which I should think very agreeable to yourself. You can never want something to say. The history of your nursery, if you had no other subject to write on, would be very acceptable to me. I am such a stranger to every thing in England, I should be glad to hear more particulars relating to the families I am acquainted with—if Miss Liddel* marries the Lord Euston I know, or his nephew, who has succeeded him; if Lord Berkeley† has left children; and several trifles of that sort, that would be a satisfaction to my curiosity. I am sorry for H. Fielding's death, not only as I shall read no more of his writings, but I believe he lost more than others, as no man enjoyed life more than he did, though few had less reason to do so, the highest of his preferment being raking in the lowest sinks of vice and misery. I should think it a nobler and less nauseous employment to be one of the staff-officers that conduct the nocturnal weddings. His happy constitution (even when he had, with great pains, half demolished it) made

* Married Augustus Henry Duke of Grafton, January 29, 1756.

† Augustus Earl of Berkeley died January 9, 1755, and left two sons and two daughters.

him forget every thing when he was before a venison pasty, or over a flask of Champagne, and I am persuaded he has known more happy moments than any prince upon earth. His natural spirits gave him rapture with his cook-maid, and cheerfulness when he was starving in a garret. There was a great similitude between his character and that of Sir Richard Steele. He had the advantage both in learning, and, in my opinion, genius. They both agreed in wanting money in spite of all their friends, and would have wanted it, if their hereditary lands had been as extensive as their imagination; yet each of them was so formed for happiness it is pity he was not immortal. I have read The Cry; and if I would write in the style to be admired by good Lord Orrery, I would tell you " The Cry" made me ready to cry, and the " Art of Tormenting" tormented me very much. I take them to be Sally Fielding's, and also the Female Quixote: the plan of that is pretty, but ill-executed; on the contrary, the fable of The Cry is the most absurd I ever saw, but the sentiments generally just; and I think, if well dressed, would make a better body of ethics than Bolingbroke's. Her inventing new words that are neither more harmonious nor significant than those already in use, is intolerable. The most edifying part of the journey to Lisbon is the history of the kitten. I was the more touched by it, having a few days before found one, in deplorable circumstances, in a neighboring vineyard. I did not only relieve her present wants with some excellent milk, but had her put into a clean basket, and brought to my own house, where she has lived ever since very comfortably.

I desire to have Fielding's Posthumous Works, with his Memoirs of Jonathan Wild, and Journey to the next World; also the Memoirs of Verocand, a man of pleasure, and those of a Young Lady. You will call this trash, trumpery, etc. I can assure you I was more entertained by G. Edwards than H. St. John, of whom you have sent me duplicates. I see new story books with the same pleasure your eldest daughter does a new dress, or the youngest a new baby. I thank God I can find playthings for my age. I am not of Cowley's mind, that this world is—

A dull, ill-acted comedy:

Nor of Mrs. Philips's, that it is—

A too well acted tragedy.

I look upon it as a very pretty farce, for those that can see it in that light. I confess a severe critic, that would examine by ancient rules, might fix many defects; but 'tis ridiculous to judge seriously of a puppet-show. Those that can laugh, and be diverted with absurdities, are the wisest spectators, be it of writings, actions, or people.

The Stage-Coach has some grotesque figures that amuse: I place it in the rank of Charlotte Summers, and perhaps it is by the same author. I am pleased with Sir Herald for recording a generous action of the Duke of Montagu, which I know to be true, with some variation of circumstances. You should have given me a key to the Invisible Spy, particularly to the catalogue of books in it. I know not whether the conjugal happiness of the Duke of Bedford is intended as a compliment or an irony.

This letter is as long and as dull as any of Richardson's. I am ashamed of it, notwithstanding my maternal privilege of being tiresome.

I return many thanks to Lord Bute for the china, which I am sure I shall be very fond of, though I have not yet seen it. I wish for three of Pinchbeck's watches, shagreen cases, and enameled dial-plates. When I left England they were five guineas each. You may imagine they are for presents; one for my doctor, who is exactly Parson Adams in another profession, and the others for two priests, to whom I have some obligations.

This Richardson is a strange fellow. I heartily despise him, and eagerly read him, nay, sob over his works, in a most scandalous manner. The two first tomes of Clarissa touched me, as being very resembling to my maiden days; and I find in the pictures of Sir Thomas Grandison and his lady what I have heard of my mother, and seen of my father.

This letter is grown (I know not how) into an immeasurable length. I answer it to my conscience as a just judgment on you for the shortness of yours. Remember my unalterable maxim, where we love we have always something to say; consequently my pen never tires when expressing to you the thoughts of your most affectionate mother.

LETTER XXX.

LOUVERE, March 2, N. S., 1756.

DEAR CHILD—I had the happiness of a letter from your father last post, by which I find you are in good health, though I have not heard from you for a long time. This frequent interruption of our correspondence is a great uneasiness to me: I charge it on the neglect or irregularity of the post. I sent you a letter by Mr. Anderson a great while ago, to which I never had any answer: neither have I ever heard from him since, though I am fully persuaded he has wrote concerning some little commissions I gave him. I should be very sorry he thought I neglected to thank him for his civilities. I desire Lord Bute would inquire about him. I saw him in company with a very pretty pupil, who seemed to me a promising youth. I wish he would fall in love with my granddaughter. I dare say you laugh at this early design of providing for her: take it as a mark of my affection for you and yours, which is without any mixture of self-interest, since, with my age and infirmities, there is little probability of my living to see them established. I no more expect to arrive at the age of the Duchess of Marlborough than that of Methuselah; neither do I desire it. I have long thought myself useless to the world. I have seen one generation pass away; and it is gone; for I think there are very few of those left that flourished in my youth. You will perhaps call these melancholy reflections : they are not so. There is a quiet after the abandoning of pursuits, something like the rest that follows a laborious day. I tell you this for your comfort. It was formerly a terrifying view to me that I should one day be an old woman. I now find that nature has provided pleasures for every state. Those are only unhappy who will not be contented with what she gives, but strive to break through her laws, by affecting a perpetuity of youth, which appears to me as little desirable at present as the babies do to you that were the delight of your infancy. I am at the end of my paper, which shortens the sermon.

LETTER XXXI.

VENICE, March 22, 1756.

I have received, but this morning, the first box of china Lord Bute has been so obliging to send me. I am quite charmed with it, but wish you had sent in it the note of the contents; it has been so long deposited that it is not impossible some diminution may have happened. Every thing that comes from England is precious to me, to the very hay that is employed in packing. I should be glad to know any thing that could be an agreeable return from hence. There are many things I could send; but they are either contraband, or the custom would cost more than they are worth. I look out for a picture; the few that are in this part of Italy are those that remain in families, where they are entailed, and I might as well pretend to send you a palace. I am extremely pleased with the account you gave of your father's health. I have wrote to desire his consent in the disposal of poor Lady Oxford's legacy; I do not doubt obtaining it. It has been both my interest and my duty to study his character, and I can say, with truth, I never knew any man so capable of a generous action.

A late adventure here makes a great noise from the rank of the people concerned : the Marchioness Licinia Bentivoglio, who was heiress of one branch of the Martineughi, and brougnt ten thousand gold sequins to her husband, and the expectation of her father's estate, three thousand pounds sterling per annum, the most magnificent palace at Brescia (finer than any in London), another in the country, and many other advantages of woods, plate, jewels, etc. The Cardinal Bentivoglio, his uncle, thought he could not choose better, though his nephew might certainly have chose among all the Italian ladies, being descended from the sovereigns of Bologna, actually a grandee of Spain, a noble Venetian, and in possession of twenty-five thousand pounds sterling per annum, with immense wealth in palaces, furniture, and absolute dominion in some of his lands. The girl was pretty, and the match was with the satisfaction of both families; but she brought with her such a diabolical temper, and such *Luciferan* pride, that neither husband, relations, or servants, had ever a moment's peace with her. After about eight years' warfare, she eloped one fair morning, and took refuge in Venice, leaving her two daughters, the eldest scarce six years old, to the care of the exasperated Marquis. Her father was so angry at her extravagant conduct that he would not, for some time, receive her into his house; but, after some months, and much solicitation, parental fondness prevailed, and she has remained with him ever since, notwithstanding all the efforts of her husband, who tried kindness, submission, and threats, to no purpose. The Cardinal came twice to Brescia, her own father joined 'his entreaties, nay, *his holiness* wrote a letter with his own hands, and made use of the Church authority, but he found it harder to reduce one woman than ten heretics. She was inflexible, and lived ten years in this state of reprobation. Her father died last winter, and left her his whole estate for her life, and afterward to her children. Her eldest was now marriageable, and disposed of to the nephew of Cardinal Valentino Gonzagua, first minister at Rome. She would neither appear at the wedding, nor take the least notice of a dutiful letter sent by the bride. The old Cardinal (who was passionately fond of his illustrious name) was so much touched with the apparent extinction of it that it was thought to have hastened his death. She continued in the enjoyment of her ill-humor, living in great splendor, though almost solitary, having, by some impertinence or other, disgusted all her acquaintance, till about a month ago, when her woman brought her a basin of broth, which she usually drank in her bed. She took a few spoonfuls of it, and then cried out it was so bad it was impossible to endure it. Her chambermaids were so used to hear her exclamations that they ate it up very comfortably ; they were both seized with the same pangs, and died the next day. She sent for physicians, who judged her poisoned ; but, as she had taken a small quantity, by the help of antidotes she recovered, yet is still in a languishing condition. Her cook was examined, and racked, always protesting entire innocence, and swearing he had made the soup in the same manner he was accustomed. You may imagine the noise of this affair. She loudly accused her husband, it being the interest of no other person to wish her out of the world. He resides at Ferrara (about which the greatest part of his lands lie), and was soon informed of this accident. He sent doctors to her, whom she would not see, sent vast alms to all the convents to pray for her health, and ordered a number of masses to be said in every church of Brescia and Ferrara. He sent letters to the senate at Venice, and published manifestos in all the capital cities, in which he professes his affection to her, and abhorrence of any attempt against her, and has a cloud of witnesses that he never gave her the least reason of complaint, and even since her leaving him has always spoke of her with kindness, and courted her return. He is said to be remarkably sweet-tempered, and has the best character of any man of quality in this country. If the death of her women did not seem to confirm it, her accusation would gain credit with nobody. She is certainly very sincere in it herself, being so persuaded he has resolved her death that she dare not take the air, apprehending to be assassinated, and has imprisoned herself in her chamber, where she will neither eat nor drink any thing that she does not see tasted by all her servants. The physicians now say that perhaps the poison might fall into the broth accidentally; I confess I do not perceive the possibility of it. As to the cook suffering the rack, that is a mere jest, where people have money enough to bribe the executioner. I decide nothing; but such is the present destiny of a lady who would have been one of Richardson's heroines, having never been suspected of the least gallantry; hating, and being hated universally; of a most noble spirit, it being proverbial—" as proud as the Marchioness Licinia."

LETTER XXXII.

LOUVERE, June 10, 1757.

It is very true, my dear child, we can not now maintain a family with the product of a flock, though I do not doubt the present sheep afford as much wool and milk as any of their ancestors; and 'tis certain our natural wants are not more numerous than formerly; but the world is past its infancy, and will no longer be contented with spoon-meat. Time has added great improvements, but those very improvements have introduced a train of artificial necessities. A collective body of men make a gradual progress in understanding, like that of a single individual. When I reflect on the vast increase of useful, as well as speculative knowledge, the last three hundred years has produced, and that the peasants of this age have more conveniences than the first emperors of Rome had any notion of, I imagine we are now arrived at that period which answers to fifteen. I can not think we are older, when I recollect the many palpable follies which are still (almost) universally persisted in: I place that of war as senseless as the boxing of school-boys, and whenever we come to man's estate (perhaps a thousand years hence) I do not doubt it will appear as ridiculous as the pranks of unlucky lads. Several discoveries will then be made, and several truths made clear, of which we have now no more idea than the ancients had of the circulation of the blood, or the optics of Sir Isaac Newton.

I expect a letter of thanks from my granddaughter: I wrote to my grandmother long before her age. I desire you would not see it, being willing to judge of her genius. I know I shall read it with some partiality, which I can not avoid to all that is yours, as I am your most affectionate mother.

LETTER XXXIII.

PADUA, Sept. 5, 1757.

I wrote to you very lately, my dear child, in answer to that letter Mr. Hamilton brought me: he was so obliging to come on purpose from Venice to deliver it, as I believe I told you; but I am so highly delighted with this, dated August 4, giving an account of your little colony, I can not help setting pen to paper to tell you the melancholy joy I had in reading it. You would have laughed to see the old fool weep over it. I now find that age, when it does not harden the heart and sour the temper, naturally returns to the milky disposition of infancy. Time has the same effect on the mind as on the face. The predominant passion, the strongest feature, become more conspicuous from the others retiring; the various views of life are abandoned, from want of ability to preserve them, as the fine complexion is lost in wrinkles: but, as surely as a large nose grows larger, and the wide mouth wider, the tender child in your nursery will be a tender old woman, though, perhaps, reason may have restrained the appearance of it, till the mind, relaxed, is no longer capable of concealing its weakness; for weakness it is to indulge any attachment at a period of life when we are sure to part with life itself, at very short warning. According to the good English proverb, young people may die, but old must. You see I am very industrious in finding comfort to myself in my exit, and to guard, as long as I can, against the peevishness which makes age miserable in itself and contemptible to others. 'Tis surprising to me that, with the most inoffensive conduct, I should meet enemies, when I can not be envied for any thing, and have pretensions to nothing.

Is it possible, the old Colonel Duncombe* I knew, should be Lord Feversham, and married to a young wife? As to Lord Ranelagh, I confess it must be a very bitter draught to submit to take his name, but his lady has had a short purgatory, and now enjoys affluence with a man she likes, who I am told is a man of merit, which I suppose she thinks preferable to Lady Selina's nursery. Here are no old people in this country, neither in dress or gallantry. I know only my friend Antonio, who is true to the memory of his adored lady; her picture is always in his sight, and he talks of her in the style of *pastor fido*. I believe I owe his favor to having shown him her miniature by Rosalba, which I bought at London: perhaps you remember it in my little collection: he is really a man of worth and sense. Hearing it reported, I need not say by whom, that my retirement was owing to having lost all my money at play, at Avignon, he sent privately for my chief servant, and desired him to tell him naturally if I was in any distress; and not only offered, but pressed him to lay three thousand sequins on my toilet. I don't believe I could borrow that sum, without good security, among my great relations. I thank God I had no occasion to make use of his generosity; but I am sure you will agree with me that I ought never to forget the obligation. I could give some other instances in which he has shown his friendship in protecting me from mortifications, invented by those that ought to have assisted me; but 'tis a long tiresome story. You will be surprised to hear the general does not yet know these circumstances; he

---

* Anthony Duncombe, created Lord Feversham in 1747; which title became-extinct in 1763 on his dying without male issue. He was the nephew of Sir Charles Duncombe, Lord Mayor of London, 1709.

arrived at Venice but a few days before I left it; and promising me to come to Padua, at the fair, I thought I should have time sufficient to tell him my history. Indeed, I was in hopes he would have accepted my invitation of lodging in my house; but his multiplicity of affairs hindered him from coming at all. 'Tis only a few days since that he made me a visit, in company with Mr. Hamilton, before whom I did not think it proper to speak my complaints. They are now gone to drink the waters at Vicenza: when they return, I intend removing to Venice, and then shall relate my grievances, which I have more reason to do than ever. I have tired you with this disagreeable subject: I will release you, and please myself in repeating the assurance of my being ever, while I have a being, your most affectionate mother.

My dear child, do not think of reversing nature by making me presents. I would send you all my jewels and my toilet if I knew how to convey them, though they are in some measure necessary in this country, where it would be, perhaps, reported I had pawned them, if they did not sometimes make their appearance. I know not how to send commissions for things I never saw; nothing of price I would have, as I would not new furnish an inn I was on the point of leaving, for such is this world to me. Though china is in such high estimation here, I have sometimes an inclination to desire your father to send me the two large jars that stood in the windows in Cavendish Square, I am sure he don't value them, and believe they would be of no use to you. I bought them at an auction, for two guineas, before the Duke of Argyll's example had made all china, more or less, fashionable.

LETTER XXXIV.

LOUVERE, September 30, 1757.

MY DEAR CHILD—Lord Bute has been so obliging as to let me know your safe delivery, and the birth of another daughter. May she be as meritorious in your eyes as you are in mine! I can wish nothing better to you both, though I have some reproaches to make you. Daughter! daughter! don't call names; you are always abusing my pleasures, which is what no mortal will bear. Trash, lumber, sad stuff, are the titles you give to my favorite amusement. If I called a white staff a stick of wood, a gold key gilded brass, and the ensigns of illustrious orders colored strings, this may be philosophically true, but would be very ill received. We have all our playthings; happy are they that can be contented with those they can obtain. Those hours are spent in the wisest manner that can easiest shade the ills of life, and are the least productive of ill consequences. I think my time better employed in reading the adventures of imaginary people, than the Duchess of Marlborough, who passed the latter years of her life in paddling with her will, and contriving schemes of plaguing some, and extracting praise from others, to no purpose: eternally disappointed, and eternally fretting. The active scenes are over at my age. I indulge, with all the art I can, my taste for reading. If I would confine it to valuable books, they are almost as rare as valuable men. I must be content with what I can find. As I approach a second childhood, I endeavor to enter into the pleasures of it. Your youngest son is, perhaps, at this very moment, riding on a poker, with great delight, not at all regretting that it is not a gold one, and much less wishing it an Arabian horse, which he could not know how to manage. I am reading an idle tale, not expecting wit or truth in it, and am very glad it is not metaphysics to puzzle my judgment, or history to mislead my opinion. He fortifies his health by exercise; I calm my cares by oblivion. The methods may appear low to busy people; but if he improves his strength, and I forget my infirmities, we both attain very desirable ends.

I have not heard from your father for a long time. I hope he is well, because you do not mention him.

LETTER XXXV.

VENICE, January 20, 1758.

I am always glad to hear of my dear child's health, and daily pray for the continuance of it, and all other blessings on you and your family. The carnival hitherto has been clouded by extremely wet weather, but we are in hopes that the sunshine is reserved for the second part of it, when the morning masquerades give all the ladies an opportunity of displaying both their magnificence and their taste, in the various habits that appear at that time. I was very well diverted by them last year. I hear Rome is crammed with Britons, and suppose we shall see them all in their turns. I can not say that the rising generation gives any general prospect of improvement either in the arts or sciences, or in any thing else. I am exceedingly pleased that the Duchess of Portland is happy in her son-in-law. I must ever interest myself in what happens to any descendant of Lady Oxford. I expect that my books and china should set out, they will be a great amusement to me, I mix so little with the gay world, and at present my garden is quite useless.

Venice is not a place to make a man's fortune in. As for those who have money to throw away, they may do it here more agreeably than in any town I know ; strangers being received with great civility, and admitted into all their parties of pleasure. But it requires a good estate, and good constitution, to play deep, and pass so many sleepless nights, as is customary in the best company.

I am invited to a great wedding to-morrow, which will be in the most splendid manner, to the contentment of both the families, every thing being equal, even the indifference of the bride and bridegroom, though each of them is extremely pleased, by being set free from governors or governesses. To say truth, I think they are less likely to be disappointed, in the plan they have formed, than any of our romantic couples, who have their heads full of love and constancy.

I stay here, though I am on many accounts better pleased with Padua. Our great minister, the resident, affects to treat me as one in the opposition. I am inclined to laugh rather than be displeased at his political airs; yet, as I am among strangers, they are disagreeable; and, could I have foreseen them, would have settled in some other part of the world; but I have taken leases of my houses, been at much pains and expense in furnishing them, and am no longer at an age to make long journeys. I saw, some months ago, a countryman of yours (Mr. Adam*), who desires to be introduced to you. He seemed to me, in one short visit, to be a man of genius, and I have heard his knowledge of architecture much applauded. He is now in England.

Your account of the changes in ministerial affairs do not surprise me; but nothing could be more astonishing than their all coming in together. It puts me in mind of a friend of mine who had a large family of favorite animals, and, not knowing how to convey them to his country-house in separate equipages, he ordered a Dutch mastiff, a cat and her kittens, a monkey, and a parrot, all to be packed up together in one large hamper, and sent by a wagon. One may easily guess how this set of company made their journey; and I have never been able to think of the present compound ministry without the idea of barking, scratching, and screaming.† 'Tis too ridiculous a one, I own, for the gravity of their characters, and still more for the situation the kingdom is in; for, as much as one may encourage the love of laughter, 'tis impossible to be indifferent to the welfare of one's native country.

---

* Mr. Robert Adam, who built Caen-Wood, Luton-Park, etc., and the Adelphi in conjunction with his brother. His designs are published.

† This story has been versified by Lord Byron (Don Juan, canto iii. stanza 18), but without any reference to the source from whence he drew it. Lady Mary introduces it with some point, to illustrate her notion of the good understanding which might be expected to exist among the members of an administration composed of very discord-

LETTER XXXVI.

VENICE, 1758.

DEAR CHILD—I received yours of the 20th of February yesterday, May the 2d, so irregular is the post. I could forgive the delay, but I can not pardon the loss of so many that have never arrived at all. Mr. Hamilton is not yet come, nor perhaps will not for some months. I hear he is at Leghorn. General Graham has been dangerously ill; but I am told he is now on his return. We have at present the most extravagant weather that has been known for some years; it is as cold and wet as an English November. Thursday next is the ceremony of the Ascension: the show will be entirely spoiled if the rain continues, to the serious affliction of the fine ladies, who all make new clothes on that occasion. We have had lately two magnificent weddings; Lord Mandeville* had the pleasure of dancing at one of them. I appeared at neither, being formal balls, where no masks were admitted, and all people set out in high dress, which I have long renounced, as it is very fit I should; though there were several grandmothers there, who exhibited their jewels. In this country nobody grows old till they are bed-ridden.

I wish your daughters to resemble me in nothing but the love of reading, knowing, by experience, how far it is capable

ant materials; Lord Byron, to describe the indifference and cruelty of a corsair.

His lines are these :

A monkey, a Dutch mastiff, a mackaw,
  Two parrots, with a Persian cat and kittens,
He chose from several animals he saw;
  A terrier, too, which once had been a Briton's,
Who, dying on the coast of Ithaca,
  The peasants gave the poor dumb thing a pittance,
These to secure in this strong blowing weather,
  He caged in one large hamper all together.

* George Viscount Mandeville, eldest son of Robert Duk of Manchester.

14*

of softening the cruelest accidents of life; even the happiest can not be passed over without many uneasy hours; and there is no remedy so easy as books, which, if they do not give cheerfulness, at least restore quiet to the most troubled mind. Those that fly to cards or company for relief generally find they only exchange one misfortune for another.

You have so much business on your hands I will not take you from more proper employment by a long letter. I am, my dear child, with the warmest affection, ever your tender mother.

LETTER XXXVII.

PADUA, July 17, 1758.

MY DEAR CHILD—I received yours last night, which gave me a pleasure beyond what I am able to express (this is not according to the common expression, but a simple truth). I had not heard from you for some months, and was in my heart very uneasy, from the apprehension of some misfortune in your family; though, as I always endeavor to avoid the anticipation of evil, which is a source of pain, and can never be productive of any good, I stifled my fear as much as possible, yet it cost me many a midnight pang. You have been the passion of my life: you need thank me for nothing; I gratify myself whenever I can oblige you. I have already given into the hands of Mr. Anderson a long letter for you, but it is now of so old a date I accompany it with another. His journey has been delayed by a very extraordinary accident, which might have proved as fatal as that of Lord Drumlanrigh, or that, which I think worse, which happened to my convert Mr. Butler; fortunately it has only served to set the characters of both the governor and the pupil in a more amiable light. Mr Archer was at breakfast with six other English gentlemen, and handling a blunderbuss, which he did not know to be charged, it burst, and distributed among them six chained bullets, besides the splinters, which flew about in the manner you may imagine. His own hand was considerably wounded, yet the first word he spoke (without any regard to his own smart or danger) was, "I hope nobody is hurt:" nobody was hurt but himself, who has been ever since under cure, to preserve two of his fingers which were very much torn. He had also a small rasure on his cheek, which is now quite healed. The paternal care and tenderness Mr. Anderson has shown on this occasion, has recommended him to every body. I wanted nothing to raise that esteem which is due to his sterling honesty and good heart, which I do not doubt you value as much as I do. If that wretch Hickman had been—but this is a melancholy thought, and as such ought to be suppressed.

How important is the charge of youth! and how useless all the advantages of nature and fortune without a well-turned mind! I have lately heard of a very shining instance of this truth from two gentlemen (very deserving ones they seem to be) who have had the curiosity to travel into Muscovy, and now return to England with Mr. Archer. I inquired after my old acquaintance Sir Charles Williams, who I hear is much broken, both in his spirits and constitution. How happy might that man have been, if there had been added to his natural and acquired endowments a dash of morality! If he had known how to distinguish between false and true felicity; and, instead of seeking to increase an estate already too large, and hunting after pleasures that have made him rotten and ridiculous, he had bounded his desires of wealth, and followed the dictates of his conscience. His servile ambition has gained him two yards of red ribbon, and an exile into a miserable country, where there is no society and so little taste that I believe he suffers under a dearth of flatterers. This is said for the use of your growing sons, whom I hope no golden temptations will induce to marry women they can not love, or comply with measures they do not approve. All the happiness this world can afford is more within reach than is generally supposed. Whoever seeks pleasure will undoubtedly find pain;

whoever will pursue ease will as certainly find pleasures. The world's esteem is the highest gratification of human vanity; and that is more easily obtained in a moderate fortune than an overgrown one, which is seldom possessed, never gained, without envy. I say esteem; for, as to applause it is a youthful pursuit, never to be forgiven after twenty, and naturally succeeds the childish desire of catching the setting sun, which I can remember running very hard to do: a fine thing truly if it could be caught; but experience soon shows it to be impossible. A wise and honest man lives to his own heart, without that silly splendor that makes him a prey to knaves, and which commonly ends in his becoming one of the fraternity. I am very glad to hear Lord Bute's decent economy sets him above any thing of that kind. I wish it may become national. A collective body of men differs very little from a single man; and frugality is the foundation of generosity. I have often been complimented on the English heroism, who have thrown away so many millions without any prospect of advantage to themselves, purely to succor a distressed princess. I never could hear these praises without some impatience; they sounded to me like the panegyrics made by the dependents on the Duke of Newcastle and poor Lord Oxford, bubbled when they were commended, and laughed at when they were undone. Some late events will, I hope, open our eyes : we shall see we are an island, and endeavor to extend our commerce rather than the Quixote reputation of redressing wrongs and placing diadems on heads that should be equally indifferent to us. When time has ripened mankind into common sense, the name of conqueror will be an odious title. I could easily prove that had the Spaniards established a trade with the Americans, they would have enriched their country more than by the addition of twenty-two kingdoms, and all the mines they now work—I do not say possess; since, though they are the proprietors, others enjoy the profit.

My letter is too long; I beg your pardon for it; 'tis seldom I have an opportunity of speaking to you, and I would have you know all the thoughts of your most affectionate mother.

LETTER XXXVIII.

PADUA, July 14, 1758.

My Dear Child—I hope this will find you in perfect health. I had a letter from your father last post, dated from Newbold, which tells me a very agreeable piece of news, that the contests of parties, so violent formerly (to the utter destruction of peace, civility, and common sense) are so happily terminated, that there is nothing of that sort mentioned in good company. I think I ought to wish you and my grandchildren joy on this general pacification, when I remember all the vexation I have gone through, from my youth upward, on the account of those divisions, which touched me no more than the disputes between the followers of Mohammed and Ali, being always of opinion that politics and controversy were as unbecoming to our sex as the dress of a prize-fighter; and I would as soon have mounted Fig's theater as have stewed all night in the gallery of a committee, as some ladies of bright parts have done.

Notwithstanding the habitual (I believe I might say natural) indifference, here am I involved in adventures, as surprising as any related in Amadis de Gaul, or even by Mr. Glanville.* I can assure you I should not be more surprised at seeing myself riding in the air on a broomstick, than in the figure of a first rate politician. You will stare to hear that your nurse keeps her corner (as Lord Bolingbroke says of Miss Oglethorp) in this illustrious conspiracy. I really think the best head of the junto is an English washerwoman, who has made her fortune with all parties, by her compliance in changing her religion, which gives her the merit of a new convert; and her charitable disposition of keeping a house of fair reception for

* In his History of Witchcraft—Sadducismus Triumphans, 1681.

the English captains, sailors, etc., that are distressed by long
sea voyages (as Sir Samson Legend remarks, in Love for Love),
gains her friends among all public spirited people : the scenes
are so comic they deserve the pen of a Richardson to do them
justice.　I begin to be persuaded the surest way of preserving
reputation, and having powerful protectors, is being openly
lewd and scandalous.　I will not be so censorious to take examples from my own sex ; but you see Doctor Swift, who set
at defiance all decency, truth, or reason, had a crowd of admirers, and at their head the virtuous and ingenious Earl of
Orrery, the polite and learned Mr. Greville, with a number of
ladies of fine taste and unblemished characters ; while the
Bishop of Salisbury (Burnet I mean), the most indulgent
parent, the most generous churchman, and the most zealous
asserter of the rights and liberties of his country, was all his
life defamed and vilified, and after his death most barbarously
calumniated, for having had the courage to write a history
without flattery.　I knew him in my very early youth, and his
condescension, in directing a girl in her studies, is an obligation I can never forget.

LETTER XXXIX.

Oct. 31, 1758.

My Dear Child—I received yours of October 2d this day,
the 31st instant.　The death of the two great ladies you mention,
I believe does not occasion much sorrow ; they have long been
burdens (not to say nuisances) on the face of the earth.　I am
sorry for Lord Carlisle.*　He was my friend as well as acquaintance, and a man of uncommon probity and good nature.
I think he has shown it in the disposition of his will in the
favor of a lady he had no reason to esteem.　It is certainly
the kindest thing he could do for her, to endeavor to save her
from her own folly, which would have probably precipitately

* He died September 4, 1758.

hurried her into a second marriage, which would most surely have revenged all her misdemeanors.

I was well acquainted with Mr. Walpole, at Florence, and indeed he was particularly civil to me. I am encouraged to ask a favor of him, if I did not know that few people have so good memories as to remember so many years backward as have passed since I have seen him. If he has treated the character of Queen Elizabeth with disrespect, all the women should tear him in pieces, for abusing the glory of her sex. Neither is it just to put her in the list of authors, having never published any thing, though we have Mr. Camden's authority that she wrote many valuable pieces, chiefly translations from the Greek. I wish all monarchs would bestow their leisure hours on such studies: perhaps they would not be very useful to mankind; but it may be asserted, as a certain truth, that their own minds would be more improved than by the amusements of quadrille or cavagnole.

I desire you would thank your father for the china jars; if they arrive safely, they will do me great honor in this country. The Patriarch died here lately. He had a large temporal estate; and, by long life and extreme parsimony, has left four hundred thousand sequins in his coffers, which is inherited by two nephews; and I suppose will be dissipated as scandalously as it was accumulated. The town is full of faction, for the election of his successor; and the ladies are always very active on these occasions. I have observed that they have ever had more influence in republics than in a monarchy. 'Tis true a king has often a powerful mistress, but she is governed by some male favorite. In commonwealths, votes are easily acquired by the fair; and she who has most beauty or art, has a great sway in the senate. I run on troubling you with stories very insignificant to you, and taking up your time, which I am very certain is taken up in matters of more importance than my old wives' tales. My dear child, God bless you and yours. I am, with the warmest sentiments of my heart, your most affectionate mother.

LETTER XL.

I am very glad, my dear child, to hear of your father's health; mine is better than I ought to expect at my time of life. I believe Mr. Anderson talks partially of me, as to my looks; I know nothing of the matter, as it is eleven years since I have seen my figure in the glass, and the last reflection I saw there was so disagreeable that I resolved to spare myself such mortifications for the future, and shall continue that resolution to my life's end. To indulge all pleasing amusements, and avoid all images that give us disgust, is, in my opinion the best method to attain or confirm health. I ought to consider yours, and shorten my letters, while you are in a condition that makes reading uneasy to you.

God bless you and yours, my dear child, is the ardent wish of your affectionate mother.

LETTER XLI.

June 22, N. S.

My Dear Child—I can not believe Sir John's* advancement is owing to his merit, though he certainly deserves such a distinction; but I am persuaded the present disposers of such dignities are neither more clear-sighted, or more disinterested

* In Mr. Dallaway's edition this and the preceding letter are joined together, and make one. It may be doubted whether this, which bears the date as above, should not have been inserted in an earlier part of this correspondence, as having been written in 1752; the "Sir John" mentioned in it having probably been Sir John Rawdon, Bart., who was created an Irish Peer, April 9th, 1750, by the title of Baron Rawdon cf Moira. He was thrice married—first, in 1741, to Lady Helena Percival, daughter of the Earl of Egmont; secondly, to Ann, daughter of Trevor Viscount Hillsborough; thirdly, in 1752, to Lady Elizabeth Hastings, eldest daughter of Theophilus, Earl of Huntingdon, 26th February, 1752. December 15th, 1761, he was advanced in the peerage as Earl of Moira, in the County of Down.

than their predecessors. Ever since I knew the world, Irish patents have been hung out to sale, like the laced and embroidered coats in Monmouth-street, and bought up by the same sort of people ; I mean those who had rather wear shabby finery than no finery at all; though I don't suppose this was Sir John's case. That *good creature* (as the country saying is) has not a bit of pride about him. I dare swear he purchased his title for the same reason he used to purchase pictures in Italy; not because he wanted to buy, but because somebody or other wanted to sell. He hardly ever opened his mouth but to say " What you please, sir ;"—" Your humble servant;" or some gentle expression to the same effect. It is scarce credible that with this unlimited complaisance he should draw a blow upon himself; yet it so happened that one of his own countrymen was brute enough to strike him. As it was done before many witnesses, Lord Mansel heard of it; and thinking that if poor Sir John took no notice of it, he would suffer daily insults of the same kind, out of pure good nature resolved to spirit him up, at least to some show of resentment, intending to make up the matter afterward in as honorable a manner as he could for the poor patient. He represented to him very warmly that no gentleman could take a box on the ear. Sir John answered with great calmness, " I know that, but this was not a box on the ear, it was only a slap o' the face."

I was as well acquainted with his two first wives as the difference of our ages permitted. I fancy they have broke their hearts by being chained to such a companion. 'Tis really terrible, for a well-bred, virtuous young woman to be confined to the conversation of the object of her contempt. There is but one thing to be done in that case, which is a method I am sure you have observed practiced with success by some ladies I need not name : they associate the husband and the lap-dog, and manage so well, that they make exactly the same figure in the family. My lord and *Dell* tag after madam to all indifferent places, and stay at home together, whenever she goes into company where they would be troublesome. I can assure you I equally contemn a woman who can forget she was born a gentlewoman, for the sake of money she did not want. That is indeed the only sentiment that deserves the name of avarice. A prudential care of our affairs, or (to go further) a desire of being in circumstances to be useful to our friends, is not only excusable but highly laudable ; never blamed but by those who would persuade others to throw away their money, in hopes to pick up a share of it. The greatest declaimers for disinterestedness I ever knew, have been capable of the vilest actions ; and the greatest instances of true generosity, given by those who were regular in their expenses, and superior to the vanity of fashion.

I believe you are heartily tired of my dull moralities. I confess I am in very low spirits ; it is hotter weather than has been known for some years, and I have got an abominable cold, which has drawn after it a troop of complaints I will not trouble you with reciting. I hope all your family are in good health, I am humble servant to Lord Bute, I give my blessing to your children, and am ever your most affectionate mother.

LETTER XLII.

GENOA, Dec., 8, 1759.

MY DEAR CHILD—I received yours of October 24 yesterday, which gave me great pleasure, by the account of the good health of you and yours ; I need not say how near that is to my heart. I had the satisfaction of an entertaining letter from your father, out of Germany, by which I find he has had both benefit and amusement from his travels. I hope he is now with you.

I find you have many wrong notions of Italy, which I do not wonder at. You can take your ideas of it only from books or travelers. The first are generally antiquated or confined to trite observations, and the other yet more superficial · they return no more instructed than they might have been at home, by the help of a map. The boys only remember where they met with the best wine or the prettiest women ; and the governors (I speak of the most learned among them) have only remarked situations and distances, or, at most, statues and edifices, as every girl that can read a French novel, and boy that can construe a scene in Terence, fancies they have attained to the French and Latin languages, when, God knows, it requires the study of a whole life to acquire a perfect knowledge of either of them : so, after a tour (as they call it) of three years, round Europe, people think themselves qualified to give exact accounts of the customs, politics, and interest of the dominions they have gone through post ; when a very long stay, a diligent inquiry, and a nice observation, are requisite even to a moderate degree of knowing a foreign country, especially here, where they are naturally·very reserved. France, indeed, is more easily seen through ; the French always talking of themselves, and the government being the same, there is little difference from one province to another ; but, in Italy, the different laws make different customs and manners. There are many things very particular here, from the singularity of the government ; some of which I do not care to touch upon, and some are still in use here, though obsolete in almost all other places, as the estates of all the great families being unalienable, as they were formerly in England. This would have made them very potent if it were not balanced by another law, that divides whatever land the father dies possessed of among all the sons, the eldest having no advantage but the finest house and best furniture, which occasions numerous branches and few large fortunes, with a train of consequences you may imagine. But I can not let pass in silence the prodigious alteration, since Misson's writing, in regard to our sex. This reformation (or, if you please, depravation) begun so lately as the year 1732, when the French overrun this part of Italy ; but it has been carried on with such fervor and success that the Italians go far beyond their patterns, the Parisian ladies, in the extent of their liberty. I am not so much surprised at the women's conduct as I am amazed at the change in the men's sentiments. Jealousy, which was once a point of honor among them, is exploded to that degree that it is become the most infamous and ridiculous of all characters; and you can not more affront a gentlemen than to suppose him capable of it. Divorces are also introduced, and frequent enough; they have long been in fashion in Genoa, several of the finest and greatest ladies there having two husbands alive.

I am afraid you will think this a long letter; but you tell me that you are without company, and in solitude, though yours appears to me to be a sort of paradise. You have an agreeable habitation, a pleasant garden, a man you love and who loves you, and are surrounded with a numerous and hopeful progeny. May they all prove comforts to your age! That, and all other blessings, are daily wished for you by, my dear child, your affectionate mother.

LETTER XLIII.

VENICE, March 18, 1760.

MY DEAR CHILD—I am afraid some letters, both of yours and mine are lost, nor am I much surprised at it, seeing the managements here. In this world much must be suffered, and we ought all to follow the rule of Epictetus: "Bear and forbear." General Wolfe* is to be lamented, but not pitied. I am of your opinion, that compassion is only owing to his mother and intended bride, who I think the greater sufferer (however sensible I am of a parent's tenderness). Disappointments in youth are those which are felt with the greatest anguish, when we are all in expectation of happiness, perhaps not to be found in this life. I am very much diverted

* General Wolfe was killed at the siege of Quebec, September 16, 1759.

with the adventures of the three graces who are coming to London, and am heartily sorry their mother has not learning enough to write memoirs. She might make the fortur*e* of half a dozen Dodsleys. The youngest girl (called here *Bettina*) is taller than the Duchess of Montagu, and as red and white as any German alive. If she has sense enough to follow good instructions, she will be irresistible, and may produce very glorious novelties. Our great minister has her picture in his collection—*basta!*

My health is better than I can reasonably expect at my age, but my life is so near a conclusion that where or how I pass it (if innocently) is almost become indifferent to me. I have outlived the greatest part of my acquaintance; and, to say the truth, a return to crowd and bustle, after my long retirement, would be disagreeable to me. Yet, if I could be of use either to your father or your family, I would venture the shortening the insignificant days of your affectionate mother.

LETTERS TO

SIR JAMES AND LADY FRANCES STEUART.*

LETTER I.

May, 1758.

I AM in great pain both for your health and situation, and wish you would permit me to be of any service to you. I know what it is to be without servants in a strange country, and how far people are imposed on that bear the name of English, and heretics into the bargain; the folly of British boys, and stupidity or knavery of governors, have gained us the glorious title of Golden Asses, all over Italy. I never was in the Padua locanda, but except they are more virtuous that any I ever met with, you will be very ill-served and very well robbed. Here is a fellow recommended to me by Baron Talmua, who says he will answer for his honesty and capacity;

* The following was written by Lady Frances Steuart upon the parcel containing these letters:

"Letters from Lady Mary W. Montagu, which are decisive of the short acquaintance necessary to the adhesion which generally takes place when superior minds are brought together. Lady M. W. Montagu was blessed with such a mind as led her to make a short (very short) acquaintance with my dear Sir James become to her a time of noted value. They reciprocally improved it, and neither of them ever lost the recollections which were so gratifying to both.

"Nor can I ever forget the thankful sensibility of the time, which appeared to me so fortunate, so fit, and so *apropos* to enliven (and very highly) his elevated but dejected spirit—feeble and dejected by a severe illness."

he can serve as cook, valet-de-chambre, purveyor, and steward. He speaks no German, but is very willing to follow you, and presumes-he shall soon learn it. I think recommending servants almost as dangerous as making matches (which, I thank the Lord, I never engaged in): nothing could oblige me to venture on it but your distress, and the good opinion I have of the probity of Baron Talmua, who is a German man of quality I have known some time, and am obliged to. He has earnestly pressed me to make you this offer, on hearing me lament the seduction of your woman.

This minute I am shown a letter of my Gastaldi (in French, Concierge ; I know no proper title for him in English). I can assure you, sir and madam, his *stile grossier* gave me more pleasure than ever I received from the points of Voiture or the puns of Swift or Pope, since my secretary assured me that it contained an account of your well-being, and having honored my mansion with your presence ; he brags of having done his duty in waiting on the two milordi ; and that you found the palazzo very clean ; and he hopes you took nothing ill, though you refused the portantina. In this manner were his hieroglyphics explained to me, which I am forced and pleased to give faith to, as I do to the translators of Hebrew, though I can make nothing of the figures myself. I have read over your book, Sir James, and have a great deal to say about it, though nothing to object ; but must refer to another time, having literally six people in the room, according to their laudable custom, talking all at once, I hardly know what I say, but I know what I think ; that I will get to Padua as fast as I can, to enjoy the best company I ever knew.

LETTER II.

This letter will be solely to you, and I desire you* will not communicate it to Lady Fanny ; she is the best woman in the

* This is clearly said in joke.

world, and I would by no means make her uneasy; but there will be such strange things in it that the Talmud or the revelations are not half so mysterious; what these prodigies portend, God knows; but I never should have suspected half the wonders I see before my eyes, and am convinced of the necessity of the repeal of the witch act (as it is commonly called), I mean, to speak correctly, the tacit permission given to witches, so scandalous to all good Christians : though I tremble to think of it for my own interests. It is certain the British islands have always been strangely addicted to this diabolical intercourse, of which I dare swear you know many instances; but since this public encouragement given to it, I am afraid there will not be an old woman in the nation entirely free from suspicion. The devil rages more powerfully than ever : you will believe me when I assure you the great and learned English minister is turned Methodist, several duels have been fought in the Place of St. Marc for the charms of his excellent lady, and I have been seen flying in the air in the figure of Julian Cox,* whose history is related with so much candor and truth by the pious pen of Joseph Glanville, chaplain to King Charles. I know you young rakes make a jest of all those things, but I think no good lady can doubt of a relation so well attested. She was about seventy years old (very near my age), and the whole sworn to before Judge Archer, 1663 : very well worth reading, but rather too long for a letter. You know (wretch that I am) 'tis one of my wicked maxims to make the best of a bad bargain; and I have said publicly that every period of life has its privileges, and that even the most despicable creatures alive may find some pleasures. Now observe this comment; who are the most despicable creatures ? Certainly, old women. What pleasure can old woman take ? Only witchcraft. I think this argu-

---

* In one of her letters to Lady Bute she dwells on the same idea. All this must allude in some way to her quarrel with Mr. Murray, the Resident and to the reports which she accused him of spreading concerning her.

ment as clear as any of the devout Bishop of Cloyne's metaphysics; this being decided in a full congregation of saints, only such atheists as you and Lady Fanny can deny it. I own all the facts, as many witches have done before me,.and go every night in a public manner astride upon a black cat to a meeting where you are suspected to appear : this last article is not sworn to, it being doubtful in what manner our clandestine midnight correspondence is carried on. Some think it treasonable, others lewd (don't tell Lady Fanny); but all agree there was something very odd and unaccountable in such sudden likings. I confess, as I said before, it is witchcraft. You won't wonder I do not sign (notwithstanding all my impudence) such dangerous truths : who knows the consequence? The devil is said to desert his votaries.

Nota bene. You have dispossessed me of the real devils who haunted me. I mean the nine Muses.*

LETTER III.

PADUA, September 7, 1758.

MY DEAR LADY FANNY—I have been some time in pain for your silence, and at last begun to fear that either some accident had befallen you, or you had been so surfeited with my dullness at Padua you resolved not to be plagued with it when at a distance. These melancholy ideas growing strong upon me, I wrote to Mr. Duff to inquire after your health. I have received his answer this morning; he tells me you are both well and safely arrived at Tubingen; and I take the liberty to put you in mind of one that can never forget you and

----

* It seems almost needless to observe that this letter is writen in a spirit of jesting, or, to use a lower word, of *fun*. *Antonio*, or Signor Antonio Mocenigo, being mentioned elsewhere as eighty-six years of age, and the head of a great Venetian family, we may conclude that what is said of the two other persons named was as lud'crously impossible as his singing at the opera.

the cheerful hours we have passed together. The weather
favored you according to your prayers ; since that time we
have had storms, tempests, pestilential blasts, and at this moment such suffocating heat, the doctor is sick in bed, and nobody in health in my family, excepting myself and my Swiss
servants, who support our constitutions by hearty eating and
drinking, while the poor Italians are languishing on their sal-
ads and lemonade. I confess I am in high spirits, having succeeded in my endeavor to get a promise of assisting some
very worthy people whom I am fond of. You know I am
enthusiastic in my friendships. I also hear from all hands
of my daughter's prosperity ; you, madam, that are a mother,
may judge of my pleasure in her happiness : though I have no
taste for that sort of felicity. I could never endure with tolerable patience the austerities of a court life. I was saying
every day from my heart (while I was condemned to it), " the
things that I would do, those I do not, and the things I would
not do, those do I daily," and I had rather be a sister of St.
Clara than lady of the bedchamber to any queen in Europe.
It is not age and disappointment that has given me these sentiments ; you may see them in a copy of verses sent from
Constantinople in my early youth to my uncle Fielding,* and
by his (well-intended) indiscretion shown about, copies taken,
and at length miserably printed. I own myself such a rake
I prefer liberty to chains of diamonds, and when I hold my
peace (like King David) it is pain and grief to me.

> No fraud the poet's sacred breast can bear,
> Mild are our manners and our hearts sincere.
> Rude and unpolished in the courtier's school,
> I loathe a knave and tremble at a fool.

With this rusticity of manners I do not wonder to see my
company avoided by all great men and fine ladies. I could
tell your ladyship such a history of my calamities since we
parted, you will be surprised to hear I have not despaired and

* Vide p. 171.

died like the sick lion in Æsop's fables, who so pathetically cries out—*Bis videor mori*, when he was kicked by a certain animal I will not name because it is very like a paw word. *Vale!*

LETTER IV.

TUBINGEN, Sep. 5, 1758.

This day, September 5, I have had the pleasure of a most agreeable and obliging mark of your remembrance : but as it has no date, I neither know when nor from whence it was written.

I am extremely sorry for dear Lady Fanny's disorder. I could repeat to her many wise sayings of ancients and moderns, which would be of as much service to her as a present of embroidered slippers to you when you have a fit of the gout. I have seen so much of hysterical complaints, though heaven be praised I never felt them, I know it is an obstinate and very uneasy distemper, though never fatal, unless when quacks undertake to cure it. I have even observed that those who are troubled with it commonly live to old age. Lady Stair* is one instance; I remember her screaming and crying when Miss Primrose, myself, and other girls were dancing two rooms distant. Lady Fanny has but a slight touch of this distemper : read Dr. Sydenham, you will find the analyses of that and many other diseases, with a candor I never found in any other author. I confess I never had faith in any other physician, living or dead. Mr. Locke places him in the same rank with Sir Isaac Newton, and the Italians call him the English Hippocrates. I own I am charmed with his taking off the reproach which you men so saucily throw on our sex, as if we alone

---

* The Lady Stair here alluded to, was probably the wife of the third Earl of Stair, eldest daughter of Sir Andrew Myrton, of Gogar, in the county of Edinburg, Baronet. She died at Edinburg, July 8th, 1761, at sixty-two.

were subject to vapors : he clearly proves that your wise, honorable spleen is the same disorder, and arises from the same cause ; but you vile usurpers do not only engross learning, power, and authority to yourselves, but will be our superiors even in constitution of mind, and fancy you are incapable of the woman's weakness of fear and tenderness. Ignorance ! I could produce such examples—

> Show me that man of wit in all your roll,
> Whom some one woman has not made a fool.

I beg your pardon for these verses, but I have a right to scribble all that comes at my pen's end, being in high spirits on an occasion more interesting to me than the election of popes or emperors. His present Holiness* is not so much my acquaintance, but his family have been so since my first arrival at Venice, 1740. His father died only last winter, and was a very agreeable worthy man, killed by a doctor; his mother rather suffered life than enjoyed it after the death of her husband, and was little sensible of the advancement of her son, though I believe it made a greater impression on her than appeared, and it may be, hastened her death ; which happened a fortnight after his elevation, in the midst of the extraordinary rejoicings at Venice on that occasion. The honors bestowed on his brother, the balls, festivals, etc., are they not written in the daily books called newspapers ?

I resisted all invitations, and am still at Padua, where reading, writing, riding, and walking find me full employment.

I accept the compliment of the fine young gentleman with the joy of an old woman who does not expect to be taken notice of : pray don't tell him I am an old woman. He shall be my toast from this forward, and (provided he never sees me as long as he lives) I may be his. *A propos* of toasting, upon my honor I have not tasted a drop of punch since we parted · I can not bear the sight of it ; it would recall too tender ideas,

* Cardinal Charles Rezzonia, Bishop of Padua, became Pope Clement XIII., 16th July, 1758, and died in 1769.

and I should be quarreling with fortune for our separation, when I ought to thank her divinity for having brought us together. I could tell a long story of princes and potentates, but I am so little versed in state affairs I will not so much as answer your ensnaring question concerning the Jesuits, which is meddling at once with Church and State.

This letter is of a horrible length, and what is worse (if any worse can be) such a rhapsody of nonsense as may kill poor Lady Fanny, now she is low-spirited, though I am persuaded she has good nature enough to be glad to hear I am happy; which I could not be if I had not a view of seeing my friends so. As to you, sir, I make no excuses; you are bound to have indulgence for me, as for a sister of the quill. I have heard Mr. Addison say he always listened to poets with patience, to keep up the dignity of the fraternity. Let me have an answer as soon as possible. *Si vales, bene est, valeo.*

P. S. Do not be offended at the word poet, it slipped out unawares. I know you scorn it, though it has been dignified by Lord Somers, Lord Godolphin, and Dr. Atterbury.

LETTER V.

VENICE, May 4, 1757.

Here is a fashion sprung up entirely new in this part of the world ; I mean suicide : a rich parish priest and a young Celestine monk have disposed of themselves last week in that manner without any visible reason for their precipitation. The priest, indeed, left a paper in his hat to signify his desire of imitating the indifference of Socrates and magnanimity of Cato: the friar swung out of the world without giving any account of his design. You see it is not in Britain alone that the spleen spreads his dominion. I look on all excursions of this kind to be owing to this distemper, which shows the necessity of seeking employment for the mind, and exercise for the body ; the spirits and the blood stagnate without motion.

You are to be envied whose studies are not only useful to yourself but beneficial to mankind ; even mine (good for nothing as they are) contribute to my health, and serve at least to lull asleep those corroding reflections that embitter life, and wear out the frail machine in which we inhabit.

LETTER VI.

PADUA, July 19, 1759.

Your letters always give me a great deal of pleasure, but particularly this, which has relieved me from the pain I was in from your silence.

I have seen the Margrave of Baden Dourlach ; but I hope he has forgot he has ever seen me, being at that time in a very odd situation, of which I will not give you the history at present, being a long story, and you know life is too short for a long story.

I am extremely obliged for the valuable present you intend me. I believe you criticise yourself too severely on your style : I do not think that very smooth harmony is necessary in a work which has a merit of a nobler kind ; I think it rather a defect, as when a Roman emperor (as we see him sometimes represented on a French stage) is dressed like a petit-maître. I confess the crowd of readers look no further ; the tittle-tattle of Madame de Sévigné, and the *clinquant* of Telemachus, have found admirers from that very reason. Whatever is clearly expressed, is well wrote in a book of reasoning. However, I shall obey your commands in telling you my opinion with the greatest sincerity.

I am extremely glad to hear that Lady F. has overcome her disorder : I wish I had no apprehensions of falling into it. Solitude begets whimsies ; at my time of life one usually falls into those that are melancholy, though I endeavor to keep up a certain sprightly folly that (I thank God) I was born with : but alas ! what can we do with all our endeavors ! I am afraid we are little better than straws upon the water; we may flatter ourselves that we swim when the current carries us along.

Thus far I have dictated for the first time of my life, and perhaps it will be the last, for my amanuensis is not to be hired, and I despair of ever meeting with another. He is the first that could write as fast as I talk, and yet you see there are so many mistakes, it wants a comment longer than my letter to explain my insignificant meaning, and I have fatigued my poor eyes more with correcting it than I should have done in scribbling two sheets of paper. You will think perhaps, from this idle attempt, that I have some fluxion on my sight; no such matter; I have suffered myself to be persuaded by such sort of arguments as those by which people are induced to strict abstinence, or to take physic. Fear, paltry fear, founded on vapors rising from the heat, which is now excessive, and has so far debilitated my miserable nerves that I submit to a present displeasure, by way of precaution against a future evil, that possibly may never happen. I have this to say in my excuse, that the evil is of so horrid a nature I own I feel no philosophy that could support me under it, and no mountain girl ever trembled more at one of Whitefield's pathetic lectures than I do at the word blindness, though I know all the fine things that may be said for consolation in such a case: but I know also they would not operate on my constitution. "Why," (say my wise monitors) " will you persist in reading or writing seven hours in a day?" "I am happy while I read and write." "Indeed one would suffer a great deal to be happy," say the men, sneering; and the ladies wink at each other, and hold up their fans. A fine lady of threescore had the goodness to add, "At least, madam, you should use spectacles, I have used them myself these twenty years: I was advised to it by a famous oculist when I was fifteen. I am really of opinion that they have preserved my sight, notwithstanding the passion I always had both for reading and drawing." This good woman, you must know, is half blind, and never read a larger volume than a newspaper. I will not trouble you with the whole conversation, though it would make an excellent scene in a farce; but after they had in the best bred way in the world convinced me that they thought I lied when I talked of reading without glasses, the foresaid matron obligingly said she should be very proud to see the writing I talked of, having heard me say formerly I had no correspondents but my daughter and Mr. W.* She was interrupted by her sister, who said, simpering, "You forgot Sir J. S." I took her up something short, I confess, and said in a dry stern tone, "Madam, I do write to Sir J. S. and will do it as long as he will permit that honor." This rudeness of mine occasioned a profound silence for some minutes and they fell into a good-natured discourse of the ill consequences of too much application, and remembered how many apoplexies, gouts, and dropsies had happened among the hard students of their acquaintance. As I never studied any thing in my life, and have always (at least from fifteen) thought the reputation of learning a misfortune to a woman, I was resolved to believe these stories were not meant at me : I grew silent in my turn, and took up a card that lay on a table, and amused myself with smoking it over a candle. In the mean time (as the song says),

> Their tattles all run, as swift as the sun,
> Of who had won, and who was undone
> By their gaming and sitting up late.

When it was observed I entered into none of these topics, I was addressed by an obliging lady, who pitied my stupidity. "Indeed, madam, you should buy horses to that fine machine you have at Padua; of what use is it standing in the portico?" "Perhaps," said another, wittily, "of as much use as a standing dish." A gaping school-boy added with still more wit, "I have seen at a country gentleman's table a venison-pasty made of wood." I was not at all vexed by said school-boy, not because he was (in more senses than one) the highest of

* Wortley.

the company, but knowing he did not mean to offend me. I confess (to my shame be it spoken) I was grieved at the triumph that appeared in the eyes of the king and queen of the company, the court being tolerably full. His majesty walked off early with the air befitting his dignity, followed by his train of courtiers, who, like courtiers, were laughing among themselves as they followed him: and I was left with the two queens, one of whom was making ruffles for the man she loved, and the other slopping tea, for the good of her country. They renewed their generous endeavors to set me right, and I (graceless beast that I am) take up the smoked card which lay before me, and with the corner of another wrote—

> If ever I one thought bestow
> On what such fools advise,
> May I be dull enough to grow
> Most miserably wise.

And flung down the card on the table, and myself out of the room, in the most indecent fury. A few minutes on the cold water convinced me of my folly, and I went home as much mortified as my Lord E. when he has lost his last stake of hazard. Pray don't think (if you can help it) this is an affectation of mine to enhance the value of a talent I would be thought to despise; as celebrated beauties often talk of the charms of good sense, having some reason to fear their mental qualities are not quite so conspicuous as their outside lovely form.

LETTER VII.

VENICE, Oct. 13, 1759.

You have made (what I did not think possible) writing to you uneasy to me. After confessing that you barbarously criticise on my letters, I have much ado to summon up courage enough to set pen to paper. Can you answer this to your

15*

conscience, to sit gravely and maliciously to examine lines written with rapidity and sent without reading over? This is worse than surprising a fine lady just sat down to the toilet: I am content to let you see my mind undressed, but I will not have you so curiously remark the defects in it. To carry on the simile, when a beauty appears with all her graces and airs adorned for a ball, it is lawful to censure whatever you see amiss in her ornaments; but when you are received to a friendly breakfast, 'tis downright cruelty or (something worse) ingratitude, to view too nicely all the disorder you may see. I desire you would sink the critic in the friend, and never forget that I do not write to you and dear Lady Fanny from my head but from my heart. I wish her joy on the continuance of her taste for punch, but I am sure she will agree with me that the zest of good company is very necessary to give it a flavor: to her it is a vivifying nectar, to me it would be insipid river-water, and chill the spirits it should raise, by reflecting on the cheerful moments we once passed together, which can no more return. This thought is so very disagreeable I will put it as far from me as possible. My chief study all my life has been to lighten misfortunes and multiply pleasures as far as human nature can: when I have nothing to find in myself from which I can extract any kind of delight, I think on the happiness of my friends, and rejoice in the joy with which you converse together, and look on the beautiful young plant from which you may so reasonably expect honor and felicity. In other days I think over the comic scenes that are daily exhibited on the great stage of the world for my entertainment. I am charmed with the account of the Moravians, who certainly exceed all mankind in absurdity of principles and madness of practice; yet this people walk erect and are numbered among rational beings. I imagined after three thousand years' working at creeds and theological whimsies, there remained nothing new to be invented; I see the fund is inexhaustible, and we may say of folly what Horace has said of vice:

> Ætas parentum, pejor avis, tulit
> Nos nequiores, mox daturos
> Progeniem vitiosiorem.

I will not ask pardon for this quotation ; it is God's mercy I did not put it into English : when one is haunted (as I am) by the Dæmon of Poesie, it must come out in one shape or another, and you will own that nobody shows it to more advantage than the author I have mentioned. Adieu, sir ; read with candor ; forgive what you can't excuse, in favor of the real esteem and affection with which I am Lady Fanny's and your most humble servant.

LETTER VIII.

VENICE, March 1, 1760.

I have at length received your valuable and magnificent present. You will have me give my opinion ; I know not how to do it without your accusing me of flattery (though I am sure no other person would suspect it). It is hard to forbear praising where there is so much due ; yet I would rather talk of your performance to any other than yourself. If I durst speak out, I would say that you have explained in the best manner the most difficult subject, and struck out new lights that are necessary to enforce conviction even to those who have studied the points you treat ; and who are often misled by prejudices which fall away, while your instructions take place in every mind capable of distinguishing truth from falsehood. Upon the whole, permit me to say I never saw a treatise which gave me so much pleasure and information. You show yourself qualified by nature for the charge of first minister : how far that would recommend you to a minister I think problematic. I am beginning to read over your works a second time ; my approbation increases as I go on ; the solidity of your reflections would overbalance a defect in style, if there was any, but I sincerely find none. The nervous man-

ner in which you write is infinitely preferable to the florid
phrases, which are always improper in a book of this nature,
which is not designed to move the passions but to convince
the reason.

I ought to say a great deal for the honor you have done
me in your dedication. Lord Burleigh, or even Julius Cæsar,
would have been proud of it; I can have no pretense to deserve it, yet I may truly say nobody can be more sensible of
the value of your present. It is pity the world should be
deprived of the advantage of so useful a performance; yet
perhaps it may be necessary to wait some time before you
publish certain truths that are not yet popularly received.

I hope our dear Lady Fanny is in good health, and your
young gentleman daily improving both by nature and instruction. I flatter myself that your affairs will soon take a more
agreeable turn. Wherever you are I wish you every happiness; and wherever I am you will ever have a faithful humble
servant, engaged both by inclination and obligation to be
always at your command.

LETTER IX.

VENICE, April 7, 1760.

I have now with great pleasure, and I flatter myself with
some improvement, read over again your delightful and instructive treatise; you have opened to me several truths of
which I had before only a confused idea. I confess I can not
help being a little vain of comprehending a system that is
calculated only for a thinking mind, and can not be tasted
without a willingness to lay aside many prejudices which arise
from education and the conversation of people no wiser than
ourselves. I do not only mean my own sex when I speak of
our confined way of reasoning; there are many of yours as
incapable of judging otherwise than they have been early
taught, as the most ignorant milkmaid: nay, I believe a girl

out of a village or a nursery more capable of receiving instruction than a lad just free from the university. It is not difficult to write on blank paper, but 'tis a tedious if not an impossible task to scrape out nonsense already written, and put better sense in the place of it. Mr. Steuart is very happy to be under the direction of a father who will not suffer him to entertain errors at an age when 'tis hard to distinguish them. I often look back on my past life in the light in which old Montaigne considered it; it is, perhaps, a more useful study than it is generally imagined. Mr. Locke, who has made the best dissection of the human mind of any author I have ever read, declares that he has drawn all his observations from reflecting on the progression of his own ideas. It is true a very small proportion of knowledge is allowed us in this world, few truths permitted, but those truths are plain; they may be overseen or artfully obscured from our sight, but when pointed out to us, it is impossible to resist the conviction that accompanies them. I am persuaded your manuscript would have the same effect on every candid reader it has on me: but I am afraid their number is very small.

I think the omission you desire in the act of indemnity can not fail of happening; I shall take every opportunity of putting people of my acquaintance in mind of it: at present the real director* (at least of home affairs) is a countryman of yours; but you know there are certain circumstances that may disincline from meddling in some nice matters. I am always with gratitude and the truest esteem, both to Lady Frances and yourself, a faithful humble servant.

---

* Lord Mansfield is probably here alluded to. He was a member of the Cabinet during the last years of George the Second's reign, and supposed to have great influence with the Duke of Newcastle, the nominal head of that administration. The circumstance of his having been himself attached on the score of early Jacobinism, might make him cautious of appearing to protect persons in Sir James Steuart's situation.

LETTER X.

VENICE, January, 13, 1761.

1 have indulged myself some time with day-dreams of the happiness I hoped to enjoy this summer in the conversation of Lady Fanny and Sir James S.; but I hear such frightful stories of precipices and hovels during the whole journey, I begin to fear there is no such pleasure allotted me in the book of fate: the Alps were once mole-hills in my sight when they interposed between me and the slightest inclination; now age begins to freeze, and brings with it the usual train of melancholy apprehensions. Poor human-kind! We always march blindly on; the fire of youth represents to us all our wishes possible: and, that over, we fall into despondency that prevents even easy enterprises: a stove in winter, a garden in summer bounds all our desires, or at least our undertakings. If Mr. Steuart would disclose all his imaginations, I dare swear he has some thoughts of emulating Alexander or Demosthenes, perhaps both: nothing seems difficult at his time of life, every thing at mine. I am very unwilling, but am afraid I must submit to the confinement of my boat and my easy chair, and go no further than they can carry me. Why are our views so extensive, and our power so miserably limited? This is among the mysteries which (as you justly say) will remain ever unfolded to our shallow capacities. I am much inclined to think we are no more free agents than the queen of clubs when she victoriously takes prisoner the knave of hearts, and all our efforts (when we rebel against destiny) as weak as a card that sticks to a glove when the gamester is determined to throw it on the table. Let us then (which is the only true philosophy) be contented with our chance, and make the best of that very bad bargain of being born in this wild planet; where we may find however (God be thanked) much to laugh at, though little to approve.

I confess I delight extremely in looking at men in that light. How many thousands trample under foot honor, ease, and pleasure, in pursuit of ribbons of certain colors, dabs of embroidery on their clothes, and gilt wood carved behind their coaches in a particular figure? Others breaking their hearts till they are distinguished by the shape and color of their hats; and, in general, all people earnestly seeking what they do not want, while they neglect the real blessings in their possession, I mean the innocent gratification of their senses, which is all we can properly call our own. For my part, I will endeavor to comfort myself for the cruel disappointment I find in renouncing Tubingen by eating some fresh oysters on the table. I hope you are sitting down with dear Lady F. to some admirable red partridges, which I think are the growth of that country. Adieu!

LETTER XI.

VENICE, January, 25, 1761.

SIR—I have not returned my thanks for your obliging letter so soon as both duty and inclination prompted me; but I have had so severe a cold accompanied with a weakness in my eyes, that I have been confined to my store for many days. This is the first use I make of my pen. I will not engage in a dispute with you, being very sure that I am unable to support it against you; yet I own I am entirely of your opinion in relation to the civil list. I know it has long been a custom to begin every reign with some mark of the people's love exceeding what was shown to the predecessor: I am glad to see this distinguished by the trust and affection of the king to his people, and am persuaded it will have a very good effect on all our affairs foreign and domestic. It is possible my daughter may have some partiality; the character of his present majesty needs only be half so perfect as she describes it, to be such a monarch as has never existed but in romances. Though I am preparing for my last and longest journey, and stand on the threshold of this dirty world, my several infirmities like post-horses ready to hurry me away, I can not be insensible to the happiness of my native country, and am glad to see the prospect of a prosperity and harmony that I never was witness to. I hope my friends will be included in the public joy; and I shall always think Lady Fanny and Sir James Steuart in the first rank of those I wish to serve. Your conversation is a pleasure I would prefer to any other, but I confess even that can not make me desire to be in London, especially at this time when the shadow of credit that I should be supposed to possess would attract daily solicitations, and gain me a number of enemies who would never forgive me the not performing impossibilities. If all people thought of power as I do, it would be avoided with as much eagerness as it is now sought. I never knew any person that had it who did not lament the load; though I confess (so infirm is human nature) they have all endeavored to retain it, at the same time they complained of it.

LETTER XII.

July 22, 1761.

Sir—I expect you should wish me joy on the good fortune of a friend I esteem in the highest manner. I have always preferred the interest of those I love to my own. You need not doubt of my sincere affection toward the lady and young gentleman you mention. My own affairs here grow worse and worse; my indiscreet well-wishers do me as much harm, more harm than any declared enemy could do. The notable plan of our great politician is to make me surrender my little castle; I, with the true spirit of old Whiggism, resolve to keep my ground, though I starve in the maintaining it, or am eat up by the wild beasts of the wood, meaning gnats and flies. A word to the wise; you understand me. You may have heard of a facetious gentleman vulgarly called Tom Earle, *i. e.*, Giles Earle,* Esq. His toast was always:

* A Lord of the Treasury. See Honorable Horace Walpole's letters

"God bless you, whatever becomes of me!"

> The day when hungry friar wishes
> He might eat other food than fishes,
> Or, to explain the date more fully,
> The twenty-second instant July.

LETTER XIII.

October 1, 1761.

MADAM AND SIR—I am now part of my way to England, where I hope to have the pleasure of seeing you ; it is so long since I have heard from you, I can not guess where you are. I venture this to Tubingen, though I fancy two letters I have directed thither have miscarried, and am so uncertain of the fate of this I know not what to say. I think I can not err in repeating a sincere truth, that I am, and ever shall be, faithfully your most humble servant.

Since I wrote the above I am told I may go by Wirtemberg to Frankfort. I will then take that road in hopes of seeing you.

LETTER XIV.

ROTTERDAM, Nov. 20, 1761.

SIR—I received yesterday your obliging and welcome letter by the hands of Mr. Simpson. I tried in vain to find you at Amsterdam : I began to think we resembled two parallel lines, destined to be always near and never to meet. You know there is no fighting (at least no overcoming) destiny. So far I am a confirmed Calvinist, according to the notions of the country

to Sir Horace Mann, Dec. 16, 1741, for an account of a debate and a division upon the occasion of the election of the Chairman of the Committees of the House of Commons, in which some account of this gentleman is to be found.

where I now exist. I am dragging my ragged remnant of life
to England. The wind and tide are against me; how far I have
strength to struggle against both I know not; that I am arrived
here is as much a miracle as any in the golden legend; and if
I had foreseen half the difficulties I have met with, I should
not certainly have had courage enough to undertake it. I have
scrambled through more dangers than his M. of P.,* or even
my well-beloved cousin (not counselor) Marquis Granby;†
but my spirits fail me when I think of my friends risking either
health or happiness. I will write to Lady Fanny to hinder
your coming to Rotterdam, and will sooner make one jump
more myself to wait on you at Antwerp. I am glad poor D.
has sold his medals. I confess I thought his buying them a
very bold stroke. I supposed that he had already left London, but am told that he has been prevented by the machina-
tions of that excellent politician and truly great man M——
and his ministry.

My dear Lady Fanny, I am persuaded that you are more
nearly concerned for the health of Sir James than he is himself. I address myself to you, to insist on it to him, not to
undertake a winter progress in the beginning of a fit of the
gout.

I am nailed down here by a severe illness of my poor Mari-
anne, who has not been able to endure the frights and fatigues that we have passed. If I live to see Great Britain, you
will have there a sincere and faithful servant that will omit no
occasion of serving you; and I think it almost impossible I
should not succeed. You must be loved and esteemed wherever you are known. Give me leave, however, dear madam,
to combat some of your notions, or more properly speaking,
your passions. Mr. Steuart is in a situation that opens the

---

* Majesty of Prussia.

† Lord Granby married the daughter of Charles, sixth Duke of Som-
erset, by his wife the youngest daughter of Daniel, Earl of Winchelsea
and Nottingham, whose wife was the daughter of Basil Earl Fielding,
and Lady Mary's first cousin.

fairest prospect of honor and advancement. We mothers are all apt to regret the absence of children we love: Solomon advises the sluggard to go to the ant and be wise; we should take the example of the innocent inhabitants of the air, when their young are fledged, they are delighted to see them fly and peck for themselves. Forgive this freedom. I have no other recipe for maternal fondness, a distemper which has long afflicted your ladyship's obliged and obedient humble servant.

LETTER XV.

ROTTERDAM, December 26, 1761.

SIR—The thaw is now so far advanced I am in great hopes of moving in a few days. My first care at London will be your affairs: I think it almost impossible I should not succeed. You may assure Lady Fanny no endeavor shall be wanting on my side: if I find any material objection I shall not fail to let you know it; I confess I do not foresee any. A young gentleman arrived here last night, who is perhaps of your acquaintance, Mr. Hamilton; he is hastening to London in expectation of an act of grace, which I believe will be granted. I flatter myself with the view of seeing you in England, and can affirm with truth it is one of the greatest pleasures I expect there. Whatever prosperity my family now enjoys, it will add much to my happiness to see my friends easy; and while you are unfortunate I shall always think myself so. This very dull weather operates on my spirits, though I use my utmost efforts to support them: I beg dear Lady Fanny to do the same; a melancholy state of mind should never be indulged, since it often remains even when the cause of it is removed. I have here neither amusement nor conversation, and am so infected by the climate that I verily believe, was I to stay long, I should take to smoking and drinking, like the natives. I should wish you the compliments of the season, a merry Christmas, but I know not how to do it while you remain in so disagreeable an uncertainty yet, if you have the company of Mr. Steuart, his bloom of life will insensibly communicate part of his gayety. If I could have foreseen my stay in this part of the world, I would have made a trip to Antwerp to enjoy a conversation ever honored and remembered by, sir and madam, your most faithful and obedient humble servant.

LETTER XVI.

ROTTERDAM, January 2, 1762.

I have been half way to Helvoet, and was obliged to turn back by the mountains of sea that obstructed our passage: the captain, however, gives me hopes of setting out in two or three days. I have had so many disappointments I can scarce entertain the flattering thought of arriving at London. Wherever I am you may depend upon it, dear madam, I shall ever retain the warmest sentiments of good-will for you and your family, and will use my utmost endeavors to give you better proofs of it than I can do by expressions which will always fall short of my thoughts.

Many happy new years to you, madam. May this atone for the ill-fortune of those that are past, and all those to come be cheerful. Mr. Hamilton, whom I mentioned, has, I believe, got a particular pardon; his case is extraordinary, having no relation to public affairs. I am sorry for poor Duff, and fear that wherever he moves there will be little difference in his situation; he carries with him such a load of indiscretion, it is hardly in the power of Fortune to save him. We are crowded with officers of all ranks, returning to England. The peace seems to be more distant than ever: it would be very indifferent to me if it did not affect my friends; my remaining time in this world is so short I have few wishes to make for myself, and when I am free from pain ought to think myself happy.

It is uncommon at my age to have no distemper and to retain all my senses in their first degree of perfection. I should be unworthy these blessings if I did not acknowledge them. If I am so fortunate to see your ladyship and Sir James in good health at London, it will be a great addition to the satisfaction of, dear madam, your faithful and obedient humble servant.

LETTER XVII.

GREAT GEORGE-STREET, March 5th, 1762.

DEAR MADAM—I have written several letters to your ladyship, but I perceive by that I had the honor to receive yesterday they have all miscarried. I can assign no reason for it but the uncertainty of the post. I am told many mails have been taken, and the letters either thrown away or suppressed. We must suffer this among the common calamities of war. Our correspondence is so innocent we have no reason to apprehend our secrets being discovered.

I am proud to make public profession of being, dear madam, ever your most faithful humble servant.

In writing to you, I think I write to your whole family; I hope they think so too.

LETTER XVIII.

July 2d, 1762.*

DEAR MADAM—I have been ill a long time, and am now so bad I am little capable of writing, but I would not pass in your opinion as either stupid or ungrateful. My heart is always warm in your service, and I am always told your affairs shall be taken care of. You may depend, dear madam, nothing shall be wanting on the part of your ladyship's faithful humble servant.

* Lady Mary died on the 21st of August, following.

SELECTIONS FROM VARIOUS LETTERS.*

THE SMALL-POX AND INOCULATION.—*A propos* of distempers, I am going to tell you a thing that will make you wish yourself here. The small-pox, so fatal and so general among us, is here entirely harmless by the invention of *ingrafting*, which is the term they give it. There is a set of old women who make it their business to perform the operation every autumn, in the month of September, when the great heat is abated. People send to one another to know if any of their family has a mind to have the small-pox : they make parties for this purpose, and when they are met (commonly fifteen or sixteen together), the old woman comes with a nut-shell full of the matter of the best sort of small-pox, and asks what vein you please to have opened. She immediately rips open that you offer to her with a large needle (which gives you no more pain than a common scratch), and puts into the vein as much matter as can lie upon the head of her needle, and after that binds up the little wound with a hollow bit of shell ; and in this manner opens four or five veins. The Grecians have commonly the superstition of opening one in the middle of the forehead, one in each arm, and one on the breast, to mark the sign of the cross ; but this has a very ill effect, all these wounds leaving little scars, and is not done by

* These extracts are made on the same plan as those in the " Letters of Madame de Sévigné," viz., to bring together whatever was of real value in the omitted Letters of Lady Mary, and thus make a clear exposition of her talents and character.—AM. ED.

those that are not superstitious, who choose to have them in the legs, or that part of the arm that is concealed. The children or young patients play together all the rest of the day, and are in perfect health to the eighth. Then the fever begins to seize them, and they keep their beds two days, very seldom three. They have very rarely above twenty or thirty in their faces, which never mark; and in eight days' time they are as well as before their illness. Where they are wounded there remain running sores during the distemper, which I don't doubt is a great relief to it. Every year thousands undergo this operation; and the French embassador says pleasantly, that they take the small-pox here by way of diversion, as they take the waters in other countries. There is no example of any one that has died in it; and you may believe I am well satisfied of the safety of this experiment, since I intend to try it on my dear little son.

I am patriot enough to take pains to bring this useful invention into fashion in England; and I should not fail to write to some of our doctors very particularly about it, if I knew any one of them that I thought had virtue enough to destroy such a considerable branch of their revenue for the good to mankind. But that distemper is too beneficial to them not to expose to all their resentment the hardy wight that should undertake to put an end to it. Perhaps, if I live to return, I may, however, have courage to war with them. Upon this occasion admire the heroism in the heart of your friend.

LIFE AT VIENNA IN 1716.—It is not from Austria that one can write with vivacity, and I am already infected with the phlegm of the country. Even their amours and their quarrels are carried on with a surprising temper, and they are never lively but upon points of ceremony. There, I own, they show all their passions; and 'tis not long since two coaches, meeting in a narrow street at night, the ladies in them not being able to adjust the ceremonial of which should go back, sat there with equal gallantry till two in the morning, and were both so fully determined to die upon the spot, rather than yield in a point of that importance, that the street would never have been cleared till their deaths, if the emperor had not sent his guards to part them ; and even then they refused to stir till the expedient could be found out of taking them both out in chairs, exactly in the same moment. After the ladies were agreed, it was with some difficulty that the *pas* was decided between the two coachmen, no less tenacious of their rank than the ladies.

This passion is so omnipotent in the breasts of the women that even their husbands never die but they are ready to break their hearts, because that fatal hour puts an end to their rank, no widows having any place at Vienna. The men are not much less touched with this point of honor, and they do not only scorn to marry, but even to make love to any woman of a family not as illustrious as their own ; and the pedigree is much more considered by them than either the complexion or features of their mistresses. Happy are the shes that can number among their ancestors counts of the empire ; they have neither occasion for beauty, money, nor good conduct, to get them husbands. 'Tis true, as to money, it is seldom any advantage to the man they marry ; the laws of Austria confine the woman's portion to two thousand florins (about two hundred pounds English), and whatever they have beside remains in their own possession and disposal. Thus, here are many ladies much richer than their husbands, who are, however, obliged to allow them pin-money agreeably to their quality ; and I attribute to this considerable branch of prerogative the liberty that they take upon other occasions.

*　　*　　*　　*　　*　　*　　*　　*　　*

If I should undertake to tell you all the particulars, in which the manners here differ from ours, I must write a whole quire of the dullest stuff that ever was read, or printed without being read. Their dress agrees with the French or English in no one article but wearing petticoats. They have many fashions peculiar to themselves ; they think it indecent for a widow ever to wear green or rose-color, but all the other gayest colors at her own discretion. The assemblies here are the only regular diversion, the operas being always at court, and commonly on some particular occasion. Madame Rabutin has the assembly constantly every night at her house; and the other ladies, whenever they have a mind to display the magnificence of their apartments, or oblige a friend by complimenting them on the day of their saint, they declare that on such a day the assembly shall be at their house in honor of the feast of the Count or Countess —— *such a one.* These days are called days of gala, and all the friends or relations of the lady, whose saint it is, are obliged to appear in their best clothes, and all their jewels. The mistress of the house takes no particular notice of any body, nor returns any body's visit; and whoever pleases may go, without the formality of being presented. The company are entertained with ice in several forms, winter and summer; afterward they divide into several parties of ombre, piquet, or conversation, all games of hazard being forbidden.

MARRIAGE OF THE GRAND SEIGNIOR'S DAUGHTER.—The Grand Seignior's eldest daughter was married some few days before I came hither; and, upon that occasion, the Turkish ladies display all their magnificence. The bride was conducted to her husband's house in very great splendor. She is widow of the late vizier, who was killed at Peterwaradin, though that ought rather to be called a contract than a marriage, since she never has lived with him; however, the greatest part of his wealth is hers. He had the permission of visiting her in the seraglio, and, being one of the handsomest men in the empire, had very much engaged her affections. When she saw this second husband, who is at least fifty, she could not forbear bursting into tears. He is indeed a man of merit, and the declared favorite of the sultan (which they call *mosàyp*), but that is not enough to make him pleasing in the eyes of a girl of thirteen.

ARBITRARY GOVERNMENT.—The government here is entirely in the hands of the army: the Grand Seignior, with all his absolute power, is as much a slave as any of his subjects, and trembles at a janizary's frown. Here is, indeed, a much greater appearance of subjection than among us : a minister of state is not spoken to but upon the knee ; should a reflection on his conduct be dropped in a coffee-house (for they have spies every where), the house would be razed to the ground, and perhaps the whole company put to the torture. No *huzzaing mobs, senseless pamphlets, and tavern disputes about politics ;*

> A consequential ill that freedom draws ;
> A bad effect—but from a noble cause.

None of our harmless calling names ! but when a minister here displeases the people, in three hours' time he is dragged even from his master's arms. They cut off hands, head, and feet, and throw them before the palace gate with all the respect in the world ; while the sultan (to whom they all profess an unlimited adoration) sits trembling in his apartment, and dare neither defend nor revenge his favorite. This is the blessed condition of the most absolute monarch upon earth, who owns no *law* but his *will.*

I can not help wishing, in the loyalty of my heart, that the parliament would send hither a ship-load of your passive-obedient men, that they might see arbitrary government in its clearest and strongest light, where it is hard to judge whether the prince, people, or ministers, are most miserable.

———

TURKISH HOUSES.—Every house, great and small, is divided into two distinct parts, which only join together by a narrow passage. The first house has a large court before it, and open galleries all round it, which is to me a thing very agreeable. This gallery leads to all the chambers, which are commonly large, and with two rows of windows, the first being of painted glass : they seldom build above two stories, each of which has galleries. The stairs are broad, and not often above thirty steps. This is the house belonging to the lord, and the adjoining one is called the *harem*, that is, the ladies' apartment (for the name of *seraglio* is peculiar to the Grand Seignior); it has also a gallery running round it toward the garden, to which all the windows are turned, and the same number of chambers as the other, but more gay and splendid, both in painting and furniture. The second row of windows is very low, with grates like those of convents; the rooms are all spread with Persian carpets, and raised at one end of them (my chambers are raised at both ends) about two feet. This is the sofa, which is laid with a richer sort of carpet, and all round it a sort of couch, raised half a foot, covered with rich silk according to the fancy or magnificence of the owner. Mine is of scarlet cloth, with a gold fringe; round about this are placed, standing against the wall, two rows of cushions, the first very large, and the next little ones; and here the Turks display their greatest magnificence. They are generally brocade, or embroidery of gold wire upon white satin; nothing can look more gay and splendid. These seats are also so convenient and easy, that I believe I shall never endure chairs as long as I live. The rooms are low, which I think no fault, and the ceiling is always of wood, generally inlaid or painted with flowers. They open in many places with folding-doors, and serve for cabinets, I think, more conveniently than ours. Between the windows are little arches to set pots of perfume, or baskets of flowers. But what pleases me best, is the fashion of having marble fountains in the lower part of the room, which throw up several spouts of water, giving at the same time an agreeable coolness, and a pleasant dashing sound, falling from one basin to another. Some of these are very magnificent. Each house has a bagnio, which consists generally in two or three little rooms, leaded on the top, paved with marble, with basins, cocks of water, and all conveniences for either hot or cold baths.

THE CHURCH OF ST. SOPHIA—The next remarkable structure is that of St. Sophia, which is very difficult to see. I was forced to send three times to the *caimaikam* (the governor of the town), and he assembled the chief *effendis*, or heads of the law, and inquired of the *mufti* whether it was lawful to permit it. They passed some days in this important debate; but I insisting on my request, permission was granted. I can't be informed why the Turks are more delicate on the subject of this mosque than on any of the others, where what Christian pleases may enter without scruple. I fancy they imagine that, having been once consecrated, people, on pretense of curiosity, might profane it with prayers, particularly to those saints who are still very visible in mosaic work, and no other way defaced but by the decays of time; for it is absolutely false, though so universally asserted, that the Turks defaced all the images that they found in the city. The dome of St. Sophia is said to be one hundred and thirteen feet in diameter, built upon arches, sustained by vast pillars of marble, the pavement and stair case marble. There are two rows of galleries, supported with pillars of particolored marble, and the whole roof mosaic work, part of which decays very fast, and drops down. They presented me a handful of it; its composition seems to me a sort of glass, or that paste with which they make counterfeit jewels. They show here the tomb of the Emperor Constantine, for which they have a great veneration.

THE ARMENIANS.—Now I have mentioned the Armenians, perhaps it will be agreeable to tell you something of that nation, with which I am sure you are utterly unacquainted. I will not trouble you with the geographical account of the situation of their country, which you may see in the maps, or a relation of their ancient greatness, which you may read in the Roman history. They are now subject to the Turks; and, being very industrious in trade, and increasing and multiplying, are dispersed in great numbers through all the Turkish dominions. They were, as they say, converted to the Christian religion by

St. Gregory, and are perhaps the devoutest Christians in the whole world. The chief precepts of their priest enjoin the strict keeping of their lents, which are at least seven months in every year, and are not to be dispensed with on the most emergent necessity; no occasion whatever can excuse them, if they touch any thing more than mere herbs or roots (without oil) and plain dry bread. That is their constant diet. Mr. Wortley has one of his interpreters of this nation; and the poor fellow was brought so low by the severity of his fasts that his life was despaired of. Yet neither his master's commands nor the doctor's entreaties (who declared nothing else could save his life), were powerful enough to prevail with him to take two or three spoonfuls of broth. Excepting this, which may rather be called a custom than an article of faith, I see very little in their religion different from ours. 'Tis true they seem to incline very much to Mr. Whiston's doctrine; neither do I think the Greek Church very distant from it, since 'tis certain the Holy Spirit's proceeding *only* from the Father, is making a plain subordination in the Son. But the Armenians have no notion of transubstantiation, whatever account Sir Paul Rycaut gives of them (which account I am apt to believe was designed to compliment our court in 1679); and they have a great horror for those among them that change to the Roman religion.

THE PARADISE OF WOMEN.—As to your next inquiry, I assure you it is certainly false, though commonly believed in our parts of the world, that Mohammed excludes women from any share in a future happy state. He was too much a gentleman, and loved the fair sex too well, to use them so barbarously. On the contrary, he promises a very fine paradise to the Turkish women. He says, indeed, that this paradise will be a separate place from that of their husbands; but I fancy the most part of them won't like it the worse for that; and that the regret of this separation will not render their paradise the less agreeable.

RELICS AT RATISBON.—I have been to see the churches here, and had the permission of touching the relics, which was never suffered in places where I was not known. I had, by this privilege, the opportunity of making an observation, which I doubt not might have been made in all the other churches, that the emeralds and rubies which they show round their relics and images are most of them false; though they tell you that many of the *Crosses* and *Madonnas*, set round with these stones, have been the gifts of the emperors and other great princes. I don't doubt, indeed, but they were at first jewels of value; but the good fathers have found it convenient to apply them to other uses, and the people are just as well satisfied with bits of glass. Among these relics they showed me a prodigious claw set in gold, which they called the claw of a griffin; and I could not forbear asking the reverend priest that showed it whether the griffin was a saint? This question almost put him beside his gravity; but he answered they only kept it as a curiosity. I was very much scandalized at a large silver image of the *Trinity*, where the *Father* is represented under the figure of a decrepid old man, with a beard down to his knees, and a triple crown on his head, holding in his arms the *Son*, fixed on the cross, and the *Holy Ghost*, in the shape of a dove, hovering over him.

A GOOD RULER.—I am sincerely afflicted for the death of the doge.* He is lamented here by all ranks of people, as their common parent. He really answered the idea of Lord Bolingbroke's imaginary patriotic prince, and was the only example I ever knew of having passed through the greatest employments, and most important negotiations, without ever making an enemy. When I was at Venice, which was some months before his election, he was the leading voice in the senate, which would have been dangerous in the hands of a bad man: yet he had the art to silence envy;

* Pietro Grimani died 1752. He was elected Doge of Venice in 1741, and was succeeded by Francesco Loredano.

and I never once heard an objection to his character, or even
an insinuation to his disadvantage. I attribute this peculiar
happiness to be owing to the sincere benevolence of his heart,
joined with an easy cheerfulness of temper, which made him
agreeable to all companies, and a blessing to all his dependents. Authority appeared so humble in him, no one wished it
less, except himself, who would sometimes lament the weight
of it, as robbing him too much of the conversation of his
friends in which he placed his chief delight, being so little ambitious that, to my certain knowledge, far from caballing to
gain that elevation to which he was raised, he would have refused it, if he did not look upon the acceptance of it as a
duty due to his country.

PARIS AND LONDON IN 1718.—In general, I think Paris has
the advantage of London, in the neat pavement of the streets,
and the regular lighting of them at nights, and in the proportion of the streets, the houses being all built of stone, and
most of those belonging to people of quality being beautified
by gardens. But we certainly may boast of a town very near
twice as large; and when I have said that, I know nothing
else we surpass it in.

THE RULING PASSION.—I arrived this morning at Dover,
after being tossed a whole night in a packet-boat, in so violent
a manner that the master, considering the weakness of his
vessel, thought it proper to remove the mail, and give us notice
of the danger. We called a little fishing-boat, which could
hardly make up to us; while all the people on board us were
crying to heaven. It is hard to imagine one's self in a scene
of greater horror than on such an occasion; and yet, shall I
own it to you? though I was not at all willing to be drowned,
I could not forbear being entertained at the double distress of a
fellow-passenger. She was an English lady that I had met at
Calais, who desired me to let her go over with me in my cabin.
She had bought a fine point-head, which she was contriving to

conceal from the Custom-house officers. When the wind grew high, and our little vessel cracked, she fell very heartily to her prayers, and thought wholly of her soul. When it seemed to abate, she returned to the worldly care of her head-dress, and addressed herself to me: "*Dear madam, will you take care of this point? if it should be lost! Ah, Lord, we shall all be lost!—Lord have mercy on my soul!—Pray, madam, take care of this head-dress!*"

To See is to Know.—The description of a face or figure is a needless thing, as it never conveys a true idea; it only gratifies the imagination with a fantastic one until the real one is seen. So, my dear, if you have a mind to form a true notion of the divine forms and features of the Venus and Antinous, come to Florence.

La Trappe.—Between Bologna and Florence I went out of my road to visit the monastery of La Trappe, which is of French origin, and one of the most austere and self-denying orders I know of. In this gloomy retreat it gave me pain to observe those austere men, who have devoutly reduced themselves to a worse condition than that of the beasts. Folly, you see, is the lot of humanity, whether it arises in the flowery paths of pleasure or the thorny ones of an ill-judged devotion. But of the two sorts of fools, I shall always think that the merry one has the most eligible fate; and I can not well form a notion of that spiritual and extatic joy that is mixed with sighs, groans, hunger, and thirst, and the other complicated miseries of monastic discipline. It is a strange way of going to work for happiness to excite an enmity between soul and body, which Nature and Providence have designed to live together in union and friendship, and which we can not separate like man and wife when they happen to disagree. The profound silence that is enjoined upon the monks of La Trappe, is a singular circumstance of their unsociable and unnatural discipline; and were this injunction never to be dispensed with, it would be needless to visit them in any other character than as a collection of statues; but the superior of the convent suspended in our favor that rigorous law, and allowed one of the mutes to converse with me, and answer a few discreet questions. He told me that the monks of this order in France are still more austere than those of Italy, as they never taste wine, flesh, fish, or eggs; but live entirely upon vegetables. The story that is told of the institution of this order is remarkable, and is well attested, if my information be good. Its founder was a French nobleman, whose name was Bouthillier de Rancé, a man of pleasure and gallantry, who was converted into the deepest gloom of devotion by the following incident: His affairs obliged him to absent himself, for some time, from a lady with whom he had lived in the most intimate and tender connections of successful love. At his return to Paris, he proposed to surprise her agreeably, and, at the same time, to satisfy his own impatient desire of seeing her, by going directly and without ceremony to her apartment by a back stair, which he was well acquainted with: but think of the spectacle that presented itself to him at his entrance into the chamber that had so often been the scene of love's highest raptures! his mistress dead—dead of the small-pox—disfigured beyond expression—a loathsome mass of putrid matter—and the surgeon separating the head from the body, because the coffin had been made too short! He stood for a moment motionless in amazement, and filled with horror—and then retired from the world, shut himself up in the convent of La Trappe, where he passed the remainder of his days.

FREE TOWNS.—I have already passed a large part of Germany, have seen all that is remarkable in Cologne, Frankfort, Wurtsburg, and this place. 'Tis impossible not to observe the difference between the free towns and those under the government of absolute princes, as all the little sovereigns of Germany are. In the first, there appears an air of commerce and plenty. The streets are well built, and full of people, neatly and plainly dressed. The shops are loaded with merchandise, and the commonalty are clean and cheerful. In the other you see a sort of shabby finery, a number of dirty people of quality tawdered out ; narrow nasty streets, out of repair, wretchedly thin of inhabitants, and above half of the common sort asking alms. I can not help fancying one under the figure of a clean Dutch citizen's wife, and the other like a poor town lady of pleasure, painted and ribboned out in her head-dress, with tarnished silver-laced shoes, a ragged under-petticoat, a miserable mixture of vice and poverty.

SUMPTUARY LAWS.—They have sumptuary laws in this town, which distinguish their rank by their dress, prevent the excess which ruins so many other cities, and has a more agreeable effect to the eye of a stranger than our fashions. I think after the Archbishop of Cambray having declared for them, I need not be ashamed to own that I wish these laws were in force in other parts of the world. When one considers impartially the merit of a rich suit of clothes in most places, the respect and the smiles of favor it procures, not to speak of the envy and the sighs it occasions (which is very often the prinpal charm to the wearer), one is forced to confess that there is need of an uncommon understanding to resist the temptation of pleasing friends and mortifying rivals ; and that it is natural to young people to fall into a folly which betrays them to that want of money which is the source of a thousand basenesses. What numbers of men have begun the world with generous inclinations that have afterward been the instruments of bringing misery on a whole people, being led by vain expense into debts that they could clear no other way but by the forfeit of their honor, and which they never could have contracted if the respect the many pay to habits was fixed by law only to a particular color or cut of plain cloth ! These reflections draw after them others that are too melancholy.

FRENCH LADIES IN 1748.—*A propos* of countenances, I must tell you something of the French ladies; I have seen al the beauties, and such —— (I can't help making use of the coarse word) nauseous creatures! so fantastically absurd in their dress! so monstrously unnatural in their paints! their hair cut short, and curled round their faces, and so loaded with powder that it makes it look like white wool! and on their cheeks to their chins, unmercifully laid, on a shining red japan, that glistens in a most flaming manner, so that they seem to have no resemblance to human faces. I am apt to believe that they took the first hint of their dress from a fair sheep newly ruddled. 'Tis with pleasure I recollect my dear pretty countrywomen: and if I was writing to any body else I should say that these grotesque daubers give me still a higher esteem of the natural charms of dear Lady Rich's auburn hair, and the lively colors of her unsullied complexion.

GAMING.—Play is the general plague of Europe. I know no corner of it entirely free from the infection. I do not doubt but that the familiarities of the gaming-table contribute very much to that decay of politeness of which you complain; for the pouting and quarrels, which naturally arise from disputes there, must put an end to all complaisance, or even good-will toward each other.

CONVERSATION.—There are many in the world incapable of any other sort of conversation except that of remarking the mistakes of others, and are very often so much mistaken themselves they blame the most praiseworthy actions, and are so unacquainted with virtue they do not know it when they see it.

THE WORLD A CENTURY AGO.—The world is so corrupt it is difficult to meet with honesty in any station, and such good hearts as yours, which are not naturally inclined to suspicion, are often liable to be imposed on.

LIFE AT TWICKENHAM.—I am now at the same distance from London that you are from Paris, and could fall into solitary amusements with a good deal of taste; but I resist it as a temptation of Satan, and rather turn my endeavors to make the world as agreeable to me as I can, which is the true philosophy; that of despising it is of no use but to hasten wrinkles. I ride a good deal, and have got a horse superior to any two-legged animal, he being without a fault. I work like an angel. I receive visits upon idle days, and I shade my life as I do my tent-stitch, that is, make as easy transitions as I can from business to pleasure; the one would be too flaring and gaudy without some dark shades of t' other; and if I worked altogether in the grave colors, you know 't would be quite dismal. Miss Skerret is in the house with me, and Lady Stafford has taken a lodging at Richmond. As their ages are different, and both agreeable in their kind, I laugh with the one, or reason with the other, as I happen to be in a gay or serious humor; and I manage my friends with such a strong, yet with a gentle hand, that they are both willing to do whatever I have a mind to.

THE WASP OF TWICKENHAM.*—The word malignity, and a passage in your letter, call to my mind the wicked wasp of Twickenham. His lies affect me now no more; they will be all as much despised as the story of the seraglio and the handkerchief, of which I am persuaded he was the only inventor. That man has a malignant and ungenerous heart; and he is base enough to assume the mask of a moralist, in order to decry human nature, and to give a decent vent to his hatred of man and woman kind.

LORD BUTE.—Lord Bute† has attained office by a very uncommon road: I mean an acknowledged honor and probity.

* Pope.

† In the last of the letters of the Honorable Horace Walpole to Sir H. Mann, dated October 28, 1760, an account is given of King George

I have but one short instruction (pardon the word) to give on his account; that he will never forget the real interest of Prince and People can not be divided, and are almost as closely united as that of soul and body. I could preach long on this subject, but I ought to consider your time is now fully taken up, and you can have no leisure for reading my tedious letters. I shall henceforward relinquish the motherly prerogative I have hitherto indulged, of tiring your patience with long dissertations.

USEFUL KNOWLEDGE.—I congratulate my granddaughters on being born in an age so much enlightened. Sentiments are certainly extremely silly, and only qualify young people to be the bubbles of all their acquaintance. I do not doubt the frequency of assemblies has introduced a more enlarged way of thinking; it is a kind of public education, which I have always thought as necessary for girls as for boys. A woman married at five-and-twenty, from under the eye of a strict parent, is commonly as ignorant as she was at five, and no more capable of avoiding the snares, and struggling with the difficulties she will infallibly meet with in the commerce of the world. The knowledge of mankind (the most useful of all knowledge) can only be acquired by conversing with them. Books are so far from giving that instruction, they fill the head with a set of wrong notions, from whence spring the tribes of Clarissas, Harriots, etc. Yet such was the method

the Second's death, on the Friday preceding the 27th, and mention is made of the Duke of York and Lord Bute having been named by the new king to be "of the cabinet council," which was probably *the situation* to which Lady Mary refers in the beginning of this letter. He had been for some time before Groom of the Stole to the Prince of Wales, and continued in that office with the new king till he was appointed Secretary of State, on the resignation of Lord Holdernesse, on the 25th of March, 1761. On the resignation of the Duke of New-castle, Lord Bute became, on the 26th May, 1762, first Lord of the Treasury, which office he resigned on the 8th April, 1763, and never afterward took an active part in public life.

of education when I was in England, which I had it not in my power to correct; the young will always adopt the opinions of their companions rather than the advice of their mothers.

NO ONE HAPPY IN THIS LIFE.—I believe, like all others of your age, you have long been convinced there is no real happiness to be found or expected in this world. You have seen a court near enough to know neither riches nor power can secure it; and all human endeavors after felicity are as childish as running after sparrows to lay salt on their tails: but I ought to give you another information, which can only be learned by experience, that liberty is an idea equally chimerical, and has no real existence in this life. I can truly assure you, I have never been so little mistress of my own time and actions as since I have lived alone. Mankind is placed in a state of dependency, not only on one another (which all are in some degree), but so many inevitable accidents thwart our designs, and limit our best-laid projects. The poor efforts of our utmost prudence, and political schemes, appear, I fancy, in the eyes of some superior beings, like the pecking of a young linnet to break a wire cage, or the climbing of a squirrel in a hoop; the moral needs no explanation. Let us sing as cheerfully as we can in our impenetrable confinement, and crack our nuts with pleasure from the little store that is allowed us.

SOLITUDE.—People mistake very much in placing peace in woods and shades, for I believe solitude puts people out of humor, and makes them disposed to quarrel, or there would not be so many disputes about religion and liberty, by creatures that never understood the first, nor have, or are likely to have, a taste of the latter:

Crushed by the stint of thirty pounds a year.

LADY BUTE AS A MOTHER.—The conclusion of your letter has touched me very much. I sympathize with you, my dear child, in all the concern you express for your family; you may remember I represented it to you, before you were married; but that is one of the sentiments it is impossible to comprehend till it is felt. A mother only knows a mother's fondness. Indeed the pain so overbalances the pleasure that I believe if it could be thoroughly understood, there would be no mothers at all. However, take care that the anxiety for the future does not take from you the comforts you may enjoy in the present hour: it is all that is properly ours; and yet such is the weakness of humanity, we commonly lose what is, either by regretting the past, or disturbing our minds with fear of what may be. You have many blessings; a husband you love, and who behaves well to you, agreeable hopeful children, a handsome convenient house, with pleasant gardens, in a good air and fine situation, which I place among the most solid satisfactions of life. The truest wisdom is that which diminishes to us what is displeasing, and turns our thoughts to the advantages which we possess. I can assure you I give no precepts I do not daily practice. How often do I fancy to myself the pleasure I should take in seeing you in the midst of the little people; and how severe do I then think my destiny that denies me that happiness! I endeavor to comfort myself by reflecting that we should certainly have perpetual disputes (if not quarrels) concerning the management of them; the affection of a grandmother has generally a tincture of dotage; you would say I spoiled them, and perhaps not be much in the wrong.

MANKIND IS ONE SPECIES.—Mankind is every where the same: like cherries or apples, they may differ in size, shape, or color, from different soils, climates, or culture, but are still essentially the same species; and the little black wood cherry is not nearer akin to the maydukes that are served at great tables, than the wild, naked negro, to the figures adorned with coronets and ribbons. This observation might be carried yet further: all animals are stimulated by the same passions, and act very nearly alike, as far as we are capable of observing them.

First Impressions.—I have seldom been mistaken in my first judgment of those I thought it worth while to consider; and when (which has happened too often) flattery or the persuasion of others has made me alter it, time has never failed to show me I had done better to have remained fixed in my first (which is ever the most unprejudiced) idea.

Gardening.—I am really as fond of my garden as a young author of his first play when it has been well received by the town, and can no more forbear teasing my acquaintance for their approbation: though I gave you a long account of it lately, I must tell you that I have made two little terraces, raised twelve steps each, at the end of my great walk; they are just finished, and a great addition to the beauty of my garden. I inclose you a rough draught of it, drawn (or more properly scrawled) by my own hand, without the assistance of rule or compasses, as you will easily perceive. I have mixed in my espaliers as many rose and jasmin-trees as I can cram in; and in the squares designed for the use of the kitchen, have avoided putting any thing disagreeable either to sight or smell, having another garden below for cabbage, onions, garlic. All the walks are garnished with beds of flowers, besides the parterres, which are for a more distinguished sort. I have neither brick nor stone walls: all my fence is a high hedge, mingled with trees; but fruit is so plenty in this country, nobody thinks it worth stealing. Gardening is certainly the next amusement to reading; and as my sight will now permit me little of that, I am glad to form a taste that can give me so much employment, and be the plaything of my age, now my pen and needle are almost useless to me.

The two Pleasures of Life.—Between you and me, I think there are but two pleasures permitted to mortal man, love and vengeance; both which are in a peculiar manner forbidden to us wretches who are condemned to petticoats. Even vanity itself, of which you daily accuse us, is the sin against the Holy Ghost not to be forgiven in this world or the next.

> Our sex's weakness you expose and blame,
> Of every prating fop the common theme;
> Yet from this weakness you suppose is due
> Sublimer virtue than your Cato knew.
> From whence is this unjust distinction shown?
> Are we not formed with passions like your own?
> Nature with equal fire our souls endued;
> Our minds as lofty, and as warm our blood.
> O'er the wide world your wishes you pursue,
> The change is justified by something new;
> But we must sigh in silence and be true.

How the great Dr. Swift would stare at this vile triplet.

DESTINY.—I wish I knew a corner of the world inaccessible to petit-maîtres and fine ladies. I verily believed when I left London I should choose my own company for the remainder of my days; which I find more difficult to do abroad than at home; and with humility I sighing own,

> Some stronger power eludes the sickly will,
> Dashes my rising hope with certain ill;
> And makes me with reflective trouble see,
> That all is destined that I fancied free.

POLITICS.—There would be neither party nor contest in the world, if all people thought of politics with the same indifference that I do; but I find by experience that the utmost innocence and strictest silence is not sufficient to guard against suspicion, and I am looked upon here as capable of very great designs, at the same time that I am, and desire to be, ignorant of all projects whatever. It is natural, and (I think) just, to wish well to one's religion and country, yet as I can serve neither by disputes, I am content to pray for both in my closet, and avoid all subjects of controversy as much as I can.

A NOBLE POET.—I am sorry for the untimely death of poor Lord Cornbury; he had certainly a very good heart: I have often thought it great pity it was not under the direction of a better head. I had lost his favor some time before I left England on a pleasant account. He came to me one morning with a hatful of paper, which he desired me to peruse, and tell him my sincere opinion: I trembled at the proposition, foreseeing the inevitable consequence of this confidence. However, I was not so barbarous as to tell him that his verses were extremely stupid (as God knows they were), and that he was no more inspired with the spirit of poetry than that of prophecy. I contented myself with representing to him, in the mildest terms, that it was not the business of a man of quality to turn author, and that he should confine himself to the applause of his friends, and by no means venture on the press. He seemed to take this advice with good-humor, promised to follow it, and we parted without any dispute; but alas! he could not help showing his performance to better judges, who, with their usual candor and good nature, earnestly exhorted him to oblige the world with this instructive piece, which was soon after published, and had the success I expected from it. Pope persuaded him, poor soul! that my declaiming against it occasioned the ill reception it met with, though this is the first time I ever mentioned it in my life, and I did not so much as guess the reason I heard of him no more, till a few days before I left London. I accidentally said to one of his acquaintance, that his visits to me were at an end, I knew not why; and I was let into this weighty secret. My journey prevented all explanation between us, and perhaps I should not have thought it worth any, if I had staid.

A RICH WIDOW.—I pity poor Lady D——,* who, perhaps, thinks herself at present an object of envy: she will be soon undeceived: no rich widow can marry on prudential motives; and where passion is only on one side, every marriage must be miser-

* Lady Dalkeith, eldest daughter of John Duke of Argyle, widow of Francis Earl of Dalkeith, and mother by him of Henry Duke of Buccleuch; married secondly the famous Charles Townshend.

able. If she thought justly, she would know that no man ever
was in love with a woman of forty, since the deluge : a boy may
be so : but that blaze of straw only lasts till he is old enough to
distinguish between youth and age, which generally happens
about seventeen : till that time the whole sex appears angelic
to a warm constitution ; but as that is not Mr. T——'s case, all
she can hope is a cold complaisance, founded on gratitude,
which is the most uncertain of all foundations for a lasting
union. I know not how it is, whether obligers are apt to exact
too large returns, or whether human pride naturally hates to
remember obligation, but I have seldom seen friendships continue long where there has been great benefits conferred ; and
I should think it the severest suffering to know I was a burden
on the good-nature of a man I loved, even if I met a mind so
generous as to dissemble a disgust which he could not help
feeling.

TRIFLES.—I saw Mrs. Bridgeman the other day, who is
much pleased with a letter she has had the honor to receive
from your ladyship: she broke out, "*Really Lady Pomfret
writes finely !*" I very readily joined in her opinion ; she continued, "*Oh, so neat, no interlineations, and such proper distances !*" This manner of praising your style made me reflect
on the necessity of attention to trifles, if one would please in
general ; a rule terribly neglected by me formerly ; yet it is
certain that some men are as much struck with the careless
twist of a tippet as others are by a pair of fine eyes.

AMUSEMENTS IN 1738.—Public places flourish more than
ever : we have assemblies for every day in the week, besides
court, operas, and masquerades ; with youth and money, 'tis
certainly possible to be very well diverted in spite of malice
and ill-nature, though they are more and more powerful every
day. For my part, as it is my established opinion that this
globe of ours is no better than a Holland cheese, and the walkers about in it mites, I possess my mind in patience, let what

will happen, and should feel tolerably easy though a great rat came and eat half of it up.

DISAPPOINTMENTS IN FRIENDSHIP.—The most tender disposition grows callous by miserable experience : I look upon it as the reason why so many old people leave immense wealth, in a lump, to heirs they neither love nor esteem ; and others, like Lord Sundon, leave it, at random, to they know not who. He was not a covetous man, but had seen so little merit, and was so well acquainted with the vices of mankind, I believe he thought there was none among them deserved any particular distinction. I have passed a long life, and may say, with truth, have endeavored to purchase friends ; accident has put it in my power to confer great benefits, yet I never met with any return, nor indeed any true affection, but from dear Lady Oxford, who owed me nothing.

SHALL THE MOTHER NURSE HER CHILD ?—You ask my advice on this matter ; and to give it you frankly, I really think that Mr. ——'s demand is unreasonable, as his wife's constitution is tender, and her temper fretful. A true philosopher would consider these circumstances, but a pedant is always throwing his system in your face, and applies it equally to all things, times, and places, just like a tailor who would make a coat out of his own head, without any regard to the bulk or figure of the person that must wear it. All those fine-spun arguments that he has drawn from nature to stop your mouths, weigh, I must own to you, but very little with me. This same nature is indeed a specious word, nay, there is a great deal in it, if it is properly understood and applied, but I can not bear to hear people using it to justify what common sense must disavow. Is not nature modified by art in many things ? Was it not designed to be so ? And is it not happy for human society that it is so ? Would you like to see your husband let his beard grow, until he would be obliged to put the end of it in his pocket, because this beard is the gift of nature ? The instincts of nature point out neither tailors, nor weavers, nor mantua-makers, nor sempsters, nor milliners: and yet I am very glad that we don't run naked like the Hottentots. But not to wander from the subject—I grant that nature has furnished the mother with milk to nourish her child; but I maintain at the same time, that if she can find better milk elsewhere, she ought to prefer it without hesitation. I don't see why she should have more scruple to do this than her husband has to leave the clear fountain, which nature gave him, to quench his thirst, for stout October, port, or claret. Indeed, if Mrs. —— was a buxom, sturdy woman, who lived on plain food, took regular exercise, enjoyed proper returns of rest, and was free from violent passions (which you and I know is not the case), she might be a good nurse for her child; but, as matters stand, I do verily think that the milk of a good comely cow, who feeds quietly in her meadow, never devours ragouts, nor drinks ratafia, nor frets at quadrille, nor sits up till three in the morning elated with gain or dejected with loss, I do think that the milk of such a cow, or of a nurse that came as near it as possible, would be likely to nourish the young squire much better than hers. If it be true that the child sucks in the mother's passions with her milk, this is a strong argument in favor of the cow, unless you may be afraid that the young squire may become a calf; but how many calves are there both in state and church, who have been brought up with their mother's milk!

WOMEN.—If I were a divine I would remember that in their first creation they were designed as a help for the other sex; and nothing was ever made incapable of the end of its creation. 'Tis true, the first lady had so little experience that she hearkened to the persuasion of an impertinent dangler; and, if you mind, he succeeded, by persuading her that she was not so wise as she should be.

Men that have not sense enough to show any superiority in their arguments, hope to be yielded to by a faith, that, as they

are men, all the reason that has been allotted to human kind has
fallen to their share. I am seriously of another opinion. As
much greatness of mind may be shown in submission as in command, and some women have suffered a life of hardships with
as much philosophy as *Cato* traversed the deserts of *Africa*,
and without that support the view of glory offered him, which
is enough for the human mind that is touched with it to go
through any toil or danger. But this is not the situation of a
woman, whose virtue must only shine to her own recollection,
and loses that name when it is ostentatiously exposed to the
world. A lady who has performed her duty as a daughter, a
wife, and a mother, raises in me as much veneration as *Socrates*
or *Xenophon ;* and much more than I would pay either to *Julius
Cæsar* or *Cardinal Mazarine*, though the first was the most
famous enslaver of his country, and the last the most successful plunderer of his master.

A woman really virtuous, in the utmost extent of this expression, has virtue of a purer kind than any philosopher has
ever shown ; since she knows, if she has sense, and without it
there can be no virtue, that mankind is too much prejudiced
against her sex to give her any degree of that fame which is
so sharp a spur to their great actions. I have some thoughts
of exhibiting a set of pictures of such meritorious ladies, where
I shall say nothing of the fire of their eyes, or the pureness of
their complexions, but give them such praises as befit a rational
sensible being : virtues of choice, and not beauties of accident. I beg they would not, so far mistake me as to think
I am undervaluing their charms : a beautiful mind, in a
beautiful body, is one of the finest objects shown us by
nature. I would not have them place so much value on a
quality that can be only useful to one as to neglect that which
may be of benefit to thousands, by precept or by example.
There will be no occasion of amusing them with trifles when
they consider themselves capable of not only making the most
amiable, but the most estimable, figures in life. Begin, then,
ladies, by paying those authors with scorn and contempt, who

with a sneer of affected admiration, would throw you below the dignity of the human species.

LADIES IN THE HOUSE OF LORDS.—At the last warm debate in the House of Lords, it was unanimously resolved there should be no crowd of unnecessary auditors; consequently the fair sex were excluded, and the gallery destined to the sole use of the House of Commons. Notwithstanding which determination, a tribe of dames resolved to show on this occasion, that neither men nor laws could resist them. These heroines were Lady Huntingdon,* the Duchess of Queensbury, the Duchess of Ancaster, Lady Westmoreland, Lady Cobham, Lady Charlotte Edwin, Lady Archibald Hamilton and her daughter, Mrs. Scott, and Mrs. Pendarvis, and Lady Frances Saunderson. I am thus particular in their names since I look upon them to be the boldest assertors, and most resigned sufferers for liberty I ever read of. They presented themselves at the door at nine o'clock in the morning, where Sir William Saunderson respectfully informed them the chancellor had made an order against their admittance. The Duchess of Queensbury, as head of the squadron, pished at the ill-breeding of a mere lawyer, and desired him to let them up stairs privately. After some modest refusals he swore by G— he would not let them in. Her grace, with a noble warmth, answered by G— they would come in, in spite of the chancellor and the whole House. This being reported, the peers resolved to starve them out; an order was made that the doors should be fastened. These Amazons now showed themselves qualified for the duty even of foot-soldiers; they stood there till five in the afternoon, without either sustenance or evacuation, every now and then playing vollies of thumps, kicks, and raps, against the door, with so much violence that the speakers in the House were scarce heard. When the lords were not to be conquered by this, the two duchesses

* Lady Huntingdon, the same who afterward became the head, the Countess Matilda, of the Whitfieldian Methodists.

(very well apprised of the use of stratagems in war) commanded a dead silence of half an hour; and the chancellor, who thought this a certain proof of their absence, (the Commons also being very impatient to enter), gave order for the opening of the door; upon which they all rushed in, pushed aside their competitors, and placed themselves in the front rows of the gallery. They staid there till after eleven, when the House rose; and during the debate gave applause, and showed marks of dislike, not only by smiles and winks (which have always been allowed in these cases), but by noisy laughs and apparent contempts; which is supposed the true reason why poor Lord Hervey spoke miserably.*

ERRORS IN SOCIETY.—Among the most universal errors, I reckon that of treating the weaker sex with a contempt which has a very bad influence on their conduct. How many of them think it excuse enough to say they are women, to indulge any folly that comes into their heads! This renders them useless members of the commonwealth, and only burdensome to their own families, where the wise husband thinks he lessens the opinion of his own understanding, if he at any time condescends to consult his wife's. Thus, what reason nature has given them is thrown away, and a blind obedience expected from them by all their ill-natured masters; and, on the other side, as blind a complaisance shown those that are indulgent, who say often that women's weakness must be complied with, and it is a vain troublesome attempt to make them hear reason.

I attribute a great part of this way of thinking, which is hardly ever controverted, either to the ignorance of authors, who are many of them heavy *collegians*, that have never been admitted to politer conversations than those of their *bed-makers*, or to the design of selling their works, which is generally the only

* The debate to which this story relates must have been that of May 2, 1738, on the depredations of the Spaniards, which appears to have been closed by a speech of Lord Hervey.—See Parl. Hist. vol. x. p. 729.

view of writing, without any regard to truth, or the ill-consequences that attend the propagation of wrong notions. A paper smartly wrote, though perhaps only some old conceits dressed in new words, either in rhyme or prose—I say *rhyme*, for I have seen no *verses* wrote for many years—such a paper, either to ridicule or declaim against the ladies, is very welcome to the coffee-houses, where there is hardly one man in ten but fancies he has some reason or other to curse some of the sex most heartily. Perhaps his sisters' fortunes are to run away with the money that would be better bestowed at the groom-porter's; or an old mother, good for nothing, keeps a jointure from a hopeful son, that wants to make a settlement on his mistress; or a handsome young fellow is plagued with a wife, that will remain alive, to hinder his running away with a great fortune, having two or three of them in love with him. These are serious misfortunes that are sufficient to exasperate the mildest tempers to a contempt of the sex; not to speak of lesser inconveniences, which are very provoking at the time they are felt.

BUILDING.—Building is the general weakness of old people; I have had a twitch of it myself, though certainly it is the highest absurdity, and as sure a proof of dotage as pink-colored ribbons, or even matrimony. Nay, perhaps, there is more to be said in defense of the last, I mean in a childless old man; he may prefer a boy born in his own house, though he knows it is not his own, to disrespectful or worthless nephews or nieces. But there is no excuse for beginning an edifice he can never inhabit, or probably see finished. The Duchess of Marlborough used to ridicule the vanity of it by saying one might always live upon other people's follies: yet you see she built the most ridiculous house I ever saw, since it really is not habitable, from the excessive damps; so true it is the things that we would do, those we do not, and the things we would not do, those we do daily. I feel in myself a proof of this assertion, being much against my will at Venice, though I own it is the only great town where I can properly reside, yet here I find so many vexations that, in spite of all my philosophy, and (what is more powerful) my phlegm, I am oftener out of humor than among my plants and poultry in the country.

———

THE EFFECTS OF AGE.—All weaknesses appear, as they increase with age. I am afraid all humankind are born with the seeds of them, though they may be totally concealed, and consequently considerably lessened by education and philosophy. I have endeavored to study and correct myself; and as courage was a favorite virtue, I studied to seem void of fear, and I believe was rather esteemed fool-hardy.

I am now grown timorous, and inclined to low spirits, whatever you may hear to the contrary. My cheerfulness is like the fire kindled in brushwood, which makes a show, but is soon turned to cold ashes. I do not, like Madame Maintenon, grieve about the decay which is allotted to all mortals, but would willingly excuse myself to you.

———

HOW TO PRESERVE YOUTH.—I wonder with what conscience you can talk to me of your being an old woman; I beg I may hear no more on't. For my part, I pretend to be as young as ever, and really am as young as needs to be, to all intents and purposes. I attribute all this to your living so long at Chatton, and fancy a week at Paris will correct such wild imaginations, and set things in a better light. My cure for lowness of spirits is not drinking nasty water, but galloping all day, and a moderate glass of Champagne at night in good company; and I believe this regimen, closely followed, is one of the most wholesome that can be prescribed, and may save one a world of filthy doses, and more filthy doctor's fees at the year's end.

THE COUNTESS OF MAR.*

In the "Letters from Horace Walpole to Sir Horace Mann," lately published, and which were edited by the late Lord Dover, there are two passages relating to Lady Mary Wortley Montagu which require some notice, in order that the real state of the facts to which they refer may be known, as far as possible.

The first of these is to be found in Letter 231, dated Mistley, August 31, 1751, and is in these words:—" Pray, tell me if you know any thing of Lady Mary Wortley: we have an obscure story here of her being in durance in the Brescian or the Bergamesco; *that a young fellow whom she set out with keeping* has taken it into his head to keep her close prisoner, not permitting her to write or receive any letters but what he sees: he seems determined, if her husband should die, not to lose her as the Count —— lost my lady O." And in the next letter he again alludes to this report.

---

* It seems due to the pious care Lord Wharncliffe has shown, in vindicating the fair fame of his ancestress from the false imputations of envious slanderers, to give these Letters in full. Lady Mary's part in these troublesome transactions was not free from blame; but she never deserved the foul accusations of Horace Walpole, which seem to have been premeditated malice. Those who desire to see falsehood refuted, and justice done to the character of an impulsive but noble-hearted woman, will be deeply interested in these Letters.—Am. Ed

Among Lady Mary's papers there is a long paper, written in Italian, not by herself, giving an account of her having been detained for some time against her will, in a country-house belonging to an Italian count, and inhabited by him and his mother. This paper seems to be drawn up either as a case to be submitted to a lawyer for his opinion, or to be produced in a court of law. There is nothing else to be found in Lady Mary's papers referring in the least degree to this circumstance. It would appear, however, that some such forcible detention as is alluded to did take place, probably for some pecuniary or interested object; but, like many of Horace Walpole's stories, he took care not to let this lose any thing that might give it zest, and he therefore makes the person by whom Lady Mary was detained " a young fellow whom she set out with keeping." Now, at the time of this transaction taking place, Lady Mary was sixty-one years old. The reader, therefore, may judge for himself, how far such an imputation upon her is likely to be founded in truth, and will bear in mind that there was no indisposition upon the part of Horace Walpole to make insinuations of that sort against Lady Mary.

The other passage is in letter 232; and after saying that he had lately been at Woburn, where he had had an opportunity of seeing fifty letters of Lady Mary's to her sister Lady Mar, " whom she treated so hardly while out of her senses," Horace Walpole adds as follows:—" Ten of the letters, indeed, are dismal lamentations and frights on a scene of villainy of Lady Mary's, who having persuaded one Ruremonde, a Frenchman, and her lover, to intrust her with a large sum of money to buy stock for him, frightened him out of England by persuading him that Mr. Wortley had discovered the intrigue, and would murder him; and then would have sunk the trust. That not succeeding, and he threatening to print her letters, she endeavored to make Lord Mar or Lord Stair cut his throat. Pope hints at these anecdotes of her history in that line —

'Who starves a sister or denies a debt.'"

Nothing whatever has been found to throw light upon the ill treatment of Lady Mar by Lady Mary; and that accusation is supposed, by those who would probably have heard of it, if true, to be without foundation. But nine letters to Lady Mar relating to a transaction with a person whom Lady Mary calls " R., a Frenchman," are among the papers which have been communicated to the Editor, which must be the letters alluded to by Horace Walpole, although there appears to be one short of the number mentioned by him, possibly by mistake. In order that the reader may be enabled to see the actual grounds upon which a charge of so scandalous and heinous a character has been made by Mr. Walpole, these letters are now given to the public. They are in no degree interesting in any other respect; but inasmuch as the fact of their existence has been asserted in a publication which has been generally read, and that their not being produced might be taken in some degree as an acknowledgment of the charge founded upon them, the Editor has thought it only fair that they should speak for themselves, and that Lady Mary's own account of that transaction should be known.

These letters are without dates by which to fix the precise periods at which they were written; but as the fall of the South Sea stock began in September 1720, they must have been written in the latter end of that year, or the beginning of 1721.

LETTER I.

From the tranquil and easy situation in which you left me, dear sister, I am reduced to that of the highest degree of vexation, which I need not set out to you better than by the plain matter of fact, which I heartily wish I had told you long since; and nothing hindered me but a certain *mauvaise honte* which you are reasonable enough to forgive, as very natural, though not very excusable where there is nothing to be ashamed of;

since I can only accuse myself of too much good-nature, or at worst of too much credulity, though I believe there never was more pains taken to deceive any body. In short, a person whose name is not necessary, because you know it, took all sorts of methods, during almost a year, to persuade me that there never was so extraordinary an attachment (or what you please to call it) as they had for me. This ended in coming over to make me a visit against my will, and as was pretended, very much against their interest. I can not deny I was very silly in giving the least credit to this stuff. But if people are so silly, you'll own 'tis natural for any body that is good-natured to pity and be glad to serve a person they believe unhappy on their account. It came into my head, out of a high point of generosity (for which I wish myself hanged), to do this creature all the good I possibly could, since 't was impossible to make them happy in their own way. I advised him very strenuously to sell out of the subscription, and in compliance to my advice he did so; and in less than two days saw he had done very prudently. After a piece of service of this nature, I thought I could more decently press his departure, which his follies made me think necessary for me. He took leave of me with so many tears and grimaces (which I can't imagine how he could counterfeit) as really moved my compassion; and I had much ado to keep to my first resolution of exacting his absence, which he swore would be his death. I told him that there was no other way in the world I would not be glad to serve him in, but that his extravagances made it utterly impossible for me to keep him company. He said that he would put into my hands the money I had won for him, and desired me to improve it, saying that if he had enough to buy a small estate and retire from the world, 't was all the happiness he hoped for in it. I represented to him that if he had so little money as he said, 't was ridiculous to hazard it all. He replied that 't was too little to be of any value, and he would either have it double or quit. After many objections on my side and replies on his, I was so weak as to be overcome by his entreaties, and flattered myself also that I was doing a very heroic action, in trying to make a man's fortune though I did not care for his addresses. He left me with these imaginations, and my first care was to employ his money to the best advantage. I laid it all out in stock, the general discourse and private intelligence then scattered about being of a great rise. You may remember it was two or three days before the fourth subscription, and you were with me when I paid away the money to Mr. Benfield. I thought I had managed prodigious well,in selling out the said stock the day after the shutting the books (for a small profit), to Cox and Cleave, goldsmiths of a very good reputation. When the opening of the books came, my man went off, leaving the stock upon my hands, which was already sunk from near £900 to £400. I immediately writ him word of this misfortune, with the sincere sorrow natural to have upon such an occasion, and asked his opinion as to the selling the stock remaining in. He made me no answer to this part of my letter, but a long eloquent oration of miseries of another nature. I attributed this silence to his disinterested neglect of his money; but, however, I resolved to take no more steps in this business without direct orders, after having been so unlucky. This occasioned many letters to no purpose; but the very post after you left London, I received a letter from him, in which he told me that he had discovered all my tricks, that he was convinced I had all his money untouched; and he would have it again or he would print all my letters to him; which though, God knows, very innocent in the main, yet may admit of ill constructions, besides the monstrousness of being exposed in such a manner. I hear from other people that he is liar enough to publish that I have borrowed the money from him; though I have a note under his hand, by which he desires me to employ it in the funds, and acquits me of being answerable for the losses that may happen. At the same time, I have attestations and witnesses of the bargains I made, so that nothing can be clearer than my integrity in this business; but that does not hinder me from being in the utmost terror for the consequences (as you may easily guess) of his villainy; the very story of which appears so monstrous to me that I can hardly believe myself while I write it; though I omit (not to tire you) a thousand aggravating circumstances. I can not forgive myself the folly of ever regarding one word he said; and I see now that his lies have made made me wrong several of my acquaintances, and you among the rest, for having said (as he told me) horrid things against me to him. 'Tis long since that your behavior has acquitted you in my opinion; but I thought I ought not to mention, to hurt him with you, what was perhaps more misunderstanding, or a mistake, than a designed lie. But he has very amply explained his character to me. What is very pleasant is, that, but two posts before, I received a letter from him full of higher flights than ever. I beg your pardon (dear sister) for this tedious account; but you see how necessary 'tis for me to get my letters from this madman. Perhaps the best way is by fair means; at least they ought to be first tried. I would have you, then (my dear sister), try to make the wretch sensible of the truth of what I advance, without asking for my leters, which I have already asked for. Perhaps you may make him ashamed of his infamous proceedings, by talking of me, without taking notice that you know of his threats, only of my dealings. I take this method to be the most likely to work upon him. I beg you would send me a full and true account of this detestable affair (inclosed to Mrs. Murray). If I had not been the most unlucky creature in the world, his letter would have come while you were here, that I might have showed you both his note and the other people's. I knew he was discontented, but was far from imagining a possibility of this thing. I give you a great deal of trouble, but you see I shall owe you the highest obligation if you can serve me: the very endeavoring of it is a tie upon me to serve you the rest of my life and with eternal gratitude.

LETTER II.

I can not forbear (dear sister) accusing you of unkindness that you took so little care of a business of the last importance to me. R—— wrote to me some time ago, to say if I would immediately send him £2,000 sterling, he would send me an acquittance. As this was sending him several hundreds out of my own pocket, I absolutely refused it ; and, in return, I have just received a threatening letter to print I know not what stuff against me. I am too well acquainted with the world, (of which poor Mrs. Murray's affair is a fatal instance), not to know that the most groundless accusation is always of ill-consequence to a woman ; besides the cruel misfortunes it may bring upon me in my own family. If you have any compassion either for me or my innocent children, I am sure you will try to prevent it. The thing is too serious to be delayed. I think (to say nothing of either blood or affection) that humanity and Christianity are interested in my preservation. I am sure I can answer for my hearty gratitude and everlasting acknowledgment of a service much more important than that of saving my life.

LETTER III.

I give you many thanks (my dear sister) for the trouble you have given yourself in my affair ; but am afraid it is not yet effectual. I must beg you to let him know I am now at Twickenham, and that whoever has his procuration may come here on diverse pretenses, but must by no means go to my house at London. I wonder you can think Lady Stafford has not wrote to him : she showed me a long plain letter to him several months ago ; as a demonstration he received it, I saw his answer. 'Tis true she treated him with the contempt he deserved, and told him she would never give herself the trouble of writing again to so despicable a wretch. She is willing to do yet further, and write to the Duke of Villeroi about it, if I think it proper. R—— does nothing but lie, and either does not, or will not, understand what is said to him. You will forgive me troubling you so often with this business; the importance of it is the best excuse; in short

> —— 'tis joy or sorrow, peace or strife,
> 'Tis all the color of remaining life.

I can foresee nothing else to make me unhappy, and, I believe, shall take care another time not to involve myself in difficulties by an overplus of heroic generosity.

I am, dear sister, ever yours, with the utmost esteem and affection. If I get over this cursed affair, my style may enliven.

LETTER IV.

TWICKENHAM, September 6.

I have just received your letter, dear sister; I am extremely sensible of your goodness, which I beg you to continue. I am very glad to hear of the good health of your family; and should be only more so to be a witness of it, which I am not without some hopes of. My time is melted away here in almost perpetual concerts. I do not presume to judge, but I'll assure you I am a very hearty as well as humble admirer. I have taken my little thread satin beauty into the house with me; she is allowed by Bononcini to have the finest voice he ever heard in England. He and Mrs. Robinson and Senesino lodge in this village, and sup often with me; and this easy indolent life makes me the happiest thing in the world, if I had not this execrable affair still hanging over my head. I have consulted my lawyer, and he says I can not, with safety to myself, deposit the money I have received into other hands, without the express order of R——; and he is so unreasonable that he will neither send a procuration to examine my accounts, or any order for me to transfer his stock to another name. I am heartily weary of the trust, which has given me so much trouble, and can never think myself safe till I am quite got rid of it : rather than be plagued any longer with the odious keeping, I am willing to abandon my letters to his discretion. I desire nothing more of him than an order to place his money in other hands, which methinks should not be so hard to obtain, since he is so dissatisfied with my management ; but he seems to be bent to torment me, and will not even touch his money, because I beg it of him. I wish you would represent these things to him ; for my own part, I live in so much uneasiness about it I am sometimes weary of life itself.

Mrs. Stoner will be a good person to send things by. I would have no black silk, having bought some.

LETTER V.

Dear Sister—Having this occasion, I would not omit writing, though I have received no answer to my two last. The bearer is well acquainted with my affair, though not from me, till he mentioned it to me first, having heard it from those to whom R——— had told it with all the false colors he pleased to lay on. I showed him the formal commission I had to employ the money, and all the broker's testimonies taken before Delpecke, with his certificate. Your remonstrances have hitherto had so little effect, that R——— will neither send a letter of attorney to examine my accounts, nor let me be in peace. I received a letter from him but two posts since, in which he renews his threats, except I send him the whole sum, which is as much in my power as it is to send a million. I can easily comprehend that he may be ashamed to send a procuration, which must convince the world of all the lies which he has told. For my part, I am so willing to be rid of the plague of hearing from him, I desire no better than to restore him with all expedition the money I have in my hands ; but I will not do it without a general acquittance in due form, not to have fresh demands every time he wants money. If he thinks he has a larger sum to receive than I offer, why does he not name a procurator to examine me ? and if he is content with that sum, I only insist on the acquittance for my own safety I am ready to send it him, with full license to tell as many lies as he pleases afterward. I am weary with troubling you with repetitions which can not be more disagreeable to you than they are to me. I have had, and still have, so much vexation with this execrable affair, 'tis impossible to describe it. I had rather talk to you of any thing else, but it fills my whole head.

I am still at Twickenham, where I pass my time in great indolence and sweetness. Mr. W—— is at this time in Yorkshire. My fair companion puts me oft in mind of our Thoresby conversations; we read and walk together, and I am more happy in her than any thing else could make me except your conversation.

LETTER VI.

I have just received your letter of May 30th, and am surprised, since you own the receipt of my letter, that you give me not the least hint concerning the business that I wrote so earnestly to you about. Till that is over I am as little capable of repeating news, as I should be if my house was on fire. I am sure a great deal must be in your power ; the hurting me can be no way his interest. I am ready to assign, or deliver the money for £500 stock, to whoever he will name, if he will send my letters into Lady Stafford's hands ; which, were he sincere in his offer of burning them, he would readily do. Instead of that, he has written a letter to Mr. W—— to inform him of the whole affair : luckily for me, the person he has sent it to assures me it shall never be delivered ; but I am not the less obliged to his good intentions. For God's sake, do something to set my mind at ease from this business, and then I

will not fail to write you regular accounts of all your acquaint.
ance. Mr. Strickland has had a prodigy of good fortune befallen him, which, I suppose, you have heard of.

My little commission is hardly worth speaking of; if you
have not already laid out that small sum in St. Cloud ware, I
had rather have it in plain lutestring of any color.

Lady Stafford desires you would buy one suit of minunet
for head and ruffles at Boileau's.

LETTER VII.

I can not enough thank you, my dear sister, for the trouble
you give yourself in my affairs, though I am still so unhappy
to find your care very ineffectual. I have actually in my present
possession a formal letter directed to Mr. W——— to acquaint him
with the whole business. You may imagine the inevitable
eternal misfortunes it would have thrown me into, had it been
delivered by the person to whom it was intrusted. I wish you
would make him sensible of the infamy of his proceeding,
which can no way in the world turn to his advantage. Did I
refuse giving up the strictest account, or had I not the
clearest demonstration in my hands of the truth and sincerity
with which I acted, there might be some temptation to this
business; but all he can expect by informing Mr. W———, is to
hear him repeat the same things that I assert; he will not re-
trieve one farthing, and I am forever miserable. I beg no
more of him than to direct any person, man or woman, either
lawyer, broker, or a person of quality, to examine me; and as
soon as he has sent a proper authority to discharge me on
inquiry, I am ready to be examined. I think no offer can be
fairer from any person whatsoever: his conduct toward me is
so infamous that I am informed I might prosecute him by law
if he was here; he demanding the whole sum as a debt from
Mr. Wortley, at the same time I have a note under his hand
to prove the contrary. I beg with the utmost earnestness that

you would make him sensible of his error. Observe 'tis very necessary to say something to fright him. I am persuaded if he was talked to in a style of that kind, he would not dare to attempt to ruin me. I have a great inclination to write seriously to your lord about it, since I desire to determine this affair in the fairest and the clearest manner. I am not at all afraid of making any body acquainted with it; and if I did not fear making Mr. Wortley uneasy (who is the only person from whom I would conceal it), all the transactions should have been long since enrolled in Chancery. I have already taken care to have the broker's depositions taken, before a lawyer of reputation and merit. I deny giving him no satisfaction; and after that offer, I think there is no man of honor that would refuse signifying to him that as 'tis all he can desire, so, if he persists in doing me an injury, he may repent it. You know how far 'tis proper to take this method. I say nothing of the uneasiness I am under, 'tis far beyond any expression; my obligation would be proportionate to any body that would deliver me from it, and I should not think it paid by all the services of my life.

LETTER VIII.

I am now at Twickenham: 'tis impossible to tell you, dear sister, what agonies I suffer every post-day; my health really suffers so much from my fears that I have reason to apprehend the worst consequences. If that monster acted on the least principles of reason, I should have nothing to fear, since 'tis certain that after he has exposed me he will get nothing by it. Mr. Wortley can do nothing for his satisfaction I am not willing to do myself. I desire not the least indulgence of any kind. Let him put his affair into the hands of any lawyer whatever. I am willing to submit to any examination; 'tis impossible to make a fairer offer than this is: whoever he employs may come to me hither on several pretenses. I desire nothing from him but that he would send no letters or messages to my house at London, where Mr. Wortley now is. I am come hither in hopes of benefit from the air, but I carry my distemper about me in an anguish of mind that visibly decays my body every day. I am too melancholy to talk of any other subject. Let me beg you, dear sister, to take some care of this affair, and think you have it in your power to do more than save the life of a sister that loves you.

LETTER IX.

I send you, dear sister, by Lady Lansdown this letter, accompanied by the only present that was ever sent me by that monster. I beg you to return it immediately. I am told he is preparing to come to London. Let him know that it is not at all necessary for receiving his money or examining my accounts; he has nothing to do but to send a letter of attorney to whom he pleases (without exception), and I will readily deliver up what I have in my hands, and his presence will not obtain a farthing more: his design then can only be to expose my letters here. I desire you will assure him that my first step will be to acquaint my Lord Stair with all his obligations to him, as soon as I hear he is in London; and if he dares to give me any further trouble, I shall take care to have him rewarded in a stronger manner than he expects; there is nothing more true than this: and I solemnly swear that, if all the credit or money that I have in the world can do it, either for friendship or hire, I shall not fail to have him used as he deserves; and since I know his journey can only be intended to expose me, I shall not value what noise is made. Perhaps you may prevent it; I leave you to judge of the most proper method; 'tis certain no time should be lost; fear is his predominant passion, and I believe you may fright him from coming hither, where he will certainly find a reception very disagreeable to him.

There can be no better specimen of the manner in which a story gains as it passes through the hands of those who delight in gossip, or who are prepared to believe the worst of the person concerned. Horace Walpole refers to these letters as the ground of his story, and so far as they go, they do not support any one of his statements. According to these letters Lady Mary did not persuade Mons. R. to intrust her with a considerable sum of money to buy stock for him, but she yielded to his earnest solicitations in that respect with considerable difficulty. Neither did Lady Mary " frighten Mons. R. out of England, by persuading him that Mr. Wortley had discovered the intrigue, and would murder him ;" but, on the contrary, Mons. R. having returned to France, endeavored to frighten Lady Mary into the payment of his losses in his South Sea speculations, by threatening to print all her letters to him, and to make Mr. Wortley acquainted with every thing. Nor would Lady Mary " have sunk the trust," for she repeatedly calls upon him, through Lady Mar, to appoint persons to examine her, before whom she is ready to submit her accounts, and to be questioned. And lastly, Lady Mary never did " endeavor to make Lord Mar or Lord Stair cut Mons. R.'s throat." She certainly threatened him, through Lady Mar, in case of his coming to England ; but no one who reads that threat can imagine that it is meant to convey the idea of her intending to have his throat cut by anybody.

Horace Walpole's accusations, therefore, are none of them warranted by these letters ; but at the same time, even upon her own showing, Lady Mary can not be acquitted of allowing her vanity to overcome her judgment, and of placing her character at the mercy of an adventurer. Nor can her gambling in the South Sea funds be defended ; the only excuse for which is, the very general prevalence of a spirit of that kind, almost amounting to madness, in all classes of society at that period. To those who know by tradition the severity of Mr. Wortley's principles in regard to every thing connected with money— a feeling produced by the recklessness of his father in those matters, against which he had, in the earlier part of his life, constantly to contend—Lady Mary's strong fears of this transaction coming to his knowledge will be readily intelligible. A consciousness of her own imprudence in the whole affair may also be naturally supposed to have added to her fears, without imputing them to a sense of actual criminality. More than once, indeed, in these letters, Lady Mary offers to submit to any examination to which Mons. R. may choose to expose her; and in one of them she even says that if he will only send over a procuration to examine her accounts, she will abandon her letters to his discretion. Such an offer appears to be incompatible with there being any thing in her letters which could really affect her character; but it is at least quite clear that Horace Walpole had no right to found upon these letters to Lady Mar so gross and exaggerated an accusation.

Mr. Cole, in his MSS. now in the British Museum, repeats this story; but it is evident that he derives his information from Horace Walpole, his friend and correspondent, as, in the same collection, he states of Lady Mary, that he "heard from Mad. Geoffrin and Mr. Walpole, *who knew her well*, that she was the vilest of womankind, notwithstanding her talents for wit, vivacity, and genius, and elegance of taste, were unexceptionable." It may be doubted, however, whether Horace Walpole ever did *know Lady Mary well*. She went abroad in the year 1739, at which time he was only just of age, when he could scarcely *know well* a woman of nearly fifty years old; and she did not return to England till just before her death. In truth, he could have had but a very slight personal acquaintance with her."

LETTER TO THE LORD BISHOP OF SALISBURY.*

(WITH HER TRANSLATION OF EPICTETUS.)

July 20, 1710.†

MY LORD—Your hours are so well employed, I hardly dare offer you this trifle to look over; but then, so well am I acquainted with the sweetness of temper which accompanies your learning, I dare ever assure myself of a pardon. You have already forgiven me greater impertinencies, and condescended yet further in giving me instructions, and bestowing some of your minutes in teaching me. This surprising humility has all the effect it ought to have on my heart; I am sensible of the gratitude I owe to so much goodness, and how much I am ever bound to be your servant. Here is the work of one week of my solitude—by the many faults in it your lordship will easily believe I spent no more time upon it; it was hardly finished when I was obliged to begin my journey, and I had not leisure to write it over again. You have it he.e without any corrections, with all its blots and errors; I endeavored at no beauty of style, but to keep as literally as I could to the sense of the author. My only intention in presenting it, is to ask your Lordship whether I have understood Epictetus? The fourth chapter particularly, I am afraid I have mistaken. Piety and greatness of soul set you above all misfortunes that can happen to yourself, except the calumnies of false tongues; but that same piety which renders what happens to yourself indifferent to you, yet softens the natural compassion in your temper to the greatest degree of tenderness for the interests of the Church, and the liberty and welfare of your country; the steps that are now made toward the

* Dr. Gilbert Burnet.

† Lady Mary was about nineteen when she wrote this letter. It is a powerful argument for the education of women. Even the excuses she feels obliged to urge on her own behalf for venturing into the then (to her sex) forbidden field of learning are eloquent of the need of mental cultivation.   S. J. H.

destruction of both, the apparent danger we are in, the manifest growth of injustice, oppression, and hypocrisy, can not do otherwise than give your lordship those hours of sorrow, which, did not your fortitude of soul, and reflections from religion and philosophy, shorten, would add to the national misfortunes, by injuring the health of so great a supporter of our sinking liberties. I ought to ask pardon for this digression; it is more proper for me in this place, to say something to excuse an address that looks so very presuming. My sex is usually forbid studies of this nature, and folly reckoned so much our proper sphere, that we are sooner pardoned any excesses of that, than the least pretensions to reading or good sense. We are permitted no books but such as tend to the weakening and effeminating of the mind. Our natural defects are every way indulged, and it is looked upon as in a degree criminal to improve our reason, or fancy we have any. We are taught to place all our art in adorning our outward forms, and permitted, without reproach, to carry that custom even to extravagancy, while our minds are entirely neglected, and, by disuse of reflections, filled with nothing but the trifling objects our eyes are daily entertained with. This custom, so long established and industriously upheld, makes it even ridiculous to go out of the common road, and forces one to find as many excuses, as if it were a thing altogether criminal not to play the fool in concert with other women of quality, whose birth and leisure only serve to render them the most useless and most worthless part of the creation. There is hardly a character in the world more despicable, or more liable to universal ridicule, than that of a learned woman; those words imply, according to the received sense, a talking, impertinent, vain and conceited creature. I believe nobody will deny that learning may have this effect, but it must be a very superficial degree of it. Erasmus was certainly a man of great learning, and good sense, and he seems to have my opinion of it, when he says, *Fœmina quæ vere sapit, non videtur sibi sapere ; contra, quæ cum nihil sapiat sibi videtur sapere, ea demum bis stulta est.* The Abbé Bellegarde gives a right reason for women's talking over-much, that they know nothing, and every outward object strikes their imagination, and produces a multitude of thoughts, which, if they knew more, they would know not worth their thinking of. But there is a worse effect than this, which follows the careless education given to women of quality, its being so easy for any man of sense, that finds it either his interest or his pleasure, to corrupt them. The common method is, to begin by attacking their religion; they bring them a thousand fallacious arguments, which their excessive ignorance hinders them from refuting; and I speak now from my own knowledge and conversation among them, there are more Atheists among the fine ladies than the loosest sort of rakes; and the same ignorance that generally works out into excess of superstition, exposes them to the snares of any who have a fancy to carry them to the other extreme. I have made my excuses already too long, and will conclude in the words of Erasmus, *Vulgus sentit quod lingua Latina non convenit fœminis, quia parum facit ad tuendam illarum pudicitiam, quoniam rarum et insolitum est, fœminam scire Latinam, attamen consuetudo omnium malarum rerum magistra. Decorum est fœminam in Germania natam discere Gallice, ut loquatur cum his qui sciunt Gallice, cur igitur habetur indecorum discere Latine, ut quotidie confabuletur cum tot autoribus tam facundis, tam eruditus, tam sapientibus, tam fidis consultoribus. Certe mihi quantulumcunque cerebri est, malim in bonis studiis consumere, quam in precibus sine mente dictis, in pernoctibus conviviis, in exhauriendis capacibus pateris, etc.*

I have tired your lordship, and too long delayed to subscribe myself your lordship's most respectful and obliged friend.

...cations.

THE LETTERS

OF

MADAME DE SÉVIGNÉ

TO HER DAUGHTER AND FRIENDS.

EDITED BY MRS. HALE.

12mo.   Price $1.50.

"The charm of Madame de Sévigné's letters has so long been acknowledged that criticism is uncalled for in referring to them, nor would it be easy to find a word of admiration or praise that has not already been pronounced in their favor.   For spontaneity, tenderness, playfulness, sweetness, they are unequalled. The style is all that is most simple and natural and graceful.   Madame de Sévigné has no variety of inspiration, and but little profundity of thought. She is inspired by only one sentiment, her love for her daughter; but this single note is so sweet, and is sung in so many keys, and with such a pleasing accompaniment of spicy gossip and pensive meditation, that its monotony is never unpleasing.   The influence which these letters have exerted upon the development of the French language and French literature has again given them a classical reputation, which works of far greater pretension and power have never attained.   They will ever be classed with the works of a few great authors, who founded in France the distinctive literary school that at a later period obtained a development so varied and so brilliant.   By the simplicity and sincerity of her genius, Madame de Sévigné corrected the false taste and feeble sentimentality of her day, while the purity of her style exerted an immense influence in forming the language in which she wrote." — *Miss Vaughan, in The Leader.*

MEMOIRS AND CORRESPONDENCE
OF
MADAME RÉCAMIER.

TRANSLATED FROM THE FRENCH AND EDITED BY ISAPHENE
M. LUYSTER.

With an elegant Steel Engraved Portrait. One volume.
16mo. Price $1.50.

From the Boston Transcript.

"The biography of a woman who admirably fulfilled a great social mission, by virtue not so much of intellectual genius or personal charms as by the *essentia womanhood* which she conserved and consecrated. It is idle to attribute the influence she exerted, the comfort she gave, the encouragement she inspired, the rational pleasure and progress she promoted, to mere blandishments or dexterous coquetry. Life-long friendships with the gifted and the brave are not so realized ; enduring memories of grace and congeniality are not so bequeathed. It was because Madame Récamier, instead of being hardened by worldliness, or soured by baffled affection, or irritated by adversity, lived through her best womanly instincts, kept pure and vivid her highest and quickest sympathies, and so placed herself in true relations with ife and literature, with genius and character, that her agency was so benign, her presence so inspiring, and her memory so dear."

Mrs. Hale in Godey's Lady's Book

"The letters, of which the book is mainly composed, are delightful to lovers of detail. Those of Chateaubriand in particular are almost a record of the las' twenty years of his life. Those who would see the influence upon great men of a fascinating, accomplished, intellectual woman, will find it in these letters."

From the New York Evening Post.

"Madame Récamier held her undisputed and marvellous sway, over men and women alike, by her exceeding loveliness of person, her kindness of heart, her good sense and exquisite tact, — a sway that was recognized when she was suffering from reverses of fortune, as well as when she was enjoying the greatest prosperity. Perhaps no biography was ever written in which there are anecdotes and glimpses of so many and such widely differing characters as in these memoirs. Covering a period of more than half a century, full of rapid and strange changes, Madame Récamier's "life" has a historic value, and the letters addressed to her take us behind the scenes and enable us to understand not a little of the intrigues that governed and the actors who took part in the political struggles of France and Europe. The chief value of the volume will be found in its autobiographical portions and its rich and diversified correspondence."

Sold everywhere, by all booksellers. Mailed, post paid, by the Publishers,

ROBERTS BROTHERS. Boston

THE LIFE AND LETTERS OF MADAME

SWETCHINE. By Count de Falloux. 1 vol. 16mo. Price $1 50.

THE WRITINGS OF MADAME SWETCHINE.

Edited by Count de Falloux. 1 vol. 16mo. Price $1.25.

MADAME SWETCHINE.

BY LUCY LARCOM.

A well-written history of an excellent and gifted woman, like the "Life and Letters of Madame Swetchine," by Count de Falloux, will naturally meet with a welcome among people of the truest culture. Madame Swetchine was not a woman who courted publicity; but the thread of her life was so interwoven with the political and religious movements of her time, it was impossible for her to escape notice. And it brightens that dark period of strife between France and Russia, with which the present century opened, to follow the life-track of this Russian lady, who seemed to have been equally at home in both countries.

She was intimately acquainted with the noblest men and women of that remarkable period, and there is not one of them upon whom her friendship does not cast a beautiful glow.

She was one of those rare beings who seem to have been created to draw out what is best in others, by the power of sympathy and self-forgetfulness. She was a woman of uncommon intellect, and of wide reading; and every thing she read was brought to the standard of a judgment remarkably clear and penetrative Indeed, her conversion to the Roman Catholic faith seems to have been mostly a matter of the head, — a choice between the Greek and the Roman ecclesiasticisms Long before her decision was made, her life shows her to have been a humble and earnest Christian; and, as such, as one whose sympathies took wing higher and wider than the opinions in which she had caged herself, her history has a rare value

One wonders at the amount of good accomplished by her, always a weak invalid. In order to understand how she lived, and what she did, the book must be read through; but some extracts might give a hint of it : —

"She rarely gave what is called advice, — an absolute solution of a given problem : her humility made her shrink from direct responsibilities. She did not lecture you. She did not set herself up as a model or guide. She did not say ' Walk thus;' but sweetly, 'Let us walk together;' and so, without making the slightest pretensions, she often guided those she seemed to follow. Young and old acknowledged her sway. She never evoked a sentiment of rivalry, because no one ever detected in her a temptation to win admiration at the expense of others. or to eclipse any person whatever. Her disinterestedness won pardon for her superiority

"Sick and erring hearts came and revealed themselves to Madame Swetchine in all sincerity ; and she shed upon them, sweetly and gradually, light and truth and life.

"In her turn she drew from this intimate intercourse, added to her own exquisite penetration, a knowledge of the human heart which amounted almost to divination. She knew the science of the soul as physicians know that of the body.

"Her charity was not a careless and mechanical practice. She consecrated to it all her strength and all her skill. Almsgiving was not, with her, the mere fulfilment of a duty. She liked to give pleasure besides doing good, and her heart always added something to what her hand gave."

Madame Swetchine lived a little beyond the boundaries of threescore and ten It is only ten years since she died. Heaven does not ask to what communion she belonged, neither will posterity. The memory of her saintliness is a possession to the church universal, in the present and in the future. Such a record as hers is an inspiration to all who read ; such an example, the most imperative " Go thou and do likewise."
